Bloodthirst in Babylon

About the Author

David Searls lives in Cleveland, Ohio with his teenage son, Evan. He is the author of *Yellow Moon* and hundreds of magazine articles, columns and essays. Look for *Malevolent* to be published by Samhain Horror in the summer of 2012. You can reach him at davidsearls.com and on Twitter @davidsearls1.

Coming Soon:

Malevolent

Bloodthirst in Babylon

David Searls

Samhain Publishing, Ltd.
11821 Mason Montgomery Rd., 4B
Cincinnati, OH 45249
www.samhainpublishing.com

Bloodthirst in Babylon
Copyright © 2012 by David Searls
Print ISBN: 978-1-60928-740-5
Digital ISBN: 978-1-60928-734-4

Editing by Don D'Auria
Cover by Angela Waters

First Samhain Publishing, Ltd. electronic publication: January 2012
First Samhain Publishing, Ltd. print publication: May 2012

Dedication

This one's for my folks, Roger and Doris Searls. Mom fed my love of storytelling with all of those rich Irish family tales. Dad introduced me to the magic of dark and speculative fiction.

And for Annie. Always for Annie
Ann Horky Searls (1962-1988)

Home Before Dark

Doyle Armstrong sneaked another quick peek at his watch. It would have looked less obvious if there'd been a clock hanging on the wall, but he'd never seen one in the department store.

"You coming out for drinks afterwards?"

She wasn't talking to him, of course, but to a heavyset sales clerk who shook her head.

"I want to get home before dark."

"Come on. *You* don't have anything to worry about."

"Still..." the heavyset chick replied doubtfully.

"Lighten up, Charlotte." The first girl chuckled, as if setting the example.

Doyle puzzled over the slimmer girl's odd inflection: *You* don't have anything to worry about.

"Your attention, please. The store will be closing in fifteen minutes. Thank you for shopping at Chaplin's."

The girls yelped with unconcealed glee, then went to work on their cash registers.

Closing out before nine o'clock was a no-no, but everyone did it, and rather openly. As he quickly surveyed the store's first floor, Doyle witnessed little activity except for huddled pairs of employees rummaging in their tills, counting, recording and pouching excess cash for delivery to the department store's office at the precise strike of nine. Doyle had the vague notion that one of his duties was to at least discourage early closing out, but he'd never gotten in trouble for ignoring the violation.

He had what should have been a cushy job, so why did he feel like the world's biggest fool? Prowling the store's three floors all day with the same battered and nearly empty shopping bag for a prop. But with his skin tone and stranger status in the pale-faced town, he felt as inconspicuous as a Jew wearing a yarmulke at a Klan rally. There couldn't be a person within fifteen miles who didn't know he was the new Chaplin's Department Store plainclothes security guard.

But, as Carl had pointed out on more than one occasion, the job paid well enough, so who cared whether or not the store actually needed security? Long as those paychecks kept coming...

Doyle took another quick peek at his watch. Twelve minutes to go. God, had it only been three minutes since the PA announcement?

II

"I'm telling you, Carl, it's weird," he'd said a week ago, after getting a fifty-cent-an-hour raise for no reason he could see. "I'm already making more money than I ever seen in Philly, and now they want to stick more of it in my pockets."

"Those heartless bastards," Carl said.

The early summer sun was warm and cloudless. They'd pulled lawn chairs and a six-pack up to the edge of the empty swimming pool where they sat drinking and bullshitting. Carl Haggerty had been a friend of Doyle's brother, Winthrop, in a section of North Philly known as the Badlands. After Win caught a fatal one in the chest in a drive-by, bunch of coked-up kids misidentifying their target in the dark, Carl and Doyle had drawn closer. When, months later, another whizzing stray shattered Carl's picture window, the two decided to find a place where bullets weren't more common than jobs.

Such a place, they'd found quite by accident, was Babylon, Michigan.

They'd been chasing the rumor of employment in Gary, Indiana, but after a series of wrong turns and an hour or so of highways that just kept getting narrower and lonelier, they'd found themselves in a town where they could stop for directions. Doyle had hoped, as he spied all those white faces gawking their way, that no one misplaced any money or young children until he and Carl were long gone.

Only, it hadn't been like that.

"I swear I don't understand you," Carl told him that night more than a week ago, by the pool. "You do nothing but piss and moan about Philly...the gangs, the drugs, the poverty. So we end up here. You see anyone flashing colors? Heard any gunshots in the night? And now you taking home a raise. Tell me again, how bad you being treated here?"

Had a point. Still...

Doyle squeezed finger dents into his empty beer can. "Yeah, about that raise. You know what I do in that store? I walk. They got no shoplifters, so I walk ten, twelve miles a day with a blank stare."

"Paid to exercise."

"Then I hang around a few minutes after closing time to make sure everyone gets out. I don't set the alarms or even turn out the lights. They got store managers and Mr. Chaplin for that."

"They got no shoplifters 'cuz you on the job, Bob. Sure, everyone knows you the man, but you ever hear 'bout those towns got dummies sitting in police cars?"

Doyle shook his head, clueless as to where this was going.

"Usually it's, they got no budget for overtime, so they park a police car with some dumbass mannequin in the driver's seat. Everyone knows the deal, but they still slow down till they get out of the dummy's sight. Habit, I guess. You get it, Doyle? Sometimes just being there's enough."

"What I get is you calling me a dummy."

"Not what I meant."

"You know how I got that job? Well, I don't, either. No pissing in bottles, no background check. Didn't even fill out an application form. Just got it."

"Random good fortune. Rich white folks get it all the time. 'Bout time we did, too."

Doyle wasn't buying it. He waved an arm to take in the empty pool and the low-slung, two-story building behind them. "Putting us up in here for practically nothing...these people are trying to put something over us 'cuz they think we're stupid."

"Oh boy, here we go. Good jobs, cheap lodging, just another example of the white man sticking it. How does that explain D.B.? Huh? He ain't black, and they're putting him up here, too. And Judd. And a buncha others. There go that theory, whatever it was."

Doyle licked his lips of beer foam. "Ain't just *my* job makes no sense. Tell me again how busy you are with that paint crew you follow around. What is it, you hold brushes, move ladders? How much you making to do that? I forget."

"Now it's me getting screwed 'cuz the job's too easy and I'm getting paid too much. You see how it sounds?"

"Well." Doyle took a final swig. "There ain't no Santa Claus, and I'm clearing out of here some day soon, with or without you."

There were all kinds of additional thoughts churning away in the back of Doyle Armstrong's troubled mind, but none made sense enough to be pulled out in the open. Carl was right, lately always telling him how he was getting old and cynical. But it was hard-earned cynicism. He'd had so much bad news in his life he couldn't accept anything without questioning it to death. But if he got on the phone to whatever was left of his bullet-riddled family and described to them his job and his eighteen—no, make that eighteen-fifty an hour—pay, no one would believe his good fortune. He knew that; he wasn't stupid.

So what, exactly, was the problem?

III

The biggest thing was the way they looked at him.

As the last of the few remaining customers shuffled for the exits, Doyle examined his watch. Openly, no danger of being accused of clock-watching. It was all but impossible to get fired, judging from his experience of the night before. Just six minutes till closing time.

He decided on the spot that he'd gotten it all wrong. It was the way the white citizens of Babylon *didn't* look at him and Carl that gave him the creeps.

There was literally not another black face in town, so he wouldn't have been surprised to have been gawked at. But it was nothing like that. He only felt eyes when his back was turned. If that made any sense. All other times, the townsfolk looked right through him as if he wasn't there.

Like now, for instance. Four minutes to go and the store virtually deserted of customers. While a few employees had heads buried in cash drawers, others paced about impatiently, examining their watches or chatting in small groups. None made eye contact as Doyle strolled by.

The hell with them, he thought as he made his way to the doors that opened out onto the parking lot. Employees would be scrambling for this exit in another minute or so. One of his night shift duties was to guard the door while the on-duty manager locked up elsewhere. Make sure everyone made it safely to their cars and no one tried to enter from the street.

But there were no other security guards on the payroll, so who performed this task when Doyle was off?

No one, that's who. Security wasn't a real concern here. Mr. Chaplin didn't need him, and the department store didn't look so prosperous that it could afford the unnecessary cost. So why, he mentally asked absent buddy Carl, did they hire me?

Don't question good fortune, he replied on absent buddy Carl's behalf.

Doyle stepped just beyond the open doorway and breathed deeply of the clean night air. He couldn't take any more of the fresh, monotonous smell of the fabrics and shoe leather on display, or the choking scent of dueling perfumes lining the makeup counters where the hottest chicks worked. He had to get out. Maybe tomorrow. With or without Carl, as he'd warned on more than one occasion.

The heavyset girl wasn't going to make it home before dark after all, he thought as he watched big purple splotches of shadow overtaking the handful of cars that remained in the lot.

And what had she meant by that, anyway? The town was so small and quiet—eerily so after Philly—that most people, including himself, walked everywhere.

Home before dark.

Something flickered, quick activity to his left, but gone when he turned.

Laughter.

Doyle craned his neck and, yes, heard it again. Deep-throated male chuckles from the shadowy depths of the parking lot.

"Hey there, bro."

Doyle took an involuntary step back. Now he saw them. Three figures in the lot where there'd been nothing but the shadowy forms of cars the last time he'd looked.

"Purcell," he mumbled to himself as his eyes adjusted.

Not the one who'd spoken, but the middle of the three still figures staring at him from the lot. Doyle recognized him by the way the short, muscular figure wore his ball cap, pulled low on his head and straight-on. And by the way the shadowy figure posed, loose-limbed, seeming to loom over the others despite his height disadvantage. The one who'd called out to him and was now hooting at his own dumbass wit was Jason Penney, still more or less hidden in the gathering darkness.

Hell, Doyle snorted. The Badlands had scarier creatures than them. By far.

It hadn't been true that the entire town had ignored him. There were a loud bunch of redneck assholes who liked to talk trash at him as he passed. Doyle had gotten the names Purcell and Penney by quietly asking around. At first he thought there were only three or four of the loudmouths, but the number seemed to have grown over the last several days. Or nights, rather. They didn't seem to hold down jobs, and had their nights free to hang out mostly at the Winking Dog Saloon on Middle View.

"Be seeing you later, bro," Penney called out.

His eyes now accustomed to the near-dark, Doyle could make out the wiry, blond-haired man with the high, jeering voice. He was sitting on a car that, in the near absence of light, resembled the mid-seventies Impalas that could be found on cement blocks all over the Badlands. Doyle would have liked nothing more than to knock the smug bastard from the hood, but then he'd have the others to contend with.

More laughter erupted from behind him, and Doyle backed out of the way of a stream of joyously released sales clerks who would have trampled him if he'd impeded their summer evening plans.

They were young, for the most part. Students earning a little cash for the fall semester, most likely. Doyle heard voices calling out for others to meet up in this or that bar, and for just a moment he wished he was going with them, sitting his ass down somewhere cool, downing

11

frosted drafts while listening to music and talking about what a bitch college was.

Yeah, right. The closest he'd ever come to stepping foot on campus was almost getting hired to the Temple University grounds crew. But then they'd looked at his record from his much younger days, and there went that job.

No, he wouldn't be meeting anyone for brewskis at the Winking Dog. What he and Carl and maybe the white dudes D.B. and Ponytail Pete and some of the others were going to be doing was sitting around a grimy pool, sharing six-packs and smoking too many cigarettes. Like most nights. Doyle sighed. Least he'd be off the job. No more walking empty aisles, roaming past half-filled racks and display cases, guarding the lingerie department, the junior misses and teen shop from no one.

Change the subject, he told himself, still standing in the doorway, staring at the rapidly emptying parking lot. That's how Carl told him to deal with just about everything: change the subject.

So think about the girl. Kathy Lee something or another. Scrawny-ass white chick, not so young anymore, but not bad to look at. She'd just moved into town. Checked in at the Sundown, like him and Carl and all the others. Had herself a couple kids, but no man. Who knows...

The stream of exiting employees had been trickling out while his thought went to his gonads, and now there was no one. He nudged the metal employee door closed before searching the premises for stragglers.

Whichever manager had night duties had already turned off most of the old-fashioned hanging globe lights, actually improving the look of the place. Chaplin's Department Store's color scheme consisted mostly of putrid pink and pastel green, the entire place a throwback to the eighties. A perfect setting for the bland and outdated merchandise.

Doyle wondered when the town would eventually see a Wal-Mart. Couldn't be soon enough. Hell, you couldn't even get cell phone reception in this throwback burg.

Doyle suddenly became aware of muffled voices from the virtually unlit back, from the corridor beyond the cashier's window where the managers had offices. He deliberately didn't go to investigate.

"Anyone need me?" he called out from a distance.

"No, you can go," someone shouted back. Sounded like Chaplin himself, the storeowner who'd certainly talked *about* him, but hadn't exchanged a half dozen words *with* Doyle.

"I'm leaving, then."

Doyle was the lone security guard, but he didn't have a key to the place. He would have offered this fact to Carl as another point of suspicion, but it was like talking to a wall.

"Go ahead," the voice from the inner sanctum called out.

Doyle let out a sigh of relief. He hadn't been anxious to wait around or to go back there behind the cashier's counter after what had happened the evening before.

IV
The evening before...

"I don't want him here. I don't need him, and I can't afford him. Get yourself someone else to—"

"Come on, Mr. Chaplin. He's useful, you know that. Pilferage happens in even the best of communities. And it's such a charitable act, don't you think?" This last comment ended with a dry chuckle.

"I've decided to take it up with Mr. Drake."

"It's not an issue that concerns Drake."

"Doesn't concern him?" Chaplin barked in disbelief. "Everything in Babylon concerns him. You know that."

"Of course we value his opinion," replied the second voice, bending just a little.

"What's this 'we?' Just how closely are you identifying with that man these days?"

"Wait just a minute, Mr. C. You're making it out to be a Drake versus Purcell thing, and it's not. Duane's going his own way and he invites Mr. Drake to do the same."

"In other words, butt out. Is that it?"

Doyle camouflaged his eavesdropping by bending over a drinking fountain near the cashier's window. The two voices were coming from behind the doorway that served as the entry point to a warren of small and uninteresting offices. It was afterhours, Doyle was closing up, and, as far as he knew, only the two men in the offices beyond remained with him.

That second voice was irritatingly familiar, but he couldn't place it.

And then it hit him. The wheedling tones of the younger man belonged to McConlon, the cop he and Carl had flagged down the month before for directions to a major highway, but who'd instead persuaded them to settle in Babylon.

He kept sipping. Kept listening.

"I can't tell you how sick I am of hearing that name. Purcell this, Purcell that," Chaplin was saying. "And now you. Marty, how do you think your brother feels about your new loyalties? No wonder they want out so badly."

"Let's leave my brother out of this." Then the voice softened. "Hey, I'm just trying to maintain the peace. That's my job. I'm serving as an intermediary between the two parties, that's all."

"I thought you said it wasn't a Drake versus Purcell kind of thing."

"Look, I'm tired of playing games here. We're not asking so much of you."

"It doesn't seem as though you're *asking* at all, Marty. If I thought I had a choice in the matter, I'd have turned you down on the spot."

"I think we're wasting time, Mr. C. You're not in the mood to discuss matters, so let's take a break and pick it up later. Whaddya say?"

Nothing followed but a strained silence. Then the young cop shuffled out of the room, nearly colliding with Doyle, still bent over the water fountain, and grunted in surprise. McConlon was in street clothes, a loud shirt and tacky pair of shorts that ballooned around him, bringing even more attention to his pudgy middle.

"Oh," said Doyle, trying his best to act startled.

The cop stared. "Hey, it's you," he said, sounding amiably unable to come up with a name.

Doyle wiped water from his lips, reinforcing the notion that it was only his thirst that had brought him to within earshot. "Everyone's gone and the place is locked up 'cept for the employee door," he said. "If someone wants to lock up after me…"

The young cop broke into a broad grin. "You're a curious one, aren't you, Doyle? Like to hear what's going on?"

Well, at least the cop knew his name.

The tall, white-haired department store owner came out, apparently drawn by the voices. He had the physique of a runner and crystal-clear eyes.

He stood behind the cop and muttered angrily, "For God's sake, this is the sort of thing I've warned against." His comments and glare were addressed to the cop, as if the subject of his simmer wasn't standing right there.

There goes the job, Doyle Armstrong had thought at the time. He had the sinking, panicky sensation of someone on the verge of unfair termination—but then the feeling was replaced by one of buoyant relief: He was free of Babylon at last.

"Mr. Chaplin, you have a key," the cop said, as carefree as usual. "Doyle here is anxious to get home. It's 'Doyle,' right?"

Doyle nodded as the elegant older man grunted and retreated to his inner sanctum, soon to return with a thick ring of keys, which he slapped into the cop's hand.

Marty McConlon rolled his eyes, still smiling, as if the two of them were weathering Chaplin's storm together. The cop ambled toward the parking lot exit with Doyle silently in tow. Shadowy mannequins loomed from every crooked bend of the narrow aisle. Ceiling blades swirled high overhead, the ancient store's answer to central air.

The cop held the door and presented the night with a flourish.

"I didn't hear nothing," Doyle had mumbled on his way out. For some reason, it seemed important.

"Okay," the young cop breezily replied. "You didn't hear a thing." He grinned.

V

That had been the night before. Tonight, the frozen-limbed mannequins still creeped him out as he groped his way to the employees' exit, this time alone. He made it safely and turned to search the shadows for the on-duty manager who was supposed to lock up after him.

Doyle saw and heard no one, but he'd been told to leave, so he shrugged and stepped partially out of the doorway and peered at the parking lot. It stood nearly empty in the foggy yellow glow of a pair of tall sodium vapor lights. Past the lot, on Main View, traffic moved fairly steadily. It was a few minutes after nine, and dark.

"I want to get home before dark."

Now what the hell had the fool girl meant by that? Doyle pushed his way out and clanged the metal door closed behind him. His ears perked for even the smallest sounds. Habit, most likely, from the Badlands. He took a sharp right onto the pavement in front of the three-story building, then another onto the sidewalk of well-lit Main View Road.

It was like day out here, people of all ages—but mostly older— strolling and eating ice cream cones and walking dogs and gazing into lit store windows displaying shoes, hardware, rugs, books, banking and dry cleaning services, jewelry, food and coffee.

Nothing like his neighborhood, where folks really did need to get home before dark.

A car horn sounded and someone on the sidewalk playfully yelled at the driver.

Both sides of the street were lined with birch and maple saplings tethered to tree lawns to form skimpy green arches in front of the brick and wood-frame storefronts.

"...home before dark."

Funny, a young girl like that, afraid of walking alone with all these folks out on the streets.

"What a night."

The voice chilled him, nearly stopping him in his tracks. An old lady passed, dragging a yellow poodle that walked as though its feet hurt. Not her. The voice was young, insolent and male.

The blond-haired man came from nowhere to sidle up to Doyle. Said nothing now. Just smiled brightly in the streetlight.

He fell in and matched Doyle's pace. They wound their way

through outdoor tables filled with ice-cream eaters and coffee sippers.

The street looked less well-lit the next block down.

The blond man snickered. He slowed, fell behind until Doyle couldn't see him without a glance over his shoulder. Jason Penney, in his early twenties, couldn't have gone more than one-fifty sopping wet. Doyle could take him easy if he had to—but where were Purcell and the others? He had to know.

An extended family out for a stroll made room for Doyle and the trailing Penney in front of a tire store still open for business. With the incandescent light leaking from a display window fully illuminating the scene for brief seconds, Doyle saw what looked to be four or five generations of a family, one member more wizened and slow-moving than the one before. Their lively chatter died as the two groups passed.

Penney laughed like he'd been expecting that reaction. "Finally some respect from this goddamn town," he said. He had a high, tight voice that would have seemed insolent just commenting on the weather.

Doyle said nothing. He watched a white-eyed figure on a painted bench. As he got closer, it became a slender, raven-haired young woman with a cigarette dangling between her lips. She caught his gaze.

"There you are," she said.

Huh?

She drew the cigarette from her lips, tapped out the ash on the ground and grinned as Doyle hurried on.

Another shadow, smaller than the girl, disengaged itself from a tree larger than the saplings in the previous block, and a boy in his early teens made Doyle veer. The boy snorted.

Footfalls. More pairs of feet than just Penney's following him like echoes. He forced himself to maintain a steady pace and not look back. He was nearly to Third Street. Half a block away, four elderly people sipped cool drinks at a café table set up in front of a bookstore. Three younger men drew around the seated figures and the four hurriedly rose and finished their drinks.

"Stay awhile, Grandma," one of the newcomers called out, and the others hooted.

His deep rumble identified him immediately as the notorious Purcell.

Doyle had seen him with the cop, McConlon, on other nights. Just hanging, the two of them with heads together. Purcell's rigid face was now blue with stubble.

"How ya doing, Doyle?" Purcell said, eyes locked in on him as the old folks scuttled away.

Doyle wouldn't have even guessed that Purcell knew his name. *Bro;* that's all he'd heard from them before now.

"Hey, Duane, don't he look like the dude on TV?"

Coarse laughter. Lots of it.

Doyle whirled to see too many young men. They came closer, clustered around him in a claustrophobic circle. No, not just men. There was the slender dark-haired girl with the cigarette, and the younger boy. And still others coming at him from out of the darkness.

"You mean the comedian dude?" said Purcell. Then to Doyle: "Say something funny, bruthuh."

Doyle jerked backwards as something touched his foot. He looked down in disgust as he felt the rat's cold belly and sorry-assed tail slithering across his shoe and touching up against one bare ankle. He stepped back quickly as the thing ambled into the night.

"Jesus," he said.

The town was full of the things.

More wild laughter. Keep walking, he told himself. They wouldn't do anything with all these town folks out. Doyle had been stopped just out of the business district, and most of the strolling townspeople seemed to have found other placed to be, but he still saw the occasional car on the street out front and hand-holding couples quickly squeezing past the crowd on the sidewalk. It was too busy out here for him to be in any real danger.

Besides, the Sundown was just a couple more blocks to the east. Not far at all in a car. Course, he was on foot. And currently surrounded by eight or ten townies who didn't look like they were there to safeguard his way back.

Purcell broke from the circle and took a seat at the outdoor table the two elderly couples had hurriedly vacated. He made a quick hand motion and someone from the back of the cluster dropped something heavy onto the tabletop. He grunted at the effort and the glass-topped table shuddered.

Doyle swallowed to wet the cement that had formed in his throat. "Okay, a suitcase," he said, trying to keep it light.

Yeah, a scuffed leather suitcase that—

"Hey," he said in the next moment. "That's mine!"

Something squealed as more fat, long-tailed bodies rolled across his feet. Doyle tried to back up, but he'd run out of space. He could feel hot breath huffing down his neck, and smelled the strong scent of rancid meat.

"What the hell?" he snapped, anger momentarily overruling fear.

He moved in to snatch the suitcase—*his* luggage—but Purcell swatted it off the table. It fell heavily and someone scooped it up and made it disappear in the crowd.

Something about the feeble streetlight out front made Purcell's eyes shine white-hot.

"How did you...?"

Doyle's anger had already started to turn to leaden dread as he considered what it meant that Purcell had his things. First, that they'd broken into his room at the Sundown, and had obviously packed his bag. Where was Carl during all this? Had they hurt him?

He could hear the sound of a zipper unzipping, and then the slender-haired girl said, "Check this out."

She'd opened his suitcase and now held up a pair of his wildly patterned undershorts, drawing hoots of laughter.

Catching quick peeks at the street, Doyle could see a few cars cruising by without slowing to investigate the sidewalk mob. Maybe even speeding up.

"So now you're all packed up with nowhere to go," said Purcell, still seated.

"You broke into my place."

"Not me," said Purcell. "Friend of mine, this afternoon. And he didn't break in. He used a key. Left the place looking as neat and tidy as he found it."

Doyle's fury got him moving. He wheeled and headed straight for the nearest body, determined to steamroll through it if he had to. But he didn't. The crowd unexpectedly parted. That's all they wanted to do, just tease him. Freak him out, scare the scary nigger away.

Their plan had worked to perfection. He wouldn't even go through the motions of filing a police report. Let them keep his underwear and toothbrush and ragged suitcase. Small price to pay. He'd be out of there by morning. Carl could tag along if he wanted. Or stay. That was fine, too.

It took a few seconds for Doyle to realize he was leading a crowd. He heard Penney giggling behind him and a few others muttering, but they kept their distance. Kept it until they drew even with a parking lot fronting a florist shop with three customers chatting away on the other side of an inviting expanse of warmly lit display glass.

As they closed in, Doyle threw his elbow back and connected with Jason Penney's throat. He enjoyed the hell out of hearing the townie gagging and puking, but everything went very bad very quickly after that.

As they fell on him, Doyle's first thought was that this was going to be the worst beating of his life. But that was interrupted by other thoughts, much darker ones, when the first set of teeth nestled into his groin.

Part One
Boomtown

What an object of horror Babylon has become among the nations!
  Jeremiah 50,23

Chapter One

Black and white with a cherry on top.

Melanie's first and still-favorite riddle sprang to Todd Dunbar's mind as the squad car pulled the weary Olds to the shoulder of a highway somewhere north of Toledo and I-90, the turnpike they'd left early to save a few bucks. Joy's idea, and a clever one if you didn't count the extra fuel cost in cruising a highway to nowhere.

The "cherry" flashed red and blue on the dome of the marked Crown Vic that had pulled behind them on the road's saggy shoulder.

"Uh oh," Joy murmured from the seat next to him.

Yeah. Uh oh. The too-late warning got passed around in the backseat, first taken up by ten-year-old Melanie, then echoed by her five-year-old sister, Crissie, and finally picked up by four-year-old Todd Junior, or simply Little Todd.

"Quiet," Todd told all of them as he pawed through glove box litter for the car's title or registration or whatever the hell paperwork he had to prove the pile of junk was his.

Like anyone else would claim it.

He found a plastic packet of official-looking documents under layers of fast food napkins, crumpled packs of cigarettes and creased maps of states through which he couldn't recall traveling.

The mess bothered him, as if the cop would consider neatness when doling out punishment for whatever violation he'd witnessed. Maybe nothing more than the general condition of the beater itself. It wouldn't be the first time they'd been pulled over for that in the last eight months.

Todd sneaked quick peaks out the rearview while the rest of the family gawked in open curiosity at the flashing vehicle behind them. Men were raised as boys to look bored rather than guilty or excited when caught in the sights of the law, even when innocent. Women and girls craned their necks every time they saw a fucking strobe light.

"What's he doing?" Joy demanded in her high, tight voice.

If they were a band of outlaws, she'd be the one copping a plea even before they got read their rights.

Todd drew a cigarette from the one crumpled pack that still held a few and held it between grim lips while he depressed the car's lighter. His first instinct had been to hold off. Nothing to be gained by pissing off a non-smoking cop, but the wait was making him crazy.

"He's running the tag," he said, knowing his brief response would only draw more questions.

He was right. They came, like a hard rain, from wife and daughters alike.

"Easy," Todd muttered, trying to stem the chatter while wrestling once again for an explanation.

So many possibilities, beginning with the muffler that had finally burned through the wire coat hanger he'd used to prop it in place a state or two ago. It had been, for the last ten or fifteen miles, sparking pavement like a butane lighter. Or maybe it was the stickers on his West Virginia plates. Todd couldn't remember if he'd renewed them on time, but he suspected the worst. When you don't have cash for such luxuries as car insurance, tires and sticker renewal, you fly under the radar screen as much as possible.

He glanced once more out the mirror, but three bobbing heads in need of washing obstructed his view. Dunbar sighed. Pack of hill rats from West Virginia: in some places, reason enough to get pulled over.

"I told you we should have paid that ticket," Joy said with a strained urgency that suggested she'd admit to anything if they'd let her walk.

"No one here cares about Parkersburg parking tickets," he said between clenched teeth.

"Afternoon, folks. See your license, please?"

Todd jumped at the cop's sudden appearance in his open side window. One of the girls yelped, a sharp sound like a hiccup. The lighter popped up from the dashboard mount to indicate its red-hot availability, but Todd ignored it. He brushed the cigarette from his lips and let it fall to his lap while he rooted around in his back pocket for his paper-thin wallet.

All this time to kill, and he'd forgotten to dig out his license. He hoped it was current. Another expense you set aside when it's that or a bag of groceries. As he riffled through his wallet, he knew that the officer looking over his shoulder could read the family's bleak condition in the emptiness of its credit card pockets and the flimsiness of the billfold compartment. That is, if he hadn't already detected destitution in the migrant meanness of the car and family. Todd found and pulled free the laminated card and hurriedly stuffed the wallet in his pants.

As he handed over the license, he caught his first glimpse of the man standing there. His face was round and smooth and young, the expression on it unexpectedly open.

"Thanks," he said.

Todd watched the cop study the license for a minute or more, moving his lips while reading the bare-bone details of Todd Dunbar's life. The cop stopped once or twice to peer into the backseat as if he held in his hand a family history that could be verified with a glance.

"Mr. Dunbar," he said tentatively, like he was trying out the name for effect. He straightened up, popping his back and grimacing. This one wasn't nearly as trim or muscled as many of the young cops with whom the Dunbars had become acquainted of late.

He bent again and brought his soft face level with the window. "A ways from Parkersburg, huh?"

Todd nodded. "A ways."

He knew what the cop was getting at, but it wasn't any of his goddamn business why he'd brought his family down from the hills. This was still America, wasn't it?

"We're looking for work," Joy blurted in the stubborn silence following her husband's scant response. "We were in Akron—in Ohio— 'cuz I got a cousin back home who's friends with a man who said he was working for this polymer company there that was hiring. But we got there and they wouldn't even take our application, so we're heading to Detroit. I got a brother-in-law who knew a guy…"

By the time even Joy realized she'd missed her train of thought, Todd had his gaze fixed on a billboard fifty yards up the road. It was faded and pockmarked with small caliber bullet holes outlined in rust. It said there'd be an ice cream stand at the next mile, but Dunbar doubted it. Things changed. You couldn't stop it.

"Detroit," the cop said. "Guess you folks are unfamiliar with the area or you would have taken the turnpike to 280 and caught I-75. This way, you pass through every forgotten little town in southeastern Michigan. And there's a lot of them."

"We never been there. To Detroit," Joy said. "We were looking for a shortcut to save money on tolls, so we got off the interstate before Toledo and headed north. One highway led to another." She shrugged, wisely letting the rest go.

"Rough, being out of work," the cop said.

Todd gripped the wheel, said nothing.

"So you got a lead or something in Detroit, eh?" the cop asked him encouragingly. Just two old friends bullshitting.

"Yeah, we—"

"Not really," Joy broke in. "But it's a big city with lots of factories and warehouses, and we'll do just about anything, so—"

"Uh oh." The cop's tone of alarm and his troubled look as he propped his arms on the window silenced Joy. "I don't want to jinx you folks or anything, but you're doing it the hard way. You can't imagine the number of people trekking *out* of Detroit while you-all head in. You know about the auto industry, right? Not so healthy. Used to be, folks in the city headed for Vegas or down South for work. Sun Belt, so they say. But nowadays, hell." The cop shrugged. "Where they should be going, I guess, is India or China. You'll make five dollars a day, but at least you got a job."

23

The cop finished with a hard chuckle at the cruel irony.

Todd could hear his wife sucking in air and knew he'd later have to justify his desperate decision to try the so-called Motor City. A decision he'd made without a whole lot of confidence in the first place, but what else was there?

A van rumbled past, braking so hard at the sight of the blue and red dome lights that it shimmied slightly.

They all seemed to be waiting for Todd to say something. To somehow justify his employment-seeking strategy.

"We're not *broke* or anything," he replied carefully, parsing the word in his mind. "We're fine till we find something."

Todd knew the stereotype: the small town cop who'd bust you for vagrancy if you didn't have cash to flash. Hell, probably no less accurate than the one about the West Virginia migrant family in desperate need of work.

Thirty-seven dollars, most of it borrowed from his folks: that's how fine they were.

"What's it you do?"

Todd took longer than Joy to figure a response.

"My husband drives a front-end coal loader for contour strip mining," Joy answered for him. She sounded so proud, puffing up his grimy job description like he ran Caterpillar itself.

"Mmm," the cop said. "Not much call for strip mining in Detroit."

Asshole, Todd said, but wisely only to himself.

"Todd can do anything," Joy said, pushing the claim too hard. "So can I."

The car got quiet. Even the kids stopped fidgeting in back, though Todd could have used the distraction.

At least three generations of Dunbar men had worked a shaft in the mountains before it got played out and closed by the EPA. Todd, who'd been the first of his family to graduate from high school, now remembered in embarrassment the family celebration that had followed that feeble accomplishment. A high school diploma and two bucks got you a cup of coffee. Long as you weren't looking for espresso.

"Nice car," said the cop as though sensing Todd's humiliation and working his fingers into the open wound.

It sure felt like sarcasm, but the uniformed officer peering in at him looked way too earnest. He was the Pillsbury Doughboy, but with a nine millimeter on his padded hip.

He took a step back, straightened and arched his back, spread his small pink hands to take in the Olds. "You take care of them, you'll be driving these Detroit beasts long after your Japanese SUV's been towed to the junkyard. How many miles?"

Todd stared up at him.

"On the odometer."

He glanced down. His hand found the discarded cigarette in his lap and he palmed it like a magician. "Uh, one-eighty-six, five...almost," he answered after scanning the frightfully long string of numbers. Numbers he'd trained his eye not to see.

The cop let out a burst of high laughter. "Wow. That's a lot even for one of these road warriors."

Not to Todd. Generations of Dunbar men had held their rides together for decades with duct tape and prayer.

"That kind of mileage, the problems start adding up quickly." The young cop's twinkly eyes seemed to take in every inch of the vehicle's ragged interior, including its five ragged occupants. "You don't put any money into a car like this, the brake shoes burn up, tires go bald, muffler droops, bulbs and lights blink out. Wiring troubles. Lots of things. And I'd say—" he added extra wattage to his grin—"you're riding on all of the above."

Todd felt a lump of panic growing deep and malignant in his belly. It wasn't just the toll-road savings that had put him on the back roads. He hadn't told Joy, but he'd also wanted to avoid just this kind of attention.

"Truth is," he said, seething at the need to plead his case before this plump badge, "it's been a little hard lately scraping together the cash for repairs."

"No shit," said the baby-faced cop. "Pardon the language, kids," he added dipping his head toward the backseat where the three sat in awestruck silence. It wasn't even close to being the first time they'd heard that word, but never before uttered to their dad by a man with a gun on his hip. "But that's exactly the point. Without a good job...well, I've got a steady paycheck and there's still stuff I need done on my car. Money's tight for everyone, even folks with regular work, so I don't blame you folks for the condition of this car."

For some reason, that lump in Dunbar's belly just kept growing.

"What if you did have a job? You, Mr. Dunbar. Or the both of you. However you'd want to work it."

The cop twitched his head like a sparrow as he tried deciding whether to settle his gaze on driver or front seat passenger.

"You saying you know who's hiring?" Todd hoped his doubt wasn't as apparent to the police officer as it was to his own ears.

The cop chuckled. "Stranger things, my friend. Stranger things. You got the whole family in here?" He dipped his head again to the backseat.

When Joy assured him that he was indeed looking at one entire branch of the Dunbar clan, he said, "Weird thing about Babylon, Michigan, it's probably the nation's best-kept secret. Almost a boomtown, but I'll deny it if word gets out. Last thing we want is to end up like Detroit...congested and dirty and crime-ridden. Know what I'm saying?"

No, Todd hadn't the slightest idea. He had a hard time imagining anywhere around here to be so bustling it had to be kept under wraps.

The air shuddered as an 18-wheeler slammed past. Crissie gasped, which made Melanie giggle, and Little Todd felt suddenly free to broadcast his bathroom needs.

Todd looked up to find the young cop with his face positioned in the driver's window frame as though patiently awaiting a response, but Todd didn't remember the question or even if one had been asked. He didn't need any of this. He was twenty-eight freaking years old, with three good kids who could seriously get on his nerves at times, and a wife who was four years older and hadn't lost the water weight from her last pregnancy. Or the two before it, for that matter. He had thirty-seven borrowed dollars and a dying car.

There were men his age still in school, their biggest decisions being which bar to head off to when exams were taken. These other men, they could look forward to wearing suits and working in air-conditioned offices for fat paychecks and different women every night. Women who spoke good and worked out and had nice teeth and didn't—

"Of course, we don't have any front-end coal-loading jobs in Babylon, but if you're not quite so picky..."

Todd blinked out of his frat-boy thoughts. He could feel Joy's glaze clinging to him. A car cruised by, honked, and three or four teen boys pumped their arms out open windows in testosterone glee at the fact that, for once, it wasn't them being pulled over.

The elms and oaks bordering the pastures and scrubland falling off to one side of the road drooped their changing leaves to block the sun and turn mid-afternoon to premature evening. He saw a tree with a faded orange 'X' sprayed on it, pointing out the presence or threat of Dutch elm disease. Someone had forgotten, decades ago, to cut it down, but it looked healthy enough to Todd.

"Thanks, but we're moving on," he said, avoiding eye contact with his wife.

At some point she'd lit another cigarette and now the smoke was drifting under his nose and making him itch for one of his own. He wished he hadn't tossed it aside, the one in his lap.

"To Detroit," the cop said, sounding like he still found it hard to believe.

Todd nodded. To Detroit, simply because it was a one-tank distance from their last wasted stop. No hot rumors this time, no inkpen-circled help-wanted ads, no nothing except pure desperation and a stubborn determination to not return to West Virginia without at least a glimmer of hope.

"Yeah, Detroit," Todd muttered.

"Well that's alright," the cop said graciously, as though forgiving a personal affront. "Thought you folks could have used a sure thing, but I was wrong. And for all I know the Ford plant's hiring or you find yourself some construction work. What do I know except what I read? Nothing. I keep hearing bad news, but I haven't actually *been* there. And it's only a couple hours away. You might be able to get someone from town to run you up there for not much more than gas money."

The hard lump in Todd's stomach moved just slightly.

"What?" Joy asked before he could.

The cop smiled, but said nothing. His eyes found Todd's, and Todd knew he was waiting to be asked the obvious. If he could have avoiding giving the son-of-a-bitch the satisfaction, he would have.

But he dry-swallowed his resentment and said, "Why would we need a ride?"

The cop raised both hands as though in supplication. "Well, because of the condition of this Olds, of course. What is it, a ninety-one? Ninety-two? Jesus, let's face it, Mr. Dunbar, you're driving a road menace and a rattletrap threat to your entire family. I wouldn't be doing my job if I didn't insist on you first completing a shopping list of repairs before you hot-tail it out of here. But something tells me you can't exactly whip out that battered wallet of yours and slap the proper change on the counter. Am I wrong?"

Thirty-seven dollars, Todd repeated to himself. That wouldn't quite cover the cost of opening the hood.

"Todd," Joy said softly, like she was just sitting there waiting for him to solve everything.

"Don't you worry, ma'am," said the cop. "I'm just trying to help, here."

Todd felt his fingers tightening on the steering wheel. He stared at the faded sign outside the windshield. It made him hungry for an ice cream stand that must have disappeared years ago, and which he couldn't afford even if it still existed. But it sure would have been nice to be able to take the kids there and watch their eyes light up at the biggest fucking whipped cream-covered banana floats they'd ever seen.

He listened to insects screeching in the weeds outside Joy's rolled-down window, and felt the sweat trickling down his face, tickling his neck, crawling into his shirt. There was something wrong here. Something badly wrong, but he couldn't put his finger on it.

"Tell me again about those jobs in town," his said, voice devoid of emotion.

"What I could do, I could send for a tow truck from Zeebe's. Jim'll take good care of you. Then I'll drop you folks off at a motel with real

27

cheap rates and she won't collect till you cash your first paycheck. In the meanwhile, I'll make a call to a guy owns a small, corrugated packaging shop on Sennett Street, which is where the factories are. What I heard, he's looking to pay maybe twelve, fifteen an hour to start. Not a fortune, but you don't need any experience and he's eager to hire."

The cop leaned further in the window, if that was possible. "There might even be a town job for you, ma'am. Seems I recall one of the city's departments needing someone to answer phones, but I'm not promising. You can answer phones, can't you?"

Joy nodded with such zest that Todd felt the car wobble.

Staring straight ahead, he said, "Maybe we'll stay for a few days." Like he had a choice in the matter. "Only till we get the car fixed and the repairs paid for."

It was important to maintain the illusion of being able to accept or reject the terms placed before him.

"Absolutely," the cop agreed.

They beckoned the kids from the back of the car, Todd shushing each puzzled query. They grabbed suitcases from the trunk, Todd trying his best to block the worst dings and scuffs from view.

The cop opened his own trunk and carefully tucked the pitiful load inside it.

"I'm going to get right on the radio to Jim Zeebe and have him come out here and hook you up so you don't have to worry none about your car just sitting here."

The cop held open the passenger door with the legend, 'Babylon, Michigan Police Department,' in white against the black panel, and they all piled in, Joy and Little Todd in front, Todd with the girls chattering excitedly in back. A ride in a police car: the thrill of their young lives.

"Marty McConlon," said the uniformed driver.

"Huh?"

"My name."

The radio crackled ominously in the space between the cop and Joy. Todd noticed that Little Todd wasn't buckled in, but, due to the absence of the third belt, sitting on Joy's lap. He was surprised that a police officer would allow that.

The squad car did a sharp U-turn that made the kids squeal, then turned down an asphalt road off of the highway, a road that Todd hadn't noticed before. Darrow Road, the sign read. The hard lump in his stomach made itself known once again when he saw the rusted sign just on the side of this new road: Babylon, 5 miles.

Now why would a Babylon cop have flagged them down that far out of his jurisdiction?

Chapter Two

Paul Highsmith tried to avoid gawking like a tourist as he stood in front of the four-story arched entrance to the Penobscot Building on Fort and Griswold in downtown Detroit. Its immense bronze, limestone, granite and glass face twinkled in the cloud-covered sunlight, its straight-edge styling an ode to Art Deco and the Roaring Twenties. Paul could smell the silty Detroit River blocks away. He'd had an office within walking distance for years and used to love making excuses to visit what had at one time been America's eighth tallest building—all forty-seven stories of it.

When someone bumped him and scurried past, Paul brushed his hand against his wallet, reassuring himself it was still there. Old habits. It broke his reverie and he pushed his way in.

Again, he had to downplay his appreciation for the familiar marble-lined corridors, the rich mahogany woodwork and soaring ceilings, all of which seemed to impress no one else in the workday crowd jostling him left and right in their race for the elevators.

It had only been eight months since his final commute to downtown Detroit's commercial district and barely two since the move to Babylon, but he already missed this. It felt good to be in a linen suit in a big city again. A city that was, hopefully, still big enough for him to go unobserved by former co-workers and associates.

No, he didn't miss everything back here, but certainly the architecture. The city flair.

The elevator took him to the thirty-sixth floor and the offices of Knoll Sullivan/Weldman Group LLP. Floor-to-ceiling glass, polished concrete floors, exposed brick walls and pounded copper and tin highlights. When he'd started coming here, everything had been rainforest hardwoods, plush Oriental carpets, rich Corinthian leather. But the finest comfort had given way to iron foundry edge at a point whose beginnings had escaped him. The battered red brick looked like it had been torn out of a road, only to be installed over the ivory grasscloth and smoothly plastered walls he'd known previously.

He didn't recognize the receptionist, though the smile and youthful appeal were familiar fixtures at such firms. It felt funny having to give up his name and tell this strange young woman that he had an appointment to see Freddie Brace.

"Thank you, Mr. Highsmith," she said. "I'll tell Mr. Brace you're here."

Mr. Brace? As their surrounding had grown more proletarian in appearance, it seemed that the culture had formalized.

He felt slightly distressed in the distressed leather chair he sank deeply into while waiting. People came and went, some vaguely familiar, but there was no sign of the one face he most needed—and dreaded—to see.

"Hey, old man," said Freddie, who came out to get him in only a few minutes. He sounded as heartily British as ever, that clipped, over-enunciated way of discarding his Alabama-by-way-of-Africa roots.

He wore summer-weight wool slacks and a pullover cotton shirt, both in a shade of black that complemented his cocoa skin tones. The tight, short-sleeved shirt actually made him look buff despite his narrow shoulders, a feat suit and tie had never accomplished. Maybe there was something to the new fashion, after all.

Paul walked down a meandering hallway and into an airy office where he was directed to a chair so deep he didn't know how he'd ever extract himself from it. Lights streamed in through windows high enough up the face of the building that the sun was only nine or ten miles away. No bother; it was tinted glass.

Freddie took a similarly overstuffed chair on the opposite side of a copper and glass coffee table that looked heavier than Paul's car.

"Nice suit," said the lawyer after they settled in. It was hard to say whether the line was ironic or not. With him, it could go either way.

After Paul declined the offer of coffee or tea or bottled water, Freddie took a longer look and said, "You look good."

Had it come to that? At just fifty-two, was he already to the point of being complimented for his apparent health and relatively slow rate of decay?

"You do, too," he told his lawyer.

That was followed by more small talk, questions about the welfare of Darby and Tuck, baby pictures peeled from his wallet and shown to the no-doubt disinterested bachelor. Comments about common acquaintances. None of it could distract Paul from his purpose for being here. Today, *he* was the client, not the Detroit office of Boston-based Anchor/Tatum Financial Services, the deep-pocketed firm to which he'd devoted his defunct career.

He'd had an office in a nearby building back in the day. Less than a year ago, actually, before the bottom dropped out of the market and fortunes and life savings got lost and reputations got ruined. Or at least severely scarred.

"So," said Freddie into a brief lull in their shared reminiscences, and Paul knew this was the moment he was supposed to grab. Freddie wouldn't go there until he did.

Paul shifted in his overly accommodating chair. He'd sunk so deeply into its inviting fabric that he felt wedged into comfort, not an

30

altogether good feeling. After squirming briefly, he said, "So what have you found out, Freddie?"

Freddie nodded, as though the right question had been posed. "I've had conversations—informal, and off the record—with people at the SEC and in the attorney general's offices of two states."

God, could it get any more ominous than that last sentence?

"The good news," Freddie was saying, "is that it's not quite a Ponzi or Madoff situation."

Yes, it could get worse. Your lawyer could start throwing around two names that Paul, as a former investment broker, didn't like to hear even when being told that the comparison to his own situation was inapt. It was obvious that this small morsel of good news was only a prelude to the rest of the story. For instance, that phrase, *not quite,* would have to be dealt with.

He waited for it.

"The *un*fortunate thing," Freddie continued after a moment, "is that some of Veck's investment decisions were..." Here he hesitated, pawed through all of the possibilities before selecting the right word. "...aggressive, to say the least."

Paul nodded. "Of course they were aggressive, Freddie. How could our investors earn the kind of returns they were seeing for seven years if the fund was risk-averse?"

"Yes, those returns." Freddie leaned back and his hooded eyes slid over his office.

The latte-colored walls and bleached wood surfaces held framed photographs of Freddie Brace with women. At various times and places he posed with his mother, his sister and with a recent governor of the state. In others, he shared banquets, balls and fundraisers with attractive females in evening attire, some of whom he'd casually referred to, at one point or another, as girlfriends. However, those women were just as likely to refer to Freddie, in conversation, as friend or business associate.

His lawyer had never addressed his sexuality in Paul's company, and that was a blessing. Still, Paul had come to believe from early in their friendship that Freddie lived more or less happily in a closet he had no intention of leaving anytime soon.

Fine with Paul. His thoughts were mainly, at this moment, on one Dominick Veck.

Seven years ago, Veck had seemed like a godsend from Manhattan. They'd been introduced by someone in the Pittsburgh office of Paul's firm who'd raved about the returns his clients were getting. Paul started small, just investing a small portion of the funds of his most aggressive clients, just to see what happened. He earned returns a percentage point or two higher than his other funds. Not high enough to make him suspicious, but Veck definitely earned more of his business.

As Veck outperformed the market, quarter after quarter, Paul's own reputation grew with the satisfaction level of his private, commercial and institutional clients. His success had not gone unnoticed. Three years ago, he'd been made managing partner of the Detroit office and had already, by that point, received a couple seven-figure bonuses and several more in the high six figures.

"It wasn't a...scheme?" Paul said forcefully, as though he could turn the question into a statement of fact.

"The problem," said Freddie, who hesitated before answering, "is that Veck's returns were always high—even when the market dipped. Forensic accountants can trace those early returns to his smart, though high-risk strategies. In other words, he really knew what he was doing—and the market helped. However, in the last year or so, the market went in one direction and he continued in the other."

Which was how Paul had pocketed a significant raise the previous December and an eight-hundred-thousand dollar year-end bonus even while the firm lost money for the first time in decades.

"Veck is talking," Freddie said. "He's telling investigators that he had to keep returns high. His reputation demanded it. He also had multiple mortgages and, naturally, a mistress that had to be kept as comfortable as his wife."

Freddie chuckled at that last comment, then retrieved the humor when he seemed to reflect on how close to Paul's situation he'd hit.

He cleared his throat and started again. "It was only in that last year that Veck started manufacturing returns. Sending out his own balance statements. Figuring that he'd make good when the markets ran bullish again. Only..."

Here, Freddie shrugged. The rest needn't be said. Paul knew as well as everyone what had happened to Wall Street when basic laws of mathematics had caught up with all of that balls-out borrowing and investing and lending. It didn't take more than an hour after Dominick Veck's name had come up in a defensive press release by his firm that an emergency meeting of the board at Knoll Sullivan/Weldman Group LLP had been called in Boston and Paul had been invited to appear.

"I didn't know anything about it, Freddie."

"Of course not, man. You just operated a feeder fund."

Paul winced. *Feeder fund.* A phrase that had become an indictment in and of itself. He was screwed.

"The political climate is such that I can't say the risk of prosecution is non-existent," said Freddie.

Paul had to read between the cautious legalese to hear what was really being said: You *might* go to jail, but the risk is minimal for now.

Meaning that it wasn't a problem that he hadn't brought a toothbrush to this meeting. About all the good news he'd get that day.

"There are, however," Freddie went on, "a couple areas of threat."

"Only a couple?" Paul said, trying for grim humor.

Freddie saw it and flashed an accommodating smile before continuing. "First, there are the investors who lost money. Hundreds have already grabbed attorneys."

"I didn't do anything wrong, Freddie."

The lawyer nodded in full agreement. Charles Manson's attorney had nodded the same way.

"Lawsuits of this nature tend to take a shotgun approach, Paul. Let's hit everyone and see who bleeds. So, in this case we're talking about Dominick Veck and his firm, Knoll Sullivan and you. Hell, they've probably managed to work your office landlord and your window washing service into the action, but, as I like to say, 'suing ain't getting.'"

"Meaning you don't think I'm vulnerable."

Here, Freddie momentarily slipped eye contact. When he returned it he said, "More like, I think all the lawsuits will get consolidated and they'll take one lump-sum settlement from you. You have liability insurance, don't you?"

"My company has—had—coverage on me. But now that I don't work there..."

Freddie studied his face for a long time. Or his eyes remained on Paul and his thoughts drifted elsewhere. Hard to say. Finally, he said, "Which gets us to our second area of concern. Your former employer."

While they'd thrown money at him and promoted him to the top during the good times, Anchor/Tatum had terminated him on the spot during that final board meeting, branding him as the sole culprit of unspecified crimes, instantly obliterating his reputation in the market.

"And now they want their money back," said Paul, thinking his thoughts out loud. "How much?"

Freddie waved a hand in his face. "I don't want you to get bogged down with that at this point, Paul. Their lawyers throw out figures and so do we."

"Meaning you want to settle?"

"It's all theoretical right now, man. Everything is part of the discussion. We'll know more—"

"How much?"

Freddie's gaze wavered. "The latest figure they've handed us is seven million."

Paul would have fallen out of his chair if he wasn't so tightly wedged into it. "Seven million *dollars*?" he asked stupidly. Not the right question, but he had so many it was hard to figure where to start.

33

Now Freddie was waving both hands. "That's why I didn't want to talk specifics," he said. "It's like suing McDonald's for a hundred mil for hot coffee. It's just a starting point."

"I don't have liability coverage," Paul said. "I'm still getting two girls through college and my wife—my ex-wife—won spousal support for the next eight years."

She hadn't *won* it, Paul corrected himself. He'd told his divorce lawyer to agree to it without a fight. Just like he'd volunteered to buy her the Grosse Pointe Woods condo that replaced the family home. He'd staved off guilt with checkbook.

"I know, I know," said Freddie. "That's why you have to leave it to the lawyers. You pay me to do the worrying so you won't have to. We, after all, have grounds for suing your former employer for liability coverage since you were obviously an employee when this happened. There's room for negotiation here."

Paul had been paying a lot of lawyers to assume a lot of worrying lately. Two years ago he'd started with the divorce lawyers and had found that Meredith was in no mood to settle peacefully. Soon after that came the corporate litigators fighting to make sure Paul's name wasn't spoken in the same sentence with such words or phrases as Madoff and feeder funds.

The jury was still out on that one—almost literally.

Even Freddie had been a legal victim of sorts. His close working and personal relationship with Paul had been the main reason Anchor/Tatum had voided their contract with his law firm. Paul didn't even want to think about how Freddie's partners must have reacted to *that* loss of business.

"Okay, okay." He held out his hands, palms out in surrender. "I'll let you take care of it. Just make sure you at least leave me enough to pay you."

"That's always in the forefront," Freddie said, tapping his temple and grinning.

Paul made himself share the laugh. Then, suddenly wanting out of the law office, out of the ornate building and the congested city just as quickly as possible, he said, "I'm glad that's taken care of for now, Freddie. It's a relief knowing you're working on this, and it's really the only reason I came here today. I mean, I had to close out a storage unit in town and run a few errands, but it was this face-to-face that really brought me here."

"Babylon," Freddie said. Part statement but a whole lot more question. "Where the hell and why the hell?"

Paul had gotten used to the question, and he'd managed to come up with a different answer for everyone. The truth was, it was far enough away that he couldn't hear the gossip, but close enough to his girls—if they ever showed any real interest in seeing him and the new family.

"It's not all that far from here," he said. "Maybe an hour south."

"So why have I never heard of it?"

Paul would have told him that the town was so far off the beaten path that it didn't get cell phone service. Would have explained that its obscurity, lost in the woods as it was, had been Babylon's main attraction at the time—although, after barely a couple months, some of the appeal had worn off. He was just starting to make some of those points when she walked in the door.

"Freddie, I'm returning the Huntington file. It's—"

She stopped when she caught sight of him. Tall and slender as ever in a pair of jeans and a black blazer—an outfit that went perfectly with the stone and concrete and copper and exposed brick.

"Oh," she said.

Her sandy hair, not worn as long as he was used to, looked stylishly tangled.

"Hi, Connie," he said.

"Come on in and join us," Freddie said heartily. To Paul it sounded forced. "I was just about to call, tell you you had an important visitor."

Paul could hear the lie in his voice and he knew that she could, too.

"Hello, Dad," she said.

Chapter Three

"I want to see your kids in swim suits. If they don't suit up they're gonna be sorry 'cuz all the other kids're gonna be flapping around in the cool water, and they'll be high and dry, all alone. Sound good, kids?"

That's what the cop, McConlon, had said on the way to the Sundown, but fifteen minutes later he was staring into the brackish water of the motel swimming pool and nodding as though he'd found the situation to be exactly as expected.

"My guess?" he said. "The pump broke down and Mona hasn't gotten around to replacing it yet. But that's more than I know about swimming pool mechanical systems."

The Sundown Motel sat high off the road, at the end of a long, twisting driveway and in front of a green patch of woods. The building was a low-slung plaster bunker, two stories accented by an ugly metal balcony that had started to rust. It was dirty white with a little pink trim, vaguely Latin in design, as if trying to entice vacationers into thinking they'd stumbled upon a Mexican villa. But not trying too hard. The cars in the parking area looked as beaten down as Todd's.

All the way up Darrow Road, into the town and along the dubiously named Pleasant Run Avenue that twisted between tall pines and oaks and green brush, Officer McConlon—"Marty" to his new friends—had bragged about the legendary hospitality afforded guests of the Sundown Motel.

"We get lots and lots of out-of-towners that Mona Dexter puts up for like twelve bucks a night, don't know how she can do it," he'd told Todd and Joy. "And she'll let the bill slide till you cash that first paycheck. I'd like to know how many motels you folks ever stayed at lets you pay when you can afford it."

Todd couldn't think of a one, but the arrangement seemed less generous after his first look at the place. Stuck out five, six miles from the nearest half-ass highway, and not really even in the town, the sad-sack feel of the building and grounds dropped the value of the deal considerably in Todd's estimation.

It was while the Dunbars and Marty McConlon and three disappointed little kids were checking out the algae-infested swimming pool that the motel owner put in her appearance. She was petite, fit and tan, with high cheekbones and a charcoal pair of eyes. McConlon introduced her as Mona Dexter.

"Pool's off-limits. Broken," she said, her voice the sultry growl of a smoker past forty who could still command attention.

Joy sidled a step closer to Todd as Mona puffed on her cigarette and looked them over without seeming to make eye contact.

"No problem," the plump cop sang out. "Hell, when you're only paying twelve a night, a pool's just frosting on the cake."

"The cake costs fourteen a night," said Mona.

"Fourteen," repeated the cop. "I see. You must have raised the rate."

Todd had a hard time reading the other man's expression. The motel owner tapped out an ash on the cracked cement that passed for a pool deck, and crushed it with a slender sandal-clad foot.

"That's alright," said the cop into the silence. "Big family like yours, you'll want two adjoining rooms with connecting doors, and Mona's got a pair like that available for eighteen a night for both."

"It's twenty now, the adjoining rooms."

Mona and the cop exchanged glances that made Todd wonder, not for the first time, what was going on. He'd initially considered the possibility that the cop dragged travelers off the highway for a commission, but that hardly seemed likely now. It didn't look like Mona Dexter even wanted the business.

Three noisy kids thudding about on the other side of the paper-thin wall and Todd and Joy still had more privacy than they'd experienced since last leaving Parkersburg seven months ago. They'd spent all too many nights with his folks in West Virginia, with her sister's family near Knoxville, and with a childhood friend in Richmond. In every case, the whole family had been packed together in a single room. They'd also spent a handful of nights in the Olds, and had been forced to bunk down in homeless shelters on two horrific occasions.

A room to themselves, even in a seedy joint like this, was a luxury to which the Dunbars were unaccustomed.

Todd sat at the cheap desk, absently pawing through empty drawers while Joy showered. No motel stationery, no postcards, not even a Gideon Bible, but what had he expected for the nineteen-dollar-a-night rate for both rooms that Marty McConlon had haggled for them?

He felt itchy and trapped as he listened with mild annoyance to Little Todd and the squealing girls releasing their pent-up energy in the next room. Todd rapped on the shared wall in an effort to lower the volume a notch so he could concentrate on the creased sheet of paper he spread flat on the desktop. It held the awkward, almost childish scribbles that marked the writing effort of the typical male. A company name and address, a boss's name and a crude map.

Marty McConlon had made some phone calls from the motel office while the Dunbars were settling in, and had come back with the scrawled information that Jack Traynor of Corwin Corrugated out on Sennett Street would be expecting him at eight o'clock the following morning, Wednesday.

Just like that, Todd had a job after months of searching, and it wasn't the end of the good news. The cop had also placed a call to the Babylon Town Hall in something called the Drake Municipal Complex and found that the Water Department did indeed need someone to answer phones. It wasn't a sure thing yet, but it looked pretty good. Paid only seven dollars an hour to start, but there'd been plenty of times the family had survived with that much as a primary income.

Yeah, things were looking up. Which made Todd wonder why he felt so uneasy.

The bathroom door clicked open, startling him out of his tense mood. He hadn't even heard the shower water being turned off.

"I was thinking," Joy said, her voice so high and girlish that Todd knew he wasn't going to like where this was going. "The kind of money we'll be making, it's not going to be long before we can afford a house. I mean, it's a possibility, right? Maybe we could start looking now. You know, just window shopping at this point. Checking out neighborhoods and schools, that sort of thing."

Todd didn't know what to say, but he finally came up with, "Houses are expensive." He was speaking to his wife's twisted reflection in the mirror, and it came out more sullen than he meant it.

"Well, not a house then. A trailer. They don't cost much."

"It's the down payment that's beyond us. And credit checks are tougher these days. Besides, we're not talking about staying here."

Joy was rubbing her wet scalp with a thin towel, but she stopped to stare at him, her mouth opening and closing. Her robe, as threadbare as the towel, opened to partly expose one heavy breast. She pulled it tighter and notched it.

"Why do you always do that?" she asked him quietly.

He frowned his confusion at his wife's distorted image.

"Why are you always so eager to point out the downside? Why can't you for once be happy with not one job, but two?"

"You don't have the job yet. The cop said it wasn't a sure thing."

"See? That's what I mean."

Todd swiveled to face her. His anger was dissipating somewhat at the thought of their private room. The kids occupied and unseen. When was the last time that had happened?

"Come here," he said, burying his irritation as deep as he knew how.

Joy sighed as if beginning her litany of reasons why now wasn't the time or place, but she plopped into his lap. Her robe fell away, once again, from that heavy breast. His mouth met hers and he tried to gauge the degree of enthusiasm with which she returned the kiss. Her lips parted slightly and she flicked at his tongue with her own.

He liked the way she was breathing now. Soft, shallow hitches. Shower moisture from her hair dripped to his face. He tried to wipe it dry without killing the moment. One hand snaked to her naked breast as furtively as he'd done it in high school. She stopped his progress like she had on too many occasions back then.

"The kids," she said, still breathing hard enough to suit him. She pulled her face away and gripped her robe with one fisted hand. "The kids."

Todd wiped her shower water from the side of his face and shimmied his hips so she'd leave his lap. The moment was over.

As she stood and moved away he said out of plum irritation, "Don't you see anything funny about this town? Why would they roll out the red carpet like this, give us two jobs and connected motel rooms on credit?"

Not that he was expecting an answer. Joy would ignore him until his mood lightened.

Fine. Todd returned his attention to the cop's scribbled directions. Could there really be so much work in this burg that they had to recruit out-of-town labor? Was it like that *anywhere* in America today?

"Listen," Joy ordered.

He did, then shook his head. "I don't hear anything."

"Neither do I," said Joy before flying out the door in her robe. "The kids," she said again, tossing it over her shoulder.

Chapter Four

Hello, Dad.

Not exactly throwing herself at her father's feet, but what had he expected? His daughter Connie had met Darby Kinston when both worked at Anchor/Tatum, Darby as an account executive in the trading department and Connie still in law school and spending the summer in the firm's compliance department. They'd bonded, two attractive young women thrown together at a stodgy investment banking boutique overrun with middle-aged men.

They weren't the only ones bonding at that time. Paul liked to think that his marriage was already unraveling when he began to take notice of the twenty-seven-year-old beauty and noticing she didn't seem to mind the attention.

As Paul exited I-75 and approached the inexplicably named South Dixie Highway he thought about how poorly he'd handled that day's surprise contact with his eldest daughter. And yet it had, in many ways, seemed consistent with their personal dynamics. Not so different than the awkward way he'd interacted with each of his daughters from their teenage years forward. It seemed that the space between him and them had always been filled with stilted discourse and uncomfortable silences.

The longest silence had started just over two years ago. Paul remembered it to the day: Darby informing him that she'd missed her period that month. It wasn't late; it was nonexistent. So she'd gone out and bought an early pregnancy test kit to confirm her suspicions and the world had changed irretrievably for both of them.

He was a father-to-be at fifty. A man with three grown—or nearly grown—daughters and a forty-eight-year-old wife who wasn't the one expecting. He'd had a lot of explaining to do and it looked like he'd failed on all counts.

There was hope, though, wasn't there?

He pictured Connie after she'd blundered into Freddie Brace's office earlier that day, no idea that she'd find her father there. Coming to a standstill, mouth open and fingers fidgeting with the case file she'd been caught in the act of returning.

After such painfully awkward introductory comments as "You look good," and "I like what you've done with your hair," Paul had tried this one: "Tuck is walking now."

Not expecting much from it, Tucker Highsmith being the girl's most unexpected little brother, but her face had broken into its first honest smile. "Really?" she'd said. "I'll bet he's cute. I'd love to see him again."

Maybe *that* was something to build a new relationship upon.

He gasped and jerked in his seat as his phone vibrated against his crotch where he'd laid it to be sure he was aware of incoming calls.

"Yeah. Hey, Freddie, what's up?"

"You sound...startled or something."

His lawyer didn't miss a thing.

"It's nothing. Just...driving. Wasn't expecting a call, that's all."

"Oh. Okay. Listen, I wanted to..." White noise could be heard washing over the other end of the line while Freddie tried to pick his way through his thoughts. "I just wanted to make sure you were cool with Connie dropping in. I mean, it's none of my business but things seemed a little..."

Again, struggling to put words to his thoughts, but this time Paul put him out of his misery with an interruption. "No, it's fine, Freddie. Connie and I, we just, she's still a little tender, that's all."

Paul crossed the South Dixie Highway and headed deeper into the woods. Fewer cars, more scrub land, narrower, twisting roads. A sharp crunch of static on the line.

Freddie said, "She loves you, man. You raised one hell of a daughter, one hell of a human being."

He raised her? Not really. He'd been stuck at work most of the time. It had been Meredith who'd taught all three of his girls to be decent and gracious and polite. To smile even when using diplomatic language to tell their old man to fuck off for what he'd done to their mother. To grow distant and formal while avoiding phone calls and courteously and succinctly responding to emails.

"Freddie..." Paul had slipped onto the barely marked Darrow Road. It grew so narrow after a couple twists, century oaks and elms crowding the shoulder, that he was thankful he'd never seen a big rig coming the other way. He pictured himself reversing all the way back to the highway. "I never meant all of this to happen." Meaning, he supposed, the cheating, the unplanned pregnancy, the legal troubles, the divorce, the estrangement with his daughters. "Jesus," he said as it all hit him at once. "I've really screwed up, haven't I?"

His phone barked static again.

"Things happen," Freddie replied after a moment. He sounded farther away than before. "Bad things to decent people. If that wasn't the case—"

"You'd be out of business."

"Exactly," said his lawyer with a sad laugh. "But listen, man. I just called to tell you...I'm there if you need me."

A long pause followed. Nearly as long as a few of the silences

between Connie and himself back in Detroit, but not nearly as
awkward.

"You're not billing me for this call, are you?" Paul asked.

"I hadn't planned on it. But you're making me second-guess myself
on that, asshole."

Both men laughed comfortably.

"I appreciate that. I really do," Paul said. "Now you gotta hang up
so I can call Darby and tell her I'm on my way. The whole town seems
to be in a cell phone dead zone so I've got to call when I can."

"Uh huh. Tell me again why you moved to Babylon, Michigan?"

Paul wore a grin as he hung up. The same uninhibited grin he'd
pasted on his face while exiting the Penobscot Building and leaving
Detroit as a man who'd lost all he could possibly lose and was now in
full, triumphant retreat. Headed back to his new life, the one he was
trying to construct upon the brightly burning bridges of all of his
fucked-up yesterdays.

Chapter Five

"The kids."

Todd's stomach dropped. He flew out of the room right behind his wife and found the front door to the adjoining room standing open. The room dead quiet. Empty. No wonder they'd heard nothing bus suspicious silence from that shared wall. Todd felt his face freezing into the sullen expression he wore when he felt emotions building, and knew he'd have to keep his thoughts from Joy. From himself, even.

"Find them," she said, the girlishness long gone as she clutched at her thin robe.

"They're around," he said over his shoulder as he began gobbling up cracked sidewalk with big strides of his short legs.

The family had been lodged on the ground floor at the rear of the motel, their view an open field before a steep ravine overgrown with scrubby woods and dissected by a swift creek that could be heard rather than seen, somewhere below.

God, not the creek.

Todd's mind watched his kids slipping, sliding, flailing in the swift water. He called out, "Melanie Crissie Todd!" in a single burst of contained panic. Nothing came back from the wooded ravine but his own sharp echo.

He saw rooflines a mile or more away on the opposite side of the cut, and wondered with vicious despair if the town liked little kids too much. That would explain the cop, McConlon, stopping strangers' cars: to snatch children for perverts.

But that was crazy.

"Melanie Crissie Todd!"

Nothing. Todd got back to the narrow sidewalk flanking the back of the motel and followed it around to the front, to a niche tucked under the metal stairs to the second floor balcony, and found them.

His breath caught in his throat and he felt his vision threaten to go gray as he fought to catch up with his spent adrenaline.

They stood in still fascination, watching a hollowed-out woman and two scraggly kids beat up a snack food vending machine. The woman was young, but as scrawny as some middle-aged Depression-era Oakie from photos he'd once seen in an admission-free museum in southern Ohio or Kentucky when he wanted to get the family out of the rain. He'd studied those stark photos with a burning sensation deep in his belly.

The woman with the scraggly kids was wrapped in a pair of jeans that could have fit a fifteen-year-old girl, giving her an unwholesome agelessness. Smoke curled around her face from the cigarette dangling from her lips. Todd watched her miserly breasts twitch as she wrestled with the machine.

She uttered something that had to have been a curse, but the words got twisted by her cigarette. Just as well for the sake of the kids who still watched the transaction in open-mouthed fascination.

"You gotta shake it just right," she drawled, apparently to Todd. Then she went back to hand-to-hand combat with it.

The kids with her, a boy and a girl, looked as rode-hard as the woman. Their hair and clothing were dirty and they seemed underfed, underamused. They'd mirror his own kids after a couple more years of this, Todd admitted to himself with brutal honesty.

He remembered the shame he'd felt about their grimy condition while parked on the shoulder of the narrow highway, waiting for the Babylon cop to approach. Now, as he watched Melanie, Crissie and Little Todd milling around the scrawny woman and her dirty kids, like the vending machine antics were the most excitement they'd experienced in a long while, Todd asked himself where things had gone so wrong.

His life, he realized, kept coming back to this. He'd been born and raised in a mountain town where louse-ridden dogs and cars on blocks were part of the landscape. He felt like he'd been the only one in his big, extended family who'd even noticed how different their lives were from what he saw on TV. But then he'd perpetuated the hillbilly stereotype by getting Joy pregnant before they'd finished high school. A hurried marriage and the mine job, soon to follow. By the time his third child was born, Todd was making eighteen an hour plus overtime and Joy was working part-time taking appointments at a beauty salon in Parkersburg. Hardly the Trumps, but they'd saved up most of the down payment for a new home they'd already picked out and pre-qualified for.

Then the economy went to shit and the ax fell at the coal mine and the salon. Story of Todd Dunbar's life.

"I *said*, is it okay if yours have some?"

The scrawny but not altogether unattractive woman was dangling packages of chips and pretzels just out of reach of Crissie and Little Todd. Like taunting chimps at the zoo. Melanie hung back, but only slightly.

"Oh...yeah," he said. He wasn't sure if there would be a supper that could be spoiled. He glanced at his watch. Not quite five o'clock. "Late summer days," he said. "Hard to keep track of time." Some sort of apology, but he wasn't sure what for.

She watched him like she didn't have a clue what he was talking about, and he didn't blame her. But the day had been something of a fog from the moment the Olds got pulled over.

Trying to find a foothold back into the conversation, Todd told his girls to thank the woman for the snacks she quickly tossed at them. In seconds, all five kids—the woman's and Todd's—had pealed out of sight in one noisy clump. Todd hoped the lady wasn't going to hold out her hand for reimbursement.

"Nice kids," she said.

"Todd...Todd! Did you find them?"

Oh Jesus, he'd forgotten. And now Joy appeared on the balcony almost overhead, still trying to grasp that thin robe around her no longer narrow hips.

"I'm sorry," he said. "I...yeah, I found them. They're okay, Joy. Everything's fine."

"Thanks for telling me," she said. Pissed royally.

"Joy, would you put some clothes on," he said, feeling as ridiculous as his wild-eyed wife should have felt.

She said something he didn't quite hear—probably for the best—before stomping down the stairs and back to the room. Too angry and embarrassed to face the woman who'd grabbed Todd's attention.

"Your wife," the woman said with the cigarette and a trace of a smile.

She turned and plinked more coins into the vending machine.

"Listen," said Todd. "I'll get you some money back at the room for what the girls ate. I just have to break a single." Had to offer, at least.

The woman gave a little laugh and shrugged her bony shoulders. "Money," she said. "I got enough of it, finally."

"Well, I guess I should—"

"Kathy Lee Dwyer."

She turned, hugging a bundle of cellophane-wrapped munchies from the suddenly amenable machine to her meager chest and took a seat on one of the metal stair steps leading up to the balcony. She dropped her stash next to her and looked up. "I guess it's your turn now."

"Oh," he said after an uncomfortable pause. "Sorry. Todd Dunbar."

"Glad to meet you, Sorry Todd Dunbar," she said with a wink in her voice.

With her sitting there, he couldn't help noticing her bitter little nipples poking through the thin fabric of her tank top while she ripped into a bag with tiny, nicotine-stained teeth.

"Dinner," she said. "You work six, eight hours a day in a restaurant, last thing you want is restaurant food. Not that this is any better."

Nonetheless, she munched contentedly for half a minute.

45

"You folks are new," she said.

"Just got in today, my wife and kids." He half-waved toward the balcony above them as if reminding her of her near-meeting with his better half.

"Yeah," she said, that half-smile returning.

Groping for more, Todd said, "I'm starting work here tomorrow."

"About as surprising as learning it snows in Alaska."

Todd leaned against the rust-flaked metal railing and watched Kathy Lee Dwyer finish one bag, crumple and toss it into a nearby waste container, and tear into another.

It wasn't a subject he wanted to delve deeply into, but Todd found himself saying, "There seems to be a lot of work here in Babylon."

The woman shook her head slightly and let out a chuckle that turned wet with cigarette phlegm. "It's just like everywhere else. Not a lot of work at all." She took a draw on the butt she'd let mostly burn away between two fingers. "There's lots of *jobs*. Big difference."

"Uh huh," he said, suddenly not anxious to hear more.

Other voices and coarse male laughter started up, and Todd took a few steps toward the sounds. Beyond the alcove housing the vending machine, he could see a dozen people across the patch of brown lawn. They were gathering on the weed-choked pavement surrounding the pitiful swimming pool.

Men, mostly, with working men's tans and jeans plastered to their legs by a day's accumulation of dust and sweat. They gripped six-packs and lawn chairs. One hoisted a big Eighties-style radio on a broad shoulder as he cut across the dead grass to join the others. A battered pickup truck churned up the long driveway from Pleasant Run and expelled more men, more beer.

When he returned to the thin woman sitting on the stair she said, "After five. Place starts to fill up fast about now, when the factories and such shut down for the day."

She crumpled up another snack bag and sat it next to her. She licked the salt from her chapped red fingers, stubbed out her smoke, expertly flicked it into the trash container and produced another and a lighter in a flash of nicotine magic.

Todd peeked around the alcove wall again. There were more of them now. Even a few kids mucking about by the stagnant water. Mental note: keep the kids away from there. Someone turned on the boom box and the twang of old-style country drifted their way.

"They all work here?" he asked, thrusting a thumb in their direction.

"They have *jobs* here," she said, as if intent on making that point clear.

Todd was now very conscious of the electric hum of the vending

46

machines. It vaguely annoyed him.

"Except for Carl Haggerty and D.B., I been here the longest, a couple months. Guy named Doyle-something came with Carl, before me and after D.B., but I barely knew him and he just up and disappeared one day, so I s'pose he don't count. A couple others have left the same way, all of a sudden." She shrugged. "Drifters."

She watched him watching her, and went on. "I work at a diner on Main View Road, which is what Pleasant Run becomes once it rolls into the heart of town. Maybe a mile from here. Town's got like four or five blocks of gas stations, bars, small offices, a department store, post office and what have you." She sucked on her cigarette. "Place I work, it's the Old Time Café. I get six dollars an hour on top of the tips, which ain't bad. Not bad at all. Sometimes three bucks on a seven-dollar breakfast check. Figure it out."

Todd had no idea where she was going with this.

She shrugged off his blank stare. "I'm not saying I'm getting rich, but they let me work my own hours and even pay basic medical for my kids and me. Ideal job, right? And yet they're so desperate to fill the position, they get Marty McConlon to flag me down and make me the offer right there on the spot. I mean, like this whole town ain't got a single person wants a waitressing job with the best tips, benefits and working conditions I ever seen."

Todd felt his chest tighten. He grabbed his pack and plugged a cigarette between his lips, lit it and dragged deep. He still had no idea what the woman was getting at. Didn't know what she wanted from him.

"Did he tell you your car was a road hazard?" he asked her.

She laughed. "That's what he used on you, huh? That's how he got Denver Dugan and Jamey Weeks and some of the others. But with me—" She stopped, her eyes flitting from his gaze. "It was different with me," she mumbled. She stubbed out her cigarette and flicked it so that it sparked hard on the pavement. "Let's just say—"

She never finished. Her eyes went as wide as Todd's when the screaming started. Maybe she thought it was one of her own ragged children, but it wasn't.

It was Melanie.

Chapter Six

The road tilted upward enough to get a faint whine out of the smooth engine of the Lexus, and Paul had to stay alert to follow the multiple curves taking him up Darrow Road until it became Pleasant Run and took him into his still largely unfamiliar home.

It was a few minutes after five as he fiddled with a radio that had turned to static mush at the same point as always, just before that seedy motel sitting high on the edge of town.

Although Savannah Easton, their real estate agent, had hinted that Babylon didn't exactly lay down the welcome mat for newcomers, there seemed to be quite a few of them staying at the Sundown Motel. He could see them as he drove by, lounging by the barely visible swimming pool. At first he'd taken them for locals in that the town couldn't possibly draw that many overnight lodgers, but they didn't look like everyone else he'd seen about town. Mostly men, they looked rough. They looked like outsiders imported to do the town's heavy lifting during the day, then dispatched to the outskirts as evening approached. Like third-world laborers in some oil-rich nation.

The Lexus flew past the motel and negotiated a slight bend where Pleasant Run smoothed out and changed names to Main View, one of Babylon's two main drags. Paul hung a left onto Third Street and cut to Middle View where he took a right. It was nearly as busy as Main View here, but fewer restaurants and retail and more modest commercial space.

With too much time on his hands since he and Darby and Tuck had moved here, he'd burned off some of his energy with long, aimless walks that had gradually uncovered the town's delightfully skewered sense of time. A curious number of shops, restaurants, offices and service providers only came alive after sundown. There seemed to be as many Babylonians walking the streets at midnight as could be found in the middle of the afternoon.

Stopping for the light on Fifth and Middle View, just before Crenshaw, their own street, his attention was drawn to a plate glass window. He frowned as his thoughts returned to a minor, though unsettling, event of the week before.

Babylon hadn't been Paul's first choice, but he loved strolling its moonlit streets. The Detroit suburb he'd formerly called home consisted of a couple square miles of cul-de-sacs with pseudo Tudors and sprawling McMansions on imposing lots, the residential pockets bordered by cookie-cutter malls and franchise restaurants.

Babylon, by pleasant contrast, actually had its own distinct downtown, five or six blocks of unzoned brick and wood storefronts from a mishmash of eras. The pubs and specialty shops and service stations, the theater and bowling alley and department store and funeral home carried names that would most likely be known only to fellow residents: Crenshaw, Chambers, Chaplin, Buck, Tolliver—all evidently prominent names in Babylon, perhaps for decades or a century or more. It was a place with its own unique history, with a story attached to every faded brick, each carved cornice and pilaster.

It was on a night of exploration the week before that he'd stumbled upon the colorfully named Winking Dog Saloon. The same bar that his Lexus now idled uncomfortably near while the damned red light refused to change.

He wasn't sure what had drawn him to the Winking Dog that other night except that he carried a romantic picture of planting his ass on a barstool just like the regulars, and knocking back a beer. Make it a shot and a beer if that was the local custom. The night being cool and clear and inviting, he could see himself as the transplanted city boy, hailed for his sophistication and youthful charm. He'd meet people who knew nothing about him—his soap-opera relationships and suddenly rocky career—and talk sports and local gossip with them. They'd later tell their friends and neighbors, "That new guy, Highsmith, he's not so bad for a rich city guy. Drinks beer, slams shots and tells dirty jokes."

And he—and by extension, Darby—would finally find the acceptance that had eluded them since moving day.

Right in line with his fantasy, the locals did take notice as soon as he walked in the door of the Winking Dog. All heads had turned, and conversations stopped.

Paul stood frozen in the doorway, his psychic hairs bristling like a cat sensing danger from the shadows. It was as if he'd intruded on an orgy, the closest image his mind could come up with for what was going on.

And yet there was nothing happening in there. Darts were being thrown, girls chatted up, cigarettes smoked. At the bar sat a cluster of men in their twenties. They were dressed in the summertime attire of young men everywhere: baggy shorts, loose T-shirts, ball caps. But they watched him with glittery-eyed interest. Grinning, unshaven, one or two with long, greasy hair jutting beneath their caps.

"Hi, Paul," one of the grinning men said, his voice like gravel at the bottom of a wheelbarrow. His whiskers and brim-shadowed eyes shone black against his pale face.

Paul nodded. More than once he'd made sales presentations to grim, hard-faced clients and plowed on as though he couldn't read their doubts. He'd held the shocked or sullen glances of employees while terminating them on more occasions than he liked to recall, but he failed this time and this time only. He couldn't force a return greeting from his locked jaw.

Then another sound goosebumped his arms and the back of his neck. A low rumble, something you felt in your feet before your eardrums caught notice. The slow warning growl of a threatened animal. A big animal. A sound you'd take very seriously if it came out of the dark woods.

Just as intimidating coming out of a dark bar.

Paul backed up a step until his spine pressed against the door that had closed behind him.

It had come from the dark-whiskered man who'd spoken to him.

"Purcell," warned the bartender, a rangy, broad-shouldered man with a jewel twinkling in one earlobe.

Paul gave his watch an exaggerated glance, shook his head and mumbled something that was supposed to imply a need to leave the premises as suddenly as he'd entered.

Someone snickered. "Guess you got places to go." He had a male model's sharp, clean features under a spike of unwashed blond hair, and a high taunt of a voice.

Without his eyes deviating from the crowd, Paul reached behind him and found the doorknob. As he did, he heard the unearthly, deep-throated growl again, a sound so untamed that he would have been sure it came from the television over the bar except that it relayed nothing more beastly than a Tigers ballgame.

"Stop in again, Paul, when you have more time," the one named Purcell said, his voice still faintly tainted with the sound that had worked its way up his throat seconds before.

"Ooh, Duane, you gonna get us in trouble with Drake," sneered the blond man.

The last thing Paul Highsmith heard as the door swung shut behind him was a chorus of high, insolent laughter.

Recalling that evening of a week or so ago as he still idled in front of the interminable light, Paul locked his car doors. When he finally got the green, he accelerated away from the Winking Dog Saloon, took a left on Crenshaw and cruised home.

Chapter Seven

As Todd wheeled around the corner several steps ahead of Kathy Lee Dwyer, he steeled himself for the worst. The high-pitched screaming had stopped, but only to be replaced by the snarling profanity of an adult male. Whatever he was about to find, he wasn't going to like it, Todd told himself.

His fatalism was an effective habit. He'd survived long stretches of unemployment by visualizing his family homeless and hungry. With that future planted firmly in mind, the reality of the situation never seemed quite so severe.

Just like the mental picture of his daughter squirming in the grasp of a lust-fueled child molester thoroughly overpowered the reality of a barrel-chested man pounding a large stick against a garbage bin while Melanie stifled her sobs behind one hand she'd planted to her mouth.

Todd wrapped an arm around her while a chorus of "What'sa matter, what happened?" erupted around them. Almost instantly, Todd, Melanie and the cursing lunatic were surrounded by sweat-stained workmen and a handful of bedraggled women.

"I'll tell you what's the goddamn matter," roared the enraged man with the stick. "It's those fucking rats again. They nearly took off that little girl's foot this time." He turned from his Dumpster-beating to reveal a blunt pair of arms with bunched muscles and a thick beard that hid a good deal of his contorted anger.

All eyes fell on Melanie's sandal-clad feet. Todd could only breathe again after counting ten intact toes.

"What's going on, Judd?" calmly asked a tall man with wide shoulders and a pink face.

"I'm telling you, D.B., it's getting worse around here. About time we did something ourselves 'cuz they sure as hell ain't gonna take care of it."

The man apparently known as D.B. winked at Melanie as he ambled over to his infuriated friend and laid an arm casually on his shoulder. "Come on, Judd. Whatever it was, it's long gone. And there's no damage, thank God."

"There really is a bite mark there," mumbled a very thin, middle-aged man with pinched voice and a ponytail.

As all eyes turned to her exposed red polished toenails, Melanie buried her face in her father's hard belly in mortification.

"Yeah, right," a black woman drawled.

"Well, not on her feet, maybe," the ponytailed man admitted. "But on her sandal. See?"

Todd squatted for a closer look. Yes, there seemed to be some kind of mark on the dirty white strap separating her big toe from the rest.

"It almost got me," Melanie murmured into her father's neck.

"What'd I tell you?" said the enraged man with the stick and fire in his eye. "What did I tell you? The fuckers nearly got her. You heard her."

"Judd Maxwell, don't you be using language like that in front of a little girl," Kathie Lee snapped. "Where the fuck is your common sense?"

Judd glared at the garbage bin, then exchanged glances with everyone gathered around them, a fairly large crowd by now. The man's body quivered like he'd just grabbed a power line. Todd was glad that the wild beard contained at least some of his intensity or he'd have scared Melanie even further.

"I'm leaving if we gotta keep putting up with this shit," the man snarled.

His eyes seemed to blame everyone in his path for whatever calamity had befallen them. "The good news, D.B.," he said, "is I finally got one of them little fuckers." His tone now indicated the possibility of a smile lurking within all that hair, but who could tell?

The tall, pink-faced man showed a shade or two of interest. "Yeah? Let's haul it into the open."

Todd watched the two men paw through the garbage in and around the big metal bin. They yanked at bags that had fermented in the late-summer sun, and he backed away from the hot stench of rotting vegetables and sour milk, the wave of repulsion blending uncomfortably with the sweat and grime of the off-duty laborers. He clenched his daughter even tighter, wondering if this was what it was always going to keep coming back to: body odor and beer and cigarettes and raging rodents.

"So what's all this fuss about?" called out a black guy with square shoulders and round belly. "Like you never seen rats before, fer crissake."

Judd, sitting like dislodged royalty on a throne of garbage bags, his big stick in hand like a scepter, stopped directing D.B.'s efforts long enough to glare at the disbeliever. "No doubt you got rats where you come from, Carl, and maybe they're even big enough to cart off little kids, but in my neck of the woods we tend to take care of problems like this."

"What I see is a little girl with, at worst, a nibbled-on sandal. Mice, probably. Let's not call out the National Guard, huh?"

Excellent point, thought Todd. He patted his daughter's head, wordlessly sending the point home to her.

"That's right," said a big man of about fifty. "You want to make waves 'cuz the town's got rats? Hell, what town don't?" He had the kind of voice that began life as a rumble from deep inside his immense chest cavity and grew to enormous proportions by the time the words broke free.

"Rodents big enough to wear dog collars, and twice as mean," Judd grumbled as he pointed out new places beneath the bin and in the shadowy corners of the building for D.B. to look.

"Judd, I don't see nothing," his friend said.

The compact man sitting in garbage cursed, then hopped down to take a more active role in the investigation. "I gotta do everything," he grumbled.

Todd bent to his daughter and, speaking close to her ear, said, "Tell me about it, Mel. What happened out here?"

He felt her nuzzling his face as she found his ear with her lips. "Rat," she stage-whispered. "Big one with huge teeth."

Or mouse, Todd thought. You couldn't blame her for confusing the one with the other. Especially after hearing the guy with the beard blowing it all out of proportion. He patted her shoulder, then pulled her to the fringes of the crowd.

"What the hell's going on here? Judd Maxwell, you'd better have some damned good excuse for tearing through my trash. And why are all these people here?"

Silence descended like midnight snow. It sizzled out the fire in Judd's eyes. He lowered his gaze from the fiery Sundown Motel owner to the thick stick he tapped on one foot. D.B., meanwhile, became one with the shadows gathering between the motel's stucco wall and the overflowing bin.

"I see you, Don Brandon," Mona Dexter bellowed, apparently using the man's proper name. "You get out here with Judd and explain to me what you're doing throwing my trash around like that."

"It's the rats, Mona," Judd whined as the tall man with the fine red hair and an even rosier face than before shuffled reluctantly into full view.

Todd watched the motel owner's face twitch, briefly lose its frozen rigidity, then gain it back with a vengeance. "Rats," she said.

"It's true, Mona," Judd sputtered. "I'm tired of being called a liar."

"I seen 'em too, Mona," said the big man with the big voice. "I'm not complaining or nothing, 'cuz your day rates suit us fine, but—"

"I'm glad to hear you're not complaining, Denver," she said, advancing on him as quick as a hound dog going after bear.

Denver backed up. He looked like he would have gladly climbed the nearest tree.

"This time I got proof," Judd volunteered. He twirled his big stick, rested it on one shoulder and waited for a reaction.

D.B., looking no more intent on getting further involved than the bear of a man Mona Dexter had just treed, said, " Judd thinks he got one this time."

Judd said, "Mona, you got rats here. You need to get an exterminator."

The motel owner's dark eyes pierced Judd's. "What do you mean, you got one?" she finally asked, hitting every consonant.

Making Todd somehow glad he wasn't the asshole with the stick.

Judd, for his part, seemed to sense a trick question. The triumphant glint died in his eyes as the big stick left his shoulder. He pointed it toward Todd, standing along the outer ring of crowd, Melanie clinging to him. "The damned thing bit the little girl," he said, putting more of a whine into it than he probably would have liked. "We got evidence this time, Mona. Look at her shoe."

She did no such thing. Her dagger stare never left Judd. "What do you mean, you got one?" she repeated, even slower, even harder this time.

"Well, I thought I did, but..."

"Apparently, it got away," D.B. finished softly. "But Judd did get in a few licks, judging by this fresh yellow shit smeared on the wall back here. Pus, I guess. Or something."

"You wanna see?" Judd asked, and of course everyone did. Even the women who looked revolted and held their kids back.

Todd melted from the surging crowd, but his ears picked up murmurs of "Gross," and "Ooh, what is it?" He'd have gone for a quick peak himself, but Melanie's grip held him in place. Besides, his attention was drawn elsewhere.

As set adrift from the crowd as Todd and Melanie, the motel owner seemed unaware of anyone around her as she stared vacantly into the distance.

Paul watched her lips move.

"I'm not responsible for this," Mona Dexter mumbled to herself. "I didn't even want 'em here."

Chapter Eight

Paul sighed at the sight of the sky-blue Escalade in his driveway. What reason could Savannah Easton possibly have for paying them an unannounced visit tonight? She'd already put in her requisite housewarming appearance, presenting Darby and him with a bottle of moderately priced champagne and an oversize basked of fruit when they'd moved in. Paul had seen so much of the real estate agent over the past several months that, unless she was here to pay off their next month's mortgage out of gratitude for the commission, he really wasn't interested.

"Paul, come in, come in," Savannah commanded as exuberantly as though it was the real estate agent's home he'd accidentally entered. "Darby's brewing coffee. I'll make sure she's making enough for three. I certainly know my way around the kitchen by now."

The interior of their new home was a spacious expanse of glass and white stone with a balcony overlooking the two-story foyer. Less than five years old, it was no accident that it looked absolutely nothing like the 1930s Tudor in which Paul and his former wife had raised three kids. A month after moving in, it was still stacked with half-empty boxes and neatly folded piles of clothing. Darby's potted plants were everywhere, including weirdly flowering cacti he couldn't even identify and would never know how to water. There were bamboo and granite floors, walls of windows and high, swooping ceilings. Some, like the one in the family room, had hidden tract lighting aimed at blank walls in need of expensive artwork yet unpacked or un-envisioned.

Savannah Easton returned from her kitchen errand and tucked herself, one shapely leg under her, in a wicker love seat in what had been christened the sunroom by Darby. Not that it contained any greater glass exposure than just about any other room in the massive house.

"No thanks," Paul said, belatedly turning down the offer for coffee.

Savannah languidly held out her arm to him and he forced a smile as he took her hand in a loose embrace. He was never quite sure how to shake a woman's hand and always suspected that he was somehow insulting female executives with a too-weak or too-firm grip.

"So how are you finding your new neighbors?" she asked him when he'd returned her hand to her. "Have you met anyone yet?"

The real estate agent's expressive eyes were violet today. Paul suspected tinted contact lenses. He glanced toward the doorway, hoping to see Darby approaching. No such luck. He eased into a fabric easy chair across from her.

"We really haven't had a chance to get out," he said. "As busy as we've been around here."

The truth was, they'd met literally no one. Not a single neighbor had dropped by, unless Darby had struck up a stray conversation without telling him, and he doubted it.

"It's the times we're living in," he said, more or less thinking out loud. "It's been that way in the cities for a long time, people keeping to themselves, avoiding their neighbors. It's just that television and the Internet let small town residents see how it's supposed to be everywhere, and they've become as isolated as everyone else."

Where that came from he wasn't sure, but it rang true.

"I'm sure you're right, Paul. But even beyond that, the residents of Babylon have something of a reputation for maintaining their distance. That's why you don't hear of outsiders moving in here."

That included Savannah herself, who lived closer to the lake. She'd tried talking the Highsmiths into lakefront living, which suited Paul fine. In fact, he had a fantasy of moving to one of the Lake Erie islands and living the life of a beach bum. It had been his younger but far more practical wife who'd reminded him of the need for good schools and easy access to the mainland in case of emergency.

Savannah shared very little about the odd town the Highsmiths had stumbled into by accident during the course of an aimless drive, but she'd helped them find their property and close the sale. Of course, there hadn't been any frank discussions about the reclusive nature of the locals when they'd been considering the house and the area. Or the lack of cell phone coverage and spotty Internet access, for that matter.

Darby floated into the room with two steaming mugs.

"Hi, honey," she said as she planted a kiss on his cheek and set down a stone mug on a stand in front of their visitor.

Darby Kinston-Highsmith always rushed her entrance as though it was part of her latest workout routine. It appeared to be such a routine that had been interrupted by the unannounced arrival of their real estate agent, for Darby's face was still flushed with cardiovascular strain, her ash-blond hair tangled with sweat and hanging in her crystal-blue eyes. She was a black, skintight body stocking under a baggy number 23 LeBron James jersey.

"What's this about the neighbors?" she asked. "Oh, shit. I forgot the cream."

"Doesn't she look wonderful," Savannah murmured as Darby dashed from the room.

Paul looked for signs of sly bitchiness in the other woman's face, voice or body language, but found nothing. He was chronically beset with imagined scenarios spinning in small minds: married boss with three grown children lays eyes on the sexy new girl in the office. Things start innocently enough with meetings after work, and escalate quickly into overnight business trips, quick promotions and suspicious cell phone records and credit card charges. Eventually comes the discovery, tears, lawyers, painful talks with the kids, and divorce of a middle-aged wife who'd let herself gain a few pounds over the years. Then, an engagement announcement, a ring with a rock twice the size of the ex-wife's, and remarriage with baby shower suspiciously soon to follow.

Although that had pretty much been the sequence of actual events, it gave no one the right to air their nasty little thoughts. There'd been so much more to it that couldn't be reduced to mere facts. For instance, his and Meredith's marriage had, in reality, died at least six years before Darby Kinston had ever walked into the firm. And it really had been her sharp mind that had drawn him to the much younger woman—though he didn't expect even his closest friends to believe that one.

"Much better," said Darby, returning just as swiftly with spoons and cream in a silver pitcher she must have frantically dug through an unpacked box to find. "I've been trying to use skim milk lately, but it makes the coffee look like mud. So cream remains my one vice, or at least the only one I'm admitting to right now. But I apologize for it."

It was impossible that Darby carried more than 110 pounds on her five-four frame, but she carefully monitored her fat grams.

Savannah was a beautiful woman in her own right, but at about fifty, she'd started to use tricks of makeup and wardrobe and coloration to gain the effect that the Darbys of the world got without yet thinking about it. Savannah's raven hair came from a salon, not a bottle. And of course there were those eyes, large and almond-shaped and violet today.

"Honey, how about you? Have you met anyone yet?"

Paul forced himself back into the conversation. He'd missed the last minute or two of it, but managed to catch up quickly enough. "No. That's what I was just telling Savannah. But I also told her we've been busy around here. Unpacking and putting the house together. And then there's Tuck, of course. We really haven't had time to get out."

Why did he sound so defensive? It was as though he found it important to convince Savannah that their shunned state was their own doing. Yes, that was it. After he'd lost the respect and companionship of so many friends and neighbors and business associates following the dramatic breakup of his marriage and career, it seemed important to show that he wasn't still experiencing rejection.

Maybe that's why they'd moved to this hidden, reclusive little town in the first place: to escape further shame.

Savannah sipped delicately, then carefully set her mug down on the table. "Well, I hate telling the both of you this because of the unfortunate timing, but Paul, do you remember that darling renovated Victorian you commented on in North Shores?"

Paul shrugged. "Yeah, I guess so." Wondering where this was going.

"Well, as I told you both at the time, it positively wasn't for sale. Even in the declining real estate market, you authorized me to make an offer that was incredibly generous—but they never batted an eye."

"Yeah, now I remember," said Paul.

"Well, the unfortunate thing is—or fortunate, depending on how coldly you want to look at it—the husband lost his job a couple weeks ago. He feels he's priced out of the job market here, and the Michigan economy being what it is, they're thinking about cashing out and moving."

"We're so sorry," said Darby, as though it were somehow their fault.

"Yes," said Savannah. "But the reason I bring it up is that they remembered how you'd shown interest and they called me out of the blue. I took the liberty of quoting a price that was just a few thousand dollars higher than what we'd offered before, and they sounded very interested. Now, obviously that wasn't a firm offer since I hadn't first approached the two of you. But with what I think I can get for your place here..."

Paul watched the woman. Studied her lips for the smile that must eventually break through. Glancing away momentarily, he saw that Darby was studying their guest with equal intensity. Savannah gave no hint of noticing their disbelief as she prattled on about interest rates, declining market values, tax bases and financing options. No, she didn't seem to be joking.

"Hold it, hold it, Savannah," Paul said, finally stemming the flow of words with an arm extended like a traffic cop. "If I'm hearing you right, you're suggesting..."

He looked at his wife for help, but she seemed to be waiting for Paul to make some sense of the matter.

The real estate agent laughed, a gracious tinkle of a sound. "I know how it sounds," she said, "and I'm not trying to get you to sign anything this very moment. But you'll recall that I was pulling for North Shores right from the beginning. Darling little community, much friendlier than Babylon. But then, what town isn't?" Savannah tittered merrily. "We have a sort of unwritten rule at our office to ignore Babylon altogether. And you've got to admit, I never encouraged you two to take your search here. But once you did, I could hardly dissuade you. There are housing laws, you know. But I did my best."

As her voice rose higher, she sounded desperate to avoid blame—but for what?

Paul and Darby exchanged quick glances before Darby said, "Tell me, Savannah, is there anything wrong with the town? I mean, beyond it being a bit aloof."

"Absolutely not, dear," came the reply, too quick, too loud, too emphatic.

The Highsmiths had not only discovered Babylon without their real estate agent's help—but also without her support, as Paul now thought about it. The town, as Darby said, "looked like home." It wasn't "picturesque," "quaint" or "postcard-perfect," and it wouldn't ever be referred to as a "village." But it was authentic and, with few of the national chains seen in every other town large and small in America, it didn't look like any other place. That was a selling point.

And don't forget the town's obscurity.

"It's home," Darby had said during that first drive-through as they passed clean, tree-lined neighborhoods and new schools.

In one particular pocket to the north of the business district could be found scores of comfortable-looking homes on large lots. None had for-sale signs in front, but Paul figured there must simply be local ordinances against signage and he'd found what he wanted on the Internet. A home privately listed.

"If you recall," Savannah was saying, "I only showed you this place as a last resort. It was less expensive than many of the homes along the coastline though I warned you it might not hold its value nearly as well."

Darby held up a hand. "Savannah, we're not blaming you for putting us out here. We love our home."

Paul watched the other woman's face as she worked over whatever was really on her mind. After a long, uncomfortable silence, Savannah said, "Okay, here's the thing. I have a very interested buyer."

Paul noticed that both he and Darby had leaned forward as their visitor's volume dropped. Like all three were in on the conspiracy.

"I know, I know," Savannah said, her voice rising as if to ward off objections both of her listeners had apparently raised with their stiffened body language. "You just moved in and the last thing you want to do is even think of leaving. I quite understand."

"I don't think you do," Darby said softly. "Or you wouldn't even suggest such a thing."

Paul watched his wife with new respect. She rarely showed annoyance, but when she did, people listened.

"Darby, dear, I wish you'd just hear me out. My buyer is quite prepared to pay for your relocation costs. And the opening offer he quoted me was forty thousand dollars more than you paid. But I don't think I'd have any problem getting him to boost it another ten thousand. How about that? A fifty-thousand dollar profit for a few weeks of aggravation."

Paul stared at the woman. Her makeup seemed to glisten over a thin sheen of sweat. Her smile was still in place, but it didn't reach her eyes.

He cleared his throat. "Savannah, we all know what the housing market's like. My Detroit area home is still on the market. So I'm, well, surprised at the very least, that we'd get such an offer."

"Yes, it's quite amazing," she said.

Her hand went for her coffee mug. She brought it to her lips before seeming to discover it was empty. Just something for her hand and eyes to do.

"Who's your buyer?" Paul asked quietly.

Her hand returned the mug to the table. She revolved it a quarter-rotation. "I don't know if I can divulge that information."

"Paul, what are you doing?" Darby asked. "What difference does it make who the buyer is? We just moved here. This is crazy."

"There's a possibility I could get more," Savannah blurted. "I said another ten thousand, but it's entirely possible—"

"No," Darby said.

Paul stared into those violet eyes, now holding his gaze as though she were afraid to let go. He thought about his car payment on the Lexus and Darby's on the Jeep. He thought of their unsold home in St. Clair Shores and Meredith's new condo in Grosse Pointe Woods and seven-figure lawsuits. He thought about his thirteen-month-old son and two daughters still in college and potentially three weddings to be paid for at some point in the not-too-distant future. He thought about alimony payments and about being fifty-two years old and potentially unemployable.

"Paul, tell her," Darby said, obviously aware of the faraway look that had crept into his eyes.

He shook his mind clear and said, "Thank you, Savannah, for continuing to work on our behalf, but we really have no problems with the house or the town. Even if we did, we'd be unlikely to move after such a short time. You can check with us again in a few years, but—"

"What if I could get seventy-five?"

"What?" Paul asked. Almost dreading the answer.

"A seventy-five-thousand dollar profit."

"Why?" he asked, sounding every bit as befuddled as he felt.

"It doesn't matter," Darby warned.

But the real estate agent's violet eyes were only on him now. He was the weak link here, not Darby.

"The house," the woman said, "is worth much more than you paid for it. The sellers were highly motivated, and there were no local buyers. I now have a buyer who's extremely anxious to own your home, and he's willing to pay a much higher price.

Anxious to own it. A curious choice of words, Paul thought.

"Think what you could do, Paul," she went on. "You really wanted the lake and now you can afford it."

"Crazy, just crazy," Darby mumbled.

Paul looked hard into those desperate violet eyes. "Once more, Savannah, who's the buyer?"

He thought at first that she was returning eye contact, but her intense gaze was actually focused miles through and beyond him. "I should have followed my instincts," she said dully. "Sometimes you get greedy in this business."

Now there was a concept Paul could buy into. He waited for more, but she continued to stare, glassy-eyed, at something or nothing.

"It's not a person," Savannah finally replied, her focus now reined in to the sunroom.

Paul became suddenly aware that his fingers could no longer feel the chair armrests he'd apparently been clenching. "What could you possibly mean by that?" he asked as he pried his fingers free.

"It's not a person who wants you two out," she repeated. "It's the entire town."

Chapter Nine

He'd done this many times in the past. Park in a gravel lot and walk more confidently than he ever felt toward a tumbledown building that either looked like it had been there forever or got prefabbed and plopped down there yesterday and would be carried away with the next strong wind.

Todd liked working with tools and machines, the smell of lubricating oil and diesel engines. It was always being the new guy he didn't treasure. Always the temp, checking in for a day or a week or a month of employment. Sometimes just getting into the routine, making a tentative friendship and learning the best places to eat, when the boss calls him into his office. Sales have died, the work's caught up, the budget's blown. Whatever the case: out on the street again. Bills piling up, landlords threatening, kids whining. Helluva life.

Before getting out, Todd observed the Corwin Corrugated Company from the cracked windshield of Kathy Lee Dwyer's borrowed boat of an Impala. She'd insisted on him taking it after he first dropped her off at the Old Time Cafe. He'd practically watched the gas needle drop. If his usual luck held, he'd owe Kathy Lee more for fuel than he'd make for the day. Then get told not to report back tomorrow.

Sales died, work's caught up, budget's blown.

There was no lobby, just a single-file row of battered metal desks piled high with paper crap. Behind the desks he could see ten-foot stacks of cardboard and hear a forklift sputtering into action, its propane tank filling Todd's nostrils. Just light a match, he thought.

A fat girl sat behind a computer at one of the desks.

"Uh huh," she said, as though confirming a fact Todd hadn't raised. He asked her for Jack Traynor, and she wordlessly pointed. "Jack," she said.

She'd pointed to a cubical that seemed to be the equivalent of a corner office, the only thing here with walls. When he got to the doorway and saw the thin, balding man sitting at a desk that faced the back wall, Todd cleared his throat to start some kind of greeting that wasn't readily coming to mind.

The balding man heard him. He swiveled his desk chair to face his doorway and Todd and offered a smile that looked equal parts guilty and confused. "Yes?"

Todd said, "The cop, er, police officer—Marty?—he told me to see you." Nothing. "That you'd have a job for me." He stared at the blank face, then thought of a much better starting point, one that he should have used from the get-go. "I'm Todd Dunbar."

"Oh. Marty. Yeah, he said something."

Jack Traynor shoved his glasses back up his nose and shot so quickly out of his office chair that it wheeled backward and crashed into the back wall of the rattly metal office cubicle, shuddering the entire flimsy structure to the point that Todd was sure it was going to collapse. Fine way to begin his first day.

But the thin man hardly seemed to notice. His shoulders were boyishly narrow, the arms coming out of his short-sleeved shirt hairless and stick-like. Standing, he stooped like a man covering up excess height, but went five-seven stretched out. He gestured with a flick of his head for Todd to follow him deeper into the building.

"Marty said something," Traynor mumbled as he led the way down a poorly lit hall and into a break room with two vending machines against a water-stained wall. A countertop held a coffeemaker, stacks of styrofoam cups, stir sticks and a powdered cream container. The company boss motioned Todd to a rickety table where they took opposing seats.

Traynor leaped up almost immediately, muttering, "Forms. I gotta...you gotta fill out..." He left, and returned seconds later. "Forms," he repeated, dropping tax forms, insurance forms and God-knew-what-else on the table.

When Todd pawed his shirt front for a pen he knew wouldn't be there, the new boss waved him off. "Don't worry. Fill 'em out...whenever. Come on."

And that was, apparently, the end of the interview.

"Um, aren't there any other, um, details?" Todd asked as he followed the other man out of the break room.

"Let's see," Jack through over his shoulder. "Work hours are eight-thirty to five. Be prompt. Pay's eleven-fifty an hour to start. Overtime if you get called in weekends."

"Eleven-fifty?" Todd asked stupidly. Hardly a fortune, but frankly more than he was expecting to make at the decrepit-looking building.

Traynor stopped in the dark hallway and made eye contact for what seemed like the first time. "I think that's the rate," he said slowly. "But if Marty McConlon promised you more we could...I could check..."

"No. No, that's not it," Todd said. "It's just...nothing. Everything's fine."

There wasn't as much noise as he'd expected in the cavernous work space. The cement floor sharply echoed what sounds there were: loud radio music and conversational male voices under the rumble of a forklift and two or three machines. The air smelled dry and dusty with cardboard accumulation and sharp with engine oil.

"We're not as busy as we'd like, but wait here," Jack said. "I'll see where we can fit you in."

Todd felt foolish, holding up the concrete block wall just inside the large room. He watched Traynor approach a bearded man in a big-ass cowboy hat with jean-clad legs wrapped around a metal stool. He was wrestling flat cardboard panels into the back of growling machinery. The man's back was to Todd. From that view, his beer belly hung so low as to resemble round ears on either side of his hips.

The two turned and stared openly at Todd, then Beerbelly shook his head. Traynor said something into the man's ear, the machine still roaring. Beerbelly shook his head again, sharper this time. Traynor shrugged—obviously not worth arguing about—and walked away. Beerbelly didn't need or want help, and he wasn't shy about it.

A yellow diesel forklift whined into view and wheeled to a stop not ten feet from Todd. The man glaring down at him from the driver's seat had a face that looked like it had been rubbed raw with steel wool. Trying to cover it, he'd added a scraggly beard and attitude. Lava Face fluttered the accelerator pedal, gunned the engine.

"Mark."

Lava Face, aka Mark, twisted in his seat to turn his glare upon Jack Traynor before releasing the clutch and pealing away without a word.

Traynor sighed, shook his head and said to Todd, "Follow me."

Men of few words. About a dozen feet from Beerbelly's machine stood another. Long and narrow and yellow, it seemed held together by conveyor belts. At the head—or the back—of the machine, a man in a ball cap stood on a short platform. His job seemed to be to feed die-cut cardboard from a flat stack into the works. When it came out the other end it was picked up and restacked by another man on the opposite end of the conveyor belt. All Todd could see of the man in the ball cap was his back and the silver chain that dipped into his back pocket, no doubt keeping his wallet in check.

Traynor broke into his thoughts with another barely heard comment, and Todd had to cup one ear to get it repeated.

"It's a taper," Traynor screamed against the twin rumble of machinery. "One guy holds the ends together and sends the cardboard through, and it comes out taped."

The machine made a rhythmic snap of a sound as it automatically cut lengths of tape and slammed them onto the boxes shoved through by Ball Cap.

Traynor indicated with the twitch of a finger that Todd should follow. "The second guy," his new boss was saying, "takes the cardboard off the belt and ties them in stacks of twenty. The third guy—that's you—takes and piles the stacks on top of this pallet here."

Todd turned his attention to the second worker, who currently seemed to be having no problem handling both of those last tasks by himself. He was easily accepting the taped panels off the conveyor, stacking them, counting off twenty, looping twine around the stacks, and filling the pallet.

Jack stooped over the second guy and spoke. A round-faced man who'd managed to keep most of his baby fat, this second man glanced over his shoulder at Todd, then lowered his head and moved away from the pallet.

"Okay, you can get started," Jack called to Todd.

Time crawled. Chain Pocket kept stopping to get Lava Face on the fork lift to bring him more die-cut stacks or to refill the taper when it ran dry of water for sealing. It seemed the only practical way to know that the taper was dry was to wait till it started spitting out a bunch of unsealed panels, at which point Chain Pocket would let loose with a string of oaths and kick the machine in its ass before calling a temporary halt to matters.

But even when production ran smoothly, there was simply too little work. To pass the time, Todd tried making a comment or two to the round-faced man sweating and wheezing next to him, but got nothing. So he did like everyone else and, despite the floor to ceiling stacks of dust-dry flat cardboard, smoked to fill the empty time.

He also had a chance to figure out Beerbelly's machine across the room. The man in the cowboy hat was feeding it long, flat cardboard panels which came out scored for folding and tabbing, and printed. Similar to the working arrangement of the taper crew, Beerbelly had two co-workers at the end of the machine stacking and loading pallets that Lava Face, in his rumbly forklift, picked up now and again and exchanged for empty pallets.

One more similarity between the two crews: neither needed three workers.

The third wheel on the printer-slotter seemed to be one of the black guys Todd had seen at the Sundown. Seeing the man carefully stacking panels that didn't need his attention, Todd recalled Kathy Lee Dwyer's words about getting overpaid for waitressing. There'd been something else she'd been about to say. Something about what had drawn her to the town, but that's when Melanie had screamed, and Kathy Lee had never finished.

Todd made a mental note to ask her about it.

He dragged on a cigarette and strained to think. What companies went out of their way to pay strangers to take jobs that didn't need taking? In *this* economy?

Both machines cut off just then and startled him with sudden, deafening solitude.

"What is it?" he called out to Roundface.

"Break," the man grunted.

The men gathered by the open bay door, several tearing off their shirts and raising their faces to the mid-morning sun. Todd hesitated, then figured they'd think even worse of him if he didn't at least try to fit in. He took a few steps in their direction.

"I wouldn't."

The black guy from the Sundown perched on a pile of pallets. He was about thirty-five, with forearm muscle that bunched up as he scratched his jaw. He reached into his pocket, popped a breath mint and said, "They're not too friendly to the likes of you and me."

As if the men sunning themselves on the loading dock had heard, they turned and glared at the outsiders with expressions that seemed to support the statement. Todd could hear the black guy's teeth clinking against his breath mint.

"What do you do here?" he asked. Something to say.

The man grinned. "Well let me tell ya, massah, I done push a broom. I steps and fetches tools, I empties trash barrels. But mostly I just stands around looking helpless."

Todd jerked a thumb at the machine behind them. "You were helping out there a few minute ago."

"On the printer-slotter? Yeah. That's because ol' Jack heard me bitching and moaning 'bout having nothing to do. He nearly passed out in a dead faint 'cuz he's thinking I'm thinking of quitting. First thing he does, he ups me to twelve-fifty an hour."

He waved a finger at Todd. "I see you got your own bullshit job." He grinned. "It's like one of them light bulb jokes: how many Sundowners it take to screw in a light bulb? Answer...as many as you can hire. You stick around, man, you gonna see how funny it really is."

The crowd at the loading dock had forgotten them in a haze of cigarette smoke and throaty chuckles.

"What's your name?" Todd asked.

"Jermaine." He sucked noisily on the breath mint slowly disappearing on his tongue. "Jermaine Whittock."

"You with that other guy? Little older than you, a bit of a gut?"

"You mean the other black guy, right?"

"No, not, well yeah, but—"

"Don't worry about it. No, that's Carl Haggerty. He's from Philly or Pittsburgh or something. I'm here with my old lady."

Jermaine swung his head for another look at the work crew on the loading dock. "Carl hit town with another guy. The buddy, he slipped out after his first paycheck, I guess." Jermaine clicked the mint between his teeth for a few thoughtful seconds. "That other guy? He's the smart one."

"How come?"

"For disappearing like he did. Ain't the world's friendliest town."

Todd thought it over. It was hard to find disagreement, but the pieces didn't fit. "If they don't like strangers, how come they draw us here? Cheap lodging. Good pay. Busy work just to keep us on the payrolls."

Jermaine stood, and Todd followed his gaze to the crowd coming toward them.

"Break's over," Beerbelly grunted before starting up his printer-slotter.

Jermaine Whittock moved in so as not to be overheard. "Now you asking the right question," he said, no longer grinning.

Chapter Ten

Todd's stacking job ran out about a half hour before lunch and job assignments seemed to shift, leaving him out entirely. The hell with it, he thought as he reached for his smokes. He plunked his ass down on an idled forklift near an open bay and puffed away. Let them tell him to get back to work.

He was still there by lunchtime.

Conversation stopped when he entered the break room, so he stuffed a fistful of change into the vending machine and retrieved soda pop, chips and a single-serve can of peaches, then joined Jermaine. He'd arranged piles of cardboard into a makeshift table and chair where he sat with napkin, plastic utensils and a paper plate piled high with deviled egg, potato salad and rice-stuffed pepper.

Todd's stomach rumbled as he stared at the other man's set-up and twisted the lid off his cold peaches. "Makes you hungry doing nothing," he said.

Jermaine smacked his lips, but didn't reply.

Todd formed his own stacked-cardboard chair and sat. "So what brought you here?"

Jermaine dabbed almost daintily with his napkin. "Place called the Time-Out Market and Deli. One of them twenty-four-seven convenience stores near the famous 8 Mile Road in Detroit. And in case you don't know Detroit, it ain't Mister Rogers' Fucking Neighborhood."

"Never been there," said Todd. "Been thinking about it a little. My brother-in-law's heard Ford's going to be hiring again soon."

Jermaine's laugh sounded high and genuine. "I bet your brother-in-law don't know who tole him this or remember any of the details. He don't have a phone number or a hiring manager's name. You get an economy this bad for this long and rumors send you traipsing the country to that next place on the map jus' dying for help. 'No experience? No training? Ain't had a full-time job in three years? No problem. We're hiring!'"

He laughed again, but this time it didn't sound so genuine. "I was telling you about the Time-Out Market and Deli." He popped his deviled egg in his mouth and spoke around it. "Place was run by about four Arab guys. Cousins, brothers, I don't know. 'Bout half of them named Mohammed. They was hiring, that's the thing. They only paid five or six bucks an hour, but all off the books. And for the graveyard shift, ten to six, they went up to a whole seven bucks. Well, I hadn't had any work but an occasional day-labor gig for months, and my old lady—Tonya— she'd lost her job at this lamp assembly plant 'cuz—get this—the feds fined them like a hundred-thousand bucks or something for not having enough brothers on the payroll. So they shut the goddamn thing down and moved to, I don't know, India or some goddamn place where the wages are lower."

"Anyway," said Todd, trying to move it along before lunch break ended.

"Point is, I took the graveyard shift on Murder Avenue cuz we got three kids and really needed the money. Okay?"

He crumpled up his paper waste and dumped it into a nearby trashcan. "First night, I'm scared shitless but everything's cool. Next night, same thing. Night after that, not so good. There's a kid, eighteen or nineteen, at the end of the aisle when this other brother comes striding in in a long coat. He goes, 'Hey, Roosevelt,' and the first kid looks up. This first kid gets a real serious expression on his face, then he breaks into a grin."

"A grin," said Todd, wanting to know if he heard right.

"Yeah. A grin. Like 'shit, what else can I do.' Then this dude that called out his name whips out a sawed-off from in his coat. He pumps it and starts spraying shots at the kid. I mean, it's this roar of sound like an explosion that won't stop. The kid, like, steps back a little so he's kinda behind an aisle, but that's all he does."

Jermaine stopped to wipe at the sweat sheen that covered his face. Maybe from the heat, maybe not. "I'm standing there behind the counter like a statue, man. Like if I stay real quiet and still, the shooter won't see me. But he don't give a shit I'm there or not. All he's interested in is putting bullets in my beer cans, my soup and chips and feminine napkins, everything but this kid standing there with a stupid grin on his face."

Jermaine was also grinning at the telling.

Todd said, "The shooter ever get the kid?"

"That's just it," Jermaine all but shouted, then glanced around nervously as if fearing he'd been overheard. "He fires four, five times, whatever the motherfucker had in that hogleg of his. By the time he's finished, my ears was ringing so loud I barely hear my beer cans still exploding. The shooter just stares at this kid standing there, grinning. He goes 'Shit' one time, the shooter dude does, then he splits. Runs like hell. The kid, the grinning kid, starts stroking his body and I figure after awhile he's looking for bullet holes. When he don't find any, he walks out the door still smiling his stupid-ass grin. He's stepping over shattered glass, but it's like it's no big deal. Just a tough day at work, you know?"

Jermaine's eyes shone. "No big deal 'cept last thing I notice is the kid's got this dark stain on the crotch of his baggies."

Todd finished his inadequate lunch and lit another cigarette. "Jesus, I understand you splitting after that."

Jermaine shook his head. "You don't understand jack shit, partner. Wife and three kids, remember? I go back there the next night, only this time I got my .38 stuffed in my pocket. Just in case. Just like the Arabs had tole me to do all along."

"You registered to carry?"

"Man, you ain't never lived in the city. The Arabs gave me the job, they called it the Shotgun Shift. They was all proud of having had a cousin get wiped out on the Shotgun Shift 'cuz he'd taken a shooter with him." Jermaine paused. "Maybe that's why they hired a nigger. They'd lost too many Arabs by then."

"Weren't they pissed off about the shooting the night before?" Todd glanced at his watch.

"Don't worry about it. The time, I mean. Lunch is officially a half hour, but usually goes over. Not much to do on the floor anyway. But to answer your question, the Arabs musta had their insurance all paid up 'cuz they treated it like a joke. They sweep up the glass and they're teasing me about the bullets flying. I filed a police report, of course, but they treated it like someone stole a bike, you know? I'm sure the Arabs doubled the actual damage on their insurance claim, so everyone's happy, right? Everyone but me."

"But now you got your gun," said Todd, prodding.

"Yeah. Now I got my gun. And the very next night, two kids come in." Jermaine took a deep breath. Let it out. "They're, I dunno—fifteen? Plenty old enough for the streets. I'm watching them real close 'cuz I don't like the way they're huddled together at the back of the store, whispering. They take turns popping their heads up to look at me and my one or two customers. And they got these long coats, right? And their hands stuffed into the pockets, and I'm trying my damnedest to hold onto my only two customers, but then they're both gone and it's just me and the punks."

Jermaine's face was glistening again, making Todd picture how it must have gone down.

"One of 'em drifts by the door—the lookout guy, right?—while the other one comes slowly up the aisle toward me. He got that nigger swagger going, this cold, dead look on his face. 'Bout to become a player, you know? So I'm slowly bringing my gun out of my hip pocket and kinda aiming it at him, but under the counter. I know I can't shoot through the wood like in the movies, so I gotta lift it high enough to get him before he gets me. That's gonna take time, but then I get this crazy idea."

They both looked up guiltily as Beerbelly ambled past them

without a sideways glance. When he started up his machine, Todd pulled closer to hear the rest.

"I'm thinking to myself, I'm thirty-four, too old for this shit. I ain't Wyatt Earp. I gotta wait for him to draw on me first and gamble on being able to get my Smith & Wesson up over the top of the counter before he plugs me? Bull*shit*. Why not just plug him first, then get the bastard at the back of the store? Element of surprise, right? Not the way the gunfighters do it, but what you do if you got no quick-draw practice and you wanna live. Then go through their coats and take out their guns and put 'em in their dead hands and everything's cool."

Todd's throat had started to tighten as the story went on. He could barely croak out the obvious question. "Did you kill them?" Lie to me, he was thinking.

To his surprise and relief, the other man shook his head. "The store security camera saved those boys' lives. I don't even know if the damn thing worked, but if it did I was screwed. So I had to wait and let the kid draw first and hope his friend wouldn't get me from the doorway before I finished off the first one. It's high noon in Detroit, right? I was ready for anything, 'cept my gun hand is going numb and heavy and I got these black spots in front of my eyes like I'm gonna pass out."

Jermaine stopped. Pausing for dramatic effect, most likely, but Todd couldn't stop himself from playing along. "So what happened? Huh?"

"So the kid, the one that's approaching. He says in this real nervous voice, 'You got condoms?' See, we kept 'em behind the counter."

Jermaine let out a high, keening wail of a laugh that could be heard even above the roar of the printer-slotter. "That's right. The punks want rubbers and they're embarrassed about asking. And I almost blew 'em away for it. Talk about effective birth control."

He erupted with one more peal of laughter, then his smile died. "Time to leave town, what I tell my ole lady. Can't do this no more. We left the kids with Tonya's ma and pa and tole 'em we'd be back when we gets some jobs somewhere and saved up some money."

Todd blinked aside a million questions before settling on one. "Your wife found a job here, too?"

"Took her all of two days. She's filing books away at the town library for nine-fifty an hour."

Todd mulled this over. "You send for the kids yet?"

Jermaine stared at a point far beyond Todd. Stared so long that Todd didn't think he'd give up an answer. Then he said, "Tonya wants 'em with us, but I'm not so sure. I keep putting it off."

There were lots of ways to respond to that, but Todd's next

71

questions sounded odd even to him. "Still got that .38?"

"Oh yeah." Jermaine Whittock nodded very slowly. "I keep that motherfucker greased and in prime working order back at the motel."

For some reason, that didn't strike Todd as being the least bit strange.

Chapter Eleven

The Babylon Police Department was housed in an impressive red brick structure on Middle View Road known as the Drake Municipal Complex. It sat behind a startling expanse of green lawn flanked by rows of bright yellow daffodils and accessed by a dazzling white circular drive. Park benches sat under century-old sycamores along an inviting sidewalk. Despite the aesthetics, Paul's affection for anything having to do with the town had been dulled by yet another conversation with Savannah Easton.

It was time for action.

He coasted up the drive and pulled the Lexus behind a long bus. He scanned the curb for a sign denying him the parking space so close to the brick walk leading to the front door, and was almost disappointed to find none.

Paul Highsmith was in a law-defying mood.

Darby's expression had been difficult to read earlier that day as she'd handed him the phone. Paul, trying to paint his study with Tuck wailing in the background, had at first welcomed the interruption.

"It's Savannah," Darby muttered, evidently eager to dash his good feelings. "She insists on talking with *you*." This last part sounding like a vague accusation.

He deliberately sighed into the receiver. "Yes, Savannah."

"Paul, you must sell," she said, skipping her customarily bubbly preliminaries.

His first thought was that the pressures of the legendarily slow market had caused the poor woman to lose it. After an empty pause in which he waited for her to explain herself, he finally had to ask the obvious.

"You were clever to hold out for so long," she said, now sounding unconvincingly girlish. "I told my buyer that you'd turned down their very generous offer. Well, I'd expected him to tell me to forget it, but he says, 'Savannah, let's quit playing games.' That's what he says. He tells me, 'Let's make it an even eight-hundred-thousand dollars.' Can you imagine that, Paul? The town's willing to buy your home for nearly double what you paid for it just a couple months ago."

He glanced at Darby and found her trying to entice Tuck's attention away from the open paint can with a rag storybook he showed no interest in whatsoever.

"Paul? Paul?" The real estate agent sounded panicky at the

thought of losing him.

"I'm here, Savannah." He caught a glimpse of Darby listening in as unobtrusively as possible. "I'm sorry, but as we told you—"

"You have to," she said, all soft-sell pretense gone. "They won't leave me alone until you do."

The line went silent, as though she'd realized she'd misspoke. After several beats, she issued a throaty chuckle. "My, I get dramatic, don't I? Sorry, Paul. It's just that they're so insistent. I never should have let you buy in Babylon in the first place. Sometimes I see dollar signs and ignore my better judgment. But now I'm thinking about you, Paul, and your lovely family."

He didn't like the sound of that at all. "Savannah, who's behind all of this?" he asked her crisply.

"I told you. It's the town. The whole town wants you to leave."

Paul sank into an overstuffed chair. What did the town" know about him? Had someone Googled his name and not liked what they came up with? He closed his eyes and tried to imagine how bad it might get.

"Savannah, towns don't speak. People do." God, he sounded like the NRA. "Give me a name."

"No. I can't," she said, her voice breaking.

What was going on here?

He waited her out.

"Bill Sandy," she finally said in such a low monotone that he had to make her repeat herself to be sure he'd caught the name. "He's the police chief," she added, somewhat more helpfully.

Then her voice rose again, clutching at him like talons. "But you *can't* tell him I told you. Just sell your home, Paul. Please. It's for your own good."

The Drake Municipal Complex. Paul found himself in a colorless hallway with crayon art safety posters from an elementary school serving as wall decorations along with notices of senior programs and adult education classes and swimming pool hours and refuse collection schedules. He saw a big person and little person set of drinking fountains against one wall, and a handful of open doors.

He followed pleasant chatter to its source, through a corridor leading toward the back of the building. The closer he got to the voices, the more of them there seemed to be, until the corridor was filled with the hum of conversation.

Paul found a double set of doors standing wide, and a patch of light spilling into the hallway. He stood in the doorway and watched men, woman and children milling around or laying in cots flexing cotton-bandaged arms. Still others formed crooked lines, waiting patiently to be stabbed by sharp needles.

He recalled the long bus parked in front of his Lexus, and understood. It was a blood donor service. With the understanding came another thought to complement his fantasy of several nights ago when he'd thought of joining the locals in the diner. The way this thought went, he'd stroll in here, roll up his sleeve and donate a pint or two.

How could the town reject his blood sacrifice? He'd just take his place at the end of one of those ragged lines and—

"Hey, what the hell?"

It was a uniformed cop who'd come up alongside him and now he braced Paul's arm in a painful grip. "Barry, get over here."

The second cop, Barry, was taller, slimmer and slightly younger than the first. He joined his partner on a dead run, gun belt flapping on his bony hip.

"Barry, goddamnit, you were supposed to—what the hell are you doing here?"

The question was obviously directed at Paul. Dozens of faces were now turned to him from the open doorway, conversations stopped. Pink-faced and sputtery with rage, the plump cop said, "Barry, you were supposed to watch the door. I said, what're you doing here?"

Even the younger cop seemed unsure who his partner was addressing from sentence to sentence.

"Let go of me."

There must have been steel in Paul's voice, for the pudgy cop unhanded him like he was a heated oven coil. "Sorry," the older cop said, chuckling weakly. "I just...we're supposed to...I got startled, that's all. It's kind of a private thing in there."

A private blood drive?

"Marty, I was helping Mrs. Oliver with her baby 'cuz she tole me to," Barry whined. "That's why I left the door for—"

"Shut up, Barry," his partner said. Chortling like the whole thing was a joke. "Now, Mr. Highsmith, what can I do for you?"

The cop knew his name, just like Purcell in the Winking Dog. That might not be unusual in a town of this size, but it was unnerving.

"I was looking for the police station," he said. "I only wandered in here by accident."

"Forget it, forget it," the plump cop said. "My problem? Too much coffee. " He laughed gustily, and his younger partner made a weak attempt to join in.

"Get back in there," the cop gruffly commanded Barry.

The older cop chatted amiably while he directed Paul, with only the lightest touch, back out into the sunshine. Now in back of the large complex, Paul could see a parking lot apparently full of the vehicles of blood donors.

"You know, they ought to make the sign more apparent," the cop was saying. "I mean, everyone in town knows where the police station is, so who needs a sign? Right? But someone like you comes along, what're you supposed to do—read minds?"

The plump cop babbled on, all the while leading Paul along a short brick path bordered by rose bushes. The walk ended at another door, an ass-backward entrance to one of the wings of the expansive building.

"Right here," the cop said. "We got PD, firehouse, city departments of all kinds in this monster of a building. When we need more space, we add on. It's crazy."

He stepped aside to let Paul enter first.

Most of the police station revealed itself in a single glance. The open space was painted a dull shade of white. Gunmetal gray desks occupied the floor, with old-fashioned metal and glass room dividers cubing off office space for the VIPs. A black and white framed photograph of a stern old-timer took up a significant portion of one wall. Stodgy prints of more doddering old men lined another.

"Hey, would you wait here?" the plump cop asked.

Paul sat in a cold plastic chair behind a display of news and sports magazines while the now friendly officer promised to return as soon as possible before disappearing behind a room divider.

Letting his gaze follow the low buzz of voices, Paul saw two heads bobbing in conversation behind the glass portion of one of the cubicles. The plump cop was waving his arms as he apparently explained the situation. Paul was fairly certain the younger cop, Barry, earned a mention. The second man had gray hair, a bushy mustache and a grim expression that showed itself every time he raised his head over the partition and glanced Paul's way.

Paul picked up a magazine and pretended to read it. When he heard a chair on wheels squeal, followed by slow, plodding footsteps, he innocently raised his gaze.

"Mr. Highsmith? Bill Sandy."

The chief carried most of his excess bulk right behind his gun belt. His holstered weapon, massive enough to singlehandedly end a coup, dug into the soft flesh. He wore a pained expression that seemed to speak of arthritis and career disappointment—not to mention the gun pressed deeply into his gut. His handshake was more of a touch than a grip. Both parties released quickly.

The chief nodded toward his cubicle. "Let's talk, can we?"

His voice was unexpectedly mild for someone Paul suspected of trying to bully his family out of town. Somewhat taken aback, Paul followed him past the oversize photos of long-dead civic leaders and into Chief Sandy's office. He no longer knew what to expect.

76

The space had been carved into a corner, so it featured two partitions and an equal number of plastered walls. There was a neat wooden desk, two shelves full of forms, a narrow bank of file cabinets and a fern. The nearly colorless walls carried the expected assortment of plaques and diplomas, but Paul's eye was immediately taken to two large photographs on a low cabinet behind the desk.

Where had he seen the white-haired gentleman before? It bugged him.

"Sorry. Got to get you a chair," the soft-spoken police chief said.

While he was gone, Paul approached the color photo and read the brass plate affixed to the bottom: Miles Drake. The name nagged him until he remembered he was in one wing of the Drake Municipal Complex.

Then: *Drake.* He recalled where else he'd heard the name.

"Oooh, Duane, you're gonna get us in trouble with Drake."

Chief Sandy came back, grunting softly with the weight of the metal chair he cradled. "Please, have a seat," he offered, patting the chair which he crashed in front of his desk.

"Thank you. I won't take much of your time," Paul said.

He sat and shot another glance at the white-haired man in the photo on the cabinet, just behind the chief. It was a formal portrait, the subject resplendent in a loud jacket and tie ensemble, the lapels looking to be half a foot wide. The resemblance to the huge photograph of the man in the lobby was startling. They had to have been relatives, though they looked identical. The photo in the lobby had the grainy, overly posed look of photography from the Forties, while this photo had obviously been taken in the Seventies.

"Mr. Highsmith, I'd like to apologize for the way you were treated by my young officers. Marty admitted that he came on a bit strong. He felt terrible about it, but that's no excuse. You'll get a written letter of apology."

Paul nodded. Now he really was off-guard. "It wasn't that big a deal," he said, the wind knocked out of his righteous anger. "I guess I was just taken aback that the police would be so protective of a blood drive. I was about to volunteer myself when we had the run-in."

"Well, thank you for your generosity," the chief said. "Now, how can I help you?"

The subject of the blood drive was obviously closed. Paul glanced once more at the photograph of Miles Drake. The old man was seated, back ramrod straight, both hands loosely clasping a bony knee. The pose was casual, but the subject made it look like it hadn't been any easy photo to get.

"Mr. Highsmith? Is there anything else I can help you with?" The police chief's desk chair squealed.

Paul refocused his attention and tried to gather his thoughts. "My real estate agent, Savannah Easton," he said, then paused to see if his listener gave any significance to the name. He didn't show anything. Paul continued, "She tells my wife and me that you've been pressuring her to get us to sell the home we just bought."

Only then did he recall the woman imploring Paul to keep her name out of it.

"I have *suggested* such a course of action," the chief corrected. "But I wouldn't characterize my remarks as undue pressure."

He might be a small-town cop, but he spoke like a big-city lawyer. Paul felt for the first time since meeting him that Chief Sandy might not be as soft as his voice.

"I'm just curious..." Paul let the sentence trail, waiting for the other man to pick up the slack.

The cop stared at his big hands. "People in other towns around here, if they go visiting out of state and someone asks where they're from, they might say Toledo. Or Detroit. Not because they're lying. They just consider themselves part of a larger metropolitan area, which technically they are." The chief glanced up suddenly, his eyes the weak blue of rain. "Mr. Highsmith, residents of our town don't think of themselves as living anywhere but Babylon. We're self-sufficient. We're no..." He sniffed the air as though hesitant to go on. "...bedroom community. And no one ever leaves."

"And yet," said Paul in something of a gentle tweak, "the McConlons sold us their home and moved away."

Bill Sandy leaned back, the air whooshing out of his chair. His jawline twitched as he stared Paul down. "Yes, that did catch us by surprise," he said. "Even Marty wasn't expecting his brother to move his family out like that."

Paul stared at the police chief. "Marty," he said. "You mean the cop who was hassling me? That Marty? He's Jeff McConlon's brother?"

Chief Sandy stared at Paul for several beats, managing to look at once both grim and expressionless. "Mr. Highsmith, as Detroit and Cleveland and all those other cities grow bigger and nastier, their citizens move farther and farther away. Unfortunately, they have a tendency to bring their problems with them, threatening to turn the peaceful little outlying towns into something not so peaceful, not so safe and clean. We don't want that to happen here, and that's why we're willing to pay good money to see that it doesn't happen. The McConlons should have known better than to sell to outsiders. It's something we just don't do."

Genuine shock held Paul without comment for half a minute. In his head he was explaining, *At worst, I'm a* white collar *criminal. Not someone who's going to break into the neighbors' home and steal their*

DVDs.

When he could finally formulate a rational sentence he said, "Savannah Easton broke an unwritten law, didn't she?" He stood and planted the palms of his hands on the other man's desk. "Is that why she's so afraid, Chief?"

His chair squealed as the lawman rose. "Thanks for stopping by, Mr. Highsmith. I hope you realize that the town means you no harm. We just prefer that you leave."

Paul was stunned. There were fair housing laws prohibiting such treatment, weren't there? Before now, he'd never had occasion to wonder.

With a grim chuckle, he yanked out the orange slip hanging limp, trapped between the wiper and windshield of his Lexus, and got in. He wasn't even surprised at having been ticketed for parking in an unmarked but apparently illegal space. Seemed the town was full of unwritten laws. Paul made a show of tearing the ticket and releasing it to the muggy air. He watched the scraps sink like confetti to the flawless lawn.

It was well after six, the day's shadows starting to grow and flatten. But one more thought worked him over like an ulcer before he could head home. Not every stranger in this godforsaken town was as unwelcome as his family.

He'd take one more quick drive before calling it a night.

Chapter Twelve

"Sure, it's good money," Denver Dugan was saying. "Good for these days anyhow, but I was making more than this twenty years ago at the GM plant in Cleveland. Didn't know how good I had it back then."

There were maybe twenty of them out there. Smoking, drinking, reminiscing under a fading sun by the brackish swimming pool. Todd and Joy sat side by side in borrowed lawn chairs, the kids having joined the Dwyer hooligans and a few others in whatever misdemeanors were being committed on the motel grounds.

"Hell, I owned Detroit back then," chipped in a man Todd didn't know by name. He was up there in age with big Denver, but as thin and worn as old socks. His teeth were cracked and uneven, his long hair tied back in a ponytail. "Me, I'd get bored working the same job, same shift, so I'd quit, stay away for a few months. When my money ran out, I'd get me another job at Chrysler or AMC or some supplier. They all paid more than the chickenshit wages we're taking home now and kissing this town's ass to get it."

"Hey, Denver," Jamey Weeks shouted, "what's the most you ever made?"

The big man tilted his cap back from his sweaty forehead and said, "Well, let me think about it."

It was obvious from his crooked smile that the former autoworker didn't need the thinking time. Todd figured that Denver probably reflected on those past paychecks every night while sacked out in his tiny motel room with the sweat crawling over him.

After the proper pause, the big man said, "In the late Eighties I remember a year when I booked seven twelves for six or seven months straight—eighty-four-hour work weeks. Ended up divorced over it, but I pulled in just over a hundred grand that year, pre-tax."

The pool area went silent as two dozen men and women studied the money like they could see it.

"Hundred grand," Jamey repeated softly.

"Course that was just before things went bad again," Denver added ruefully. "On top of the divorce, I didn't get any overtime the next year. I had to pay for her lawyer as well as my own, but I musta bought her a better one than me since she got the house and spousal support and child support. By that time, the automakers were all laying off again, not hiring."

Bringing them all down.

D.B. said, "Most I ever made at one time was twenty-eight an hour."

"Get outta here," snapped a muscle-bound kid with a crew cut and an attitude.

"It's true. I was working construction outside Boston just before the housing market went to shit. Bunch of us, we had more money than we ever seen, but we lived in trailer camps, some of us in tents 'cuz we couldn't afford nothing else. Most expensive town I ever been in."

"I made twenty an hour once," said a quiet guy of no more than thirty despite his shiny dome. "Made it in a lumber camp in Oregon, but the job only lasted through the summer."

"Shit," grumbled Carl Haggerty. "I ain't never took in more than eight, ten dollars an hour. Not even when times was good." Although he couldn't have been more than forty, he had the deepest forehead furrows Todd had ever seen. As he sat scowling into his beer can, the furrows dug even deeper. "Don't suspect race has anything to do with it, do you?"

"Jesus, now we get the lecture," Judd Maxwell said.

"Ain't no lecture. Just facts. Me and everyone I know been making minimum wage even during the so-called good times. And that's if we can get work at all. Which is why Doyle was so suspicious of this goddamn town. You spend your life getting shafted, then someone gives you the keys to the city. If you smart, you stop and ask why. That's what Doyle was tryna tell me, and I shoulda listened."

Judd snickered. "And right now your old buddy Doyle's standing in some unemployment line telling everyone who'll listen that he don't got no money 'cuz the white man shafted him. Not 'cuz he left a perfectly good job for worrying he's got too good a deal."

"Is that what happened?" Carl hunched in his lawn chair like he was trying to wrap his big shoulders around himself.

"Is it?" Todd asked. Every eye on him now, the first time most had seemed to notice him. "What happened to your friend? Why *did* he leave town?"

"Cuz he a fool, that's why." Carl grumbled as though reluctant to admit Judd Maxwell had been right in his appraisal of Carl's friend.

Todd caught several people stirring, like the conversation had gone off into uncomfortable territory.

"Todd was making good money outside of Parkersburg," Joy piped in. "He drove a Caterpillar loader for a coal mine." His wife nudged him in the ribs. "Todd, tell 'em how much you was making at the mine before it closed down."

The silence now seemed unbearable.

Todd shrugged and kept his eyes on the cracked pavement. It was like being in high school and trading sex stories and worrying that your lies wouldn't hold up next to everyone else's. So what if these other assholes *used to* pull down fifty, a hundred grand a year and quit whenever they felt like it? All of their grand stories were twenty years in the past. What had they all been up to for the last couple decades? Same as him, Todd thought. Scrabbling. Avoiding phone calls. Paying off the interest on payday loans so you could borrow more. It didn't matter how great life used to be, so why torture yourself talking about it?

He thought about how stifling hot it had suddenly turned, the late afternoon sun beating down on them in righteous punishment. He was still thirsty, even with a longneck halfway to his lips. Then he thought about the silence his wife had brought down on all of them just by feeling a need to contribute. To build her husband up to people he barely knew and didn't give a shit about.

"Who the hell is that?" Tonya Whittock asked.

All heads turned, as much to change the subject as it was out of curiosity.

"Never seen him before," Kathy Lee drawled. "Whaddya think he's doing?"

"Him and his fucking Lexus," Judd said. "You can bet he ain't checking in at the Sundown for the night."

"Cop, maybe. Think he's taking down license plate numbers?" the crew-cut kid with the attitude nervously asked.

He was young and had watched too much television or he'd know real-life cops rarely drove luxury Jap cars. Todd watched the driver slowly cruise the parking lot.

Judd said, "He ain't gonna steal nothing, is he?"

"Now you're on to something," said D.B. "Bet he smashes and grabs all that cash you're hiding in your glove box."

"Then what the hell's he up to?" said Kathy Lee.

The kid with the muscles and the buzz cut had at least gotten something right. The driver actually was checking out license plates. Looking around him, Todd saw nervous faces and wondered what was going on in their minds right then. D.B. had admitted to what he'd called "a minor warrant" on his head and plenty others had turned the conversation away from their pasts.

Compounding the problem, probably half the tags in the lot were expired.

The sleek car coasted up and down the twin rows of battered, rusted and primed cars and pickups before straightening out and coming back down the circular drive. The Lexus glided to a stop parallel to the pool, maybe sixty feet from the gathering.

"Uh oh," someone said softly.

The driver's window bounced back enough sunlight to obscure his features, but Todd could see that he sat tall and straight-backed in his glove-soft upholstery.

God, to have a ride like that. Its tires would whisper over pavement. There'd be a CD player with crystal-clear hidden speakers, the upholstery would always smell new and you'd ride on an invisible cloud of cool air, oblivious to the day's heat and the smell of the streets.

Todd licked his lips as though it had been a naked and willing woman driving his fantasy.

Judd Maxwell rose quickly, his lightweight lawn chair skittering away from him. "I've had enough of this," he growled.

Maybe the driver heard him, for the sleek car pulled away as silently as it had appeared. It coasted down the winding driveway to Pleasant Run Avenue, its tires caressing the pavement, all cylinders purring with mechanical contentment.

"Asshole," Judd mumbled, but he put nothing behind it.

And no one chimed in. It was as though each of the two dozen men and women sitting around that pool was thinking about their parking lot of cancerous metal and tailpipes suspended by hanger wire and arriving at the conclusion that the tall man wasn't such an asshole after all. Not for driving a car that purred, that taunted the summer swelter with its own pure cushion of cool air.

Which one of them wouldn't do the same?

Chapter Thirteen

"Honey, I'm sorry," she whispered later. "I didn't mean to embarrass you." Joy placed a hand lightly on his shoulder. "You had a good job, too, you know. I just wanted people to know that."

Todd silenced her with a kiss before laying his head on her cushioning breasts. She began to moan softly as his tongue flicked over an exposed nipple. Moving up, his tongue touched hers as their lips came together, stifling the sounds of her pleasure.

The walls were thin, Little Todd asleep but the girls still up, still playing just outside the door.

Joy took his hand and pressed it against the warm flesh covering her hipbone as his thoughts returned again to the silver Lexus. The cloud of cool air that would, unlike the window air conditioner rattling a few feet away, kiss the skin with a gentle, nearly silent chill.

She unlocked her tongue with his as he rolled heavily on top of her. "I just thought it would be a good way of meeting people, joining the conversation like that," she said, picking it up where they'd left it. Where he *thought* they'd left it.

For some reason, that brought to mind the condescension of her previous statement: *"You had a good job, too."*

Todd rolled off her and stared at the ceiling. He clicked his teeth in a gesture of irritation that he hoped wouldn't drag them into a fight. Why couldn't she just drop it?

"Sorry," she said again. Reading him.

He found and squeezed her hand to show more understanding than he felt, and hoped that would end it. They needed to enjoy the alone time before the girls grew bored and came knocking.

"I got a call at the room phone while you were at work," she said. "Someone who's with the Water Department at the what-not Municipal Building. I forget her name, but she wants me to come in for a job interview tomorrow."

Todd wondered how she planned to interview with the woman if she didn't know her name, but let it go. "When?" he asked her instead.

"I told her you work till five and I'd have no one to sit with the kids, so she said it was okay if I came in at five-thirty. Kind of funny, don't you think?"

"What?"

"A job interview at five-thirty on a Friday evening. I don't know."

Todd felt her shrug beside him as he continued staring at a ceiling already lost in the shadows, the days growing depressingly shorter. He could hear a radio with too much bass playing down by the pool. Voices getting louder and drunker.

"Will you do something for me, honey?" Joy asked in a warm whisper. When he made no reply, she said, "Will you go to Zeebe's Garage tomorrow and see how the car's doing?"

He nodded. "Fine. But the municipal building's so close, you could walk there. I'll give you directions in the morning. And I can always get a ride into work from someone."

"That's not why I want it," she said. If she expected him to ask, he didn't. "I just think...I think we need it."

"I told you, I'll check on it."

She'd get the job. They both knew it. That's what was scaring her...and him, too. It had never been this easy before, people calling them up and practically begging them to take jobs. He was used to sweat and grime, lung-choking smoke, toil and boredom broken up by the degradation of unemployment lines and job applications going nowhere and milk money borrowed from relatives and neighbors.

He didn't trust Babylon's brand of prosperity any more than Joy did, but he felt like a starving mouse sniffing at a smear of peanut butter. He didn't know what the contraption was around it, or how it worked, but he distrusted the hell out of it. He was so hungry, though, that he had to take a careful walk up to it and hope he could fill his belly before the damn thing bit him.

He caught a few moments of sleep before the kids burst in the door. Long enough to dream about sitting behind the wheel of a silver Lexus with buttery upholstery, riding on a cushion of cool night air.

Chapter Fourteen

Thank God for microwaves. After finding Darby taking washcloth swipes at Tuck while he splashed away in a tub of water, Paul found a chicken and broccoli casserole in the fridge and started heating it up.

"You didn't call," she said after he returned upstairs and found Darby now bracing their squealing son into some semblance of temporary inactivity so she could wash his hair. She could have entered a wet T-shirt contest.

Paul took a seat on the toilet lid. "You're all wet."

"And you're late, buster. You missed dinner."

"I tried calling, but I think the nearest cell phone tower is in the next county."

He scooted out of the way as a small tidal wave came at him.

"Daddy!" Tuck screamed. He slapped the water with both hands in some sort of nautical welcoming ceremony.

Darby rolled her eyes as she picked up their pink-skinned son in an oversize towel. She was amazing with him, ever-patient, eternally understanding of his loud enthusiasm. It was something that Paul felt was a little harder to do at fifty-two.

But that thought brought to mind his daughters, kids he'd had in his twenties and early thirties and with whom he'd bonded no better. He felt his chest tighten at the ramifications, the knowledge that he was running out of time and second chances.

He waited until Tuck had no more moisture to shake off before moving in for hugs and kisses. Hard hugs and wet kisses, as if staving off a repeat of familial history. After pajamas and bedtime stories from the both of them, Tuck was finally done for the night. Nice trick, warm water. The toddler's mouth had dropped open and his lids drooped even before his parents made it out of the room.

"So where were you?"

They were in the kitchen now, Paul scooping his chicken and broccoli into a plate. It felt only lukewarm when Paul stuck a finger in it but he decided to eat it as-is rather than reheat.

"I went to the police station to see why the town fathers hate us."

"And?"

He shook his head. "Police Chief Sandy is a reserved but decent enough sort, I gather. Way he explains it, the town's afraid of turning into the big, bad city if they don't keep out dangerous characters like us."

"Sounds illegal," she said.

"Well, that's not exactly how he put it." Though, come to think of it, the chief's message hadn't come across a whole lot more guarded or diplomatic than that.

"I guess it makes a little sense. From their perspective, anyway."

"Very little," he said, gulping at dinner. "Total strangers willing to pay eight-hundred-thousand dollars for the house just to keep us out?"

"Maybe it's worth that much."

"In this economy? And if it is, how'd we get such a great deal in the first place? I'd love to know why the McConlons were so anxious to leave. I wish we'd actually met them. By the way, the cop who yelled at me is the seller's brother."

Darby was nibbling at a fingernail. She'd long ago found a way to tame her nail-biting habit by taking such tiny portions that the damage could only be seen under a microscope. "What cop?" she asked.

He washed his lukewarm meal down with milk. He drank more of the stuff than any grown man he knew. "I'd better back up. First thing I see at that Drake Municipal Building downtown is a blood drive. Simple enough, right?"

Darby kept taking her tiny bites from a thumb nail.

"You ever seen cops guarding blood like it's plutonium? That's how this was. Weird."

By the glazed look in his young wife's eyes, he could tell she was mentally making to-do lists. He couldn't blame her when he thought about it. *You had to be there.*

"Anyway, that's how I met this Marty character. McConlon. The cop. The brother. He almost arrests me for trying to enter the blood drive room, but gets real friendly once he stops PMSing. I can't figure him out."

"Uh huh."

Yep. Definitely mentally composing one of her to-do lists.

Before he lost her altogether, he said, "Forget the blood drive. I've got a puzzle for you. If the locals hate strangers so much, why do they have a whole motel full of them at the top of Pleasant Run Avenue?"

Darby sat and folded her hands demurely in her lap, apparently to keep her teeth away from them. "You mean the Sundown Motel? I've noticed those men by the pool."

"A few women and kids, too. I drove through the parking lot on the way home, another reason I was late. The rusted heaps had plates from West Virginia, Tennessee, Ohio—even as far away as Oregon. They're obviously dirt poor and a lot easier to run off than we are. People like that, if you want to get rid of them, you throw them in jail for flicking cigarette butts from moving vehicles."

"That's awful," Darby said.

"I'm not saying it's right, but it's a fact of life. Only, it seems that the good citizens of this town would rather have the likes of them around than us." He ended it on a note of hurt disbelief that sounded more like priggish petulance than irony.

Darby stared at her slender fingers. "Maybe they're working on some kind of construction project."

"Maybe," he reluctantly agreed. He hadn't considered that. "But I've done a lot of walking and I haven't noticed anything going up. Have you?"

"Maybe an indoor project. More work in that monstrous municipal building. Whatever."

Yeah, that could explain it, but Paul hoped it didn't. A part of him—the bored, unemployed part, no doubt—was enjoying his little mystery.

The hollow two-note chime of the doorbell took them both by surprise. It was the first time he'd heard it since an earlier Savannah Easton visit. Paul found his wife's eyes and wondered if his were as wide with surprise and vague fear as hers. Even outside of this cold town it was unusual for anyone to get unexpected visitors these days...especially at night.

It was drizzling out, Paul noticed as he watched beads of water dripping down the glass over the front entry hall double doors. He hesitated briefly before cautiously unlocking and turning the knob. He heard Darby hovering in the background.

The door swung open to three old men.

Chapter Fifteen

The three stood facing Paul on the terrazzo stone front porch. The one in the middle, taller and somewhat less elderly than the others, held high a black umbrella under which his friends gathered, framing him tightly like carolers sharing a songbook.

"Good evening, Mr. Highsmith," said the old man on the right. Like the others, he wore a necktie, his creased with careless disuse. Not much occasion for one in a town like Babylon. He stood the most hunched of the three, looking oddly frail despite his wide shoulders and deep chest. "I wonder if we can come in out of the rain."

"Of course."

Paul mumbled a puzzled apology and stepped aside so the three could enter and shake themselves dry in the foyer. Like Tuck after his bath. One umbrella seemed to offer insufficient coverage over three old men. Together, they stomped imaginary mud from their feet and murmured greetings to Darby, behind him.

The tall one said, "We really should have called, but old men have old habits."

"It used to be," said the one who'd spoken first, "you wanted to chat, you took a walk, rapped on your neighbor's door and talked his ear off while his wife put the kids to bed. You folks have a kid, don't you?"

The abrupt question and the nonchalance with the harsh-sounding "kid" caught Paul by surprise.

"Won't you come in?" Darby asked.

She led them to a couch in the family room where they plunked themselves down in the same order in which Paul had greeted them at the door, then took an inordinate amount of time settling stiff bones.

"Big house," said the third guest, a dour-looking man who spoke for the first time. His voice seemed unused to the workout. "Much too big, I'd think, for just the three of you."

In the uncomfortable silence that followed, the tall umbrella owner chuckled. "John, you always get right to the heart of matters, don't you? We haven't even introduced ourselves yet."

The frail man with the massive upper body chortled an apology. "Sorry. That should have been my job, being the mayor of our little town. I'm Olan Buck. This tall fellow here is Mr. James Chaplin, and the grumpy man simply talking your ear off is John Tolliver."

The tall one, Chaplin, flapped a hand self-consciously. Tolliver barely nodded. He sat folded compactly upon himself, his features seeming to meet in the middle of his face as his scowl pulled his eyebrows down and lifted the center of his mouth nearly to his nose.

"Well then," James Chaplin said into yet another awkward silence. "Now that you know us..."

"Can I get you gentlemen something to drink?" Darby asked, springing to her feet. It was obvious that she wouldn't mind leaving Paul alone with the odd group.

"No thanks."

"Not a thing."

Obstinate head shake.

With that, Mssrs. Buck, Chaplin and Tolliver removed any excuse for Darby to abandon him. Paul could hardly contain his smug glee.

Groping for something, anything, to contribute, he finally blurted, "Chaplin's Department Store," to the tall man. "And Buck Cement Products," he added, this time addressing the town's mayor.

"Very good," the department store's namesake said.

"Yes, Buck Cement Products," the mayor contributed. "You've obviously explored the industrial area to the southeast of town."

"I've been everywhere," Paul said, enjoying, without understanding why, the stir caused by his words. It was as though the three decrepit bulls squirmed their discomfort in unison.

"Well, it doesn't take long," Olan Buck finally offered. "Babylon is so small and uninteresting." He tittered. "I'm mayor. I shouldn't be talking like this, should I?"

The department store owner patted Buck's knee. "I think we all feel the same way, Olan. I'd probably take off for greener pastures myself if I wasn't trapped by generations of Chaplins. We've always lived here and I suppose we always will."

Mayor Buck murmured his agreement while John Tolliver stared with half-closed eyes at a spot between the two chairs occupied by Paul and Darby.

"My department store, Mr. Highsmith," the taller old man continued," is a tradition here, but if you lived twenty miles outside of Babylon you would have never heard of it. That's what I'm trying to say. For nearly a century, my family's lives have been intertwined with that store. We'd be useless in the outside world."

Chaplin leaned back at the same moment the town's mayor scooted forward. "It's the same with us, Mr. Highsmith. Buck Cement Products...I hardly even know what the company does, but it's run by cousins and uncles and I get a quarterly dividend check because I'm family."

"What these two are trying to say," grunted John Tolliver from his still corner of the couch, "is that Babylon is an old town—old with family—and that's the way we like it. It's home to the Tollivers and the

90

Bucks and the Chaplins and the Drakes and the Cravens and a dozen more names. There's no place for people like you."

The dour old man remained motionless, hunched in upon himself, his wizened body almost lost in the couch. The other two smiled serenely as though applying salve to the sting of their friend's words.

"When you mention the Drake family, that would include Miles Drake, wouldn't it?" Paul asked casually, his eyes flitting from face to face to face for a reaction truer than words.

"And that would be your little boy, Tuck, wouldn't it?"

It was only after John Tolliver spoke that Paul heard the faint wailing from up in the nursery and echoing out of the baby monitor in the kitchen. Darby gasped and skipped up the stairs.

"Sorry," said Mr. Chaplin. "We'll keep our voices down."

"Wonderful boy," John Tolliver said dryly. When he spoke, only his lips moved, and just barely. "Kids, you have to watch them. You think they're safe in a small town, but that's not always so."

The sour old man's eyes shone with a touch of yellow as they focused on Paul. "Read the papers, Mr. Highsmith—or the Internet, which I guess is the thing these days. Violence, child abuse, missing children. It happens everywhere, not just in Detroit. The only thing we lack here is white collar crime."

Did a smile crack his dour countenance? Paul couldn't be sure.

"Wouldn't it be ironic," Chaplin said with a pleasant chuckle, "if you leave Detroit for the safety and serenity of little old Babylon, where nothing ever happens, and all hell breaks loose."

Was that a threat? Paul opened his mouth, but he couldn't dig words out of his storm of thoughts. He sat stunned, literally speechless, until his attention was grabbed by the sound and fury of his young wife racing down the stairs and sliding across the foyer and into the living room, screeching to a halt before the three startled old men.

"Listen and listen well," she said, the words escaping her like steam from a hot teapot. "I heard you threaten my child. That's a fact, so don't waste my time denying it." She swept the air with one trim arm. "First, you come into our home and insult me with your story of the good old days when you'd drop by for a chat with the man of the house while the little wife prepared the children for bed. Well, alright. I put up with that anachronistic bullshit from my grandfather, who didn't know any better and was slightly daffy at the time, so I'll cut you three the same slack. But don't *ever* issue even the most veiled threat against my son. Do you all understand?"

The three men sat with gaping mouths.

James Chaplin recovered first. "Mrs. Highsmith, please don't think any harm would ever come to your lovely little boy. Not from us. I think

Mr. Tolliver here was merely—"

"Mr. Tolliver here," Darby interrupted, "is a fool and a bully who's been allowed to get away with too much for too long in the guise of being old and crotchety."

John Tolliver's rheumy eyes momentarily sparkled with a heat that would hurt to the touch. "Longer than you can imagine," he said.

As soon as he'd made his inscrutable comment, the eyes seemed to cool, the lids droop to their half-mast expression of bored disillusionment.

"Now gentlemen," Darby said, "I want you to leave. Please don't forget your umbrella because it's still raining and you're not coming back for it."

The three struggled to their feet, pulling at neckties and smoothing the creases from slacks.

At the door, Mayor Buck said, "Mrs. Highsmith, I assure you—"

"No, I assure the three of you," Darby said evenly, "that I'll hunt you to hell if anything happens to my son or my husband. Please take that as a promise, and don't return. Don't make a new offer on our home or even discuss the matter with our real estate agent." She smiled engagingly. "And it would be wonderful if you could pretend not to know us if we pass on the street. We'll do the same."

As the door closed, Paul's last sight was of three speechless old men hunched under an inadequate umbrella in a steady drizzle.

Chapter Sixteen

Great, Todd thought Friday morning while standing in front of the crumbling brick and wood and concrete garage. Life just keeps getting better.

"Get back in the car," D.B. shouted. "I'll run you back out here on lunch break. He'll definitely be open by then."

Todd shook his head with the finality of a man who'd already listened to his fill of reason. He burned with a vague, smoldering anger that found targets in Joy for insisting he come out here to check on the car, but mostly in the hick who ran Zeebe's Garage for not being open at damn near eight-thirty on a weekday morning. When were working people expected to take in their cars if not before work?

"Thanks," he managed to get out from between clenched jaws, "but I'm gonna wait around. I'll walk to work if the Olds isn't done yet."

He'd caught Don Brandon on his way out that morning, and been readily granted a ride to the garage. Like most of the men from the Sundown, D.B. worked in one of the six or seven small factories on Sennett Street in the so-called Industrial Parkway.

Zeebe's was at the very end of Main View Road before it took a ninety-degree turn, exchanged pavement for gravel and became Sennett. Bean fields and gravel roads and rickety factories. A walk would be all of a mile, mile and a half. And he'd have the advantage of gloomy silence rather than D.B.'s sunny chatter.

The ride in the Ford pickup had been filled with country music rattling like broken glass from defective speakers and the driver's incessant morning cheer. The white sky and early humidity also contributed to Todd's foul mood.

Now facing an empty building, he wiped his face of the sweat already accumulating and said, loud enough to be heard above the radio twang, "Really, D.B., thanks for the ride but I'm gonna wait around."

D.B. shrugged. "Guess it don't matter if you're late. I'm thinking you gotta sleep with the boss's wife and drink all his beer to get fired in this town. Just remember, Friday's payday."

He rapped his palm against the door of the F-150, some kind of high-energy sign-off, then threw gravel as he shimmied out of the lot.

Todd saw more Sundowners in rattletrap cars and hillbilly trucks. They honked and waved at him as they screeched around the turn onto Sennett. To get out of the worse of the heat, Todd slid behind a crooked row of dead vehicles with missing grills, missing doors, missing tires, missing lights. The patch of dirt and weeds in front of the garage was a rust-flaked graveyard of American metal, unburied corpses with hoods up, engine blocks gone. Hulks with no seats sitting on cinder. If the property offered any indication of Zeebe's mechanical skills, Todd already regretted his decision to send the Olds this way.

Of course, it hadn't actually been his decision in the first place, a recollection that sent him seething. Goddamn cop.

He circled Zeebe's grounds, sinking into the mud up to his work boot laces. He made his way around the rusted corpses and the seriously leaning building, searching with all the enthusiasm of an earthquake survivor hoping not to find loved ones.

The building sat on a colorless concrete foundation, two closed bay doors in front. Todd tugged at one of the roll-up doors and wasn't surprised when it didn't budge.

"Damn," he said as he took off for the street.

Then he recalled spying a second door, to the side of the building. He turned with another curse, this one for his wife for sending him on this fool's errand. He jammed a cigarette between his lips and fired it up.

It was unlocked. It opened a crack. Todd looked up and down the road, giving the garage owner one last chance to show up if he wasn't already here. He took a big drag of good tar poison, stomped the butt underfoot and pushed the door open.

The bright white sky left him squinting in the dark interior. He stood in the doorway until his irises slitted and his vision adjusted enough to pick out six parked vehicles, one of which was his Olds Eighty-Eight. Looking no worse, at least from this view, than when he'd last seen it.

"Hello?" he called out to the shadows.

Nothing.

The cement floor was sleek with engine oil and lubricants, littered with tools that wanted to trip him up as he picked his way as carefully as possible to his car, his T-shirt glued to his back by sweat and anxiety.

The floor wasn't level—had he really expected otherwise?—and now he heard the door behind whine slowly close, another victim of gravity. Todd turned and nervously watched the sharp white line of natural light disappear. By the time the door nudged up against its jamb, daylight had fled the premises altogether, but by now his eyes had grown accustomed to the shadowy bleakness.

Or at least enough so that he could pick his way carefully past a beater of a Cadillac and to his own car's front door, which he opened for the sake of the dome light. And got nothing for his troubles.

Now fairly well accustomed to the dark, he could identify five cars and a pickup, arranged in two rows. The Olds with the burned-out dome light headed up one of those rows.

He'd lit another cigarette at some point—probably as much for the illumination as the jolt—and now he tapped the ash loose on the slick floor and called out another weak greeting to the ever-present shadows. It bounced back without comment.

Todd climbed into his car, noting with new annoyance the absence of lighting. The key was dangling from the ignition along with a yellow tag. There were greasy fingerprints on it, and scribbled numbers in a code that would mean something to the mechanic.

Not sure what he hoped to accomplish except to assure himself they hadn't stolen the battery or hoisted the engine, Todd fluttered the gas pedal and turned over the ignition. It barely even threatened to catch. He sat back. Counted to three. Tried again. Again got the mechanical drone of a starter that couldn't quite make it over the top. Like a sneeze watering the eyes but just hovering at the edges.

"Shit."

He kept fluttering, kept grinding, devoid of expectations but filled with rage and frustration. He might have kept this up until he killed what little battery juice remained, except that his attention got drawn to a winking dot in his rearview mirror.

As he stared at it, Todd's thumb and forefinger forgot their sweaty grip on the ignition key. In a few seconds the red light was gone, leaving him only with the glowing after-image burned into his mind.

He turned for a better look out his rear window at whatever he'd seen back there. He found the spacious interior of the monster Caddy parked immediately behind him. A car from the days when Detroit ruled and gasoline ran like water and success meant more horses under your hood than the neighbors.

Staring hard, Todd grew convinced he's seen nothing of any significance. Then he caught another red wink from the vicinity of where a steering wheel should be if good old Zeebe hadn't plundered it and sold it on eBay. Todd squinted, but the light was gone. Again.

"What the hell...?" he breathed.

He sniffed the air. Cigarette smoke. Maybe his own. Maybe not. He stabbed his butt out in the ashtray. Then saw the glow again.

Incensed at being spied upon, and embarrassed by his momentary shock and confusion, Todd slammed out of his car, strolled to the parked Caddy and rapped on the driver's door.

Like one of those optical puzzles where you see nothing at first and then the smiling witch suddenly shifts into view, the car's open window afforded shadows and then from the shadows emerged the chilling reality of a slouched man smoking behind the wheel. Todd jerked away from the massive head and broad shoulders, the rest still lost to shadows.

The man said nothing. Just smoked. Stared at him. Smoked. Smiled.

Todd hid his fear—more than that, his sudden and inexplicable revulsion—in chin-out aggression. "Hey, what's the deal with my car?" The effect was supposed to be forceful, but it sounded thin and whiny even to his own ears.

The man coughed up a wet, chesty substance that he caught in a used tissue., This he balled up in a grimy fist and tossed to the floor on the passenger side of his big ride. He grinned. "Kids, don't smoke," he said.

Christ, thought Todd, thankful the asshole hadn't been resting in *his* car.

The man behind the wheel gazed out the cracked windshield with the bored expression of a long-distance hauler. He took another drag on his cigarette, the glowing ash feebly lighting the car interior for a second.

It was enough. Todd stumbled back a step, choking slightly as he inhaled secondhand smoke with his startled gasp.

The seated man turned so Todd could read 'Jim Zeebe, Prop.' sewn in an unsteady hand over his work-shirt pocket.

Zeebe shaped his thick lips into a twist of a smile. "Boo."

Chapter Seventeen

"Lung cancer," he said, first hacking more dark moisture into another fisted tissue, then dragging another nicotine hit into his ruined lungs. "Forty-six." He shrugged. "Young for cancer, but what're you gonna do?"

Jim Zeebe could have been a whole lot older than 46, judging by the way his body was wasting away under the big head and wide shoulders. Todd could see the man's skull under his taut, paper-thin flesh. His grin revealed a partial set of stained teeth that already seemed to be settling into a death mask. That's what had caused Todd to react when the cigarette glow had provided too much light.

Now he resisted the urge to dab his own dry lips after seeing the blood spotting the other man's mouth. Was that normal, even for advanced lung cancer?

"Sorry to hear it," he mumbled. Not sure what else to say and knowing it wouldn't be enough, no matter what came out of his mouth.

"Oh, that's alright," Jim Zeebe rasped. "Not the end of the world."

He profiled another contorted grin, and then his lips curdled into a tortured grimace. The tissue went up in time to catch most of another blood-spurting cough. Todd backed away as Zeebe pinched off a final drag on his butt before tossing it onto the greasy pavement. Then he slumped forward far enough that his hand could reach for and find a fresh pack in the messy glove compartment.

"Might say it's the start of the world rather than the end," he said. Then winked.

Todd had grown painfully aware of the new cancer stick he'd stuck between his own lips without even thinking about it. Nicotine magic. Now he reached up to throw it away, but couldn't quite bring himself to do so. In a sort of compromise, he didn't light it, but allowed it to perch uselessly in the corner of his mouth.

"Well that's good, your attitude," he said, propping up, in a way, Zeebe's bullshit bravado.

He wasn't sure how he'd shift gears and bring the dying garage owner around to the subject of his Oldsmobile, but hell, tact had never been his strong suit anyway. "I was just looking over my car there—the Eighty-Eight you picked up for Marty McConlon?—and I was wondering when you think it might be ready."

Zeebe's thick lips crawled down his tight face in a grotesque parody of concentration. "Olds Eighty-Eight," he said, confirming the make and model. "Needs work."

David Searls

Todd waited for as long as his patience allowed, but that wasn't long. He sputtered, "I know it needs work, man. That's why it's here. What I need to know is, when'll it be done? And how much will it cost? Okay?" His voice dripped with more sarcasm than he'd intended under the circumstances, the fucker dying and all, but shit.

Zeebe didn't seem to take it personally. He continued to stare into the cracked windshield before erupting in a fresh spasm of coughs. This attack must have caught him unaware. There was no balled-up tissue. Or he just didn't give a shit anymore. He covered the glass in a fine mist of pink. "Sorry," he said, chuckling.

Finished for the moment, he soothed his blackened lungs with another drag of tobacco smoke.

Todd tried not to breathe until the blue smoke had left Zeebe's broken chest cavity and dissipated in the air.

"It needs a lot," Zeebe murmured so faintly it could have been his dying statement. "Plugs," he added after a brief pause. "Plugs and points."

"Are you kidding me? Any high school kid could've changed the plugs and points in an hour. You've had my car for two days."

If Todd had any concern about upsetting the mortally ill mechanic, it was unnecessary. Zeebe offered him another ghastly grin. "Needs other stuff, too." His voice sounded hollow, as if the chest cavity it came from was already a dry, empty husk. "The hoses are soft, brake pads and shoes worn. Muffler and pipes rusted out."

"I'll tell you what else it needs," Todd said too quietly. He leaned his head in the window, temporarily oblivious to the stench of stale smoke and motor oil and the iron scent of fresh blood. "Needs a battery. Mine was in okay shape when you brought it in, though. Newest thing on this damn car. So I'm figuring that two days of playing my radio—hell, who knows, maybe living in my car—well, that's just about kicked the shit out of that battery. What do you figure?"

The garage owner whipped his head toward Todd with more reflexive speed than Todd would have imagined he had left. His face, glistening with pain-sweat, was so pale it looked blue in the insufficient light.

"What I figure," Zeebe said, his voice sharp and brittle, "is that you're taking a hell of a chance talking to me like that."

Todd's feet stuttered away.

"I'm thinking," Zeebe continued, his voice rattling loose in his mouth, "that you'll never get yourself another good night's rest if you ever get on my bad side, little man."

"All I want is my car back," Todd said in a placating whine he hated to hear.

As if distracted by the windshield into which he stared, Zeebe said in an almost singsong voice, "No more sickness, nor death, nor fear. Hurts now, but it'll all be worth it once I'm free. I'm flying already, little man. Saw the town...the birds...the rooftops..."

He tilted his head skyward as though he could catch such fanciful sights somewhere in the vicinity of the Cadillac's smoke-stained dome.

With his neck exposed like that, Todd saw the purple welt. It look like the middle-aged mechanic might have been given a hickey by a high school girl, a possibility too disgusting to consider. Staring at it, Todd felt a desperate need to be outside again in the clean daylight.

"All I want to know," he said quietly, "is when I can pick up my car. In working condition."

Zeebe once more turned that ghastly grin on him. "It's going to be expensive, little man."

"For what, plugs and points? Brake pads? How much can it be?"

"Forgot to tell you about the transmission."

Todd felt acid gnawing away at his insides. He'd felt the engine lurch a time or two, but the transmission was fine. Jesus, it had to be, because he could guess what a new one could cost. Definitely more than he paid for the car. He was being screwed. Let the cops handle it.

That last thought made him almost giggle out loud, an outburst he feared even more than his anger.

He stumbled away from the dying man and aimed his sights on the faint crack lining the door. He knew what he'd known all along and just hadn't admitted to himself: Marty McConlon was never going to let him and his family out of Babylon without more car repairs than they could possibly afford.

And that meant they'd never get out.

He felt something black and cancerous squeezing his lungs and knew he had to get out fast. He spat his unlit cigarette to the floor, even though he knew he'd light its replacement as soon as he left the darkness.

Behind him came a phlegm-filled chuckle that ended in a painfully wet cough. "One of these nights, little man," the moist voice wheezed. "Be all fixed real soon."

The mechanic was still speaking, but Todd lost the message in the wet, choked cackle that accompanied it.

Chapter Eighteen

"Todd, when's Joy's interview? It's five-fifteen now."

"Relax," he said, sniffing Kathy Lee's lovely beer breath.

Why bust his ass to get home when all he'd get was a whiny earful about the car? He'd tried, hadn't he? Joy would never understand how he'd left Zeebe's without the Olds or some idea of what he owed or when it would be fixed.

More to the point, why was it so damn important that she make this interview when all she could talk about was getting out of Babylon?

There's something not right about this place, she'd told him the night before.

No shit. She'd never be able to imagine the terror he'd felt that morning, staring at that dying man with blood in his phlegm and nicotine staining his fingers and rotted teeth and smoke on his breath. And that bruise at his throat...

Todd would never make her understand what had propelled him out the door that morning and sent him hiking down that gravel road to a box factory that didn't need him. She wouldn't understand because even he couldn't explain his unmanly fear.

When the golden content of his first frosted mug slid down his throat and started kicking ass with his brain cells, he was able to push aside the need to know. He had cash in his pocket, thanks to his fortuitous discovery that the bearded bartender cashed local payroll checks. Todd also had a corner of the Winking Dog Saloon filled with his new neighbors and friends.

"I don't know," Kathy Lee was saying. "I think you oughta at least call and tell her you can't make it. What's she gonna do with the kids?"

"I was detained," Todd said, trying out a possible alibi for later. By not making the call just then, he could at least postpone the inevitable clash. "She'll understand," he added, a lie so boldfaced he couldn't even make himself believe it.

"You're goddamn right," shouted the pesky kid with the muscles and buzz cut. He stood behind them, throwing darts with D.B. and Judd, but somehow still managing to insinuate himself into the conversation. "These women, you gotta keep them in place or they'll run your life for you. No one's running mine."

His ever-flexed forearm sported ink that looked like a fire-breathing stag with a set of initials tattooed below it. Likely an ex-girlfriend who was no longer running his life for him.

Todd wished the kid hadn't taken his side. It made him doubt his judgment a little. He thought of calling Joy just to spite him, but didn't. She'd have plenty to say about him plunking his ass down on a bar stool with her stuck home with three hungry and bored kids and a job interview in...Todd sneaked a look at Kathy Lee's watch and saw that it was too late to worry about it. The interview was starting without her.

"We don't really even need it no more," he told a new beer bottle, one that had magically appeared on the counter when he wasn't looking. "Not with me working."

"Trust me, you need it." This came from Jermaine Whittock, sitting with Tonya and others at a table behind him, "We got three kids, too. The grandparents get our money once a month, what we can afford to send, and it's never enough." Jermaine drained the rest of his bottle in a single gulp. "Damn, I miss them," he said quietly.

"I'm making good money," Todd insisted. "Good enough for now, anyhow."

D.B. leaned over Todd's stool to chime in. "I'm up to eighteen-and-a-half an hour now for lugging cement bags. I was getting an even eighteen, but I saw that this week's check was off. In my favor. I added it up and found out they'd given me another raise they didn't even tell me about."

"Don't tell no one," Judd said. "They know about it, they'll take it away."

"I don't know," Denver Dugan said from another barstool. "I can't figure out this blasted town. Never believed in no worker's paradise, least not till I got pulled off the road in Babylon, Michigan. Now I don't know what to think."

"I'll bet you weren't even *in* Babylon when you got pulled over," Todd said. "Bet you were on a state highway when you got stopped by that Marty cop."

"Wasn't Marty," Denver drawled. "The younger one."

"My point being, it was a local cop pulling you off a state highway," Todd insisted. "Anyone see anything funny about that?"

They sat and thought and drank while .38 Special pounded from the jukebox.

Todd was feeling too good to work up any real anger. Most of two beers in him, he somehow knew the alcohol was achieving peak performance right about now and that he wouldn't stop pouring it in and it would all be downhill from here. He clicked his bottle against the top of the bar in solemn recognition of the wrongs he'd do tonight, and prepared to do them.

The Winking Dog was the kind of joint that didn't think entertainment could be found in simple conversation. It was a square, dusky room with a pine plank floor, scarred walls and decades of cigarette smoke still floating in the air. A long bar and mirror with bottle reflections occupied one wall, a few tables and a pool table with its accumulation of sticks, chalk and players taking up most of the space in the open area. Three dartboards, a video golf game, a basket-shooting game and the guitar-heavy jukebox kept bodies occupied and conversation to a minimum.

The cacophony of sound put Todd more at ease than he'd felt since being yanked into town. It didn't surprise him that no one noticed his late arrival at work that morning. He put in another long day of dust and glares, simple tasks and long smoke breaks. It felt good to be among friends now, in a commandeered corner of a loud bar.

When he broke away from his thoughts, he found yet another sweating beer bottle in front of him. Yessiree, it was going to be a fine evening—if only he could ignore the sight of the pay phone in the alcove by the restrooms.

"I got nothing to feel bad about," he told his latest beer.

"What's that?" Kathy Lee asked, dragging herself none too reluctantly out of a conversation with the buzzcut kid who'd abandoned darts to pull up a stool next to her.

"I wanted to know," said Todd, making up the question on the spot, "what you were about to tell me before Melanie got her flip-flop nibbled by the rat that first night."

She stared at him blankly.

"How Officer Marty was able to pull you into Babylon. You were starting to tell me."

"I'm getting us more beer," Buzzcut said, standing wobbly. Naturally, he was frowning. Todd couldn't tell if the kid was pissed off at having Kathy Lee's attention diverted, or if he was born that way.

"Get me another one, too," Todd said, shoving a ten dollar bill across the table.

The attitude didn't go away, but the kid and the money did.

"Dukey likes me," Kathy Lee said.

"Dukey?"

"Duke Gates. Real name's probably Ralphie or Byron, but Duke's what he goes by."

"You're not avoiding the subject," Todd said, scooting closer. He accidentally knocked his beer bottle against hers as if sealing a pact he knew nothing about. "What's he holding over you? The cop, I mean."

Kathy Lee stared at Dukey's empty stool on her other side as if willing someone interesting to take it. "He let me keep my kids," she said, still facing away.

Todd barely heard her. When he asked her to repeat it, she swiveled in her seat and said it again, right to him this time. While burning him with a look that dared him to find fault with her words.

She twirled a bottle that had been half full the last time he'd looked, but was empty now. "My kids, they're loud, obnoxious and semi-evil," she said. "I can't spend too much time around them or they'd drive me nuts. But I do love them in my way." She sucked on the bottle, her eyes so lost in thought she didn't even seem to mind that it was empty.

"Skip, he was my husband." She laughed. "Good name, now that I think of it. As in, 'he skipped.' So he's gone, and I get into a tiff with the landlord, right?"

Todd wasn't sure he was keeping up, but he nodded anyway. "Right."

"This bastard's all gung-ho about raising my rent, but he won't fix the locks on the windows—and three of the neighbors have had break-ins. So he comes over one night after work with his hand out for last month's rent which is late 'cuz I'm not getting any child support and Skip's skipped without a forwarding address. I tell him—the landlord—he's not gonna see another rent check until I get some locks on those windows. That's fair, right? He screams at me and I scream at him and the next thing I know there's cops pounding on the door. I'm busted for disturbing the peace and for assaulting my pig of a landlord. By that he means that I shoved him away when he got his face into mine. Now I've got the cops on my ass and my landlord's lawyer, too. And now Skip's back in town long enough to tell me he wants the kids 'cuz I'm obviously a violent, unfit mother."

"Here ya go, Kathy Lee," young Duke said, plopping another bottle in front of her. He wordlessly slid Todd his, but not a dime of change.

"So what happened?" Todd asked, nudging her back into the story. He squinted to narrow his field of vision and miss Duke leaning into the picture.

She shrugged. "Skip didn't want the kids. He was just pissed at me for chasing him down for child support. He'd found a job of some kind in Knoxville—miracle of miracles—and his employer was about to start garnering his wages. So..." She shrugged again and sucked down a throatful of suds. "...I packed up the demon seeds and took off for somewhere Skip wouldn't look. Knowing, of course, that he wouldn't look too hard when he learned his wages weren't going to be attached."

Kathy Lee turned the other way and let Duke ramble on about a new pair of speakers he was thinking of installing in his ride, but Todd didn't let her off that easy.

He tapped her. "I don't see why you didn't stay put. Okay, you were late with the rent and you tussled with your landlord, but compared to the way your asshole husband took off, that don't seem too bad."

She sighed. "Right. The lesser of two evils. Mommy's violent and

103

Daddy's a deadbeat. Let's flip a coin and see who wins. Skip had what passed, for the moment anyway, as a steady job, while I was tending bar. Leaving the kids alone, I might add, 'cuz I wasn't making near enough to pay a babysitter on top of everything else. Whoever's got the best lawyer wins, and I couldn't even afford a bad one."

Todd tugged her thin forearm again when she turned her attention to glassy-eyed Duke, sitting there slamming down beers like he thought the faster he drank the smarter he got. "So where does Marty McConlon come in?" he asked when he had her attention back.

She stared into space. "I had an aunt in Flint. I think she still had a job with one of the automakers—forget which one—and I needed to convince her that I just had to see her for the first time in like twenty years. Actually, I was hoping she'd let me and the kids crash at her place for awhile. Buying time, you know?" She took a healthy swallow from the new bottle. "I was keeping off the main freeways just in case anyone was actively looking for us, though, as I said, I didn't think Skip was trying too hard."

Todd felt her attention wavering again, and quickly pressed her to get to the McConlon part.

"You know, I can't even remember why he pulled me over," she said. "Probably don't matter. But while I'm waiting, he's running my plate and finding there's a bench warrant out for me." She snorted. "I'm wanted in Tennessee for snatching my own kids. Hell, if the law knew what those two were like, they'd give me a medal for taking 'em out of the state."

That was the last of it. She poured herself off of her stool too quickly for Todd to catch her this time, apparently to visit the little girl's room. Never mind. He had the rest figured out for himself. He could picture the smarmy cop telling her that she's probably unaware there's a warrant out for her arrest, that it must be a big mistake but she'll have to come with him to get it sorted out in town. Later, he'd tell her that her legal problem could stay a big mistake as long as she stayed in Babylon and took the easy job and generous tips they threw at her.

But why? Todd took a long pull. Maybe beer really did make you smarter. He was bound to find out.

"D.B.," he shouted when the man passed his line of vision.

Don Brandon plopped onto the stool that still held the shape of Kathy Lee's fine, though scrawny, ass. His little pink eyes danced with Friday night fever. "Gimme ten bucks, boss. Judd and me can take Carl and Denver," he shouted, jerking a thumb toward the Sundowners waiting at the dartboard.

Todd knew or at least recognized everyone at their section of the bar. Tonya Whittock waited listlessly for the rail-thin guy with the ponytail and messed-up teeth to quit simultaneously talking and spitting at her. Carl Haggerty and Denver Dugan stood waiting for a money match while Jamey Weeks was chalking up a stick and chatting with Jermaine and the chrome-dome young dude.

"They any good?" Todd asked, peeling away a ten from his thin stash. "If they are, and I lose my money, my wife's gonna hate me even more than she already does."

"They're good, we're good…" D.B. said, brushing aside the issue with an expansive shrug.

"Tell Carl I want to talk to him when he gets a chance," Todd said, reluctantly letting go of the bill.

D.B. winked. "Oh, he'll get a chance real soon."

Carl Haggerty was a ten-spot richer by the time he plopped into a barstool next to Todd. "The problem with those two," Carl said, jabbing a thumb at D.B. and Judd, "is that they drink when they play. You can gamble or you can drink, and do a halfway decent job of either, but you can't combine vices like that." His own gambling vice apparently put to bed for the night, Carl waved the bearded bartender for a beer. "So what you wanna see me about?"

Todd made himself ignore the ten-dollar bill on the bar in front of Carl. *His* ten. "Doyle Armstrong," he said and waited for a reaction.

"What about him?" Carl Haggerty's black skin looked combat boot tough, his half-mast lids weighing down his eyes. The deep grooves etched into his forehead heightened the image of a man with a lot of past.

"Jermaine tells me you and this Doyle were friends. You traveled into town together, but one day a month or two ago he just disappears."

"So?"

So, indeed. Not even Todd knew where he was going with this. He tried working it out by talking, not thinking. "Way Jermaine tells it, sounds like your friend Doyle just up and left."

"My friend Doyle. That's all I hear from people: 'Why'd your friend Doyle…?' How the hell do I know? He didn't tell me nothing. Just left, is all."

"Just left," said Todd. "Couldn't find work, or what?"

"All these goddamn questions."

Todd stayed stubbornly silent while Carl mulled over whether to answer him or not.

Finally, voice heavy with resignation, Carl said, "No, of course he had work. That was the easy part. Didn't like the town, though. Suspicious of everything. My way of thinking, you don't question good luck." Pointedly spoken, and not lost on Todd.

"What kind of work did he find?"

"Security guarding. Plainclothes security at that department store in town."

Something didn't sound right. "Small town like this, everyone knowing everyone, why they need a security guard? An outsider."

And a black guy at that, he almost added.

Carl whistled between his teeth, a low, haunted sound. "Man, you and Doyle. Twins separated at birth. Just like you, he'd come in with those eighteen-dollar-an-hour paychecks, pissing and moaning all the way to the bank."

"Sounds like a lot of money for keeping an eye on shoplifters."

Carl shook his head. "I heard my fill of that talk, Dunbar. But know what? I make that kind of money lugging ladders and brushes for a company that sends me out with paint crews." Carl squirmed deeper into his barstool, a cold beer in front of him. "Rains three straight days last week and we can't go out, so they tell me to stay home, stay dry. Today, after I drag out the equipment and help set up scaffolding in front of this big old house that's now an insurance agency, my job's done till cleanup. I grab me a newspaper and a coffee and go sit in the shade 'cuz that's what they tell me to do. But I get a pay envelope end of day just like everyone else. Just like every week."

Todd stared at him while formulating his next question. "Yeah, but do they like you?" he finally asked. "Do they respect you?"

"What, am I on Oprah? Here." Carl ripped a ragged cloth wallet from his hip pocket and slapped it onto the bar. He pulled bills out of it and held them up for inspection. "Here's the respect. You see this paper money here? Not a fortune, but it's more'n I was getting cashing unemployment checks about to run out. Does it all make sense to me? No. Does it have to? No again."

Todd sat back and waited for the other man's nostrils to stop flaring. For his forehead furrows to smooth out at least a little. Then he said, "You don't know shit about economics, Carl. Neither do I, but I know jobs like ours don't last forever."

"My point exactly. So let's enjoy life while it's got a little sweetness to it. Tomorrow..." Carl shrugged. He stood like he was about to leave, but then heaved his boot-leather face into Todd's. "You think you're the smart guy, don't you? Think you the only one bright enough to figure something's wrong, but lemme tell you. D.B. knows it, but he also knows he's looking at jail time for stealing from his last boss, a construction contractor who kept promising him raises that never came. Kathy Lee knows it, but the poor woman wants to keep her kids. Jermaine and Tonya know, but they already had to leave theirs behind and they want them back. So how 'bout this? How 'bout you keep your brilliant deductions to yourself, huh?"

106

With that, Carl moved away. Todd tipped his bottle to his lips in a futile effort to get his mind off of his full bladder. When that didn't work, he lurched to his feet and tried avoiding sight of the pay phone just begging for his quarter.

Two young locals in jeans and T-shirts quit talking when he stumbled into the men's room. And when he finished, zipped and came back out, a middle-aged man in a suit stopped trying to pick up a girl who could have been his daughter as Todd leaned across the bar to give his beer order to a new bartender. This one had long hair, wide shoulders and a tiny red stone set into an earlobe.

Kathy Lee was pretending she didn't know how to shoot pool so that Buzzcut Duke could demonstrate the proper technique by shoving his groin against her ass and wrapping his big strong arms around her.

Beer in hand, Todd wandered over to the basketball-shooting game and set his bottle down.

"Dontcha see the quarter?" The kid had a denim jacket with the sleeves removed and motorcycle club patches sewn here and there. The rugged look clashed with his frail build and coke bottle eyeglasses. His friends looked like they'd back him up in a fight, though, which accounted for the sneer.

Todd moved away.

The makeup of the Winking Dog had subtly changed over the timeless period in which he'd been there. With no windows, no structure to the routine of chatting and drinking—mostly drinking— there'd been no way to measure the passage of time. Well sure, he could have looked at someone's watch, but that would have just depressed him.

Now that he thought about it, he remembered a smattering of businessmen when he first got there. Now the place was overrun with the jeans and work-shirt crowd. The women were his age and younger, flaunting hips and asses and boobs, but at other locals. Not at the few remaining Sundowners.

The mood of the bar had changed, too. Voices were lower, the music more somber. It had been Seger's *Night Moves* before, but now it was a Vietnam ballad from Billy Joel that made Todd inexplicably uncomfortable. Something about holding the day in the palm of your hand and letting *them* rule the night.

The locals stood closer together now, men whispering to women, limbs intertwined. Others sat in small clusters with expression that seemed to harden by the minute as they passed quick glances at the Sundowners in their corner.

Carl and the Whittocks were gone now. Denver Dugan flapped a hand toward them as he and Jamey Weeks dragged ass out the door.

"What's going on?" Todd asked D.B. and Judd, both standing

motionless behind a tight crowd of dart players. Todd tried flagging down a waitress, but she pretended not to see him. He felt in desperate need of putting something in his friends' hands—beer, darts, something—to keep them there.

"We won, dammit," Judd growled, his fists as tightly clenched as his hairy jaw. "They gotta play us or give us the dartboard back."

D.B. patted the kid's shoulder. "Relax, Judd. If they don't want to, fuck 'em."

"That's right," Todd said, not knowing or caring exactly what the hassle was about. He tried steering both of them to the table the Sundowners had staked since happy hour. "Let's just get another round and wait them out. When they leave, we'll shoot darts ourselves, okay? Kathy Lee'll be my partner." He scanned the room and waved her over to them.

She surprised him by laying a cool hand on the back of his neck and pecking his cheek. She was braless, as usual, her nipples stiff against her coarse cotton top. The sight didn't irritate Todd as it had before. Didn't irritate him at all.

She put her lips to his ear. "Call your wife," she said.

He grabbed her hand when it was apparent she was about to get away. "What are you...?"

Duke Gates came swinging out of the bathroom, zipping up as he pranced toward them, the gesture and the smile deliberate.

Kathy Lee brushed Todd's ear again with her lips. "Dukey said he'd take me—"

"I bet he will," Todd said, laughing wildly, yet inexplicably pissed. Funniest goddamn thing he'd ever heard. He signaled again for a drink, and this time the waitress acknowledged him.

He cocked an eyebrow at D.B. as the girl sauntered their way, and D.B. said, "I don't know, man. I shouldn't spend any more."

"I got money," Todd said, pulling from his pocket not much remaining evidence of that claim.

The waitress was blond and young and uninterested as she waited for them to decide.

"I'm staying," Judd said sharply. "These town fucks ain't forcing me out."

Heads turned from the dartboard, faces hard.

"Easy, man, easy," D.B. soothed. He took one of Judd 's balled fists and held it like a lover, pulling him into the next chair. "Two more of the same," he told the waitress, eyes twinkling with counterfeit ease.

"Where's Denver?" Judd looked around, his eyes not tracking well. "Shit. If he's gone, I rode in with him and Jamey."

"I'll give you a ride," Todd said. Then echoed Judd with "Shit," as he remembered the status of the Olds.

"Never mind. I drove," said D.B.

The front door pealed open at that moment. It was almost flung off its hinges to admit a clutch of night shadows and four loud, strutting men.

"Yes!" the first of the four shouted.

Todd's eyes moved first to the darkness they'd tracked in with them. It had been close to broad daylight, the September sun sitting high and eternal in the sky, when he'd let D.B. take him here. Where'd it gone?

The front door hushed shut behind the last of the four. Todd's hand on the table rattled a graveyard of empty green bottles and sent up grainy clouds of cigarette soot from overflowing ashtrays. His head swam, his throat burned and eyelids felt braced up by everything he could put into the effort.

"Beer, Lattimer. Lots of beer."

"Outta the way, assholes. We got drinking and fucking to get to."

"Yeah!"

The four roared, grunted and barked laughter as they cleared a path to the bar by the strength of their strut, the swing of eight arms, the glint of eight glittery eyes.

"Purcell," said one of the dart players in a greeting that sounded carefully neutral. Just: "Purcell."

Todd squinted for a view that eliminated blurry multiple exposures of the four. Their eyes seemed to emit a slight white glow until they got to a place in the room where the light was strongest and Todd saw that he'd been mistaken. They were just eyes, one pair dark, one green, the others just eyes.

The one who'd burst first through the door was compact and unshaven, somewhat shorter than average stature. He wore a denim work shirt that looked too hot for the weather. It seemed to be the cause of the sheen of oily sweat across his pale face under a billed ball cap that advertised an agricultural chemical.

This one, the muscular guy with the stone eyes, just had to be the Purcell pointed out by the darts player.

The second one through the door was the noisiest. A slight man in his mid-thirties, he whooped "ha, ha!" with brazen joy. He pawed the air in quick, meaningless gestures. "Bud. Yes! Four Buds," he yowled to the bartender. His tongue played with a cigarette, whipping it from one side of his mouth to the other as he impatiently awaited his order.

The third one showed off unwashed, blond hair that hung to his shoulders. He was both younger and taller than the first two, his face paler. His green eyes were everywhere, searching for a fight.

There were no takers.

The fourth in line to the bar—

Todd's stomach lurched. "No," he whispered, his eyes unable to leave that last figure.

"Jeez, what's with you, Todd?" D.B. asked.

The last one through the door was the tallest, the broadest-shouldered of the four. It was his laughter, strong and low and dangerous, that had preceded the four into the Dog. "Beer, Lattimer, lots of beers," had been his greeting. Now he absently slapped palms with the skinny guy in the coke bottle glasses who'd hassled Todd for the basket-shooting game, the skinny guy going, "Alright, man. Good to see you back in the saddle."

"Back in the saddle," the fourth man repeated, trying it out. "Back in the saddle," he said again. He sucked the life out of a cigarette and dropped it to the floor.

"Ah, shit, it's good to be alive," he said as he climbed onto a stool, four of which had quickly become available, a few of the locals having decided to make bathroom breaks as soon as the newcomers came through the door. "Jason, gimme another," this fourth one bellowed to his buddy with the stringy blond hair, green eyes and insolent voice.

Jason tossed a fresh cigarette at him and drawled, "Watch it, man. Those things'll kill you."

The four erupted in loud laughter.

"Looking good, Zeebe," one of the dart players said to the fourth man, between jukebox tunes.

"Damn right," Jim Zeebe howled.

The compliment was a partial lie. Zeebe looked sick, though a hell of a lot healthier than he'd looked earlier in the day. While his eyes were bright and his voice strong, his greasy work clothes hung loose on his emaciated frame.

He twirled once on his stool and clapped his hands sharply. "I feel so good I could kill a half dozen of you just for the practice," he shouted.

Nervous laughter.

"It's Zeebe," Todd said so quietly he wasn't sure his remark would even be picked up.

D.B. said, "The guy in the garage? I thought you said he was dying."

"He was." Todd laid both palms flat against the top of the bar so they wouldn't shake so much. "We've gotta leave. Now."

"Bullshit," Judd cried out. "I'm playing darts. We ain't leaving on account of them pussies."

Christ. They'd draw too much attention if they tried dragging the little bastard out, and Todd knew D.B. would never leave without him. He scanned the room for familiar faces but found what he'd already suspected: The three of them were the last of the Sundowners.

In fact, they were among the last of the bar's customers of any kind. With his attention riveted on the four who'd just entered, Todd hadn't noticed all of those who'd just as suddenly exited the premises. Four dart players remained, along with the skinny guy with the glasses and motorcycle gear, and an unattractive couple that seemed oddly fascinated with one another. That and four or five others in T-shirts and shorts, everyone besides the swaggering four.

"How 'bout something from the grill?" Zeebe shouted, cupping his hands and aiming his demand through a pair of swinging doors near one end of the bar.

"Make it bloody," added the one apparently known as Jason, to which Purcell added a low rumble of a comment that Todd couldn't hear. His mates laughed appreciably.

"Let's go," Todd said.

For some reason, there was no more argument from Judd. The three left the table and glided toward the door, the state of inebriation seeming to have been drained from all of them.

Too late. The door burst open before they got to it.

Chapter Nineteen

The door to the Winking Dog Saloon suddenly opened and sucked in more shadows from the night. More flickering eyes, a teenage girl and a younger boy. Too young to drink, but it didn't look like that was going to stop him.

Four heads at the bar turned, catching Todd, D.B. and Judd in a crossfire of white, glittery eyes.

Todd's gaze strayed to Zeebe even though he'd told himself to avoid such contact.

A smile of recognition played on the lips of the sickly mechanic. "Sorry, boss. Still need more time on that Eighty-Eight. Seems to be a problem with the battery, but please don't get mad at me again."

Zeebe let his head loll so Todd could see the purple bruise at his jugular. He let go a laugh, a deep, throaty growl that sent the Sundowners a step closer to the two newly arrived strangers panting noisily behind them.

Purcell climbed off his stool and took two steps forward, to an area of the bar where the light was weakest and shadows had been allowed to gather.

The dominant of the two jukeboxes was spinning "My Generation" by the Who, the lower-volumed one trying to keep up with something gloomy from a forgotten Seattle grunge trio.

"How 'bout this," Purcell said in a bassy rumble that could somehow be heard over the music. "How 'bout we give you boys a five-minute head start?"

"Here's another idea," said Judd before Todd or D.B. could stop him. "How 'bout y'all grease up real good and go fuck yourselves?"

It couldn't truthfully be said that the room fell silent. Not with the two jukeboxes vying for attention, but it seemed that way. Purcell's eyelids shut, then popped open again a slow second later, like a cat blinking. Zeebe's mouth puckered into a shape that could erupt with laughter or rage. Blond Jason leaned back in his stool to plant both elbows on the bar while the wiry one remained in movement, limbs and lips twitching soundlessly. Behind Todd and the other two, the panting grew harsher, so that the room reeked of meaty, male breath—apparently even from the lone female.

Purcell's eyelids clenched and unclenched again, and now Todd could see that this was the way the man blinked. In slow, tight movements of contained fury that pulled at his cheek muscles. Purcell said nothing, but his eyes glimmered with white-hot fire.

Off to one side, the long-haired bartender on the late shift wore a white-toothed grin, his eyes reflecting as much light as the jewel in his ear.

Todd took hold of D.B. and Judd and steered them carefully around the panting girl and underage boy. Without turning their backs on the four at the bar, they pressed against the closed door and spilled out of the Winking Dog Saloon.

"What's that?" Todd cried in reaction to the sharp, scratching sounds he heard as soon as they stepped outside.

"Rats," Judd said. He sounded beyond fear.

Red, glowing eyes followed them into the parking lot, tiny rodent claws working to gain traction on the loose white pebbles. As a set of teeth grabbed hold of Todd's work boot, he flicked the thing into the night.

"Where's your keys?" he demanded, and watched in horror as D.B. rummaged through his jeans pockets with a bad look on his face.

He couldn't go back in in there, Todd knew. *Please, God, let him not have left them at the bar.*

"Got 'em," D.B. finally gasped, holding the shiny metal ring into the light of the three-quarters moon peeking through cloud cover.

They walked fast—very fast—to the Ford pickup parked close to the door. Five minutes, Purcell had told them, but that was before Judd's ill-chosen comment.

"You think they'll really come after us?" D.B. wanted to know as he struggled with the key in the lock.

"Let 'em come," Judd said while looking over his shoulders. Said it not loud enough to be overheard by anyone but the other two.

The driver's door squealed open and they all piled in, Larry, Curly and Moe style. They punched the lock buttons as D.B. stabbed the ignition with his key.

Todd caught flickering movement from the corner of an eye. Men entering the bar, not exiting. A wash of relief swept over him until he spied the men's eyes: bright dots of white light winking in the night.

The engine didn't even try to turn over.

"No battery," D.B. said pointlessly.

"Zeebe took it. Took it so we'd know it was him." Todd couldn't believe how calm he felt, sitting there hopelessly between the passenger door and an uncommonly quiet Judd Maxwell, and smelling the sharp odor of desperate men.

Something scratched against a door panel.

"Okay," Todd said, voice flat. "We walk."

But the truck cab was hard to leave. It seemed so safe, so high off the ground, enclosed and tightly sealed against the night's multiple threats.

113

"What are they?" D.B. asked. Maybe a stall tactic.

Todd didn't answer. Had it been five minutes yet? He unlocked the passenger door and heaved himself from the pickup. Something fat and awkward and slung low to the ground waddled out of his way. With their safehouse breached, the other two quickly poured out and joined Todd in the night.

They kept the truck between them and the saloon door, and began to walk. Todd, stiff with panic, wobbled in the loose parking lot gravel, barely keeping his footing. They stayed in motion, the short-legged and slightly more drunk Judd grunting to keep up.

The parking lot ended in a cracked cement sidewalk.

"Where to now?" D.B. wanted to know.

They all took turns with backward glances toward the bar door.

It seemed, to Todd's annoyance, that all questions had been directed at him for the last several minutes. As if he knew any better than them what to do about whatever was back there. "How the hell do I know? Anyone got a cell phone?"

He already knew the answer. Cell phones cost money and even those Sundowners who'd been there long enough to put a little cash together had found spotty tower coverage at best.

"What street is this?" he said.

"Middle View Road."

Todd closed his eyes and tried converting the town into a map. He'd had little opportunity or desire to explore the place, but he recognized Middle View as a major street running parallel to Main View. "What's around here? Is there a police station?"

"Yeah," Judd said doubtfully.

"Part of the big municipal building, maybe three blocks down and a block over," said D.B., sounding no more anxious than Judd to involve the law.

They could have debated the matter further, but dueling jukeboxes suddenly rocked the night as saloon doors were flung open.

"They're coming."

"That way," said D.B., pointing to the right.

Chapter Twenty

The sidewalk's main objective was to trip them up. The squat, unlit buildings on either side of the road sat far enough back to be only shadow witnesses to whatever was about to happen. The three quickly passed a shuttered community playhouse and a junior high school still abandoned for the dying summer.

A block later, Todd heard a car drifting toward them on whispering tires. "Other side," he ordered, and the three dashed across the street.

On this side were a succession of buildings positioned closer to the street. The farther they ran, the safer Todd felt. They moved single-file and orderly, wending their way through lit parking lots and small strip shopping centers. They dodged traffic cruising the side streets, weaved through clusters of the slow-moving elderly, broke through a line waiting at an ice cream stand and skipped past strolling lovers walking snarly little dogs.

Despite a town full of witnesses, Todd could still hear the distinctive purring engine just behind them. At least if he could hear them, he knew where they were.

Though breathing hard and sweating beer, it felt good to take action, to pit his strong legs and only slightly abused lungs against tires and pistons.

Metal doors banged shut in the distance, and D.B. said, "Jesus, they left the car," and Todd didn't feel a fraction as safe as he had moments before.

"How far to the police station?" he gasped.

"Next block this way, I think."

"Wait up," Judd said, and they slowed to give his stubby legs a chance.

They'd be alright. They had to be. The streets and sidewalks were packed with people. Even on the side street they cut down to link up with Main View. Houses and buildings blazed with light, shadowy figures moving in the windows. There were townspeople out eating, drinking, shopping, chatting. He wasn't used to seeing this much nighttime activity even in much larger cities.

"Up ahead," D.B. said.

White lighting bathed the massive municipal building. The three flew across yet another side street, their feet slapping like small caliber gunshots against the asphalt pavement that made a black ocean around a long post office building. No lights here, none in the lot, only the three-quarters moon showing the way.

They ducked around parked postal vehicles and cut to the rear of the sandstone building. Todd slowed his pace to a jog, picking his way as carefully as possible in the dim light.

Something slammed into the sandstone wall and Judd uttered a low oath. "Wait up, you guys. I can't see shit."

When they ran out of buildings to hide behind, they turned on the speed, dashed across another intersection and streaked to the next lawn. They were on the grounds of the incredibly well lit Drake Municipal Complex—according to the sign out front. Its circular drive shone white in the night and was full of cars and a long bus whose side panel bore the words, "Babylon Blood Services." Todd saw people walking stiff with age up the sidewalk, and ran to join them. Safety in numbers.

"Wait up," Judd shouted, and Todd was surprised to hear it coming from the vicinity of the post office.

Todd and D.B. paused on the moist, rich lawn in front of the impressive structure. They clenched their knees and gasped for breath while they waited for him to catch up.

Invisible footlights splashed a warm glow at the face of the building so that every brick gleamed. Pedestrians cast huge shadows against the face of the building as they exited into the night, each carrying and sipping from large plastic containers.

Turning toward their slow companion lost somewhere behind them, D.B. shouted, "C'mon, Judd. They're right behind you."

Todd giggled. What he was going to do, he decided, was get between the building and one white spotlight and wave his arms like the frigging Queen to catch the attention of the police and everyone else out in the night. No, even better: he'd dance a shuffle step while slowly extending his middle fin—

"Jesus, noooo..."

Todd wheeled, his feet gouging divots in the wet grass. He and D.B. locked eyes.

It didn't even sound human, but it was Judd, his high-pitched scream tearing a hole in the night. The shrill cry of pain mingled with the low growl of predatory beasts. The scream rose higher, and ended abruptly, in a sharp sob.

And then just the growls.

When Todd finally jerked his eyes from D.B.'s, it was because he was distracted by movement against the face of the Drake Municipal Complex. They looked like giants, the huge, spotlit shadow images of men and women, most of them elderly, pouring oversize plastic containers into their two-story faces. Against his will, Todd followed the shadow movement to its source, a dozen people with cups upturned, thick red liquid dripping down withered chins.

Something slithered underfoot to break the spell. Todd danced out of the way of thick-bottomed rats racing in two directions. Some made their way to the feet of the elderly drinkers, necks craned to catch stray red droplets. The others headed toward the screams that now only echoed in Todd's mind.

Two uniformed police officers raced from the Drake building and shouldered their way past the old people with their plastic cups.

"Over there," Todd croaked, motioning toward the post office building across the intersection.

The older and heavier of the two cops lurched into the lead, his holstered gun jammed tight against his side. "Keep the crowds back," he grunted to his partner.

Todd and D.B. followed from a safe distance. Up ahead of them, a police radio squawked.

Good, Todd thought. *Bring in the cavalry.*

Todd and D.B. pressed up tight against the front of the post office. The screams, and the low growls that had followed up until a few seconds ago, had come from the back. They slid across the face of the building and turned a cautious corner.

From the street they heard voices filled with confusion and concern as crowds gathered and exchanged information. None of the townspeople had ventured as far as the two of them.

He couldn't do this, Todd thought, locked against the wall in muscle-paralyzing fear. Then, remembering the presence of the police officers, and not hearing gunfire, shouting or any more screams, he motioned D.B. to follow him and proceeded toward the rear of the building.

What he saw back there, at first, was shadows in movement. When his eyes grew accustomed, the shadows turned into four blood-spattered men and the girl and underage boy, all ripping the flesh from Judd Maxwell's spasmodically twitching body.

They looked up at the sharp sounds of the cops' approaching footsteps and wiped Judd's red blood from their eyes for a clearer view.

"Oh, Jesus," D.B. wailed, which pulled the attention of everyone in the tableau from the dying man to the two surviving Sundowners.

Todd had already started to glow from the comforting warmth of shock when the overweight cop slammed him against the sandstone building and put the cold steel gun barrel to the back of his head.

Chapter Twenty-One

In the next instant plenty happened, but Todd couldn't later be sure of any of it. He foggily recalled the older cop kneeing him in the spine so that his shocked body flexed and an electric current of pain shot through him. He remembered being dragged to the side of the building, thankfully out of sight of the carnage, his arms being twisted almost out of their sockets so that murderously cold cuffs could be clamped tightly around his wrists.

Then there was the older cop saying, out of breath, "Goddammit, Purcell, what the fuck's the matter with you? Stay away, get back."

And another glacier-cold voice, one he knew well from the Dog, saying, "Watch very carefully how you speak to me, Sandy."

He heard the cop on top of Todd, the younger one, saying, "Easy, Duane, easy. We're all cool. It's just that...so many witnesses. You shoulda..."

And while he had his cheeks rubbed raw against the sandstone Todd could hear a similar struggle going on right next to him, the older cop having slammed D.B. against the wall, too, and slapping on handcuffs.

"Not them," someone shouted, to which the heavy cop, the one addressed earlier as "Sandy" said, "Goddammit, Ernie, I told you to keep these people away."

"You got the wrong men, Chief," the new voice insisted, and Todd got a peek at him because the cop holding him firm against the building turned to see who'd spoken.

In the act of turning, he twisted his cuffed prisoner with him and Todd caught a glimpse of a man standing tall and tan in khaki shorts and a country club knit shirt.

"These two here," the stranger was saying in his strong, clear voice, "had nothing to do with it. They were standing on the front lawn of the municipal building when the screaming started."

Todd heard most of this with his eyes closed because he didn't want to see any more. His mind retained the image of Judd Maxwell lying torn and bloody, parts of him dripping from the jaws of Zeebe and his five insane friends. Blood and steaming entrails and glistening teeth.

Then the flashing lights strobed the night as a squad car came right up the sidewalk that paralleled this side of the sandstone building and halted with tires squealing in front of him and D.B. He heard the insistent squawk of an ignored radio, and the crowd murmur growing, the older cop saying, "Ernie, keep these fucking people back." Then Ernie slamming Todd's face against the rough sandstone like it was his fault he'd gotten yelled at again.

"What's back there?" the strong, clear voice said and the older cop said, "Ernie, dammit, these people," and Todd thinking, *here it comes again*, but this time the young cop didn't hurt him.

Then he lost a slip of time and the next thing he felt was pressure on his head as he was stuffed into the back of the squawking squad car. D.B. was already seated beside him, blinking blood from his eyes.

Todd blinked, too, and that was like setting off a fresh wrinkle of time, because now he was being yanked and prodded down steep, narrow stairs and into the dark, at which point he recalled the strong, clear voice saying, "I'm not going to allow this, Sandy." Saying it sometime in the distant or not so distant past, and now, thinking back on it, Todd was wondering who Sandy was. He hadn't seen a woman on the scene, just a lot of fresh blood and ruined flesh.

Then came the memory of the strong-voiced man in country club shirt saying, "Nothing had better happen to those two in your custody, Sandy. I'm watching."

Only he wasn't watching as Todd got pulled down a steep, dank flight of stairs, the darkness outlined by naked bulbs on chains high up overhead.

"D.B.," Todd shouted. "D.B., where are you?"

"Shut the fuck up."

A voice he hadn't heard before. And then he got pushed into a cell and a metal door clanged shut behind him and Todd caught the faint whiff of sewers that must have backed up years ago. He heard harsh, ragged breathing and for a moment thought time had flipped on him again and he was back at the Winking Dog. But they'd left the Dog and Judd was dead and D.B. bleeding like Todd, sitting right there on the thin mattress of the bottom bunk in their black cell.

And D.B. wasn't the cause of the ragged breathing. Those sounds, Todd finally realized as he grew accustomed to faint lighting, were coming from the pair of white-lit eyes somewhere in the black shadows where the nearest hanging bulb couldn't reach.

The eyes were part of a police officer's uniform. They remained riveted by the blood dripping from Todd's scraped face onto the cement floor.

"I'm right here, man," D.B. whispered from the bunk, answering a question that had been posed an eternity ago.

We can do it, Todd thought as he shuffled closer to his friend bleeding with him in the dark. We *can* survive till dawn.

Chapter Twenty-Two

Daylight came as it always does, no matter how bad the night. With the sun up less than an hour before, Paul Highsmith was back at the police station, having it out with the uncommunicative cop who'd just told him he couldn't see the new prisoners until Chief Sandy arrived. The catch was, the chief wasn't expected in till noon or so, having had a particularly hard night.

"I'll bet he did," said Paul. "I had a hard one, too."

And he had, his sleep robbed by nightmares of the piercing screams and inhuman growling he'd heard, and by the sight of two innocent men slammed against a wall, bloodied and cuffed and stuffed into a waiting squad car. The evening, which had begun with a pleasant after-dinner stroll, had ended in something foul and unfathomable.

Paul clicked his tongue impatiently when the young cop continued to stare serenely at him. "If you would just pick up your phone and call your chief at his home—"

"I'm afraid I can't do that, sir."

"How'd I know you were going to say that?"

Okay, rein in the sarcasm, he advised himself as the cop's expression went hard.

"Good morning, Mr. Highsmith. How are you doing today?"

This new lobby arrival also wore a police uniform, along with a smile and an annoyingly chipper manner.

"Morning," Paul answered, keeping his expression carefully neutral. "If your co-worker or your underling—whatever he is—can't call the police chief at his home, will you do so?"

"I bet you don't remember me," the cop practically sang out. "We met the other day under slightly unfortunate circumstances. The name's Marty—"

"McConlon," Paul finished. "Will you call Bill Sandy, please?"

"Cuppa coffee?"

Paul stared at a coffeemaker that had probably run continuously since Joe Dimaggio's final TV commercial, but surprised himself by nodding.

It was practically a replay of his previous visit to the station, him sitting in front of a table of old magazines and staring at an oversize portrait of Miles Drake, circa 1940, waiting to chat with the police.

But, as he now reflected, his career had taught him not to fear being a pain in the ass.

"We had us some disturbance last night, huh?" the pudgy cop said as he handed over a paper mug with a sprinkling of powdered cream that hadn't noticeably improved the oil-sludge coloration of its contents.

"I'd like to talk with your chief and then see the two men you dragged in here last night," Paul said, equally conversationally.

"Ah, the two men." McConlon took a seat opposite Paul and balanced a cup in his lap. "That shouldn't be much of a problem." He tapped the cup. "Not with the shorter one anyway. I think his name's Dunbar. He'll just have to pay some nominal fine, twenty-five, fifty bucks, whatever it is. If there's a catch to that, it's just that Judge Mattis won't be able to see him till Monday, so I'm afraid he might have himself something of a gloomy weekend. No big deal."

Paul had so many questions, he barely knew where to start. So he sat and stared at the unruffled cop.

While the previous night had featured bloodcurdling screams and spine-chilling growls, cops and handcuffs and bloodied and bruised strangers, the crowd had reacted with nervous silence. No questions, no one besides him even trying to trespass on the scene. And this morning he'd listened to the newscast of the one local radio station, and heard not a word of the disturbance make it to the air.

Paul cleared his throat. "What's the fine for?" The least complex question he could wrap his mind around at the moment.

Marty slurped noisily at the sludgy brew. "I leave the judging to the judges, but I'm thinking he's looking at disturbing the peace. Public drunkenness, maybe. Who knows? Nothing real serious." He chuckled. "We might be a little town in the boondocks, but we outlawed public lynching a year or two ago."

"Why was the town taking blood donations late into the night?"

Paul had meant to shake the pudgy cop by pitching him a question from left field—one that would hit at a tender spot—and he wasn't disappointed. A look flashed across the cop's face as he tried to hide his obvious irritation with another long sip.

"That's off the subject, isn't it?" the cop asked, a thin and unfelt smile back in place.

"For some reason, I didn't think I'd get an answer. Is Bill Sandy on his way?"

"He'll be here."

"Yesterday afternoon, I saw mostly young people giving blood, but last night it was mostly old folks entering the building. I'm not sure what they were drinking when they came out."

"You've got a lot of questions, don't you?"

"It was a statement rather than a question. But if you prefer, I'll ask you one. Do your prisoners' families know you're holding them?"

121

Marty let out a bark of a laugh. "Prisoners. Like we're running some sort of penal colony here. Chain gangs, slave labor. What we got is a couple guys who drank too much, got out of hand and are being held till we can sort things out."

"I'll rephrase my question. Have those two wild and crazy guys been given an opportunity to notify their families or seek legal counsel?"

"I wouldn't know," McConlon answered dryly. "I went to bed after the situation died down."

"And what situation was that? What exactly happened last night?" The heart of the question. Paul awaited a response he wasn't sure he wanted to hear. In that way, he seemed like much of the rest of the town.

The cop tapped his cup against his teeth. "What happened," he said, "was that those two hard-partying boys began to see and very noisily respond to creepy-crawlies as they stumbled home."

"I heard the same creepies," said Paul, "and I hadn't had a drop."

Marty shrugged. "Maybe their drinking buddies were screwing around with them."

It wasn't something he'd considered. It would explain why the police, who had to have investigated, hadn't found anything suspicious behind the post office, where he'd been stopped from looking.

Paul sat and sipped his cooling sludge. "You told me that one of the two would soon be free. What about the other one?"

"Let me answer that one," a voice boomed from the doorway, and Bill Sandy walked into the lobby.

He hadn't shaved and his hair hung flat against his skull. The dark circles under his eyes attested to the fact that he, too, had been pulled from his sleep the previous night. He grabbed a paper cup and poured from the coffee pot. "Damn, I need this. Last night, just a little too much excitement for me."

He took the third and final chair and balanced his cup on a knee. Together, they looked like three sleepy men waiting for a dentist.

"Donald Brandon has an outstanding warrant in Pittsburgh. Grand larceny," the chief said after a moment. "Seems he stole a load of copper from a construction site. Wrapped it around his waist, under his shirt, and took out a little at a time. Kinda like that Johnny Cash song, I'm thinking. The one about the auto worker who steals a car one part at a time over a period of years."

Paul set down his cup on a tattered magazine. As badly as he'd needed a caffeine jolt, he'd barely touched it. "I asked Officer McConlon here whether the suspects had been able to contact their families or lawyers, but I'm not sure I got a response."

"I wouldn't call them suspects," Sandy said.

Paul waited for more.

"We haven't hidden them from anyone," the chief grumbled into the heavy silence. "When Mrs. Dunbar called, looking for her wayward husband, she was told that we were holding him and that she could come visit today. She could be here anytime, in fact, though we got the impression she might wait until her mood brightened. Apparently he made her late for a job interview."

Job interview. The ancient town fathers wanted Darby and him out, but these people couldn't fill out job applications fast enough to meet demand. "What about the other one?" Paul asked.

"The other one, Brandon, all he's got is an ex-wife. My guess is she'd be as thrilled to hear from him as he would be to get in touch with her."

"I want to see them," Paul said.

The chief stared at him for several beats. "Why? You're not a lawyer."

"No, but I have one." Let them take it as a threat if they wanted.

Paul watched the two cops exchange quick glances. He almost wanted to be turned down. He had no idea what he'd say to the jailed men if given a chance.

"All right," Chief Sandy said, nodding slowly. His gray head just kept nodding. "All right," he said again. "Follow me."

Chapter Twenty-Three

The door slammed behind them, trapping Paul, with the police chief, at the top of a flight of stairs that disappeared into the shadows. The light was dim, rough walls pressing in on either side. The smell of mildew hung heavy in the air. He could hear Chief Sandy a step or two above him, the key chain he'd strapped to his belt jingling his presence like a cat with a bell.

"You'll see them," the chief called out, his voice ringing off solid walls. "Down the stairs, cell to the left, halfway down the corridor."

Under the occasional hanging bulb, Paul could see a hallway lined with iron-grilled cages. Empty, until he made his way slowly to the fourth holding cell on the left. He went queasy at the sight of the two blood-caked men behind bars. He couldn't remember the last time he'd seen a bleeding adult, and he'd never viewed anyone in a jail cell before except on screen.

"G'morning, boys. You got a visitor," Sandy announced. The undertone of merriment made it seem as though Paul would be a welcome surprise, a special treat for the well-mannered prisoners.

They showed no reaction. They stood awkwardly, facing the corridor like strangers waiting for a bus, their eyes dark, bodies as rumpled as their clothing.

The police chief fiddled noisily with the latch, then swung the door wide. It actually screeched on its hinges like dungeon cell doors in some late-night Vincent Price flick. He stood back and waited, his eyes twinkling.

"Have they seen doctors?" Paul asked.

"Bumps and bruises," the cop said, as if that were an answer.

Paul let himself be locked in with the two. They waited, the three of them listening to the sounds of the chief's retreating footsteps. Only when the upstairs door slammed shut did Paul begin to study the men in greater detail.

Their faces really weren't as bad at he'd first suspected. The blood was dry and scabby. It looked like a little soap and water could wash away most of the evidence of last night's...whatever.

He had no idea what to say.

Once, when he was a kid, Paul had won a job umpiring Little League. He'd spent weeks studying the rulebook so he'd know what to do, and in his very first game, first at-bat, the chattering from the team in the field had ended as soon as the first pitch crossed the plate. It slowly dawned on young Paul that both teams and all of the parents in the rickety stands were awaiting his ball or strike decision—and he couldn't open his mouth.

Like now.

"Can we sit down?" he said, then saw the lunacy of the request. The tiny cell contained one double-stacked bed, a wall-mounted sink and a lidless toilet. "Okay," he said, but nothing else came out.

"You a lawyer or a vampire?" It was the shorter of the two, asking the odd question in an Appalachian twang.

Paul's shoulder blades pressed the cell bars. He regretted not having first discussed with the town police chief when *he'd* be released. Now he wished he hadn't been such a pain in the ass up there.

"I'm definitely not a vampire." He said it straight. They might see sarcasm in his response if they were playing with him, or take him seriously if they were seriously insane.

"Then you're a lawyer."

Despite his lack of size, this one had a dark-eyed aggressiveness about him that made Paul keep his distance. His cellmate was as tall as Paul, but wider in the shoulders. His complexion was light, his eyes looked painfully rimmed in pink and he had an absence of eyelashes. The hair on his head had the fine texture of a baby's and his gentle face held a hint of a smile despite the circumstances.

"Well?" the short one prodded. "Who the hell are you?"

Paul said, "I'm a witness to what went on last night."

The short one's eyes took on a distant stare as he seemed to consider that. "Yeah," he finally said, as if Paul had answered correctly. "I remember now."

"Sir, do you know where Judd is? What happened to him?" the taller one wanted to know.

"Judd. That's your friend, right? The one who screamed. I'm afraid I don't know."

This drew a snort and a sharp head shake from the short one. "Then what good are you?"

"I was on the sidewalk in front of the municipal building when the screaming and growling started. The two of you were just thirty, forty feet from me, so I know you didn't do anything if that's any help."

"The perfect witness: you saw nothing. So why're you here?" asked the shorter one.

Paul formed his lips around various explanations, none of which seemed adequate. "I was curious," he finally said.

If possible, the shorter man's expression soured even more. "Curious."

Paul tried again. "I've seen you two and the others at the motel on the edge of town. My family and I are outsiders just like you. There's something going on here that involves you...and us. I'd like to compare

125

notes."

"Yes, we shall compare notes," the shorter one said in archly formal voice.

Paul didn't really blame him. It all sounded so academic, so civilized when played against the screams he'd heard in the dark and the blood still caked on the faces of these two. "And I want to help you find out what happened to your friend," he added, drawing the first flicker of interest from the two.

"How can you do that?" the taller one asked.

"It's bullshit," said his friend.

He turned his back on Paul and his cellmate. For a ludicrous moment, Paul thought he was walking out on the conversation, but then he remembered where they were. He heard a zipper unzip and a steady stream splash into the open toilet bowl.

While taking care of business, the short one called over his shoulder, "Yeah, I know who you are. I saw you last night, all decked out in your country club duds. Your khaki shorts. You drive the Lexus, right? I can just recall bits and pieces of what happened, but I remember you sounding so goddamn sure all you had to do was clear your throat and those pissant cops would all snap to attention."

He zipped up and turned, smiling for the first time. "But here we are, Country Club Dude. We spent the night in jail, but I see you had a chance to go home, sleep in your own bed and change into a nice pair of Dockers so you can save us poor boys in style. Maybe write an editorial or take up a petition."

Paul took two quick steps, all the distance it took to be in the shorter man's face. "Yes, here I am. I talked my way into your cell not much past daybreak, which is more than your family and friends have been able to accomplish so far. But if the way I dress and talk repulses you so much, just tell me to get out of here and I'm gone. On the other hand, if you think I just might be able to help you, then ignore whatever you find offensive about me and prepare to cut me some goddamn slack."

The short one tried staring him down, but that would be a contest Paul wouldn't lose.

"Hey, no, man, it's cool," said the taller of the two. "He didn't mean nothing. Right, Todd? Todd?"

If the little creep's name was Todd, then the other was Donald Brandon, the copper thief. The Todd creature dropped his gaze and mumbled something that might have passed for an apology, but Paul wouldn't have bet on it.

Letting it go, he said, "Fine. I'm Paul Highsmith, and the two of you are Todd Dunbar and Donald Brandon." He pointed a finger at each in turn.

"D.B.," said the taller one, nodding amiably. "What people call me."

"D.B.," Paul repeated. He stepped down from his confrontational pose in front of Dunbar and took his place back by the bars. "Right. Now can we talk about what happened?"

"There were vampires watching us all night," Dunbar said.

The vampires again. Paul wondered if Dunbar still had a buzz going from the night before.

"It's true," said D.B. "It wasn't as bad once the blood on our faces dried up, but at first I thought we were goners. Like Judd."

Great. A shared delusion.

Paul sighed. "Okay, let's talk about that." He wanted to hear about police brutality, withheld phone calls and trumped-up charges, something Freddie Brace could sink his teeth into. He most definitely didn't want to discuss vampires.

"I can understand your skepticism," D.B. said chattily. "Hell, I'd be the same way if I didn't see the way the one cop's shiny eyes went all hungry at the sight of our blood. Like a dog drooling at a juicy steak. He stayed down here with us all night, just staring at us. Sometimes he'd be joined by one or more of the others and we'd hear them whispering in the dark but we couldn't see much 'cept the gleam in their eyes. I'd say at least half the local force is vampires."

Paul needed to sit. He even considered bracing himself on the lidless toilet until he saw the fresh urine splotches on the porcelain rim. He maintained his position. "Chief Sandy tells me they found a warrant for your arrest," he told D.B.

"Found it four months ago when Marty pulled me over for a missing taillight," D.B. said.

"They didn't take you in then?"

The tall prisoner smiled a touch sadly. "I got the distinct impression the charges would go away if I took their cushy warehouse job and kept my nose clean."

Paul nodded. "They're not in such a forgiving mood anymore, but I'll get you a lawyer and work on getting you out. But it might not be until Monday."

"Why?" Dunbar's face hardened once more. "Why you doing this for us?"

Paul stared until the shorter man's face softened a fraction. "Your wife knows where you are," he said quietly. "She'll be here soon and I'll make sure they let her visit. What's her name?"

It looked for a long time like Dunbar wouldn't answer. Then his black eyes dropped and he said, "Joy. Her name's Joy. If you see her, tell her I'm sorry. Will ya? She'll know what I mean."

Paul nodded. He was on the verge of saying more, but the door at the top of the stairs opened and heavy footsteps clumped carefully down.

"Well, I see you're okay," Bill Sandy told Paul when he came into view. "No one made you bend over for a bar of soap, did they?"

He didn't know how much he appreciated freedom until he got back upstairs and noticed how spacious and airy and light and dry the lobby was. He found Chief Sandy at his desk, fiddling with a pack of cigarettes. He'd tap one out, twirl it around his thick fingers and jam it back in the pack while Paul stared at the framed portrait of the town's leading citizen.

Lawyer or vampire? he'd been asked by the cellmates downstairs.

"Miles Drake," Paul said, not meaning anything specific.

The chief studied him. "I can't figure out why you're here," he said, ignoring the name mention. "You some kind of community activist sent by the big city lawyers to check up on us local yokels and make sure our prisoners don't end up hanging by their shoelaces?"

Paul leaned back in his chair. "I'm a...retired...investment banker."

"You mean like those guys headed to jail in New York?" the chief asked, with no idea how close he'd come.

Paul met his gaze and said nothing.

Chief Sandy decided on that cigarette after all, despite the building's probable no-smoking status. He flicked some fire at it and turned a half-inch of the tip to ash in one hearty inhalation. "I've done some talking with our prosecutor," he said. "It's looking like we'll be able to get the Dunbar character sprung earlier than I'd thought. I guess everyone figures he didn't do anything worth a weekend in jail."

"What about the other one?"

The chief shook his head. "Told you, he's got a warrant out. Grand theft."

"I understand," Paul said, rising. "Just give me the name of the prosecuting attorney and I'll pass it along."

The chief stared blankly at him. "Pass it along?"

"To my attorney, of course. He doesn't handle as much criminal defense work as he used to, but he should be able to get up to speed fairly quickly."

Bill Sandy hadn't risen with Paul. He remained slouched low in his air-cushioned seat, staring up at his visitor with an unreadable expression. Then he chuckled, but the humor didn't make it to his eyes.

"How about this?" he said. "When Dunbar's wife gets here, we'll release both of them to her custody. As long as they stay clean and sober, we'll forget everything. How does that sound?"

Bill Sandy was coming across like some Old West lawman. He'd caught the bad guys, pressed charges, locked 'em away and issued the reprieve. Paul wasn't up on the intricacies of the American judicial system, but he was pretty sure things were done differently these days.

"What about Pittsburgh?" he asked.

The chief shrugged expansively. "What about it? You think someone wants to extradite Brandon for a few rolls of copper? Think they wanna send a couple cops to Michigan to drive or fly him back for that?"

Paul awkwardly took and shook the hand extended to him and mumbled his thanks. On the way out, he held the door for a jittery-looking blond woman who looked like she could lose a few pounds. Mrs. Dunbar, he told himself as she rushed into the lobby.

There was a whole mess of unanswered questions staring him down, but he couldn't help feeling good as he found the early morning sunlight.

"Why are you doing this for us?" Todd Dunbar had asked him, and now he knew.

Because I still can. Maybe not the answer he'd give if the question got put to him again, but that was the heart of it.

There were questions to answer, obstacles to evade, goals waiting to be met. It felt like there was still a place for him out here.

He was back in the saddle again.

Chapter Twenty-Four

Early that Saturday evening, the sun was too bright and the sky too blue for conversation to have turned to vampires, but that was what Paul overheard as he left the Lexus gloating over the parking lot heaps and joined the mass of sweaty humanity on the cracked pavement surrounding the Sundown Motel pool.

A bare-chested man in his twenties with a near skinhead haircut and a fire-breathing something-or-other decorating one muscular bicep was saying, "Vampires, my ass. If you two are trying to tell me—"

That was as far as he got before catching sight of Paul as he came toward them. The kid's small eyes narrowed, both of his hands inexplicably occupied with lit cigarettes. "Hey," he said. "Who're you?"

While the others craned or twisted or scraped their lawn chairs for position, the better to see the stranger in their midst, the kid with the crew cut and tats stuffed one butt in his face and handed off the other to a scrawny woman sitting in a ragged chaise lounge next to him. She looked to be in her mid-thirties, limp chestnut hair and nipples that announced themselves against her thin shirt fabric. She wasn't unattractive, but seemed to exist on cigarettes and the Pepsi next to her.

"I'm Paul Highsmith."

As far as announcements went, it felt a little underwhelming. One man smiled and nodded slightly. D.B., from that morning. Everyone else just stared at him, some with curiosity. Others with challenge.

"I wonder if I can join you all."

Paul stood outside an irregular circle of hard, used-up men and a few weary women. A handful of kids chased each other dangerously close to the empty swimming pool.

He suddenly saw himself as they would: tall and leisurely tan, his smooth hands innocent of physical labor. Crisp linen shorts and cotton shirt in light, neutral colors. Deck shoes that still smelled of new leather. Heavy gold watch nestled in sun-bleached arm hair.

Most of the unshaven men had too much or not enough hair. They had man boobs and bellies that overran their belts. The women had faces drawn taut by bills, bad men and cigarettes.

Paul cleared his mind of distracting thoughts and said, "I already know what you're talking about, so you don't have to stop on my account. I've spoken with D.B and Todd and I'd like to be a part of seeing what needs to be done."

The kid in the crew cut flapped an arm to get the scrawny older woman to move her feet so he could perch his butt on the end of her chair. From here, he glared up at Paul as though he hadn't liked what he'd heard so far.

"Hey, it's our rescuer." This came from dark-haired, dark-eyed Todd Dunbar. He was seated next to and sharing a cigarette and a beer with the plump blond woman Paul had last seen entering the police station as he left it. Dunbar's voice was bent with insolent irony, but by now Paul was considering the possibility that it always sounded that way.

"That's right. This is the guy got us sprung," D.B. said amicably. As if unable to detect his buddy's sarcasm. "Thanks, man, but I hope you didn't come here for a reward. I kinda blew my budget at the bar last night."

One or two Sundowners chuckled while the others waited to see how the scene would play out.

A chair wasn't offered, so Paul flipped off his shoes and sat at the edge of the pool. He'd been wrong about it being empty. There were several feet of black rainwater smelling of mold and decay. He scooted back and said, "It would be in all our best interests to figure out what's going on here. Maybe we can figure it out together."

"What makes you think your best interest is ours?"

This came like the crack of a rifle from a middle-aged black man with a heavily creased forehead. Paul could imagine his pulse throbbing like a heartbeat in that furrow.

"I came to Babylon with my family," he said, trying to address everyone at once. "Bought a house and moved in a month or so ago. We've been approached a number of times since then about selling and leaving. I want to know why, and I want to know if our experience is in any way connected to what happened to you folks last night."

To his own ear, he sounded like someone too intent on making a speech and swaying a crowd. The sort of thing that might go over at a board meeting, but not at the Sundown Motel. "However wild your stories," he said, "I want to hear them."

A cooler lid slammed. Lawn chairs scraped over the weedy pavement.

"How's this for wild?" Todd Dunbar said. "Judd Maxwell got killed by fucking vampires last night and me and D.B. got snatched by the cops so we couldn't report what we seen."

His burning gaze dared Paul—dared anyone—to argue or laugh.

No one did, exactly, but the kid with the buzz haircut said, "Christ." Putting equal parts disbelief and sarcasm into it.

Dunbar shot him a glare. "You got a problem with this...Dukey?"

Dunbar's wife touched his forearm while the kid with the crew cut uttered a face-saving chuckle, but nothing more.

D.B., from his seat on a beer cooler lid, said, "I don't blame anyone for their doubts, but we saw what we saw. Poor Judd got taken down by six or seven wild men. A gal, too. It's just a fact, so now we gotta figure what to do about it."

"Holy Christ," someone muttered. "So it's true?"

Paul admired Don Brandon's quiet strength. Without raising his voice, he'd established the credibility of an incredible claim. He'd turned the conversation from the theoretical to the strategic without ruffling a single feather.

"Duke," a black woman said, "you don't like what you hear, then tell me where Judd's hanging out today."

The poolside chorus mumbled its stricken endorsement of the foul play scenario. If there was nothing to all of this, then where was Judd Maxwell? The kid named Duke didn't bother to reply. He sucked harshly at his cigarette, eyes hooded.

"That would explain the rats," growled a shirtless polar bear of a man. About fifty, he had a full head of white hair, a face grizzled and sunburned.

"What rats?" asked Paul.

"Rats," the man repeated impatiently. "They're all over the place."

"I forgot all about that," said Dunbar, his eyes widening. "With everything else going on that night, I forgot how the damn things came after me about the time the screaming started."

"And they went after the old folks, the ones with the blood or whatever the hell was in their plastic cups," added D.B.

"Well I sure as hell don't know what y'all are talking about, but it still makes sense," said the shirtless polar bear. "Rats hang out with vampires." He looked at the blank faces. "Don't you poor fools never read nothing?"

The middle-aged black man with the creased forehead barked once, an abrupt imitation of laughter that did nothing to erase the scowl. "I get it. Now we gotta study up on garlic and bats. Stakes through the heart under a full moon."

"Easy, Carl," said D.B. "Denver's just talking. But we're getting off track. We got less bickering and more figuring to do. That make sense to everyone?"

How could it not? The man's voice was an ice floe of cool reason.

Duke motioned D.B. to his feet so he could retrieve a beer from under him. "Let me play devil's advocate here," he said. It seemed the perfect role for the kid. He pulled the pull tab as he strolled center stage. "Let's say somebody or a bunch of somebodies really did tear Judd Maxwell apart last night." He made a show of flipping a cigarette ash, as though demonstrating how little weight he gave that view. "How do you know they're vampires?"

132

"Because they ripped his fucking throat out with their teeth, Dukey," Dunbar said, sounding alarmingly calm. On the verge of committing the same foul act on the dragon-tattooed kid, Paul thought.

Joy Dunbar found her husband's forearm in a move so practiced she probably didn't even know she was doing it.

"And I heard it," Paul said, surprising even himself. Not that he'd heard *vampires*, of course, but...something. Something worth talking about. "Not that I buy the official version, but what I heard was pure torment and terror. Not some drunks raising a ruckus. Besides, I stepped into the Winking Dog myself once, so I have a hard time discrediting any horror story that starts there."

Now he had their attention. Chairs shifted more quietly now. Several parents seemed to search for children who'd wandered out of sight.

Eyes downcast like she was studying the soft drink in her lap, the thin woman sharing a seat with Duke said, "I was at the Dog last night, too, and I never seen fangs or nothing." She dropped her spent cigarette into the can. "And I wouldn't mind continuing to not see nothing in that I got two kids and a job. Don't love the job—and, come to think of it, the kids aren't always at the top of my list, either." She looked up at Paul, her expression hard. "But life's been worse, mister. You might not understand that."

The rhythmic motion he caught out of the corner of an eye was heads nodding in unison.

"She's right," said the black woman who'd spoken before. Wide-hipped but attractive, she grabbed the hand of a well-built man next to her and said, "We got kids, too. Three of 'em, and they ain't seen their momma and dad for two months now. Every payday, money goes into a special envelope that'll get us all together someday. Till then, Jermaine and me ain't seen and ain't gonna see."

D.B. offered Paul a sad smile, then called out, "Jamey Weeks."

"What?" cried the wiry young guy with a fuzzy mustache standing next to Denver, the polar bear. His entire body twitched at the mention of his name, while his face carried the expression of someone who's just been called out in a police lineup.

D.B. said, "Jamey, can I see your resume a minute?"

The younger guy blinked. "My...?"

"Forget it, Jamey." D.B. gave Paul another sad smile. "Through no fault of his own, Jamey hasn't had a real job before getting hired to bag nuts and bolts for a hardware parts distributor in the parkway. No background check."

"Two years at Burger King," Jamey grumped, sensing he'd just been insulted, but not clear on the details.

"Lots of us worked fast food," said a short Hispanic man with a bandanna that sopped only some of the sweat from his eyes. "Or we stand in line all morning for sub-minimum wage, off-the-books day labor. We chase one boomtown rumor after another, always a day late. That's how things was till we pulled into Babylon. Anything suspicious about this town, sorry, we ain't seen a thing."

Having had his say, he tossed a cigarette and made a lap for one of the scraggly-haired kids who'd earlier been kicking a soccer ball in the patchy lawn.

D.B. leaned in closer to Paul and lowered his voice. "No document checks, either. Some bosses, they just pay in cash without even being asked."

"Jamey."

This time the voice making the wiry guy jump belonged to Dunbar.

"Yeah?"

"How you like your new job?"

Jamey played it like it was a trick question, taking his time before answering. "It's okay."

"You get lots of breaks and sitting-on-your-ass time when it's not too busy?" Dunbar asked.

Jamey thought again and nodded. "I guess. Sure."

Dunbar stared hard at the younger man, making him melt in the sun. "Don't they make machines these days for bagging hardware?"

"I don't know," Jamey mumbled.

"They got lots of people on the floor with you, right?"

"Regan Santana works with me," he answered brightly, pointing a beer can at the bandanna-wearing family man.

"What about local people? Lots of them?"

"What're you getting at, man?" Duke demanded.

"Answer me," Dunbar snapped, getting Jamey to shrug.

"Enough, I guess."

"Enough that you find yourself with nothing to do a lot of the time?"

Jamey looked like he was trying to see the trap, but eventually gave up and just nodded.

"And how much are you making an hour?" Dunbar pressed on.

Jamey dropped his head. "Fourteen."

"So what?" Denver barked. "Guy makes a halfway decent wage, first time in his life, and you wanna tell him he should run like hell?"

Todd set aside his latest beer can and rose, first wriggling free of his wife's forearm hold. He nodded sharply at the black couple and said, "Jermaine here knows where I'm going with this, but he ain't gonna say nothing. He's gonna sit there with a blank look on his face 'cuz he don't wanna end up in the middle of another convenience store gun battle in Detroit. But what I'm saying is, there's always a catch

134

when you get something for nothing, and we all know it."

He locked glances with several of the others, and was always the last to look away. "Sure, we're sitting here with cash in our pockets like it's Christmas, but we all know there ain't no Santa Claus. Sooner we admit that, sooner we can get down to the business of working out what to do about this."

Dunbar's speech ended as abruptly as it had begun. He plopped back down in his lawn chair and let his wife's arm flutter to his shoulders like a trainer working over her fighter.

Searching faces for reactions, Paul found mostly averted gazes. He'd kicked off his shoes and almost stirred one foot in the murky pool water to distract himself from what he was about to say, but stopped himself in time.

"My story's the opposite of yours," he told the crowd. He faced blank stares. "This town seems to be working overtime to get my family *out*. All while spending good money to keep you folks in. Frankly, it's got me confused."

He got a humorless chuckle from Dunbar. "Frankly, it's got me confused, too," he said.

His wife said something and he said something back and she handed him a cigarette from her purse. Something to calm his nerves. He lit up and dragged smoke into his lungs and stared at a sky now streaked with clouds. "Why in hell would this town choose us over someone classy like you?" he said.

"That's not what I'm saying."

Dunbar cut Paul off with a wave of his cigarette. His eyes sought something in the parking lot on the other side of the weedy lawn. Paul could tell when he'd found it. "Silver Lexus. Wonder what one of them goes for new. And I'm sure you bought yours new, right?"

Paul bit back a response.

The plump blond leaned over her husband to say something, but he shook her off. He was a man on constant simmer, his wife taking on the full-time job of keeping the heat turned low. Must be a great life for both of them.

"Bet we could live on your monthly car payment," Dunbar said with another unfelt chuckle. He took a drag from his cigarette, then flicked it, only half dead, into the pool, where it hissed sharply before the murky rainwater finished it off.

"It is a mystery," Dunbar said so quietly that the words seemed to be for his own benefit or that of his placating wife. Tracking Paul with his dark eyes, he said, "Man with your car and shorts and country club tan, man packing enough punch to waltz us two out of jail like that..." He snapped his fingers, let the rest fade, unfinished.

A fresh smile touched his lips. "You and your little wife, you sip

135

your dirty martinis with lawyers and judges and politicians. Belong to all the right clubs. Republicans, right?" Dunbar shook his head. "No, I can't imagine why this town likes us better than you."

Paul had never been accused of wealth and privilege before—had never even thought of it as something that should induce guilt—but now he saw quiet condemnation in every haggard, bloodshot eye. He looked to D.B. for support, but the most he got was a weak smile.

"Just a second," said the black family man, Jermaine.

He rose to cross the weedy lawn to the parking lot. Paul watched him rummage through the trunk of a copper Ford with plastic for a rear window. He pulled out a duffel bag.

"Oh no," said his wife.

The crowd watched him retrace his steps, their interest perked by her reaction. Jermaine reached into the canvas bag and pulled out a handgun. He aimed it at the sky and announced, "Smith & Wesson Model 15 Combat Masterpiece." He grinned. "Don't have no silver bullets, but I bet it could do some damage."

"Awesome," said the boy sitting on the lap of his father, Regan Santana.

"If you gotta have a .38 wheelgun," sniffed a lank, middle-aged man with a long ponytail and bad teeth.

The revolver, dull and dark and long, sent shivers down Paul's spine. Much like the jailhouse scene that morning, he realized that outside of a thousand movies and TV shows, he'd never seen a real gun in someone's hand before. The nonchalance with which nearly everyone else treated the sight made him see what a sheltered life he'd led.

"You really want to cause some trouble," Ponytail continued, "you get yourself what I got."

Denver sighed heavily. "Go ahead and tell us, Pete. Being as you're going to anyhow."

"Ruger Blackhawk .357 mag with a retrofitted nine millimeter cylinder for Parabellum cartridges," Ponytail snapped.

Sounding interested, D.B. said, "You got it on you?"

Pete's face changed and his gaze drifted to the pool. "Had to sell it to pay my goddamn lawyer."

"Well, the gun you used to have is certainly helpful to our situation here," Duke said.

Pete said, "So what? Best weapon 'round here's in Judd's room, and I don't think he'd have any problem with us using it on them fucks."

"What're you talking about?" asked the black man with the creased forehead.

"Talking 'bout that taped baseball bat he used to run around with."

"And you got the balls to criticize my .38," Jermaine snorted, still aiming his revolver at the sky.

"Bet I could be in Judd's room in under five seconds," Jamey, the former fast food worker, said with a wink that suggested job skills beyond burger-flipping.

"I got me an itty-bitty five-shot .38 Charco with nickel finish," D.B. said. "Kind of a girl's gun, but it conceals well in my pancake holster."

"Yeah? Well there's no concealing my Savage .30-.30 deer rifle," said Denver. "And yes, I got it with me."

"Alright!" Duke shouted. "You got a scope?"

"Yeah, but just enough shells for my eight-round clip."

"We'll put you on the balcony," said D.B. "You can be our official sniper."

"What about the rest of us?" someone wanted to know, and that sparked a lively debate over the comparative stopping power of kitchen knives, gasoline bombs and homemade shivs. It was a game now, played by drinking men who'd seen too many movies. Paul wondered how cocky they'd be going after whoever had preyed on Judd Maxwell.

He caught Todd Dunbar's troubled eyes and knew that there was at least one Sundowner who was taking the whole thing seriously. But then Dunbar flashed him a ghost of a smile.

"Thanks for the help, Mr. High Horse," he said. "But I think we got this situation under control here. Don't you?"

Chapter Twenty-Five

"You didn't have to treat him that way."

Todd looked up from the motel room desktop where he'd been playing a made-up game of field hockey with coins and beer can pull tabs, and cocked his eyebrows.

"He got you out of jail, hon. You can't forget that."

Moments before, she'd shut the room door despite the clackety room unit that barely moved any air, and left Little Todd and the girls watching television in their room next door. That meant Joy was ready for a Serious Discussion.

Jesus Lord.

He mumbled an insincere apology as a way of heading her off at the pass, but suspected he was too late.

She stood, hovered, sighed. Crossed to the window to peer at the patch of woods that separated them from the town. "Getting darker," she said.

He knew what she was thinking. The same shadowy thoughts kept crawling through his own mind. He knocked askew two nickels with a quarter while listening to the tinny murmur of the TV in the adjoining room.

"We could leave," she said.

"Yeah." Hoping that might slow her down some.

He thought about what was in his wallet, and that reminded him that he didn't really know how much he had, so he got up and pawed through the pockets of a pair of jeans on the floor and found it. He opened the bill compartment and swore.

"What?" she asked, alarmed.

He poked through more pockets of the same jeans, and then attacked more discarded clothing from the previous night. Turned out more pockets full of breath mints and used tissues and more coins, and brushed aside a bunch of crap on the desk.

"They took it," he sputtered, and swore again.

"Took what? Who did?"

"My money. Most of it."

He tore through desk drawers, tossing aside Joy's underwear, inexplicably stored there. He grabbed her purse, scattering lipstick, more tissues, creased turnpike receipts, and found three crumpled singles and more coins, mostly pennies.

"Todd, what are you doing? Leave my things alone." She snatched the purse from him, stuffed her shit back in and placed it behind her, on the mattress. Maybe thinking he couldn't do further damage if he couldn't see it.

He froze, half bent. "We aren't going anywhere, Joy. They made sure of that by stealing our money."

She gave him a crooked glance. "You mean they broke in—"

"I mean," he said, "the cops musta took my cash when they booked me." He slumped into the desk chair. "We couldn't leave this shithole even if we had a working car. We wouldn't get far with seven bucks and change."

He was ready for any kind of response but the heavy silence he got. The room was collecting too many shadows for him to be able to gauge her expression in the mirror, so he turned.

"What did you mean when you said they'd taken *most* of your money?"

"I've got four bucks," he said.

"Funny they'd take most of it, but not everything."

He saw where she was going with that, and headed her off. "I didn't spend it. I had two, maybe three beers all evening."

They'd already had it out that morning about the missed babysitting duty of the night before, but now she was back at it. Hitting at him from a different angle.

To break her brooding silence, he said again, "I didn't spend it all."

"Okay, fine," she said, but he could see that it wasn't. "It's just that when you drink..."

He placed both hands in his lap.

"I'm not saying..." she said.

"Yes, you are."

"It's just that, you go into a bar, and...two or three?"

His fist crashed to the desktop, sending their pathetic money pile fluttering, the coin stacks crumbling. She never knew when to walk away from an argument before it hit the red zone. He stood and began pacing, trying to burn through the energy fueling his anger. He could no longer hear the tinny TV in the next room. Melanie always knew when to turn it down.

"That's right," he rasped. "I'm the grade-A fuck-up who can't drink, can't hold on to his own money, can't even remember to come home at night."

"Honey, calm down," she said, but it only made him pace faster.

There was still too much fuel to burn up, so he had to throw something. But everything in the goddamn room was bolted down. He picked up his jeans from the floor and whipped them against a wall. A totally unsatisfying *whish* of a reaction.

"Honey," Joy said. "It's alright. I got the job anyway."

Coming at him from yet another angle. "What?" Stopping him cold.

"I should have told you earlier, but I was saving it."

Meaning she'd withheld the news as punishment for his lost Friday, but he tried to brush it off.

"A woman from the Water Department came and got me at about seven last night, after I called and told them why I couldn't make it. She took the girls, too. They sat and read while I was interviewed."

He stood over her, one foot propped on the bed. He was wearing shoes, and just waiting for her to complain about dirt on the spread even though it wasn't their spread. He'd never heard of an employer who'd do something like that for a job candidate. And the Water Department was open on a Friday evening?

He was going to congratulate her anyway and worry about it later. But he never got the chance. Not before the gunshot rang out and cries filled the air.

Chapter Twenty-Six

Full night had somehow sneaked up on them while he and Joy had been fighting. Now, as he shouted through the thin wall for the girls to stay where they were, Todd slipped out and followed the voices to the ravine that demarcated the rear of the motel complex, cutting it off from the woods that separated them from the town.

"Hey, get a light," Denver Dugan was shouting. "What happened here?"

Several people lit cigarette lighters, and Todd could just make out that about half of the bleary, stumbling shadows carried guns, knives or homemade weapons of some kind.

"Someone's gonna get shot out here," Joy said.

"Someone did get shot."

Todd aimed his own lighter at the voice. Kathy Lee was firing up a cigarette, her lighter hand shaking so that the flame left swirling tracers in the night. A dull, black automatic hung by her side, at the end of her other scrawny arm.

"What happened?" This from D.B., coming up behind them with a flashlight and his gentle take-charge manner.

Kathy Lee, now centered in D.B.'s beam, said, "Over there." She pointed her shaky gun at a stand of greenery just before the ravine fell away to the creek bed below.

"Who'd you get?" Duke Gates demanded, slipping his fire-breathing dragon arm around her. He stood bare-chested, his shorts unbuttoned to a wiry patch of hair below his belly button. He took the gun from her and notched it in his waistband, gangsta style.

"Heard something after you fell to sleep, so I went to see," she said. More than Todd cared to know.

"It came at me."

"What? A rat?" Carl asked.

"If it was," she said, "it was as big as you. And on two legs."

Explaining nothing.

D.B.'s eyes and flashlight beam swept the crowd before landing on two side-by-side armed men: Denver with his scoped deer rifle and Jermaine with the .38 the others had already met. "Will you two take a look? Here. Take the flashlight."

They went.

There might be fucking vampires out there, Todd thought, but all D.B. had to do was ask them nicely.

The Sundowners waited silently topside while Denver and

David Searls

Jermaine thrashed around below. Jermaine aimed D.B.'s weak flashlight beam at tangled brush that looked black as the night, the light sometimes picking up Denver's big, scared face.

Meanwhile, Kathy Lee was going on in that steady twang of hers. "It was climbing out of the ravine, right up at me, its eyes shining in the moonlight."

It, she'd said this time. Man or creature? Todd wondered.

"When it saw I had Duke's nine millimeter with me, it—he scrambled back behind that bush, but not before I nailed it once, point blank in the chest."

Flip-flopping pronouns like even she didn't have a clue.

"Duke didn't mention having no nine," Todd said.

"Why should I?" the kid replied.

"We're all in this together, you little prick."

"Hold it, you two, I wanna hear this," said D.B. He motioned for Kathy Lee to continue.

"Not much more to say."

Oh yes there was. Todd wondered where she'd stashed her kids for the evening. What if it had been one of her own little urchins she'd trigger-happily plugged?

"There's nothing here, D.B.," Jermaine shouted up at them.

By now, a couple more Sundowners had found flashlights and brought them to life. D.B. took one and joined the two men digging footholds into the cantilevered soil like mountain goats. Others followed and, with a deep sigh of annoyance, Todd did the same.

"Todd, get back up here," Joy snapped, but he ignored her.

"See. Nothing," Denver said.

"Give a woman a gun..."

"I heard that, Dukey," Kathy Lee said.

Denver, who'd been scrambling up the hill, chose that moment to lose his footing and topple backward, slo-mo style. He rolled like a playful grizzly most of the way to the creek bed below, triggering hoots of laughter, beams crisscrossing his prostrate body like footlights.

"Hey, look at this," said a man with a last name so complex that the Sundowners had taken to simply calling him Ponytail Pete.

Flashlight beams hit him. He'd slid several feet down the hill and anchored himself to a tree root. When a light found him, he was prodding at a couple saplings that had tried to cling to the side of the ravine, but failed. Their spindly trunks were snapped clean.

"So?" said Carl.

"These are recently broken," Pete said. "Crushed. Like something big fell into 'em."

"Something like a body?" Tonya Whittock asked.

"Could be," said Pete.

142

"Bull*shit*," offered Dukey.

Hating himself for appearing to agree with the asshole, Todd said, "So where's the body?"

That was the worst moment, standing there watching them all take in that question and put together what it meant. The woods seemed darker, the flashlights weaker just then. Even the creek whispering below sounded like it was against them.

"Blood," said Ponytail Pete. Still gripping what remained of the snapped-off saplings, he stared at the fingers of one hand.

And there it was. The flashlights found it. Moisture picked off a torn sapling, now turning two of Ponytail Pete's fingers black and wet.

Todd grabbed a flashlight from the nearest Sundowner and slashed the woods, the ravine and the motel grounds with its yellow beam, the sudden motion triggering gasps from all around.

"Jesus, what is it?" Jermaine Whittock asked.

It was nothing. Dark, dark woods, that's all. Unseen, on the other end of those woods, the weird, fucked-up town of Babylon, Michigan.

"As of now," said D.B., "we're setting up a night watch. We'll need four people patrolling the place front and back at all times, sundown to sunup. We'll switch off every, say, four hours."

"No way," said Duke Gates, skipping quickly up the hill. "I'm out of here."

"You're what?" Kathy Lee asked him.

Todd waited for a response that never came.

"What a chickenshit," Kathy Lee murmured.

For having incurred Kathie Lee's wrath, the overbearing Dukey Gates almost earned Todd's pity.

Chapter Twenty-Seven

The Highsmiths had turned into harmless hypocrites upon undertaking the raising of their son. That was the only explanation Paul could come up with for the visit the three of them paid to Monroe, the nearest city of any size, so they could attend Sunday services with the Episcopalians. They'd decided on that denomination after setting out early enough to find the church that charmed them most. This Sunday, the Episcopalians. Perhaps they'd become Catholics next Sunday.

"It's nice here," Darby said as they cruised aimlessly along the Lake Erie coastline in Darby's Jeep after the service. "Makes you almost not want to go home."

More than *almost*, Paul thought. He couldn't help wondering why the most commonplace amenity of any town—at least a single church—had gone missing in theirs. And whether the Episcopalians' omnipotent Creator was any match for the darker gods that seemed to be roosting in Babylon.

Tuck was getting fussy in his car seat, so they couldn't dawdle. Paul took I-75 to Michigan 151, crossing over the South Dixie Highway, the way he knew best. It occurred to him as they slipped into an unmarked road buried in the trees, that there were probably quicker routes in and out. But the thought of exploring the back roads surrounding Babylon left him vaguely ill at ease.

Taking Darrow Road into the outskirts of town, Paul made a conscious effort to ignore the Sundown Motel as they passed it. Babylon seemed both dismal and watchful that morning, but he knew his impression of it was colored by recent events. The sky was blue, the air mild as they drove through the same town that had so excited them just weeks before. It couldn't have all gone that bad that soon—could it?

Paul hooked a left blocks before the vast Drake Municipal Complex on Main View, noticing for the first time that the cut-through street he'd arbitrarily chosen was named Drake.

Why not? Everything else was.

He wished Darby would talk, really talk to him about all of this, but she had her back turned to him and was cooing with Tuck in the backseat. Anyway, what was he looking for from her? A serious conversation about vampires?

"Who is it?" she asked him sharply as the Jeep turned down Crenshaw with its other large new homes sitting as far back off the street as their own.

She meant the green Chrysler in their drive. Paul could hear the tension in her voice.

Police Chief Bill Sandy, in street clothes, stepped out of the car as they pulled up. When the Highsmiths got out to join him, he made a stilted hat-tipping motion toward Darby even though he was hatless.

"Morning, folks," he said cheerfully.

Paul provided a hurried introduction, then stood about awkwardly as Darby freed their son from his car seat. "What's up?" he asked the cop, not even trying to mask his desire to wrap up whatever business it was that required the lawman's presence on their property.

Chief Sandy turned to glance at the house as Darby steered Tuck into it, but Paul ignored the hint and waited for him to speak from the driveway.

"Both prisoners are sprung," the cop said. "Released well before yesterday noon."

Saying it like he was looking for a pat on the back, but Paul wasn't going there. "I know," he said. "I've talked to them since."

He let the cop ponder this.

Chief Sandy seemed to do so for a moment, then said, "I'd like you to meet someone."

"Oh?" Paul said it with a careful lack of inflection.

"One of the town's leading citizens. He'd like to meet you."

"Who would that be?"

"Name's Miles Drake."

Paul cocked an eyebrow. "You mean, like, Miles Junior? Or Miles the Third?"

The chief looked momentarily lost. "I mean...Miles Drake."

Paul's mind went back to those two old photos in the police station, the one mounted on the wall and the other in the chief's office. Miles Drake from the 1940s, and from maybe three decades later. In both, a tall and slender but elderly man with a head of snow-white hair and a face that looked flushed with high blood pressure. He couldn't possible still be alive. Could he?

"Mr. Highsmith?"

It brought him back. At least a little. "Um...sure," he said. "But what does he—?"

"Just a chat," the chief said. "Say tonight at eleven at the police station?"

Paul felt the lump of panic like it was a physical obstruction in his windpipe. Tonight. Eleven o'clock. Three hours past sundown.

"No," he said, getting past that lump.

The cop's face worked it over. "What do you mean, 'no'?"

"I mean," Paul said, forcing more decisiveness into his voice than he felt, "that if Miles Drake wants to see me tonight, he'll have to come here."

"To your home?"

What you must never do, Van Helsing would have warned, *is invite the vampire in.*

Unless, of course, you needed home court advantage.

"Yes," he said. "To my home."

Chapter Twenty-Eight

Darby yelped, a high hiccup of a sound, as the door chimed melodiously. "You didn't warn me," she cried out from an upstairs room.

That was his job. He'd had his face pasted to a dining room window that overlooked the driveway for the past half hour. They'd latched all of the doors and windows and had put Tuck to bed hours ago.

"He didn't drive," Paul said.

Be prepared, he'd reminded himself often that day. But already they'd been fooled.

Darby tripped down the stairs to lock sight on Paul as he came into the entry foyer, her eyes wide. "You didn't warn me," she said again, now little more than a whisper.

This was the young woman who'd laughed off the talk he'd brought home with him from his meeting with the motel residents the day before. She'd scoffed until the sun went down.

"Get back upstairs," he said thickly.

She nodded, but didn't move. He turned to the front door and stared at it. I'm walking, he told himself. Walking to the front door. And I don't believe in vampires.

The face looking in the window set into the carved door was white and craggy with age, stern as a monument. The mouth was a straight line, the eyes hard, dark.

Paul glanced over his shoulder one final time to see his wife skipping up the stairs like a schoolgirl.

His fingers moved numbly over the various locks. He gripped and turned and pulled the door handle prematurely, then had to eat up more time turning more locks until it would swing open smoothly and admit the face in the door panel.

Miles Drake was not alone. A woman stood next to him. She was middle-aged and, though moderately tall, managed to appear short and squat next to the much taller and more slender man. Her hair hung limp, her face unremarkable, her expression put-upon.

"My daughter Tabitha," the elderly man said. He seemed to know that no self-introduction was necessary.

Something chittered at the vampire's feet, and Paul caught a quick glimpse of meaty bodies and slithering tails before Miles Drake shuffled past Paul and into the house ahead of his daughter. From the white foyer with its thirty-foot ceiling, the two surveyed the premises while

Paul closed and latched the door with his eyes shut, anxious to see no more than he had to out there in the dark.

Drake turned as he did. "Well?" he rumbled. The next move was obviously Paul's.

The man's pressed blue slacks, his short-sleeved white dress shirt, dull necktie and scuffed shoes gave him the appearance of a minor bureaucrat or a fuddy-duddy grandpa.

Paul motioned and led the way through the tall arch and into the family room and to the same sofa that had held three soggy old men just days before. He considered offering food and drink, but the protocol for hosting vampires was a mystery to him.

This last thought came with a grim, hidden smile. This whole vampire thing…he was just playing along.

"Please take a…" he finally murmured, but the two had already taken such action.

While Miles centered himself on the offered sofa, his daughter sat alone on a wingback leather chair angled next to but slightly behind him. Paul backed into a chair on the other side of a Persian rug the color of sunlight.

Even seated, Miles Drake loomed. Though not quite Paul's six-two, the other man had a long neck, ramrod spine, narrow waist and lean physique, all of which seemed to lend inches.

His slender hands caressing his knees, just as he had in his formal photo, Drake said, "You've heard stories."

His voice was rich, deep. Beneath the ceiling track lighting his face lost the ghastly pallor Paul had observed in his door pane. Quite the contrary, his complexion was ruddy, even mottled. His irises were of a non-reflective blue, the whites of them tinged with yellow. His thick hair was unattractively white, more like yellow snow, his teeth primarily that same unappealing color, but brown where tooth met tooth. He looked like his photos. No better, no worse.

Meaning he closely resembled his appearance sixty years ago.

"Like with most stories, most gossip, there's truth and partial truth and untruth all mixed together until you don't know exactly what to think. And so," Drake said, rubbing his knees as tenderly as a lover's breast, "I'll tell you what to think."

Don't look up, Paul told himself. Don't lift your eyes to find Darby crouched behind the balcony railing, her sightline taking in this section of the family room visible through the tall doorway.

But of course the command only brought about the action and he let his gaze flicker to the shadow he'd thought he'd seen peripherally— but he saw nothing.

"I could do as the others," the old man was saying. "I could promise you money, more than you've yet been tempted with, but I think you're used to money and a generous offer would only make you wonder how much better the next offer might be."

As if reading Paul's career trajectory.

"There's a limit," Drake continued, "to my finances and my patience. And I won't waste time issuing silly threats like my annoying friend Tolliver." He chuckled dryly. "Oh yes, I heard about your meeting with my three ageless cronies. They do things the old-fashioned way, especially John."

Miles Drake moved his head ever so subtly, but the movement caused the track lighting to lose him momentarily, and his watery eyes to sparkle and gleam like some moist gem. Then the head turned back into the light and the sparkle was gone, and he was just an old man with rheumy eyes like his three old friends. Elderly, but strangely intense.

Discomfited by the old man's naked scrutiny of him, Paul turned his attention to Tabitha Drake. Or at least he assumed Drake to be her last name. He couldn't imagine her giving up her name to a man as she sat slumped and sullen.

"Threats from old men seem empty and toothless," her father was saying.

Drake leaned forward until he could stand all ten of his long fingers at attention on the glasstop table in front of him. "To fear a threat, you must first be convinced that the gun is loaded."

Paul heard a sound from upstairs. Maybe just Tuck tossing in his sleep. As he gave the possibility more attention, he heard everything: bumps, creaks, settling timbers, each sound more stealthy and portentous than the previous. He also thought he heard the rats outside, scratching to get in.

It had seemed so easy, so heroic, to tell the police chief that if Miles Drake wanted a face-to-face, he'd have to face him here. So dramatic an act with the sun shining, the birds singing.

But here he sat. Hunched forward to tent his long fingers, his aged eyes gleaming with unexpected depth. And the daughter so calmly contemptuous, watching him with the same detached interest and repugnance she might show apes fornicating behind glass at the zoo.

"Paul," the elderly man said, "for you to truly understand how loaded my gun is, you must hear my story."

Paul's breath went ragged. The old man's icy use of his name was like a chain binding him, as though his name had been captured, not merely spoken. He had no desire to hear whatever Miles Drake had to share. But he'd listen. He had no choice.

"I was born..." the vampire began, flicking a tongue across his brown and yellow teeth, "...on April Fourteenth, 1836."

No. Paul very definitely did not want to hear this.

Part Two

The Vampires Drake and Darrow

The few who survived were taken away to Babylon...
2 Chronicles 36

Chapter Twenty-Nine

"Those first forty-two years? There's really nothing to tell. I recall having a wife and seven children and we were rather poor, certainly by today's standards. But for the time, I suppose we were working class. There was such a chasm between the wealthy and needy back then, but I suppose there still is. America, land of opportunity. I can tell you that has not always been the case.

"I was a scrivener in Rochester, New York." The vampire let out a breath, an exasperated chuckle. "Paul, I'm not changing the subject, but how many photocopies have you made in your life? You can't even answer that, can you? You think nothing of slapping your document onto the glass and pressing a button for ten copies, whether you need them or not. What's interesting, Paul, is that while the talking heads keep insisting that the world's becoming more complicated, it's really become less so. But you'd need perspective to realize that."

Paul hadn't said a word since the old man had seated himself. He vowed to change that, to take back some of the control he'd lost, but he still couldn't force anything from his constricted throat.

The vampire said, "I was a scrivener for an insurance company, a human photocopier. I sat by a kerosene lamp all day writing longhand copies of letters, memoranda, policies, contracts, whatever was given me. Beginning at daybreak, I'd struggle through a stack of documents that never stood less than half a foot high. I was uneducated, so I scribbled all day to make neat sense of other men's more learned scribblings. Yes, beside a wood stove in the winter, my tools a pen and ink pot, at least in the earlier days. It sounds positively Dickensian, I know, but all true.

"Tell me, Paul: Did you make your own copies at that investment bank in Detroit?"

Paul shook his head, slowly. Hypnotically.

"No, of course not. You had a secretary for that. Probably called an administrative assistant in these more enlightened times, but she was almost definitely a *she,* and she invariably bitched at the occasional paper jam or complicated collating assignment. A greater sense of history would have reduced her complaints, don't you agree, Paul?"

Paul sat. Stared. Speechless.

"My old job has nothing to do with my story," the vampire grumped, as if chastising himself, "except that you must understand how dismal life was back then, mine no worse than anyone else's. Which might have a great deal to do with what was to become of me, or maybe it means nothing. I was bright, but, as I said, uneducated. My family before me had been poor, so I was to be poor. Remember, Paul, Horatio Alger's young rags-to-riches heroes of the nineteenth century were fictional characters. The poverty-stricken boys and young men reading those tales for inspiration would, for the most part, be further out the cost of the book as they lay dying in the same wretched poverty to which they'd become accustomed. Just a fact.

"Emily and I—Yes!" he cried, interrupting himself. "That was her name. Emily. I sometimes forget. Sometimes one's lifetime can exceed his memory capacity. But Emily and I, we had seven children, and that high number further accounted for our impoverished state, but there was no dependable solution for that back in my day. Unless, of course, you gave up the act altogether, but when you're poor..." he stretched his arms in mock-supplication "...what else is there?"

Tabitha Drake must have heard this story countless times. Paul watched her eyes wander to the bookcase, to one dark window, to the high ceiling...

"I'm listening," Paul said sharply, though the old man had barely paused.

"Thank you," Drake said with the mildest touch of sarcasm. He folded his long fingers in his lap, then splayed them flat on his thigh. "Consumption," he said. "You've heard of it?"

Paul nodded. "Tuberculosis."

"Tuberculosis," Drake agreed. "But the old word is the more accurate term. The disease consumes its victims in tiny, wet, messy increments, and finally eats even the will to live. You cough up lung tissue as you lay gasping, praying for just one more painful breath, and then another." A grin wobbled on the old man's face. "Very graphic, I realize, but if you fail me this early in my story, you'll miss the best parts."

Paul's face must have looked stricken. He wanted to wipe away the salty sheen he knew was gathering along his temples, but he wouldn't give Drake the satisfaction.

The vampire shrugged. "Let's just say that it didn't look as though I had a particularly serene death to look forward to."

"You were the one with TB?"

Drake slapped his thigh. "That's right, we don't even call it tuberculosis anymore, do we? TB. We'd done a fine job of cleaning up that nasty disease for public consump—" He stopped. "Sorry. The pun was unintentional.

"But to answer your question, yes, I was dying. Death was a given. Some went fast, some slower, but all died. I was forty-two, as I mentioned. The year must have been 1878. Naturally, there were no hospitalization benefits, no social security or welfare. And no life insurance to care for my family when I passed on. This despite the fact that—and the irony has only hit me now—I worked for an insurance company. Which, by the way, terminated my employment as soon as it became evident that I was gravely ill."

Miles Drake paused as he stared into the distance of memory.

Picking up the thread of storyline, he said, "It was Amanda, the second of my seven, who inadvertently arrived at a solution for the family's survival—and mine as well. Amanda, you see, had grown enamored of a pale and rather bland-featured young man who would only call upon her in the evenings."

The vampire's lips stretched into a passable smile. "I'll bet you see where this is going, Paul. But I had too much on my mind to give her Frederick Darrow more than a passing thought. I was dying, don't you see? I never heard the whispers from my wife and four other daughters or the unconcealed glares of my sons when Frederick came calling."

"Are you saying—?"

Drake nodded distractedly. "Yes. That he was a vampire."

Of course this was where the evening had been headed from the moment that morning when Chief Sandy had issued an invitation that had sounded more like a summons. Paul had blocked it from his rational mind as much as possible, much as he'd ignored the long-term economic viability of investment instruments with suspiciously generous returns.

His blood slowed in his veins as he listened and desperately tried to discount all that he'd heard that evening and over the last couple days. But at that moment he felt the presence of an ancient vampire sitting and stroking his knees, and the vampire's sulky daughter, and he wished for a drink to drink or a cigar to handle. Or just a cat to stroke. Anything to divert his attention from the sinister flow of words.

And that flow continued.

"He was a name to me, a vague impression, that's all. Frederick Darrow, medium of height, dark brown hair worn rather long and tangled, light complexion and foppish build. Brown eyes in constant motion and a rather skittish presence. That's the sum impression Amanda's young beau made on me as I slowly died, hiding the bloody cough from my employers for as long as I was able.

"By the time I was bedridden and jobless, I was consumed—that word again—with self-pitying anger."

Frederick Darrow, said the vampire, had shuffled into his bedroom after what was to have been Drake's last meeting with his weeping second eldest.

"I was dimly aware of much harsh whispering as the girl prodded, cajoled, threatened. Despite my growing mental fog, I observed her

155

gentleman friend shaking his head equally adamantly, the scene piquing my curiosity more than I might have admitted. Or perhaps it's that I had nothing else important to do but to die. Distractions were welcome, so I watched them fight. Naturally, Amanda won. She was, after all, a Drake."

He offered up a thin smile.

Frederick Darrow was all but dragged into the room to meet with Miles on his deathbed by his persistent daughter. The boy sat stiffly on the straw mattress while Amanda remained by the closed door like a posted sentinel. Keeping others out and her intended in. The dying Miles Drake figured he must be getting closer to the end, for he was now hallucinating. His reluctant guest's eyes seemed to glitter oddly, as though reflecting strong moonlight that couldn't be glimpsed through the closed drapes.

Fear went through his feverish and crumbling mind as Frederick Darrow bent closer.

"I can make you live," the strange young man whispered in a voice that coolly bathed Drake's hot body. "It's not free, and it's not eternal, but it's health and postponement. Do you want it?"

How could he not?

"Yes," the terminally ill man croaked.

"What would *you* have said?" the vampire demanded rather peevishly of Paul.

He blinked. "What?"

Paul felt as though the story—the very presence of the old man in his living room—had slowed his mental reflexes to the point that reception trailed dialog the way audio dragged behind video in a poorly dubbed film. The time was 1878, and he had to struggle back to present day to address the question.

"I asked you if you wouldn't accept the gift of life even with the price tag hidden. Of course I accepted his offer."

There it was again, the peculiar flash of white brilliance in the young man's eyes, but too quick for the dying Miles Drake to verify.

"Hurry, Frederick. Just do it," the girl hissed from her place in the doorway.

So strange...but Miles was accepting every curious event with a sort of incurious acceptance. So his daughter nervously guarded the bedroom door. So he'd been offered life and health. So her fluttery beau's eyes glittered as he loomed closer. Miles felt as though his consciousness detached to watch the ravaged, bedridden body and the tableau of daughter and lover and dying man with only mild anticipation.

156

"Now," Amanda commanded.

And Frederick's lips touched him as though it was *he* who was Darrow's lover, and not Drake's daughter.

"It's supposed to be deliciously erotic. Sensual. Enticing. Or so the books and movies would have it." Miles Drake leaned forward, letting his long arms dangle between his bony knees. "Now the truth, Paul. Vampire breath is hot and harsh and carrion-foul. More to the point, it hurts to have your jugular torn. It hurts *very* much."

Paul could see it. Could feel the teeth, the exploratory nibble that sent shivers down neck and arm. And then the bite. The excruciating bite.

"The bite," said the vampire, "is a repulsive, infectious, frenzying shot of pain, a screaming sensation that keeps intensifying until your senses finally overload and you're given the comfort of unconsciousness."

Drake tapped a knee and offered one more ghost-faint smile. "Not at *all* like it's described in the books and movies, is it, Paul? Not a *Twilight* encounter by half."

Paul forced his tight jaws to loosen enough for a few words. "Why didn't you bleed to death?"

The vampire straightened up and sat back. He looked faintly disappointed, as though he'd expected something deeper. "Properties of the blood and saliva," he said with an impatient hand gesture. "The immune system which contributes to the vampire's long life goes to work on its host, stoppering the wound and swiftly rejuvenating the body." He shrugged as though both acknowledging and dismissing the suspect science of his explanation.

"What the vampire kiss meant to *me*," he said, "was the cessation of death. I can't put it in less melodramatic terms. I don't know how my Amanda explained the puncture marks at my throat, for I remained in a groggy state until my injury had healed. Which didn't take all that long, for I now shared the rocket-boosted immune system of the man who'd saved my life."

"But your family," said Paul.

"The topic never came up, although there was much whispering among family members and young Darrow was never invited back to the house."

The vampire showed his teeth in a brief flash of yellow and brown. "I suppose Amanda and I became the black sheep of our family, and much blacker than most."

"So they...knew?"

The vampire created a part in his white-yellow hair with his fingers. "If they didn't suspect at first, they must certainly have had misgivings by the time the children started disappearing."

The vampire must have seen a look of revulsion cross Paul's face, for he added quickly, "No, no. Not *my* children. I exhibited perfect self-control at all times when it came to my own brood."

A brand new threesome hit nighttime Rochester in the winter of 1878-79. Miles Drake, his daughter Amanda and young Frederick Darrow inseparably traveled the most forlorn streets and alleys, the seediest bars, the deepest and darkest woods and loneliest harbors of the Gennessee River.

"Life grew stereophonic that winter, multi-layered with sights and sounds and odors and textures I'd never before experienced. Every coal-blackened snowflake was sculpted of the purest ice and smelled as blue as cloud frost." The vampire's eyes had gone glossy with the memory, and now focused back on Paul. "To be us," he murmured, "is to see, feel, hear, smell, touch life for the first time. Every delicious sensation a virgin experience."

Paul's tongue roved his lips, wetting and unfastening them. "You were telling me about...the children."

"Ah. You must first understand that there were no better friends anywhere than Miles and Amanda and Frederick. I no longer thought of her as my daughter, the child I'd never found time to know. She was now my dearest friend, as was her lover. We were all lovers, though not in the traditional sense, so you needn't purse your lips so. Our love was the sort that might be enjoyed by the three final souls inhabiting a breathtakingly alien world.

"No," said the vampire, correcting himself with a shake of the head. "As usual when revisiting the past, I've only seen what I want to see. There was another side as well, for as we turned away from all others, they turned from us. My wife—yes, Emily—and the other children—I'd have to think much harder to come up with all of their names—knew more than they cared to consciously admit. They avoided my presence, steering clear of the heavily cloaked bedroom where I slept alone and insentient during the day. Initially I suppose I could have explained my odd hours as some vague by-product of my illness and its miraculous cure, but no one asked. No one wanted to know.

"Money was a bigger problem, as it is to many families today. While my health had returned, my new lifestyle made it impossible to obtain traditional employment. And, to be perfectly honest, I had no desire to do so. My mind soared so far above the bosses with their smudgy little lives that to set pen to paper to document their petty thoughts was unthinkable. So I found other means of sustenance.

"Bloodthirst, like lust, is as useful as it is instinctive," the vampire said.

His matronly daughter watched him with hooded eyes, as

unimpressed with his words as Paul was thunderstruck.

"I was strong, Paul. Unimaginably so. And I could see so much. With moral constraints gone, I was a force of the night. I'd like to say that my first kill was an emotionally wrenching experience, but I can't. I remember it, just as you remember your first girl, but it's lost its larger-than-life feel with the passage of years. He was a man, small and weak with diseased, imperfect blood. He had a few dollars in his pockets, though. My dear wife learned surprisingly quickly to accept without question the small piles of money I left on her nightstand before retiring to my own room at dawn. She didn't ask, and I didn't tell, and in this way we were able to keep the hovel we called a home."

Oddly, Paul felt greater terror sitting with a thief and serial killer than upon hearing Drake's claim to be a vampire. The supernatural could be shrugged off. Murder, though, was horrifyingly mundane.

"But what I've told you so far still doesn't explain the children," Drake said. He scrunched himself deeper into the deep sofa and let his long legs stretch to the glass tabletop. He seemed to enjoy having found a new audience, perhaps his first in years. "As Frederick explained it, children only briefly quenched my bloodthirst, but they could be dispatched swifter and easier than adults. That was like my timid friend, to take the safest route.

"'In a city like this,' Frederick would say, waving his arms to take in Rochester's cobbled streets, its granite flour mills and soot-blackened buildings, 'danger is everywhere and caution is paramount.'

"So we took adults when we had to, for cash, but children for nourishment. Ragtag urchins with too many siblings, and orphans with none. What I learned from Frederick is that if we only bait our hooks for the poor, there's rarely an outcry."

Drake shrugged. "Fewer mouths to feed. We'd dump the bloodless corpses overnight in the already polluted Lake Ontario or the Gennessee River. Perhaps some of the small, waterlogged bundles were found with injuries that confounded nineteenth century forensics, but I can recall no public outcry or close calls.

"Follow me so far? Frederick and I only took the weak and unwanted. Until the night my skittish friend slipped up."

Frederick had been seen, Drake explained. From a dance hall with a side door facing the alley chosen for his solo feeding erupted besotted witnesses to the frail young vampire's struggle to drag the squirming, squawking child into the night.

"Frederick panicked and abandoned the injured boy and ran," Drake explained. "He ran straight to my home and waited for me under the front porch. When I arrived hours later with my daughter, having first tidily wiped clean my lips and face and changed shirts in an alley, I found this babbling, hysterical man with blood-spattered frock coat

159

under my house. He'd done the unthinkable: not only nearly getting caught, but dragging the police to within sniffing distance of my door.

"We fled with a single hastily packed trunk between the three of us," the vampire said. "We had a terribly close call at dawn, when we had to burrow into the darkest, smelliest corner of an abandoned chicken coop outside of town. I haven't been back to Rochester since. Not in more than a century. I hear it's changed."

Chapter Thirty

Paul looked from Drake to daughter, and back to Drake. He had to keep the man—the *thing*—talking. When the vampire ran out of conversation...Paul swallowed the hard fear and refused to finish the thought.

He said, "Then you and Tabitha have been together..."

"No, no, no," the vampire replied with the briefest chuckle. "I have—or have had—many sons and daughters. Too many to recall through the years. This one..." he waved his hand dismissively at Tabitha Drake, who sat staring at nothing. "You weren't listening, Paul, or you'd know that my second daughter's name was Amanda. This one here is my eyes during the day, I suppose, but she's no Amanda."

The three—the two vampires and Amanda—followed the Erie Canal to the Buffalo Harbor, and from there boarded a Great Lakes steamer. They stopped for brief periods in Cleveland, Toledo, Detroit. They strayed into Canada, staying only in cities where children were both a plentiful and burdensome commodity, and they reduced the burden.

Large bodies of water were important for disposal, and most industrial cities of the upper Midwest sat on such stretches. Later, as they found their way to the Northwest, the three found deep woods with soft soil and remote mountain trails, and that worked as well.

Sometimes they'd befriend and recruit rather than plunder the night inhabitants of the alleys and saloons and flophouses. And, on very rare occasions, they found others like them.

"Frederick and I were never prejudiced, like some of our kind met along the way," said Drake. "There are those who consider all daylighters to be of blood value only. Not true." He fanned one long finger in the air to emphasize this point. "I might have been quite the liberal for my time, but our present-day social system could not have evolved under the weight of such tired beliefs."

As Drake explained it, the vampires' relationship with the daylighter Amanda was uniquely close. The three shared a bond of genuine affection for one another.

"As for conversion, sure, she wanted to become one of us. Who wouldn't? But we needed her in human state. We needed a guard when we slept, someone to handle the day-to-day logistics and to make sure we had shelter from the sun. And to arrange safe passage when we had need to travel quickly."

Despite a growing sense of dread that left his shirt soaked and body smelling of panic, Paul was deeply embedded in the story. He had to keep reminding himself how amazing it was that the old man had been able to share his delusion with so many. It was during long stretches of forgetting to remind himself of this—that it was only a story, an imaginative fairy tale—that the terror set in.

Having Amanda around for so long, Drake continued, the vampires had grown accustomed to traveling with humans. As their numbers grew, the two groups lived in symbiotic harmony, a relationship that benefited the night creatures and their band of amoral cutthroats who gained the most sadistic of thrills and the promise of eventual near-eternity.

"Ah, but who could be unimpressed with our ways?" the vampire purred. "Think of it, Paul. To live vibrant lives for centuries with godlike powers. To overcome most injuries and all disease. Of course we had followers, Paul. Of course."

To overcome *most* injuries, the vampire had said. Paul latched onto that thought, but asked another question altogether. "If everything was so great, why move to Babylon and settle down?"

The vampire froze in position as his daughter shifted uncomfortably behind him. "I need a drink," he said. Petulantly, it seemed. "Water. Just water. Perhaps your wife can..."

His wife.

Paul couldn't stop his gaze from lifting to the arched doorway and the high foyer and the flight of stairs beyond it and the small patch of balcony that could barely be glimpsed from his angle. He knew the vampire had seen his gaze shift, so he said, "My wife's upstairs. She's sleeping. I'll get your water for you."

He asked Tabitha Drake if she wanted anything. Her head lolled in a slow, uninterested shake.

Paul had to keep from running to the kitchen, desperate as he was to keep the vampire from exploring his home, even if just with his eyes. He splashed the water so hard into the drinking glass that most of it sprayed back out. The couple ice cubes he added as an afterthought floated dismally to the surface, lonely as two small islands in a deep sea.

The Drakes, it would seem, hadn't moved. Tabitha sat in a brooding ball, her hands fisted in her lap, blank eyes focused on a wall where a large painting would go whenever they got around to finding and hanging it.

The vampire's delicate sip barely disturbed the ice islands. He chunked the glass down on the glass table and said, "I suppose I must tell you what happened to Amanda."

Chapter Thirty-One

"As I've mentioned," Drake began, his voice strained as though his chest was heaving forth words that didn't want release, "Amanda wished to become one of us. But it was impossible. Frederick and I were in total agreement: Ours was no life for her.

"We witnessed the changes coming over her in those first years. It was as if she became ravaged by a disease that left its mark in small increments of destruction, but it was just normal aging—a process most people never notice in others because they're going through it at the same steady rate. In our case, Frederick's and mine..." Drake waved off the rest as obvious.

"In 1878, Amanda was a girl of nineteen, but by 1893, she was thirty-four. The changes that occurred to her over those fifteen years were subtle, but she and we noticed them with utmost dread. We held, if not the cure, at least the strongest treatment known. Held it in our saliva and could have easily injected it into her bloodstream.

"But tell me, Paul," he said, "what would you have done?"

Paul fervently hoped the question was rhetorical and the vampire would get on with his terrible tale. But as the silence lengthened to the point where he could again hear his home creak and settle, could imagine the tail-dragging rodents sniffing and scratching outside, he knew that Miles Drake awaited a response.

His thoughts went to Tuck, his blue-eyed boy who lay peacefully asleep under a thin blanket some two dozen paces from the murderous creature his father had invited into their home.

"I think," Paul said. And that was it, for there were too many conflicting images in slippery black and white and gray for one sharply defined response to rise above. Everything and nothing came immediately to mind. Just: *I think.*

The vampire chuckled. "Exactly."

And then Amanda Drake was visited by another affliction. She'd taken ill, or that's what Miles and Frederick believed, until one of the women in their caravan took the men aside to explain what should have been obvious: Miles Drake's thirty-four-year-old daughter was pregnant.

Why was it so surprising? She and her perpetually youthful Frederick had lived together as husband and wife for fifteen years, and yet Drake had almost forgotten to think of his two dearest friends with bodies pressed and limbs intertwined in that earthly manner. It was true that other human and vampire couplings had resulted in births, but Frederick, with his odd mix of flighty fears and blood courage had seemed neither masculine nor feminine, but sexless.

Obviously, he'd not given the young vampire enough credit.

The condition was diagnosed in Springfield, Illinois. When they hit the outskirts of Keokuk, Iowa in her seventh month, complications arose.

"So much blood," Miles Drake murmured in a fluttery voice nearly lost to the high ceiling of the Highsmith home.

Tabitha jiggled one leg as if to circulate the blood.

Blood. Seemingly the theme of the evening.

A table clock, a metallic geometric contraption of Darby's, signified the official arrival of midnight with twelve flat electronic and anticlimactic beeps.

The vampire cleared his throat of accumulated emotion. His face settled like mottled marble. "Frederick and I were not aware of the situation as it unfolded. It was daylight and we and others of our kind had stashed ourselves away in a weather-rotted barn. At nightfall the women came to us with word that there had been complications and the baby hadn't survived. Amanda, they told us, was fighting. Their faces as they brought us this news...they were as white as our own."

Drake paused for a sip from his drinking glass. Paul could see through the bottom of the tilted glass all the way up and into the pink mouth, the yellow teeth parted to channel the water.

The old vampire gasped like a child who'd drank too fast, and wiped the chin dribble with his necktie. "They kept slipping into her tent with fresh rags which they'd then try to smuggle past us so we couldn't see their condition." He gave a wan smile. "As if they could hide the fresh scent of blood from Frederick and me."

After a brief silence, the vampire casually added, "She was dying."

He'd had well over a century to deal with it.

"Frederick was beside himself, much more distraught than I'd ever seen him—though not as much as I ever would." Drake's dry chuckle after those words chilled Paul. It alluded to yet another story he was afraid he was going to hear.

"This scene had been played out before, vampires and daylighters waiting anxiously outside a tent, listening to screams of pain while harried women scuttled about with hot water and blankets. But this time it was different. I could tell by the faces of those scuttling women under the low moon. Much later that night, one of them told Frederick and me that we should visit my daughter. This woman, she had the tired but relaxed manner of one who has graciously accepted defeat. Her urgency was gone."

Amanda lay still, her blood scent hanging wet and heavy in the air.

Drake could hear Frederick sobbing softly behind him in the gloomy tent as the panic welled like a malignancy in his own chest.

"She lay chilled by her own cooling blood on the sheets and tick mattress," the vampire reported. "She was still conscious though, her eyes so alive they were difficult to look into."

"Take me," the woman demanded of her father and lover. "Hurry," she said in a dying whisper. "Be too late...soon."

It seemed impossible to be dying with eyes so bright and shiny and expectant. When one of the midwives reentered the tent with a lantern, Drake saw sympathy and regret etched on the woman's face, but also something more uplifting. Yes, your daughter is dying, the expression said, but it was a condition her father and lover could—and obviously would—correct.

Miles Drake felt dizzy, befuddled, nearly drunk under the weight of Amanda's bloodscent. It at once enticed and repelled him. His senses reeled. It was as though he were dying himself, but much worse than slipping from existence in his own darkened bedroom with Frederick's sharp teeth and fetid breath so near.

As the battle of enticement and repugnance raged within him, he heard another choked sob. Frederick looked even less composed than usual, his jaw throbbing, nostrils flaring, his eyes brightening and dimming in the flickering kerosene light. The young vampire studied the older man's face for an answer. Finding nothing, he bent to the dying Amanda and took one limp hand.

"Frederick...now," she croaked. She tried to say more, but her jaws tightened in pain.

Drake imagined he could see a fresh black pool emerging from between her legs as her bloodscent drew stronger. He placed a hand on his friend's shoulder and tried to convince himself that this was virtually the same as holding his daughter, for he could not trust himself to come closer to the dying woman.

"Don't," he said softly so that his daughter couldn't hear, but of course she did.

Her pale, sweat-stained face met his. "Why?" she asked him, her voice little more than a breath.

She gave a strangled cry, grasping her lover with both hands. "Frederick, I'll die," she said.

Drake's bedside view was mercifully blocked at that moment by the kneeling Frederick, but he heard her calling his name. That couldn't be avoided.

"Father, you can't..." Her voice stunned.

"But I could," said the vampire in Paul's living room, salty pools forming in each eye. He rubbed swiftly, angrily at the gathering moisture. The creature's lips drew tight over his rotted teeth in a mask that turned grief to rage. "You wanted to know so much, Paul," he growled. "So now you must hear all."

His longstanding refusal to allow Amanda to join them in the most primal sense had never before been questioned by Frederick, who was all but paralyzed with self-revulsion. The last thing he'd ever wanted was for the woman he loved to truly become one with him.

"And yet, as she lay dying," Drake murmured, "my thoughts turned to the scene of fifteen years before, when a young and healthy girl had saved her father's life with the gift of her lover's kiss. It had been the ultimate act of love, and now I had the opportunity to do the same, and all I could do was stand my ground with nostrils flaring in blood anticipation. With that one short directive—*Don't*—I'd condemned my daughter to death."

Drake sat rigid, his body concave in the plush sofa. "Sentenced her to mortal death, but perhaps saved her mortal soul." His shoulders rolled. "Who knows? Who knows?"

Paul wished he'd brought himself a glass of water from the kitchen. Or something stronger. His lips parted with an audible dry-mouth smack. "I'm sorry. I didn't know..."

"Didn't know what?" Drake snarled. "That vampires have feelings? But you haven't heard the whole story, Paul. Not by any means. Hear me to the end, and see how much pity you feel for me then."

Somewhere outside the door, the night was broken by whipcracks of sound dulled by distance. A burst of crackling in the night. Something came over the old man's face, but it was soon replaced by his usual mottled rigidity.

Firecrackers, Paul told himself. *Let it be firecrackers.*

166

Chapter Thirty-Two

Frederick Darrow changed from the moment the light faded in Amanda's eyes. He became more withdrawn, less timid. They traveled faster and more frequently as the emboldened young vampire exposed the growing clan to ever-greater risks.

"There was a problem in Chicago," Drake said. "Suffice to say that we fled the slum tenements we'd temporarily called home. This was in 1895, and the arm of the law had lengthened considerably since my conversion. The telegraph wire had become the telephone line. The automobile and trains and the Pinkertons had shrunk our world, made it more difficult to elude trouble. In St. Louis, for instance, I'd read an article in the *Missouri Gazette* about a marauding caravan that seemed to precede missing persons reports across the nation.

"They were writing about us, Paul. The first time I'd ever heard of that happening. We fled to the rural South. It was like another country back then, the sticky air, the dusty roads that the best maps couldn't find. Our destination was New Orleans with its French and Spanish and Negro influences so unlike the rest of the nation. No one spoke the same language—some tongues appeared to be made up on the spot—so how organized could they be in our persecution? Besides, we imagined that the blood would run richer, hotter, darker, spicier in this exotic land."

Drake fluttered his hand. "I don't know what we were expecting," he said impatiently. "And it doesn't matter now because we weren't to discover the properties of New Orleans blood."

The vampires were under strict orders to be on their best behavior as their humid trek took them deeper into the swamp country. Although they passed sharecropper shacks housing barefoot blacks and mulattoes in rags, and knew that these people would never be missed, the clan ignored them. They made do with the lifeblood of the occasional stolen goat—a very poor and temporary substitute at best—but Chicago was too near in their memories. And so were their pursuers.

Such self-constraint came at a terrible price. The vampires, numbering some thirty in all, and cared for by a roughly equal number of daylighters, lay inert in the blaze of day, their sweltering forms covered by horse blankets and hidden under the floorboards of wagons. They awoke with teeth chattering, bathed in sweat and racked with unquenchable thirsts that left them feverish with rage and desire and eying their caregivers in ways that made some slip out before the next nightfall.

Outside of Memphis, a young vampire slipped from the caravan upon the discovery of a farmer's dry husk. A female of the species was put down near the Louisiana border when, in a frenzy, she attacked and killed her human mate. Drake, who partook of the execution along with his partner, was horrified to find that vampire blood sated his needs as readily as his usual prey. He uneasily watched Frederick's slow smile as his friend licked the last of the flow from his lips.

The daylighters who witnessed the mercy killing of the renegade must have whispered their misgivings to the others, for seven more were missing by the next sunset.

Three vampires, two men and a woman, retaliated for the betrayal by killing four clan daylighters and disappearing before Drake and Darrow could intervene.

"We were falling apart even before Chitimacha Bend, but that proved to be very nearly the end of us," Drake said. He let out a sigh. "The James Gang had their Northfield and the Daltons had Coffeeville. What we had was Chitimacha Bend, Lousiana."

The dwindling clan crossed the Mississippi River at Natchez. They drew dark, suspicious glances as they passed squalid settlements of Houma and Coctaw Indians, chain gangs clearing sugar cane and skeletal sharecroppers working tobacco fields and watermelon patches. They cut through forests of ash, pine, elm and red gum, following the rich, sluggish Atchafalaya ever southward. The air became hotter and wetter until the vampires gnashed their teeth in heated fury even in their sleep, dreaming red dreams and awakening with sore mouths and bloody gums.

"It was the relatively cool swamp of cypress and tupelos that stopped us outside of the town," said Drake. "Olan Buck was a daylighter back then and it was his decision. A good one, for under the thick canopies of Spanish moss we hid from both the sun and our pursuers, whose dogs we'd occasionally hear in the distance. It was still hot, unbearably so, and the mosquitoes took more blood than we ever did, but we were able to evade the hounds under the land's strong scents of mud, muskrat, raccoon, red pepper and wild hog. There were no more killings and no one deserted the clan for the next several days."

They'd found safe quarters for three days and nearly three nights before running into trouble. It was about the middle of that third night when a quivery young vampire burst into the clearing where Drake was inadequately feasting with some of the others on the rats within constant reach. They'd long ago found that animal blood dulled their cravings like a pacifier calms a baby anxious for mother's milk. It doesn't feed the hunger, but temporarily dims the need.

"This young vampire—his name was Tolliver; yes, the same— positively shook in his boots as he reported to me. The story we eventually got from him was that he and his young wife had accompanied Frederick on a forbidden foray into town. And yes, they'd found a lone child, and yes, Frederick brought it down while the others watched, and yes, Frederick was seen. He'd grown incautious with thirst, but that's no excuse.

"At least Frederick had the decency to draw the enraged townspeople away from our camp so that when he was caught, hours later, he was miles away."

"He traveled by day?"

The vampire smiled. Even the old man's daughter showed appreciation for the comment, or maybe it was just a play of shadows in the wee hours. "Thank you for your concern, Paul," Drake said. "But it was still an hour or so before dawn when our small scouting party saw the brave hunters drag Frederick back in chains, their hounds baying in triumph. We watched them from a copse of water oaks high on a hill overlooking the shabby town's mosquito-infested standing water and its tarpaper shacks. Underfed chickens squawked at the men's ankles as they struggled through the red mud. Truly a dreadful place. Chitimacha Bend had no jail, the nearest being in St. Martinville, the parish seat, so the townspeople decided on the earthen cellar of the general store."

Tolliver and his wife convinced Drake that they'd gone unseen— perhaps the only reason they were allowed to live. And, being certain that Frederick wouldn't turn the clan in, the master vampire retired for the day.

"Naturally," he said, "I checked in with him."

Paul stirred in a seat that had seemed comfortable when the endless evening had begun. "What do you mean, you checked in with him? You went back?"

Drake gave his host a sharp, penetrating stare. "I won't tell you all of our secrets, but we have ways of knowing things that you wouldn't even begin to understand."

"We have ways of knowing..."

Paul's eyes once more flitted to the second-story balcony beyond the doorway where one might listen in comparative secrecy.

However the feat was accomplished, Drake "saw" his old friend the following day.

"If there hadn't been so many men, so many dogs, he'd not have been taken. But fortune hadn't been with him and they now had him

David Searls

chained like an animal to a long stake pounded deep into the mud cellar floor. He'd been beaten and the hounds had taken a taste. That I'd seen earlier, but by this time I saw nearly flawless flesh as he lay there in the dirt, his clothing all but torn from his body. I could imagine the whispered rumors that would make the rounds of pig farms and chicken-wire shacks when Frederick's self-styled jailers viewed that smooth, unbruised face.

"His eyes were closed as I floated above him, but I knew he was watching my prostrate form as carefully as I watched his. Then my attention was diverted by the angry crowd gathering outside the makeshift prison, and I knew where events were leading."

Drake took a deep breath. Released it. And continued.

"The constable—I believe that was the term used for their part-time lawman—was more courageous and level-headed than I'd expected. I overheard him telling the crowd that he'd telegraphed the parish sheriff and had been promised a detail in the morning to pick up the prisoner. But as events progressed, it looked as though they'd arrive too late. I prayed to whichever gods consider the prayers of vampires that what was to happen would wait till sundown."

A single beep sounded, an electronic trill. Darby's confounded timepiece. Digital numbers in a soft shade of lavender indicated the time as, not twelve-thirty as he'd suspected, but one o'clock. He'd missed the half-hour trill and it had been a full hour since last he'd considered the time of night. His world—his very concept of physics and reality—had been upended in the space of an hour.

"Maybe our particular god was listening after all," Drake said, flippantly. "At any rate, I awoke at sundown figuring the issue was probably decided and my best friend most likely dead. But the daylighters who'd watched from the water oaks told me otherwise. I joined them under the moonlight to see that the crowd had tripled in size from the previous day as word had gotten out to the outlying farmers and travelers. They carried torches, lanterns and guns. They threw rocks and issued threats to the constable who'd refused to turn Frederick over to them, and I silently egged them on."

"What's that?" Paul said as a crack in the story brought in a little light from the outside world. "I guess I missed your last comment."

The vampire smiled. "No you didn't. You heard better than you give yourself credit. I egged them on. Keep listening and you'll understand.

"I said that the constable appeared to be a good and courageous man, and that's true to the extent that he held out all of that day and half the night before losing control of my chained friend."

"Couldn't you have...done something?" Paul asked.

"Could we have marshaled our forces and gone to war against these swamp creatures? Yes, perhaps. But our numbers had been so

170

depleted that the outcome against fists, clubs, shotguns and dogs would have been very much in doubt. But it mattered little at that point. Listen on.

"We watched and laughed softly among ourselves as we watched Frederick being dragged from his prison, pushed and shoved ahead of the crowd. His face had been freshly bruised and battered, all marks that would have cleared up in little time, but his expression of blind panic was sincere. Frederick had always been like that, a scurrying chipmunk of a man with an eye open for danger at all times, though less so after Amanda's death. That he could take the risks he took attested more to his lack of self-control than to confidence or courage.

"The swamp creatures pulled and prodded and shoved and dragged him onto the back of a horse and sallied forth like a midnight parade, heading straight toward us. At the last minute, we realized that they meant to use that very copse for their purposes, and we quickly slipped away to what we hoped was a safer patch of trees."

Drake paused. "You've probably seen lynchings dramatized in film or on television. But in real life it's much more barbarous. When the actors do it, they play the scene for outrage, for brutal, selfish justice. Real-life lynchings, on the other hand, provide the common man with an electric thrill unlike anything they've ever hoped to witness. They enjoy themselves immensely.

"Let me explain, Paul. The act of dragging Frederick out of the cellar and onto the back of a horse had stripped him of most of his clothing, giving the boys and even a handful of bold women accompanying the mob a thin and battered body to snicker and jeer at. They spilled him repeatedly from the horse, the children threw rocks and the men stomped him and dribbled foamy spit upon him.

"We were no longer smiling as we watched in hiding. This was too much. He'd survive, but it would take his body quite some time to heal from this outrage.

"The man with the foresight to bring a rope first used it like a bullwhip to lash at naked flesh till Frederick barely had the strength to writhe in pain. We heard discussions on the removals of his genitals, it being falsely assumed that the young victim had been murdered to satisfy Frederick's earthly lust. Fortunately, such retribution was considered indelicate with ladies and children present.

"I watched them, Paul," the vampire said, staring at a point beyond his host's head as if watching the offenders still. "I memorized every face and in my most carrying whisper ordered the vampires and daylighters in my charge to do the same. I vowed that we'd be back, and Frederick would lead the assault.

"In due time, the rope was slung over a low limb and the other end tied to the neck of their victim, whose blood and fear perhaps even the daylighters among us could smell from our position a hundred yards away. He had, at this point, been mounted again on the back of the horse. 'Play dead,' I whispered. We'd rehearsed this countless times, under Frederick's direction, but I didn't know how he'd act when the time actually came. If he panicked...

"But he didn't. He was perfect. His body twitched spasmodically, but he didn't overdo it. I felt it played well, as did the others. We released a collective sigh of relief and I accepted words of congratulations from the others. It sounds odd, but it seemed natural to be praised for the accomplishments of my partner, as he would have been praised for mine. We were like that, Paul. We'd been together for seventeen unforgettable years by then, in a relationship much deeper than lovers. I carried his thought and he carried mine. It was as if—"

The vampire interrupted himself with a low growl of annoyance. He drained his water glass and stared at it as if contemplating another. He leaned forward and placed the glass on the very center of the table, then looked up with eyes that glittered with rage.

"In the clear moonlight we saw the profile of his body, hanging limp and lifeless," said the vampire in a tone as slack as his friend. "'Perfect,' I told those around me, and together we watched someone in the crowd spray him from water with a bucket, apparently to make sure he couldn't be revived. Once more I sent him a mental reminder to stay still, stay still.

"Only, it was as though he'd forgotten all that we'd rehearsed. His body began to twitch again, to quiver, then to thrash violently at the end of his tethering rope as panic overtook him. Who knew? Maybe the cold water had been a shock to his system and had broken his self-control. He screamed. I heard him scream my name. 'Miles!' he said. Or tried to, through the rope constricting his words. Shocked at his outburst, I muttered for the fool to stay quiet. I didn't know."

"Didn't know what?" Paul croaked. His heart slammed his ribcage as all hope dwindled for the child-murdering night creature. Darby's goddamn electronic clock beeped again, but he ignored it.

"I smelled it in the wind moments later."

"Smelled what?" Paul demanded in a barely audible whisper.

"I told you these men and boys carried lanterns, didn't I? And torches."

"Gasoline," Paul whispered.

"Close enough. Kerosene."

"Kerosene," repeated the vampire's daughter, the single word a condemnation of all humankind like herself.

Miles Drake shrugged. "He became a torch. Frederick lit the night sky with his brutalized, cindering body and with his screams."

The old man—the creature—began to knead his knees with

gnarled hands as he'd done minutes or hours before.

Paul worked at almost physically pushing the lynching scene from his mind. He had to regain some semblance of perspective. "Yes, but...he was your friend, but...he did kill small children," he said with almost plaintive tact.

"Yes," the vampire boomed as he sprang from the sofa with the limber grace of a man half his apparent age. "Yes," he said again, pacing. "We must be perfectly candid here and acknowledge that the vampire Frederick Darrow did indeed suck the life from small children and drunks and low-life others and even from the occasional lady with purse. Yes, he was kind and loyal and a wonderful lifemate to my beloved daughter and a dear friend to me, but there was that bloodthirst thing."

The vampire strolled out of the living room and into the foyer and to the dining room across it. Paul followed meekly to find him cocking one leg on a straight-back chair. Drake twirled to face him.

"Remember this above all else, Paul. These are not fairly tales I'm telling you tonight. The good witches don't wear white and the evil ones black. You wish to deal with me, to confront me on a level you think you understand, as you dealt with our police chief. But let me tell you: I am no Bill Sandy. You have no comprehension of what you're up against." He flashed another yellow and brown smile. "And still there's so much to tell. Are you up to it, Paul? Would you like a beer, Paul? It might be a very long night."

Chapter Thirty-Three

He did. He very much wanted a beer, and Tabitha Drake surprised Paul by wanting one as well. The master vampire only drank more water as they returned to the living room and Miles Drake continued the long story of his longer life.

Frederick's agonizing death played havoc with Drake, left him yearning for his own oblivion. Maybe there really was a Hell on the other side, but there was one here as well. If that one was populated with Amanda and Frederick, it might have fewer torments than where he was stuck.

The clan fled Louisiana. Drake lost all memory of leading or being led, but they escaped. They traveled north for a hundred aimless miles before Drake was able to take command again. He'd arrived at a decision.

"Wait a minute," said Paul, vaguely irritated. "What about the lynch mob in Chitimacha Bend?"

Drake halted with the drinking glass halfway to his lips. He moved it to uncover a thin smile. "You want me to say that vengeance was mine. That we slaughtered to our hearts' content, don't you?"

"No, of course not. "I'm...curious, is all."

"You want revenge, Paul, because you've only heard our side of the story. My side demands retribution, but what if it were the mother of Frederick's final small victim telling the tale? Would you want your closure then, Paul?"

The vampire offered nothing more on this subject, and the story continued.

The clan was too ravished both physically and emotionally to do anything but flee. Day after day, night after night, their ranks thinned. Their emotionally numbed leader didn't even care when, despite his standing order, sharecroppers were harvested in Mississippi, children snatched from mountain shacks in Tennessee. But as they traveled, an idea formed.

"A new society, Paul. I talked it over with James Chaplin and Olan Buck and a handful of the others. John Tolliver was against it, of course. He opposes everything, but he's an excellent devil's advocate.

"The times had changed and the hunters had become the hunt. The days of plundering and pillaging and slipping into the night were numbered. We'd eventually all die, victim of automobile chases, telephones and newspaper reporters. We had to change. To evolve. To blend in to a civilized society."

"Babylon," Paul said, thinking that it had taken him a good deal of the night to comprehend even the smallest fraction of the vampire's history.

"Babylon," Drake echoed.

It wasn't their first chosen home. They settled initially in small towns in Tennessee, Ohio and elsewhere, but the locals always got too curious, too soon.

"It took us three more years of traveling and stopping and moving on before we discovered Babylon. In the meantime, we'd taught ourselves how to peacefully siphon blood from cooperative daylighters and, in an emergency, from a donated vein of one of our own.

"Oh, it's not the same at all," Drake said, shaking his head. "Life without the hunt is like eating without taste buds. Like seeing the world in black and white." He sighed. "It's vanilla, but it's survival."

In 1898, the Michigan town consisted of a feed store, a saloon and a handful of homes. Even then, the roads leading to it were dirt or gravel afterthoughts. The clan numbered just eleven vampires and eight daylighters by then, so it was relatively easy to fit in as a small, inoffensive religious sect.

"Babylon," Drake said, chuckling softly. "The name appealed to me from the first. *What a horror Babylon has become among nations.*" Drake winked. "Jeremiah forty, verse forty-two."

"Scriptures?" Paul asked, bewildered.

"Know the competition. The irony amused me. God cursed the Babylonians because they massacred and enslaved His Chosen. They were as accursed as us, I would like to think." Drake shrugged as if the joke might not be readily apparent to everyone. "As I say, it appealed to my sense of irony."

Paul rubbed his face. It was tingly, numb, covered in cobwebs. Thin grains of sand seemed to dig at his eyelids when he blinked. He heard tiny claws scratching at the front door. "Did you...what did you do with the locals?"

"Did I kill them, you mean? Massacre them like my Biblical predecessors? Some of them, I must admit. But not most. My intention, if you'll recall, was to fit in. And yet all you can imagine is murder. I married them." He grinned. "Well, not all of them, of course.

"The worst sin we committed in our town's early days was to cut a sickly calf from a herd or grab a dog. Our few poor daylighters must have looked a bit wan as our idea of transfusions took hold, but it kept down the crime rate. And we did something else. Something we'd never done before. We socialized. You see, it's much easier to introduce a spouse or lover to our non-traditional lifestyle than a total stranger, wouldn't you agree?

175

"By that time, I'd been what I am for twenty years. I was sixty-two years old, and still looked to be in my early forties. At worse, a couple years had been added to my appearance. The dramatic slowdown of the aging process is a powerful sales tool, Paul."

"I'll bet you had them lined up at the door," Paul replied dryly.

"You'd lose that bet," the vampire said, jumping to his feet. He paced the living room, dining room, sunroom. Paul could picture him out in the foyer, craning his neck up at the balcony that overhung it, both of them wondering at shadows up there. Drake returned to the family room, examined book covers, touched vases, studied his reflection in a mirror.

Yes, it showed.

"The key to our continued survival—and I can't stress this enough—was putting an end to the kind of violent activity that could bring attention upon us. Sure, we might feast on a lonely outsider now and then if we could be absolutely certain nobody would come looking, but for the most part we lived in peace and goodwill in our adopted community."

Drake returned to the sofa and settled into it like he meant to stay. "Can you comprehend the difficulty in refraining from such primal urges? No, of course you can't. You've never experienced bloodthirst, and I think the whole subject would be too gruesome for your sensibilities. What a madman I must seem."

Paul took his old seat and the vampire turned his head to confront him full-on, as if he expected to read the truth on his face.

"Well, so be it," Drake said after a moment. "I really should get points for good behavior because right now I can visualize you quite easily with your throat torn open. And yet, I can stifle my urges when it suits me to do so. Why? Because I'm strong, Paul. Because my desires are suborned to my superior will. Because I have age and maturity and discipline working to my advantage. So, to finally answer your question, while the daylighters might have been lining up at the door to be converted, we weren't indiscriminately opening that door."

The vampire rubbed his face as Paul had done earlier. Exhaustion perhaps catching up with him as well.

"There's another issue involved," Drake said. "A town needs daylighter activity to stay alive and to allay suspicion. What if you had driven into Babylon for the first time in the middle of the day and the streets were deserted, all the shades drawn? What would you think, Paul? How do you operate factories and sweep streets and run banks and answer phones only at night? I knew even a century ago that civilization would creep to our doorstep no matter where we holed up, so it was imperative that our town look and feet like every town in America—at least to the casual observer."

"Wait," Paul said. "I'm confused." For a moment, he'd been on the verge of comprehension, but now he had more questions than before. He took a healthy slug from his beer can and said, "If you're so cautious, how come you're practically dragging strangers off the highway and killing them in public?"

The vampire was on his feet even before the question was out. In three steps he crossed the room to pound his white fist on a wall. There might have been words in the snarl that followed, but they were incomprehensible.

"Keep it down," Paul ordered, as annoyed as he was chilled by the outburst. "There's a child upstairs trying to sleep."

The vampire turned. Sniffed the air like a dog. "I know. A woman, too."

Paul's hands fisted on the arms of his chair. He watched the vampire slowly relax until he leaned loose-limbed against the wall. His face, which had grown more mottled with his scarlet rage, faded back to a shade closer to normal for him. "The situation now developing," he said thickly, "is not of my doing."

"Purcell," said the nearly forgotten daughter, the name dribbling from her mouth like sour milk.

"Yes. Duane Purcell. It happened just four months ago. And now that I think of it, it *is* my fault. The problem, Paul, is that I'm too compassionate for my own good."

Laws, Drake had told his people on more than one occasion, must be obeyed, for the law is the heart of a civilized society. Those who'd remained with him after Chitimacha Bend gave him no argument for they were the most fiercely loyal. There were no major transgressors for more than a century.

Until the night Frank Dexter killed Duane Purcell.

"I believe John and I were bloodletting a rat at the time," Drake reminisced, "when James Chaplin blundered in to tell me in that officious manner of his that we had a situation. That's how James would have put it, too: *'We have a situation.'*

"The two daylighters had been feuding for years. I don't know why, and quite frankly I don't care. That was my downfall: not keeping closer tabs on my town. Anyway, I let James drag me to the Winking Dog Saloon, which is where, if anything tawdry happens around here, it will take place."

"My head reeled with bloodscent as soon as I walked in. Frank Dexter held a dripping knife blade, and that ocean of blood...he must have hit an artery.

"I'm going to use that bloodlust as a partial excuse for my foggy thinking. At least I didn't do like John Tolliver and Vern Chambers and

177

drop to my knees to lap the pooling liquid from the bare floorboards. But when I saw that the bloody mass at my feet was Duane Purcell, I wanted to celebrate then and there. White trash, Paul. Riffraff, as we called it in my day." He snickered. "Or at least one of my days."

The vampire wiped his mouth. "The point is, the entire Purcell clan should have been wiped out long ago. No loss."

But Purcell's mother had been called and by now she'd thrown herself down on the floor with her dying son, sobbing.

"He lived with her. Almost thirty years old and he still lived with his mother. Typical Purcell. But like I say, I'm too compassionate for my own good."

Since the town's daylighters were all converted as they matured and therefore expected to live exceedingly long and glorious lives, premature death was a particularly grisly prospect. The onlookers gaped in horror as the life pumped from the twitching man on the floor. Take him, the man's mother implored in the presence of the master vampire.

"Anyone who tells you that rules are made to be broken leads an undisciplined existence," said Drake.

"You converted him."

The vampire's eyes flashed. "I might as well have put a loaded gun into the hands of a disturbed child. I knew it was a mistake as soon as I'd done it. Even before. But that woman...she was relentless."

There was more to it than that, Drake admitted. With eventual conversion being the basis of the vampires' unwritten pact with the humans, there was no telling what affect an eyewitness account of that pact being broken would have. Anything from mass exodus to open rebellion would devastate the community.

After a review of the assault, it was determined that Frank Dexter had been provoked by Purcell and his friends, and since no permanent injuries had been sustained, the matter was officially closed.

"Then we heard rumor that Jason Penney and Gary Leckner, two cronies of Purcell's, were spending their days behind closed blinds and prowling the streets after dark.

"Naturally, I confronted Purcell and he apologized. He pointed out—quite correctly, though impertinently stated, as it turned out—that conversion of the young was not strictly forbidden in our community. We hadn't had to establish such formal laws before his kind came along. We'd always let common sense dictate that anyone under the age of at least fifty was too young to have the self discipline to assume such grave responsibilities."

Again, Drake stopped. He sipped water, almost daintily, and stared into the distance.

"I should have cut him down then and there, while I was still stronger than him. But the truth is, my killer instinct had been dulled over the years, and I took my time thinking about it. Trying to be fair."

The next rumor to befall the town was that Jason Penney had converted his teenage girlfriend, Patty Craven, and that she'd taken her younger brother, Ethan. Even as the master vampire went about his business of collecting and sorting through the evidence of the latest conversions, Purcell changed his strategy and began threatening, cajoling and bribing daylighters.

"Imagine a society, he must have told his listeners, where you don't have to be withered and senile and near death before joining the hunt. Eternal life, he would have promised, as only the young might enjoy it.

"Not everyone listened, I'm proud to say. Plenty reported back to me, but plenty didn't." Drake frowned at the memory. "Frank Dexter disappeared four months ago and hasn't been seen since. Four months ago, the conversions took up again, this time openly. They converted one officer on the police force, and the strangers started being pulled into town by the daylighter McConlon and a couple cops working for him. But first, McConlon got hold of some of the business owners and made them donate jobs as bait. Many, like my good friend James Chaplin, agreed out of fear. Others are looking toward their final reward."

Drake ran a finger along his mouth. "I don't know how Purcell did it, but that hayseed has somehow managed to set up a competing society right in the shadow of my own. If I were younger," he hissed, "this would not be happening."

"The outsiders...they're here to be hunted," Paul said in a hushed tone. "They're here for...harvesting?"

"It's an outrage," said Tabitha Drake as she teethed her empty beer can. "Sooner or later someone important is going to be taken, and then where will we be?"

And now Paul understood, as the vampire frowned his daughter to silence, why he'd been handled with kid gloves.

"If you must know," said Drake, "a few have already fallen victim."

"Doyle Armstrong," Paul shot back. "Judd Maxwell."

"Unfortunately, all it did was feed their appetites."

Paul sprang from his chair. "You have to stop them." He began to pace the room.

"I can't." Rheumy, yellow eyes followed him. "They're young, and too strong to be stopped without triggering a vampire war." He flapped his hand in a tired gesture. "They got out of control. I should have kept better track of them and I didn't. I accept responsibility."

Paul wheeled and faced the vampire. "You accept responsibility? They're killing innocent people and you 'accept responsibility?'"

179

The eyes, which had seemed so old and weak just moments before flared with white brilliance in an instant. "Watch how you talk to me, daylighter. Purcell and the others are problems. You, on the other hand, are an irritation."

Paul fell to his seat, breathless. He'd almost allowed himself to forget who—or what—he'd been addressing.

Drake said, "My purpose for coming here tonight was to let you make a rational, informed decision regarding the sale of your home. I've rambled some, but I'll now get to the point. I know you have business associates and relatives and friends and bankers and lawyers and accountants, all who'd raise more questions than we'd care to answer if you were to just disappear."

The vampire stared at an index finger before nibbling the ragged nail. "But you haven't made a new and powerful friend tonight, Paul. I haven't unburdened myself because I see you as a trusted confidante. Quite the contrary, I don't trust you at all. And yet, what choice do I have? You're bright and inquisitive and quite stubborn. You've made it abundantly clear to everyone who's tried to intervene that you have no intention of leaving Babylon without answers."

"So now you have answers," said Tabitha Drake.

"And now it's very difficult for us to let you go," said Drake.

Paul's bladder felt heavy enough to release and spill down his legs, and yet he hadn't the strength to attend to the problem. There were no fully formed thoughts in his head, just cloudy, abstract images of death and dread.

"There's one more tale to tell," the vampire said softly. This one—I swear it's the last—concerns the people who lived in your home. The McConlons? You know the brother, the bastard working for Purcell. Jeff and Andrea and their two lovely kids, I don't believe you ever met. They were in such a rush to leave. If you listen carefully to this final tale of mine, I think you'll find in it a valuable lesson.

Chapter Thirty-Four

Of all the laws governing the residents of Babylon, Michigan, those concerning population control were among the most seriously observed. Word would not seep out if no one *got* out.

While some worked in surrounding towns and even as far away as Detroit or Toledo, the town's dark secrets were guarded by the fact that emigration was strictly forbidden. The obvious problem with this decree was too many births and an absence of counterbalancing deaths. Even after annexing nearby farm acreage, not always voluntarily, civic leaders could foresee the town outgrowing all available expansion space.

To postpone a population crisis, the families of Babylon were limited to a maximum of two children.

"We're quite progressive," the vampire quietly boasted. "Condoms and a variety of female contraceptive options are widely available and inexpensive, and abortions are free and safe at Babylon Community Hospital. As a result, we've rarely had a problem."

Paul's eyes felt scratchy, prickly for the need for sleep. For the first time, he was struggling to keep up. "Rarely," he said.

The vampire's face grew more mottled. "Again, I was kept in the dark. The first I knew of the situation was Olan Buck telling me that the McConlons wanted special dispensation to have a third child. Such permission has never been granted, but I had Tabitha look into it."

"They'd already conceived. Apparently, the laws of the land are not meant for such as them," she spat.

A dark glance from her father returned the woman to her sullen silence.

Drake turned back to Paul, his white brows low over his eyes. "After careful consideration, I decided that making the one exception would only encourage disregard for the laws of logic that bind our society. The situation was handled firmly, but with compassion. An appointment was made for Mrs. McConlon at our hospital."

"The bitch never showed," Tabitha muttered.

"The next we knew, they were gone and the house was sold," said Drake, with all the hurt indignation of the offended party. "In a whirlwind of activity, they took off three weeks before you moved in."

Paul nodded. "The real estate agent said it was a highly motivated seller." Understatement of the year.

Very softly, the vampire said, "Oh, we know all about Savannah Easton."

"She's not responsible," Paul said. "We found the place ourselves, online, and she recommended against it."

"No matter. The house should not have even been on the market. There are certain things that area brokers have just picked up on without anyone having to hit them over the head with a hammer about it." Drake offered up a ghastly smile. "Or maybe that's exactly what we should have done."

The vampire scooted forward in the sofa and fixed his listener in his sights. "Here comes the part I want you to pay especially close attention to, Paul. It provides the moral that holds this entire long evening together. Listen carefully, please."

He could hardly do otherwise. Paul was snared in those twin beams under the thick set of brows.

"You and your lovely family moved in almost five weeks ago, and yet it's only in the last few days that we've begun to pressure you to leave. Why do you think it's taken that long, Paul?"

The long hours and the vampire's cool voice had nearly lulled him to sleep, but Paul managed to shake his head into wakefulness and provide a response: He had no idea.

"Of course not. It's because we had other things to do. Other activities occupying our time and attention and resources. Think hard, Paul. Why do you suppose it's taken this long?"

He would have liked to have said he didn't know, but he had a horrible suspicion. He broke eye contact with the vampire and stared at the bamboo floor. His voice rasped painfully in response. "You were hunting. The McConlons."

"Right!" the vampire shouted. "Right on the money, son!"

The only significant time Jeff McConlon had ever spent away from Babylon, Paul was told, was during a three-year Army stint (*"We don't discourage patriotism, Paul"*), and Andrea had never been out. Therefore, the fleeing family had few avenues of outside assistance.

"His brother is a rat's ass, but he came up with the identity of Jeff's best friend from his service days. With the help of our police department computers, we were able to track this man down to a trailer outside of Ithaca, New York. He was divorced and living alone on a weed-choked field owned by an alcoholic widower of a farmer whose own tumbledown home was at least a mile away. It couldn't have been a better setup."

The last thing Paul wanted was the details, but, as before, he couldn't stop himself. "You wiped out the entire family."

The vampire looked hurt. "You didn't give them enough money, Paul. You found your motivated seller and low-balled even their ridiculously low selling price in a terrible market. I'm not blaming you, just stating the facts. By the time their mortgage was paid off, well..."

Drake shrugged. Smiled, as Paul felt his stomach clench up.

"I'm sure young Jeff and Andrea planned to take the money and run for as long as it held out. Disappear for months, years, however long it took us to forget. That's easy enough to do with ample funds, but like I said, you found yourself in a well leveraged position. I think that's the term you use. I can picture the young couple, their two young children and a third on the way, trying to survive with nothing. No job, no plans and no experience on the road. That's the main thing, Paul: experience. It's taken me a century to learn that. But the McConlons had this one friend in the whole huge, scary outside world, so where are they likely to end up?"

Paul wanted the night to end, for dawn to break and the new sun to shatter either the vampire whom he'd invited into his family's home or his own delusion about the old man's power.

"I'm picturing Andrea protesting her husband's plans," Drake went on. "She'd tell him that it was too obvious, too risky. But Jeff would tell her that it'd been several weeks and that it looked like the town had forgotten them. Now, he'd probably know otherwise, but he was without options, Paul, so it was a lie he had to pull over both of them. Can you picture it, Paul? Can you see how two intelligent people can delude themselves out of a sense of desperation?"

The vampire chuckled. "Jeff and Andrea grew up here. They should have known we'd never give up looking for them."

Paul's system felt burned out on spent adrenalin. Listlessly, almost beyond caring, he said, "So you people slaughtered the entire family in the trailer home."

"And their host, too, of course. "But you're getting ahead of the story."

The family had most likely chosen such a desolate spot to avoid prying eyes, and yet it worked just the opposite.

"It was such a remote hideaway that we were able to take our time, set the stage. Our daylighters had preceded us to stake the place out, and I arrived with a handful of old men after sundown. We'd traveled by night and stayed at a nearby motel, but not so near that we'd be remembered, you understand. I recall it being such a lovely, cool evening that we could barely pull ourselves out of the tall grass where we'd been talking politics and philosophy and waiting for the children to be called in.

"The young ones, you see, had been playing outside for hours, tussling in the dirt and weeds under a full moon, chasing fireflies, just being kids. They looked lightning-quick, much too swift for old men like ourselves. We couldn't risk them flitting away in the dark, which is why we waited so patiently.

"But finally bedtime arrived—much too late for children so young,

183

but that's just my old-fashioned opinion—and the whole family came together one last time."

The vampire's eyes twinkled. "Paul, I don't think you have a stomach for the details, so I'll spare them. But there is one thing I must tell you."

Drake shimmied his hips so that he edged farther forward on the sofa. His eyes looked painfully red-rimmed, as though the bright fires within had burned holes through his lenses. "Since Mrs. McConlon had missed her appointment at the hospital, I performed the surgery myself. No charge, in keeping with our community's generous family planning tradition." The vampire again gave up that yellow and brown grin. "It was a most tender meat."

Then he glanced at his watch and said, "Look at the time."

Father and daughter rose together and headed into the foyer. Paul found himself, as though floating rudderless, following them to the front door.

It was all a lie, he told himself. A dark and mad parable designed to strike fear in his heart. And yet he knew the truth was otherwise.

"I probably don't have to spell out the lesson to be learned from all of this, but I'll do so anyway."

The vampire's voice boomed from his powerful chest, under the cathedral ceiling. Though not quite as tall as Paul, the thing seemed to look down at him with eyes that had yellowed with age, irises wide and shiny with exhaustion. He looked like a time-ravished old man who'd stayed up too long.

"We recognize the irrationality of killing you for what you've learned about us, so we must trust you to keep our dark secrets. And yet I trust no one, so hear me now: If Babylon is to be destroyed by you, there's no place to hide that we won't find you. We want you and your lovely family—your attractive young wife, Darby—I'm sure there's a story there—and your beautiful son, Tuck—to accept our generous offer for your home. We want you to take your capital gain and move quickly and quietly. But talk to Police Chief Sandy rather than Savannah Easton to complete the transaction. I shouldn't think the whole process would take more than three weeks. We'll cut through the red tape."

"Why not Savannah?" Paul asked quietly as his heart juddered in his chest.

The vampire pulled open the door to the night. "You know the answer to that, Paul."

He stepped out, setting off an alarm of squealing rodents. Paul could see dozens of the plump night shadows slithering across the vampire's feet, dragging long tails in their ponderous wake. Drake cocked one leg and launched a kick into the ribs of one. It cracked like a hardshelled nut, and Paul could hear its breath wheezing from ruined lungs.

"Damned things," the vampire said with an absence of heat. He spread his arms to indicate the creatures just out of reach of his long legs. "When my ego is running dangerously high, Paul, I'll glance down and see my most fervent disciples." He issued a tired chuckle. "That always puts me in my place."

Chapter Thirty-Five

"Did you—?"

"Yes," she hissed, flying down the stairs. "My God, he must be insane. There's got to be—"

"Shush," he warned. "Don't say anything. We don't know what he can pick up or how he does it."

"That's right, Paul." Darby kept coming until she stood before him. She looked up, her eyes raging with a fire that seemed as lethal as anything the vampire had shown him. "We don't have any idea what that thing sees or hears. For all we know, he's already aware of what we have in mind. And then what, Paul? What do we do if he knows?"

Paul checked the door. He'd locked it, of course, when the vampire and his daughter left, but he checked again. "I don't know," he said.

He felt utterly defeated by the night, by a century of tales.

"You don't know." She spoke in a slow, heavy whisper. "You don't know, and yet you invited that thing into our home." Her voice turned to a strained rasp, a shout without volume. "Then we have to stop, Paul. We can't go on with it. You heard what happened to that other family."

The windows at each wing of the entry door were without curtains, and now the glass looked too inviting, too black with intrusive night.

"I can't," he said finally. "I can't just leave those people."

He was trapped. Every thought, each plan was blocked by those two competing nests of vampires in which he still didn't allow himself to fully believe, and by the fate of the people in the Sundown Motel. And, more than anything else, by his wife and child in the house with him.

"I can't," he said again. "I won't leave them. We're relatively safe compared to them. We have to go through with it."

Darby continued to glare up at him, but at least she didn't ask him if he was sure that they'd be okay.

So he didn't have to lie.

Part Three

War

Against the walls of Babylon raise a signal, make strong the watch; post sentries, arrange ambushes!
Jeremiah 51,12

There will be weeping there, and gnashing of teeth...
Luke 13:28

Chapter Thirty-Six

Sunday night, all hell broke loose at the Sundown.

Later, after they'd buried the dead in a shallow grave, Todd followed D.B. through a door behind the counter in the motel office and into Mona Dexter's living room.

The air was frosty as the Sundown's only working window unit hummed contentedly behind a fluttering pair of drapes. In a bookcase filled with knick knacks and on tables and a fireplace mantle with no fireplace—just a basket of tall dried flowers where the flames should be—were framed photos of Mona and a man with a graying beard.

"You can take a shower, take your stuff off if you want," she told him, her voice still tight.

Todd shook his head.

She took another look at his bloody clothing and said, "Well, no offense, but..." She led him to a small love seat she hastily covered with plastic dry cleaning bags. "The furniture's kind of new."

D.B. sat next to him, uncomfortably close. There was a much longer couch on the other side of the coffee table, but no plastic.

At the top of the "L," before the room took a hard right toward a doorway that seemed to lead to the kitchen, was a round wooden table with spindly legs and four blue placemats. As he sat placidly in his plastic-covered seat, Todd wondered whether she'd been expecting three guests for her next meal or if there were four settings merely because there were four chairs.

"We want answers, Mona," D.B. said. His demand began on a firm note, but ended with a slight hitch that betrayed his tamped down panic.

She'd changed into a robe, but her black hair was still damp from the shower she'd taken immediately following her part in the evening's frenzy. She'd gotten all the blood out, it looked to Todd.

As he inspected her, she did the same to him. She took in his gouged shoulder, then his drained face. Her eyes were a warm shade of brown.

Todd couldn't help thinking about her eyes. And about her indigo blue place settings and the chill of her air conditioner and the way D.B.'s arm hairs touched his and the sweaty, wrinkled feel of the plastic dry cleaning bags beneath them. He couldn't seem to focus his thoughts on vastly more important issues, no matter how hard he tried.

And that was a good thing. There was much he hadn't the strength to confront.

"Your shoulder," she said.

He wet him mouth. Shrugged. "Rat got me."

She nodded. "Sure. Lots of them. You got nibbled on your arm and wrist, too, I see. Damn things got most of the others, too. I passed around a first aid kit and disinfectant. But that one on your shoulder. I noticed it before you dressed it. It looks...different."

"It was a rat."

"Okay," she agreed quickly. But her eyes kept returning to it.

Todd had spent the earlier part of the evening squatting in front of a fire and scowling at the tops of oaks and sycamores in the ravine below, miffed at D.B. for not stationing him by the pool. At least there he could dip his feet in the stinky water to cool off some of the night heat.

The smudgy flames were supposed to ward off vampires. Todd supposed they might do the trick since no vampire in his right mind would come close to their damn bonfires when the outside temperature was still running in the heatstroke zone even with the sun gone.

Jermaine said, "I dunno, Pete. Just 'cuz movie vampires don't like fire don't mean the real ones react the same way."

"Don't mean they don't." Ponytail Pete piled on more dry pine needles and the fire crackled with fresh life and less smoke.

"Vampires," Duke Gates snorted.

He'd never gone away as promised. Todd could only guess how Kathy Lee had gotten him to change his mind. Now the kid cradled his nine millimeter Mauser on his knee as he sat Indian-style, staring into the flames.

"I don't like it here," Tonya Whittock said in a voice as soft as a night breeze. She stared off into the black woods that dropped before them.

"Ain't nothing to worry about," her husband reassured her, but none too loudly.

Todd thought about Joy and the girls, locked into a single motel room with orders to only open up to a knock that came in a prearranged code. He hadn't even taken a room key with him, in case it should somehow fall into enemy hands.

Something rustled in the brush.

"Jesus," Jermaine said, gasping. He whipped his Smith & Wesson .38 into a two-handed shooter's stance aimed at the black trees.

As Todd and the others sprang away from the noise, Duke hiccuped with quiet laughter. "Look at y'all. Jermaine's all 'ain't nothin' to worry about,' and now look at him. He's gonna blow holes in the first tree branch that moves."

"Shut up," Todd snapped and, surprisingly, the kid did.

Night is never still. Todd heard twigs snap, creek water run and the breeze—he hoped to God it was the breeze—rustle the trees. Deer and other lightfooted animals skittered over deadfalls while bats flitted low overhead. Insects screamed for love and sparse traffic sounded invisibly through the town beyond the woods.

"What is it?" Jermaine whispered to Todd.

He had no idea what he was supposed to be listening for. The others, particularly the Whittocks from downtown Detroit, seemed to think of him as some West Virginia mountain man, able to identify insects by their mating calls and a mammal by its footprint. In reality, he'd spent his nights in bars and bowling alleys or at home vegging in front of the TV like everyone else. He hadn't camped out since Boy Scouts, and hadn't liked it then.

Now, everything he heard in that dark ravine was a threat.

He shuddered at the memory of Jim Zeebe in his garage, and those hungry cops outside his jail cell. He knew exactly how bad it could get out there.

"It's nothing," he told Jermaine, maybe lying. He pawed sweat from his face and said, "Musta been a squirrel or rodent or—"

"Rats are rodents," Tonya whispered. "And according to Denver Dugan, rats hang out with vampires."

"And he's the expert," Todd muttered.

"What's that?" Ponytail Pete was pointing an unsteady finger at a spot in the woods below them.

The spot looked to Todd no less black that everything else down there. He peered intently at the dark and was about to chew Pete out for scaring everyone when he saw it.

"Eyes," Tonya whimpered.

"I don't know," Todd said, barely breathing. He shivered, chilled by the shirt plastered to his skin.

Twin dots of light that flickered like tiny white-hot flames.

"It might be eyes," he reluctantly agreed. Reflecting moonlight, maybe.

Jermaine whispered, "Another pair," and this time Todd had no doubt. More white-hot eyes, and now the others were hoarsely pointing out pinpricks of light in several places in the ravine. The lights moving slowly, steadily uphill.

"Stay cool," Todd said with a calm he could barely muster. "They're too close-set and low to the ground to be human."

"Yeah...rats," Tonya whispered.

Todd said, "Stay close to the fire and they'll leave us alone."

Which was when he learned just how little he knew about the subject.

191

Chapter Thirty-Seven

The first thing he later recalled was the way Duke Gates scrabbled away, pushing off, crablike, elbows and feet in motion, moving him quickly away from the fire. Todd wanted to warn him to stay close, but all at once he had his own problems to deal with. Lots of them.

The first one landed softly in his lap, knocking him onto his back. The weight of its fat, hairy body sent dull pain settling into Todd's stomach and groin. It smelled like the dead dog Todd had found in a ditch near his home when he was a kid, but it was the sharp little teeth gnashing at the clothing protecting the soft of his belly that disturbed him most.

He felt his bruised groin involuntarily retract, away from the teeth. He arched his back to keep his face out of peril as the rat scrambled up his torso. The hands he flung up in front of his face drew quick stabs of pain. Grabbing the attack rat in a loose grip, its teeth already pink with his blood, Todd flung it like a cow chip back down the ravine.

"Goddamn," someone squealed in high-pitched male panic.

Shaky flashlight beams crisscrossed Todd's vision in drunken patterns. A muffled scream came from Tonya as three of the things tried to shimmy up her legs. Jermaine was beating Ponytail Pete about the head and shoulders with a thick stick in an effort to dislodge a snarling rodent that had hold of an ear.

Todd felt heat close to his face as Duke Gates swung a crackling tree limb snatched from the flames. With a quick fanning motion he swooped it low over an invading platoon of bright-eyes rodents. One of the creatures sprouted flames and screamed in near-human agony as it dashed for cover.

Todd threw himself on Tonya. He grabbed a sleek rat that had nearly won the race to her face. It wiggled from his grasp, slashing the back of his wrist. He dropped it, poked at it with an off-balance sissy kick that couldn't have done much damage, but sent it down the gully with a squeal of rage.

Todd could hear gunshots in the distance, the sounds coming from the front of the motel. He thought wildly, *Gunshots? How do you fight rats in the dark with bullets?* Then came the footsteps crashing through the underbrush, climbing up out of the ravine and coming for him.

Shadows. Large, bulky shadows. And the same guttural growls he'd heard when Judd Maxwell was taken down behind the post office building on Main View.

At least three human-shaped figures climbed out of the ravine.

They made odd rasping sounds as they charged the flailing Sundowners.

Todd rolled away as one headed straight at him. The figure froze in a predatory crouch, waiting for Todd to come to a stop. As he did so, he saw Tonya Whittock kick at the campfire, scattering ashes and flaming branches right at the crouching shadow. The thing stumbled backwards, grunting, as sparks grabbed its socks and bare legs.

It was the most ludicrous sight of the evening, the arthritic old vampire in shorts, black socks and preppy boat shoes jerkily dancing to put out his hot foot.

Something exploded, roared, and a red spot grew in the center of the elderly attacker's chest. Arms jerking, it crashed to the ground.

Todd rose shakily and watched more of the creatures scramble up and out of the ravine. He smelled burning flesh as campfire sparks took hold of another downed vampire's leg. More gunshots sounded in the distance.

The Sundowners were facing attack from all sides.

Duke Gates' Mauser roared again and again and again, three flat explosions that knocked a pair of charging vampires on their asses. One was flung back down the ravine while the other, a frail, white-haired woman, remained in a seated position, clutching her stomach and gasping for air.

A hand seized Todd's ankle, and his muscles froze rigid. It was the old fart with the shorts, black socks and gaping chest wound, but the carnage didn't look half as bad as before. On hands and knees, the night creature dragged Todd toward him with one unexpectedly strong arm. His mouth hung slack, displaying two rows of ragged teeth. From his throat came a growl of animal lust, a gurgle of pain and carrion desire.

Todd braced himself and lashed out to free his leg. The vampire's grip was loosened, but his other arm whipped out to lock Todd's ankle in a two-handed embrace. Then the first withered hand let go long enough to snatch a better grip just below Todd's knee, and in this way the vampire pulled itself steadily toward him.

Ponytail Pete struck like a placekicker, his running shoe making solid contact with the old vampire's face. Bones snapped, teeth flew, pink spittle sprayed the air from a suddenly slack mouth. The creature's snarl turned to a pitiful gargle, Todd momentarily forgotten. He scuttled out of the way as the vampire's hands explored its own ruined face.

Branches broke like rifle shots. The creature who'd been shot and launched into the ravine had laboriously regained altitude and now its head could be seen over the top as it clutched, with a muddy fist, a maple sapling that bent under its weight. Jermaine jogged several steps toward it to swing a charred log that made excellent contact with the thing's face. It toppled back into the ravine with a howl of injured fury.

The Mauser went off several more times, until the white-haired woman on the ground stopped twitching. Her bloody housedress covered her like a shroud, her spindly pale limbs grotesquely twisted beneath her.

Nothing else moved.

Todd heard the rhythmic, hydraulic hiss of machinery and realized it was him and the others, gulping air together in harsh, frantic gulps. Someone picked up a flashlight and its shaky yellow light outlined their terror. They bled from an assortment of tiny punctures. Clothing torn, faces streaked with sweat and dirt, eyes black with shock.

"They get you?" Jermaine gasped, bending to cradle his wife while his eyes never left the ravine.

Tonya shook her head, her spasming lungs choking on a more verbal reply.

"Bastards," Duke croaked, head craning and body twisting to see everything everywhere. The Mauser turned with him, the hammer locked back and ready for another assault wave.

"You did good," Todd muttered to him, not believing he'd said it.

"Damn right," the kid replied.

"What about the others?" This came from Ponytail Pete, who held the flashlight.

They seemed to realize together that the distant gunfire had ended. Then the muffled cries broke the night. Shocked Sundowners calling for help, pleading for the safety of loved ones.

"I gotta get back," Todd said. "Make sure my wife and kids—"

Someone screeched in a voice so high-pitched that at first he thought it was Tonya, but it wasn't. It was one of the men, and he never did learn which one. Todd saw their eyes first—Jermaine and Tonya, Duke and Ponytail Pete—wide and horror-struck, and Todd's world slowed so that he seemed to have all sorts of time to wonder what it was that had terrified them so.

Whatever it was, it was right behind him.

Before he had time to fully execute a turn, something crashed into the center of his spine, pile-driving him to the ground and punching the air from his lungs. Todd could hear a ruined jaw flopping open and shut close to his ear. He caught a sideways glimpse and found that the old vampire's mouth wasn't half as broken as he'd remembered it. The thing had recovered quickly.

They can't be killed, he thought, just before the thing sank its teeth into his shoulder.

Todd closed his eyes, kept them shut, didn't even much care when

Duke Gates' gun roared again and again, blasting his hearing to hell and running warm wet matter down his cheek and neck. The vampire bucked and was lifted off him by the force of the multiple blasts.

"Jesus, they keep getting up," Todd heard Ponytail Pete say. All sounds were bass-heavy, muffled in cotton, the upper ranges lost in the incessant ringing. "What're we gonna do if we can't keep 'em dead?"

Todd still kept his eyes shut, rode out the ringing. He remembered slipping his dad's new Buick out of the garage one night, releasing the brake and rolling it down the driveway before getting shitfaced with his friends and wrapping it around a telephone pole. He'd kept his eyes sealed the next morning on that occasion, too, in the impossible hope that when he opened them again the old man's Le Sabre would be unmarked and back in the garage where it belonged.

"Hey man," said Duke. "You okay?"

He opened his eyes. His cheek nuzzled black grass. He smelled the rich, wet aroma of the neglected lawn, but also the acrid scent of gunpowder, the sour odor of body sweat and the metallic tang of blood. He felt a solitary tear trickle from one eye and roll into his ear. And in the distance the voices, drawing nearer.

"Todd, you all right?"

Tonya dropped a warm, sticky hand onto the back of his neck, a hand that shook in delayed reaction to her wide-awake nightmare.

The vampire lay motionless on the grass and weeds at the edge of the ravine, its skull as shattered as a stolen pumpkin.

Todd nodded slowly, though it was a motion that would be difficult to see. He heard running footsteps drawing near and rose to his feet to see a biped shadow approaching fast. Duke had his Mauser pointed, Jermaine a burning torch cocked over one shoulder. Tonya said "Don't," just as Pete took aim with his flashlight and the shadow turned into Carl Haggerty.

"Over here, there's five of them," Carl shouted to someone out of the light, waving a smoldering log like a beacon.

Jermaine asked what had happened elsewhere, and Carl rattled on about rats and vampires and gun battles, a tale that, for all its familiarity with their own situation, Todd had a hard time following.

"We kept hitting them and they kept coming," Carl was saying, but Todd found that he could repeat the words verbatim without fully comprehending the message.

He couldn't concentrate, couldn't form or hold a thought. Couldn't care. His shoulder throbbed. He felt warm drool form a trail from the corner of his mouth to the end of his chin. He shuddered, gasped, sobbed.

Tonya Whittock laid a hand on his undamaged shoulder, but didn't seem to know what to do when the sobbing didn't stop. "I don't

195

think no one got killed," she said, as if that addressed his concerns.

"The goddamn thing's still moving," someone called out hoarsely, and that's what cut Todd out of his personal fog.

He leaped to his feet to watch with the others as the ancient vampire stirred yet again. It was on its back, flailing its wrinkled limbs like an overturned turtle. The old woman who'd taken a bullet in her chest had crawled into the ravine and they could hear her stumbling away.

"You can't kill them," Todd said with listless calm.

"You're not doing it right."

If motel owner Mona Dexter had been a vampire, they would have all been dead. No one knew she'd joined them until she spoke. "You have to take more permanent action," she said.

On her hip she balanced a long object that suddenly roared to life. She advanced slowly on the wounded vampire, holding her snarling chainsaw in a two-handed grip as gasoline fumes filled the still night air.

The vampire rose on two elbows to utter a growl that changed to a squeal of panic as she kept coming. A plea heard even above the gas-fueled roar of the chainsaw.

"No, no, no, get away," he screamed.

Yes, it now possessed a human pronoun in Todd's mind: *he* rather than *it*. The old man began to crawl, inching his broken body toward the edge of the ravine. Pleading for his life as the motel owner advanced. Twin flashlight beams picked him up along with the red smear of blood that trailed him.

"Jesus, no," he cried out shrilly.

Under the vampire's screams and the roar of the two-cycle engine, Todd heard what sounded like a foot grinding eggshells into cement: the vampire's cracked skull shifting back into place.

She kept coming. The vampire made a weak grab for her foot, but she shook him off easily.

"Let me live," he screamed, throwing a hand up in front of his face as Mona Dexter swung like Paul Bunyan taking down a tree.

The blade caught the old man under the chin, immediately snarling up in muscle, bone matter and tendons. The screams ended in a short bleat as the old vampire lost his windpipe in a spray of blood. The chain slowed momentarily as it tangled up in the wrist bone of a defensively thrown hand, but Mona worked her way past the obstruction. Blood and chunks of unidentifiable organic material so gummed up the works that the saw nearly stuttered out before rallying through the wet congestion like a mower through high weeds. The overtaxed motor whined as the saw shot a fine mist at the dark sky. It had even more difficulty cutting through the spine at the base of the neck, and finally did throttle out as Mona Dexter tore up ground beneath the dead man's head.

She wrestled the silent chain free and stepped back.

"That's for Frank," she said.

Gore clogged her tool, hair and clothing, but the cut was so clean that at first the vampire's head still seemed attached, to hang only slightly askew on the vampire's shoulders.

"Gross," Duke Gates said.

"James Chaplin," Mona said, panting heavily. "He always was an arrogant prick."

The motel owner's expression soured as she primly scraped from her blouse the worst of the creature's spilled body matter. She looked up to fasten her eyes on the horrified cluster.

"We have to talk," she said. "I'll see a couple of you in my living room in a half hour. It'll give you time to bury this thing and me a chance to take a shower and wash my hair. I hate this shit."

Chapter Thirty-Eight

"We want answers, Mona," said D.B., back in the woman's apartment behind the motel office after the head and body of the unfortunate James Chaplin had found home in the loose soil by the creek bed.

"Sit down," she said.

Several Sundowners claimed to have killed attacking vampires, but only Chaplin had stayed that way. For their part, the Sundowners considered themselves as lucky at having suffered not a single casualty more serious than rat bites.

Todd tenderly rubbed his shoulder. He and Joy had cleaned, sterilized and dressed it earlier. He stared with the dullest interest at the tidy apartment. Done in various shades of pastel, it looked as cool as it felt. There was a Navajo rug on the floor, a long couch and, on the other side of a marble table, the plastic-covered love seat anchored by D.B. and himself.

She lit up without offering to share with either of them. Her hand shook as she leaned her cigarette on the edge of a copper ashtray.

Mona had wrapped herself to the neck in a thin robe that couldn't help emphasizing her breasts. She wore a white motel towel like a turban, tied in that complicated way only women could do. With a second towel draped loosely around her shoulders, she blotted her face as if she still felt the blood and brain matter and flesh particles that had clung there just a half hour before.

"Tea? Beer?" she offered.

They shook off the suggestion, but she bounced up again, evidently to prepare something for herself while the men waited in the love seat. Todd could feel the other man's arm hairs lightly tickling his own, and kept trying to pull away from the sensation, but there wasn't room.

She came back with a tall, frosted glass. She held it for a moment against her cheek before setting it down without a sip. She towel-blotted more imaginary moisture from her face while staring at Todd. Not into his eyes, but at the point on his shoulder where his shirt was torn to expose a white bandage already showing some spotting.

"You got bit," she said, as if the subject was a new one.

"A rat." Again.

Followed by a silent standoff that only ended with D.B. saying, "Thanks for helping us, Mona, but we've gotta know what's going on. What the hell are those things, and whose side are you on?"

She tore her gaze from Todd's shoulder so she could glare at D.B. "Whose side I'm on." She studied the words. Puffed. Pulled the robe tighter as if chilled by the air conditioning.

Todd wondered why she didn't just turn the damn thing down.

"Whose side I'm on," she said again, making it neither question nor statement.

She looked away suddenly, aiming a finger at one of the framed photographs of her with the broad-shouldered, bearded man, both of them dressed for someone else's wedding. The bride was in the background, hugging an older man. Her father? Whatever. Where the hell was this going? Todd wondered.

"If anyone's, I'm on his side," she said. "Frank Dexter. No one's idea of a saint."

"Tell us," D.B. said.

She stood to move a curtain from a window. "You have guards posted out there?"

"Yeah," said both men together.

They'd spent the last half hour rallying the troops. Todd had checked in on his family and found them playing Old Maid, only Joy's eyes showing the strain. Duke Gates, so brave during the firefight, had flatly refused to leave the room he was sharing with Kathy Lee to take guard duty, and had sworn he'd be gone by morning.

Mona nodded. "Good. They lost one of their own, so that should keep them away for the rest of the night. They're not used to death. Their own, I mean. The concept's even more horrible to them than it is to us since they're so much closer to immortality. So I don't think they'll come right back, but you can't tell. It's better we keep a lookout."

"We?" D.B. asked. "So you really are with us?"

She smiled. A sad smile. "I was scared before. Still am." She examined her hands. "Can't believe I really did it, but it felt good after what they did to Frank."

"Frank was..." D.B. began.

"My husband. A loudmouth, cocky, arrogant son of a bitch. Best-intentioned and dumbest thing he ever did was try to rid the town of Duane Purcell."

It came in fits and starts. She got easily sidetracked, sometimes contradicting herself, other times spicing it up with imagined dialog. Things got especially confusing as Todd's attention kept drifting to his torn shoulder and ragged thoughts he couldn't escape. But even with all the detours and roadblocks and unmarked highways, Todd was able to piece together the story.

Frank Dexter's family had owned the Sundown Motel since the 1940s.

199

"The town vampires never objected to overnight guests, truck drivers and the like. They pumped dollars into the community without hanging around long enough to get suspicious."

It was becoming so easy to discuss vampires. Like condoms and vaginas, it was a once taboo topic that could now be raised in polite company.

Frank and Mona, the story went, had been married for seven years when they assumed control of the motel upon the conversion and retirement of Frank's parents. That had been four years ago if Todd got the chronology right.

Everything had gone well except for the Friday and Saturday nights when Duane Purcell came to unwind with his hoodlum friends.

"He and Jason Penney and the others would use the long drive and the parking lot to drag race," Mona said, staring intently at the Navajo rug under her bare feet. "Or they'd check in with some drunk-ass farm girls and keep us up all night."

Frank and Mona would usually end up in a fight because he'd want to throw the troublemakers out while his more pragmatic wife knew they literally couldn't afford to take such a stand. As a destination for travelers, the town was practically off the map. It had gotten so that Purcell's raucous business was all but the mainstay of their survival.

And there was more to it than economics. Mona shrank from the thought of confrontation. "I know I make them sound like a pack of unruly teenagers, but these 'boys' are closing in on thirty. Jim Zeebe's well into his forties."

She blotted her face again. "The way I see it, the dayligbers of this generation are a dangerously impatient lot. They see their lives stretching so far into the future that they've lost all ambition, all enthusiasm for day-to-day existence. They're guaranteed power and centuries of life, but they can't cash in that chip till they're old and useless. At least that's the way they'd see it. They see a bunch of old men holding them down. Old men who commanded much more respect and awe in the old days. The young ones won't wait any longer, and that's why I think this town's about ready to explode."

Todd's attention kept drifting to the dull pain deep in his right shoulder. Joy had helped him wash the wound and all of the tinier punctures, but he'd felt a compulsion to splash more alcohol into it in an attempt to burn away whatever ghastly poison might be coursing through him.

He tried following the conversation while mentally inventorying his body's sensations: heart beating at about normal speed...breathing unconstricted...no pain beyond the expected soreness...body chilled by the air conditioning but not numb. No alien sensations of any kind.

200

Some agitation and distraction, but that didn't seem at all unusual under the circumstances.

D.B. nudged him.

"I'm fine," Todd blurted, subconsciously aware that Mona had asked whether he was feeling alright.

"We've been through a lot," D.B. explained for him. "So tell us what happened between your husband and Purcell."

"Ah," she said.

Frank was a fighter, a carouser, an older version of Purcell himself. He'd overstayed a trip into Detroit with several of his bar buddies the night four months ago when Purcell, Jason Penney and Penney's girlfriend, Patty Craven, spent their last night at the Sundown.

"Naturally, they were drinking," Mona said. "The Craven girl was already soused, ragging Jason from the moment they checked in. I heard bottles clanking in a grocery bag they made no effort to conceal, and knew it was going to be another long Friday night. Especially with Frank gone."

There were no other booked guests that May evening, so the partying was unusually loud even for Purcell. Mona heard thrash metal pounding from speakers, loud voices and shattering glass as she marched over to confront the problem.

"They hadn't brought a radio, so they'd simply cranked up Purcell's car stereo and opened all the car and room doors so they'd hear it."

Some incoherent argument could be heard from fifty feet away. They didn't take well to Mona's stern suggestion that they lower the volume of music and conversation alike.

"There were words," she said, shrugging into her iced tea. She sucked a frail cube, swishing it around in her mouth before daintily plopping it back onto the surface of her drink.

"My worst mistake," she said, lifting her gaze to her visitors, "was telling Frank about it the next day. I don't know, maybe I was angry at him for leaving me alone all night. Or looking for my big strong man to defend my honor." She chuckled, a dry sound resembling a cough. "After telling him everything, I told him to just forget it." Another dry cough of a chuckle. "Yeah. Right."

"What happened?" D.B. asked her gently when it looked like the rest of it wasn't coming.

"Okay," she said, and went on with hardly another pause to tell how a drunken argument in the Winking Dog Saloon the next day escalated into a knife fight, a dying man and a last-second intervention by the master vampire.

"Miles Drake couldn't stand Purcell, but he saved him anyway. It's town politics and some misguided sense of responsibility on the old man's part."

She let out a heavy breath and seemed to consider wrapping it up. "First thing Frank said when he got home that night was that he was dead. Doomed. Drake had turned Frank's worst enemy into something that, for all practical purposes, couldn't be killed. Everyone knew it was the wrong thing to do, but who could tell that to Drake?"

She let out another long breath. "That's the problem with dictators. There's no one to warn them when they fuck up."

The knifing was called justifiable, and Purcell was told to go in peace.

"Frank begged me to leave Babylon, but I talked him out of it." Mona waved her glass. "This motel, this town, these people, it's all we had. What were we going to do, slip out one night with a couple suitcases and spend the rest of our lives looking over our shoulders? Sleeping under bridges? Anyway, Drake had given us his word that we wouldn't be bothered." She set her glass down on the table. "Which shows you what their word is worth."

D.B. rasped two fingers through the stubble on his chin. "Drake should have taken out Purcell long ago, before it came to tonight."

Mona frowned, then her eyebrows lifted and lips spread in a vague smile. "I see. You think Purcell's responsible for tonight."

The two men leaned forward at the same time. Momentarily, Todd's shoulder was forgotten. "If not Purcell, then who?" he asked.

Mona ran a finger through the condensation on the side of her glass and sucked it dry. She seemed to be enjoying their confusion. "The man whose head we removed tonight is—or was—a genteel old fellow named James Chaplin. The town will be buzzing tomorrow with news that one of its leading vampire citizens bit the dust. His obituary will identify him as one of the oldest and dearest friends of town founder Miles Drake."

Todd's shoulder throbbed in dull waves. He wanted to stroke the wound, but that would bring attention to it, so he forced his hand to stay at his side. The woman's words had sunk in slowly, and not all the way. "So who are the bad guys? Drake's people or Purcell's?"

"They're vampires, for chrissake." She rapped her knee with a small fist. "You can't trust any of them. Purcell wants to hunt you folks down for sport and Drake's only opposed because it might draw attention to his beloved Babylon. You want my best guess about what happened tonight?"

Todd could feel D.B. nodding.

Mona lit a cigarette found in a robe pocket and leaned back. "I'd say Drake figured the sensible thing would be to wipe out everyone before Purcell pulls another stranger off the highway. Destroy any chance of you people spreading whatever you might have seen or heard. Bury the bodies where they'll never be found, and maybe in the process put a scare into all the obstinate young vampires."

She balanced her cigarette on the rim of her iced tea glass, stood and began to move excitedly about the small room. "It's cold logic from Drake's point of view. Purcell's faction is getting too strong for direct confrontation, so Drake proves he's still got it by ripping into a bunch of clueless daylighters. Low risk, high probability of success."

"Or so he thought," D.B. said, a grin nearly breaking through.

"They're getting old," said Mona.

"He got none of us and we took out one of his best lieutenants."

Lieutenants, for chrissake. To Todd, they sounded like kids playing war games. He figured it was pretty easy sitting on your ass discussing vampire politics and military strategy when you didn't have monster spittle coursing through your bloodstream.

"So why'd you help us tonight?" he asked the woman.

She thought about it for a very long time. "I've hated the bastards ever since they killed Frank, but I kept it to myself. That's why I didn't come out of the office the time that cop who works for them—"

"Marty McConlon," Todd and D.B. said together.

She nodded. "Him. He's the main one. Anyway, one day couple months ago McConlon asks me for a key to Carl Haggerty's room when Carl was bunking with the other black guy at the time. Doyle something. Or something Doyle. I gave it to him—what else could I do? Never said a word. Let everyone think the poor guy had taken off when I knew different." She took a tiny sip of tea. It must have mostly been ice water by then. "I was paralyzed, like everyone else. A lot of us have lost confidence in Drake's ability to protect us, but we've not tried saving ourselves. When I revved up that chainsaw, though..."

She stared dreamily into the distance as she groped for words she couldn't seem to find. Then she shook her head sharply, ending the search.

The silence gave Todd too much time to think. His numb mind was drifting into dark places he didn't want to go.

Mona said something else, rescuing him from those crevices. Todd was suddenly aware that he was alone with the woman. He heard D.B. noisily splashing urine wherever the bathroom was located.

"What?" he asked blankly.

"I asked if you told your wife about it. At least *she* should know, don't you think?"

"She knows about the rats," he answered too quickly.

"I'm not talking about that." She stared at him, seemed to wait him out.

He stared sullenly back until she dropped her gaze.

"Alright," she said. She seemed on the verge of saying more, but D.B. returned.

"Todd, you and me better make sure no one's fallen asleep and that the perimeter's still secure."

His friend was still playing war games, but for once Todd was glad to do as directed.

Outside, he smelled fresh cut grass again, and tobacco smoke and the brackish swimming pool water. He watched late-season fireflies, the most desperate of bachelors, send out weak pick-up signals, and saw cigarette embers in the clean night air. He heard the comforting murmur of human voices and thought of his wife and little girls locked away, safe from the vampiric night.

I'm alive, I'm alive, I'm alive, he told himself, an exuberant thought that seemed to lead nowhere.

Chapter Thirty-Nine

Darby and Paul shared whispers till dawn, Tuck fast asleep on the mattress they'd dragged into their bedroom.

We can't go through with it, she kept insisting. Not after hearing what happened to the previous owners of their home.

It's exactly because of the McConlons that we have to stay with it, he'd replied. The slaughter had proved what vicious, merciless—and relentless—creatures they were up against. Drake and his people weren't going to forgive and forget, no matter what promises the Highsmiths were told.

But that was night talk. At daybreak, with the sun peeking in the window spaces that hadn't been covered with bedsheets during the night, things looked different. Not better, but maybe more manageable.

Paul kissed his wide-awake son ferociously and told Darby to lock the door behind him. She seemed better in the first light of day. Like him, more resolved. She hadn't wanted him to leave, but understood his need to see the Sundowners before they left for work.

"Be careful," she told him.

The front lawn winked with dew. The orange morning light bathed the town in a pattern of light and shadows that resembled dusk, and yet unmistakably reflected daybreak. The town looked new and innocent in first light, but Paul knew how deceptive appearances could be in Babylon.

He hoped to find a pot of strong coffee brewing at the Sundown Motel.

At first glance, the place looked as still and serene as the early hour suggested. But as the silver Lexus padded up the long drive, Paul spotted Tonya Whittock leaning against a second floor railing and following his progress with binoculars. He watched as she made an arm signal. Seconds later, the big old guy, Denver, tilted a scoped rifle at him in an expressionless salute from his station under the stairs to the second floor. And as the Lexus drew to a stop under the carport in front of the office, the gaunt Sundowner with the ponytail and bad teeth sidled up to the car from nowhere and indicated with the anachronistic cranking motion of one hand that Paul should roll down his window. Since the man's other hand rested a heavily taped baseball bat on his bony shoulder, Paul was quick to power it down.

"Hi. Where ya going?" The man leaned in and flashed a broken-toothed grin.

Paul said, "Where's D.B. and Todd?"

"We had us some excitement here last night," he said cheerfully.

"Thanks, Pete. Good job."

Caught by surprise, the man with the ball bat jumped at the voice. Not exactly a natural as a perimeter guard, Paul thought.

It was D.B. coming around from behind his bat-wielding sentinel. He said, "Paul, why don't you leave your car here and come visit us in the office?"

He was greeted by a blast of overly cool air. The pastel room was small, but comfortable even with the presence of four people even before he and D.B. added to the congestion. Three sat at a table in a dining alcove, as if waiting for him. The plump but pretty blond woman, Joy Dunbar, gave him a tight smile and murmured greeting. Her husband scowled, as usual.

"Everyone remember Paul?" D.B. called out.

More murmurs. Mugs of coffee and bran muffins sat in front of them, mostly untouched. The black guy with the furrowed forehead glared at the food, but it was obvious that his thoughts were elsewhere. It did not look like a party in progress.

A petite woman in her late thirties was the only unfamiliar face. Throatily, she said, "I'll get you some coffee." Her attractive, heart-shaped face framed a pair of dark eyes and perfect lips. The few careless strands of gray added striking emphasis to her styled hair.

Paul took the metal folding chair that D.B. found and squeezed into a corner between Joy and the guy glaring at the muffins.

"Carl Haggerty," the black guy said gruffly, by way of introduction.

"Mona Dexter. I'm your hostess," the attractive woman supplied. Already returning from the adjoining kitchen, she set a mug in front of Paul. Despite her soothing tones, her hand shook enough to set off a ripple wave of coffee spill. "Shit. Sorry." She hustled back to the kitchen and wiped up the spill with a paper towel. "There's cream and sugar on the table."

Dexter, Paul thought. He'd heard the name.

"We're all a little wired after last night," D.B. explained.

"The bastards attacked us," Carl said. "Caught us by surprise but didn't do no major damage 'cept rat bites. We got one of 'em though. Got lots of them, actually, but only one stayed dead. Mona taught us how. Word of advice: don't piss off *that* lady."

It made little sense that way, but Paul got them to backtrack and tell a story he was able to piece together from the morsels of it thrown his way by everyone at the table.

"Purcell," he said, nodding, when everything seemed to be out. "I learned all about him last night."

The motel owner shook her head. "Whatever you learned was off-track. It was Drake's people coming at us."

"That's impossible," Paul said.

Her face hardened at the challenge. "I saw the body before I decapitated him. It was James Chaplin, one of Drake's oldest friends. Trust me, it was old people out there."

As heads nodded in vigorous agreement, Paul's mind reeled, his thoughts going ninety miles an hour and getting nowhere. "But I was *with* Drake last night."

All eyes fastened on him.

"Miles Drake and his daughter Tabitha came to my house. We talked through the night and he told me everything."

If he'd proven he could fly, he couldn't have startled them more. All around the table he saw open mouths and troubled eyes.

"You were with him," Mona repeated. "And he told you everything."

Paul gave them the quick version. Even heavily edited for time, it took nearly a half hour.

"Jesus Christ," said D.B. when it was finished.

Paul took his first bite of muffin. It had long ago cooled, so the pat of butter he placed on it just stared at him. His coffee had achieved room temperature, making it equally unpalatable.

Unexpectedly, someone laughed. A low, humorless sound.

Todd Dunbar had remained silent from the moment Paul had joined them. He looked terrible, his face pale, eyes bloodshot. His hair was dull and tangled, whiskers bluish on his bloodless cheeks. He sat hunched as if in pain or chilled.

Without looking up, he said, "So you're sitting there bonding with the master vampire while they're climbing all over our asses." He chuckled. "Our hero."

"I can't believe Drake would do that," Paul sputtered. "He was trying to keep the peace. Maybe he didn't know what the others were up to."

The firecrackers, he thought, but shoved it aside.

"He better have known or we're in even worse trouble than we think we are," Mona said. "Those old guys, Chaplin and the others, are Drake's most loyal followers. If even they've abandoned him, there goes the balance of power that's the only thing keeping us alive right now."

"Sounds like it's already gone if both sides now want us dead," said D.B.

Paul studied his unfinished muffin. He could feel the others waiting for something from him.

"Next time you want to be a bigshot, why don't you make sure you're talking to the right guy," Dunbar said, still glaring at the table.

"Hey, he just tried to help," said D.B.

Paul pushed his cold coffee out of the way. "I don't know what happened last night," he admitted, "but I still think it's important we stick with Drake. At least he's more rational than Purcell." He looked directly at Dunbar. "Or are you forgetting what happened behind the post office?"

"Drake's a vampire," reminded D.B. "That means there are definite trust issues involved."

"We can't trust a goddamn one of them," said Mona.

Paul sat in stunned silence, forced to confront an ugly truth. Drake had ordered the annihilation of the Sundown community even while chatting in the Highsmith home. He'd done it to eliminate the possibility of the town's secrets getting out, and would unhesitatingly do the same to Paul's own family if he ever felt the need and found the opportunity.

After a stunned, helpless moment, Joy Dunbar leaned in to Paul and said, "The vampire's daughter. You said her name's Tabitha. Right?"

Paul nodded absently, still lost in thought.

She tore off a bit of muffin with her fingers and brought it delicately to her mouth. "There's a Tabitha at the Complex, where I suppose I work now. Doesn't seem like a real common name."

She had Paul's full attention now. "Tell me what she looks like."

"I only caught a glimpse. Someone called her name while I was waiting to be interviewed. Tall and kind of plain. A little plump. Probably late forties, not too personable. It's her, isn't it? I can tell by your face."

Paul thought a moment. "What time does she get in to work in the morning?"

"I wouldn't know that. I just saw her for the first time. It was after five last Friday evening."

"It's Tabitha Drake," Mona said, nodding. "She works in the Water Department, which shows how brazen Purcell's people have gotten. They're filling bogus jobs right under the nose of Drake's own daughter."

So what time do you think she gets in?" Paul pressed.

Mona shrugged. "The Complex opens to the public at nine. So then or before. Why?"

Paul didn't know why it was important, but he filed it away.

"Your life should get real interesting now that Drake has spilled his guts," Dunbar said. Looking up briefly, his eyes seemed to twinkle with something approaching amusement. "At the motel here, we only had an inkling that something ain't right and look what he did to us. What do you think the odds are he's gonna let you just mosey on out?"

Paul stood so fast that his chair folded up behind him. He pulled his cell phone from his pocket and stared at the 'No signal' message.

"The town didn't get electricity until the rest of the country had it and it would have been suspicious to go without it any longer," Mona said. "Cable TV keeps getting promised. So when you think we'll have our first cell phone tower? Forget about the Internet."

Paul traced a phone cord on the floor back to the top of a bookcase. He reached it in three strides and almost immediately resorted to the stereotypical reaction in old movies, repeatedly clicking the phone button while shouting "Hello?" into the mouthpiece.

He came slowly back to the table, unfolded his collapsed chair and sat. "How long have the lines been down?" he asked, dead calm.

"They cut them during the night," Joy replied.

"The Santana family and good old Dukey and a few others left us at dawn. We heard gunshots minutes later," said Dunbar. "A lot of them. So you see, it just keeps getting better."

Paul closed his eyes and tried to make himself ignore the black spots of panic blossoming behind his lids. It didn't work. "Gotta get to Darby," he said as he jumped up, again knocking over his chair.

A pair of hands grabbed him and braced him to a standstill.

Wheeling, he snarled, "What the hell—?"

D.B. immediately unhanded him but held up a single finger that stopped Paul in midsentence. "Your wife's okay. You don't have to worry about her."

"She's all alone with our son. I never should have left them."

"The vampires are sleeping," D.B. said.

"Yeah? What about the daylighters who work with them?"

"Daylighters," Todd snorted. "This guy speaks the language, don't he."

"They won't do anything on their own," Mona said. "If Drake wanted you dead, he'd have done it last night when he had his followers attack us."

"And when he was hobnobbing with you," Dunbar had to add.

Paul felt his muscles slacken slightly. "What about those under Purcell's control?"

Mona shook her head. "I doubt that he knows what Drake told you, so there's no great urgency on his part. His attention's on us right now."

"So who cut the phone lines?" Carl asked.

They all stared at Mona Dexter, waiting. When she spoke, it was into her coffee cup. "The police, maybe. Or the old people just before they attacked." She looked up suddenly and let her eyes flit from face to face. "You can't trust any of them. That's what I've been telling you. The only thing we even marginally have going for us is that some of Purcell's followers still fear Drake. At least for now. They won't go out of their way to antagonize him until they get stronger."

"Jesus Christ," said Carl. "We're caught in the middle of a fucking vampire war."

Now there was a comforting thought. But before Paul could fully explore the ramifications, the door from the office blew open and the bat-wielding sentry with the bad teeth staggered in, gasping for breath.

"What's up, Pete?" D.B. asked crisply.

"Better come out. We got trouble."

Chapter Forty

"You folks okay? We got reports of gunfire in the middle of the night. Someone said it sounded like a war out here. Hate to think anyone got hurt."

Marty McConlon's easy grin didn't match his words of concern. Neither did his response time. He leaned on the driver's door of the cruiser that had pulled up under the canopy in front of the office, just behind the Lexus. Stepping out of the passenger seat was the young cop, Barry, who'd intercepted Paul at the Municipal Complex days before. He stared at the Lexus, his face full of thought, but said nothing.

"Took your time checking up on us, didn't you, Marty?"

The cop turned to the motel owner and cocked his head comically. "Did you say 'us,' Mona? Interesting. Like you've joined a club or something."

She gave him nothing, so McConlon shifted his gaze elsewhere. Everywhere. "We're also hearing from a lot of pissed-off employers wanting to know where their workers are. Someone declare a holiday?"

"No one's going anywhere this morning," said Paul.

The cop's gaze caught him. "Well, well," he said, trying to keep an affable grin that kept slipping. He turned to his partner across the hood of their cruiser. "Barry, you remember Mr. Highsmith from the other day, right?"

The younger cop mumbled a stilted greeting.

McConlon's eyes fixed on Paul's again. "You're...what? A union organizer? Keeping these folks out of work."

Paul returned the hard stare, gave the officer nothing.

Carl said, "Union organizer. Maybe that's what we need. What we got us here is unsafe working conditions. We all split up and head to work, we end up vanished like my friend Doyle."

"Your friend Doyle," McConlon said. "Way I heard, he didn't take much of a shine—excuse the pun—to this town. So he packs his bag and shuffles off for greener pastures."

"Or someone packed his bags for him," Mona said. "But you wouldn't know about that, would you, Marty?"

No love lost, Paul thought as Mona and the plump cop exchanged red-hot glares.

"You wanna try packing up my shit, cop?" Carl pulled open his shirt to expose a knife with taped handle and five-inch blade in the waistband of his jeans.

David Searls

At least a dozen Sundowners now surrounded the uniformed men. McConlon kept tight control of his grin, but Barry wasn't even pretending to enjoy the attention.

Paul's stomach began to churn at the ridiculous challenge, Carl daring two armed cops to take his steak knife. They had no idea what they were up against.

It seemed that everyone at once became aware of a rhythmic beat that had been going on for some time. All heads turned to see Denver Dugan casually tapping the second floor balcony with the butt of his .30-.30 deer rifle.

McConlon gave his partner a curt nod and the younger man ducked back into the cruiser. Through the windshield glare, Paul could see the radio mic pressed close to his mouth.

Trouble, he thought. As if he hadn't seen enough of it over the last few days.

"Whooooeee," said McConlon, a high-pitched sound ending in tight laughter. "Must be the weather making everyone so hot and pissy." He mopped the back of a sleeve across his face to illustrate his point. "Not a great combination, all this Indian-summer heat and the anger and those guns I notice you all carrying. Another night like last one and we'll be filling body bags. No one got hurt, all that shooting?"

"Why don't you ask Mr. Chaplin?" Mona suggested.

McConlon's mouth puckered into an 'O' of genuine surprise. "James Chaplin? What could he tell me?"

"Not a thing," Jamey Weeks snickered.

Soft, nervous laughter tripped through the crowd. The cops' eyes danced from face to face, trying to track down the source of the humor.

As a second squad car crawled up the long drive and parked behind them, McConlon's smile broadened. Out stepped a woman in uniform who looked like she could handle herself. Before the crowd had a chance to fully absorb this shift in the power dynamic, a third marked Crown Vic pulled up to idle at the rear of the cop car convoy. Young, with traditional crewcut and cop mustache, this third driver pulled a nasty-looking scattergun out with him.

"What's up, Marty?" he asked.

McConlon locked glances again with Carl Haggerty. Still posed like an Earp facing off the bad guys at the O.K. Corral, but armed with a holstered steak knife, Carl didn't look so sure anymore.

"Maybe you oughtta take that thing out of your pants," McConlon said amiably. "Use two fingers, why dontcha, and set it down very carefully on the hood of my car."

Carl's eyes under his deeply furrowed brow flitted everywhere at once. His face was shiny with sweat, his shirt soaked through at the chest and under the arms.

212

"I don't think so."

This came from D.B., sounding as good-natured as the cop. Stepping sideways to block Marty McConlon's view of Carl, he flicked a finger high over his head and rotated it.

Then he crossed his arms and said, "As many of our people as you see, Marty, there's as many you don't."

He paused to let his words sink in, and it seemed that they did. All four cops stirred uneasily, their eyes roving the grounds, moving up the balcony and to all of the many open windows and the layout of the pool and even toward the ravine they couldn't see for the building.

Paul took a quick mental count and his stomach roiled. So much for military discipline. Other than Todd Dunbar, who he couldn't find, it seemed that every last Sundowner had left his or her post to cluster curiously around the police cars. There were no hidden sentinels. He was with the gang that couldn't shoot straight. All Paul could do was keep his face as expressionless as the others and see how D.B.'s bluff and bullshit hand signal would play.

At some point, D.B. had unbuttoned his own shirt to expose his white belly and the rubber grip of his five-shot barely peeking out of the flat holster he'd fastened to his hip.

"Maybe your man better put away his scattergun," he said.

A ballsy approach for such a little gun. Marty McConlon seemed to have the same thought. Rather than giving the order, he continued to survey the crowd. His smile had gone taut and unsure again, but his voice still held a trace of what could be mistaken for wit. "Denver, Jamey, Kathy Lee, Jermaine, Tonya. Hey, I know all of you. Ain't that something." He broke into his widest grin. "I see a face or hear a name, I never forget it. The one talent I got. Always hoped it would count for something."

Mona said, "That does come in handy, Marty. So why don't you get on the horn to the nearest state police post and call for reinforcements. You could report us all in by name and have the cavalry here in fifteen minutes."

"And Mona Dexter," the cop said as if completing his list of familiar names and faces. "You I will *never* forget."

He made a quick gesture that sent his backup back in their cruisers. He started to do the same, but then came out quickly. "Almost forgot," he said. "Found this."

He held up a tissue thin vinyl wallet and made a show of eyeballing the crowd. "Is there a Darwin Wayne Gates from Ankeny, Iowa on the premises?"

"Dukey," Kathy Lee said in hoarse panic.

"Dukey?" the cop repeated. He chuckled. "Okay, I guess if the folks gave you the name Darwin, you might take on a nickname. Anyone

213

seen Dukey lately? We found his wallet along the back roads early this morning."

Gunshots after dawn.

The crowd reacted with stunned silence. McConlon managed to look theatrically puzzled. He let the cheap wallet dangle from two fingers like a dead mouse as he pretended to examine it for the first time.

"Looks like he spilled something. Ketchup? Is this Darwin a messy eater, folks?" He grinned, tipped his billed cap to the crowd like something he must have seen in a movie. "Well, if you see him, tell him we got it."

He made another hand motion and the parade of squad cares reversed down the long drive. They turned around in the gravel lot and spat pebbles.

"Bastards," Kathy Lee said.

Chapter Forty-One

"No problem so far," Mona Dexter murmured to the armed men on the floor of her Dodge minivan.

Paul, wedged between the first two rows of seats, could glimpse Mona behind the wheel, making a big show of smiling and nodding conversationally at Kathy Lee in the seat next to her.

"I'm a local and I drive these streets all the time," she told everyone in the car. "McConlon and the others wouldn't dare touch me. Not in broad daylight."

It sounded to Paul like she was trying to convince herself. But even if she was right, it would be a different story if any of the town's rebel cops knew that Paul, Todd Dunbar and Jamey Weeks huddled out of sight of the windows, armed with hatchet and knives.

"We almost there?" Jamey whined. "My leg's cramping."

"Just stay down," Dunbar snapped.

Paul could feel the van begin to slow.

"Looks good," Kathy Lee said. "Let's get those bastards."

"Uh huh," said Mona, her voice seeming to have leaked enthusiasm for the task at hand.

They'd already passed Paul's home during the course of their semi-aimless drive to determine whether or not they were being followed. Mona and Kathy Lee had decided they were alone, but Paul wondered how much experience either woman had shaking off a tail.

The Highsmith home had looked undisturbed to the women, but again Paul was left trying to figure how they'd know otherwise.

"Alright," Mona said fifteen long minutes later. "Only a couple junkers in the lot. No lights on, no sign of activity in the building. We're going in."

It was broad daylight, so of course there were no lights on. Paul wondered what would constitute activity with a quick glance from a moving van.

He didn't ask. The answer was destined to make him once again consider abandoning the raiding party planned shortly after the three police cars had left the Sundown that morning. He couldn't pull out, he told himself firmly. He'd already looked naïve and undependable by entertaining Drake at his home while the others had been under an attack orchestrated by the head vampire. If he couldn't inspire their confidence and trust, he and Darby would have to face the town alone.

Although right now his wife was all alone anyway.

The van stopped, the engine gently idling. Paul raised himself enough to peek one eye out a side window. He studied the face of the narrow brick building. There it was, one downstairs window a concrete block slit, the large upstairs one covered by a drawn shade.

"Shit, let's do it," Dunbar whispered next to him. His face looked haggard and pale, eyes red-rimmed with sleep need, dark bags underneath.

Mona pulled into an unpaved alley behind the building and cut the engine.

"What we need," D.B. had said that morning after the police cars left, "is some kind of armed response to get their attention. To show them what they're up against."

Todd and Joy Dunbar, D.B., Mona, Carl and Paul had returned to the motel owner's tiny apartment where they'd huddled once more over the table in the dining room as if the police interruption had never occurred.

"Oh right, a road trip. Just pack up our white ash stakes and garlic cloves," said Joy, displaying uncharacteristic sarcasm.

"That's exactly what we need to do," said D.B. "We'll have the element of surprise. They think we're in here quaking in our boots."

"We are," Paul mumbled.

"Good. Then taking the battle to them is the last thing they'd expect. And don't forget, daylight's the time to catch them."

"And don't you forget," Joy shot back at him, "the reason sunup's such a good time is 'cuz we're dealing with vampires."

Good point. That shut everyone up until Dunbar scraped back his chair and stood up, still looking wobbly, but more animated than Paul had seen him lately. He slapped the table with an open palm and said, "Let's get the fuckers. Take Drake now and he'll never know what hit him."

"Good idea, wrong target," said Mona. She smoked a cigarette while her fingers played with a spoon. "You take out Drake, there's no order left in the town. We've got to keep him in power and eliminate his enemies."

"Jesus Christ, they're the ones came at us last night," Dunbar snarled.

The outburst seemed to take a lot out of him. He slumped back to his seat, his face pasty with sweat, eyes ringed in black.

Paul knew the other man had been rat-bit that night, like several of the others, but he was the only one who still seemed sapped by it. Paul briefly considered rabies, but pushed the thought aside. They had enough to worry about as it was.

Dunbar propped himself on his elbows. "It's that old fuck who attacked us, so why're we screwing around with the others?"

A fair question.

Mona set aside her spoon. "As bad as you think Drake is, Purcell's worse. We can at least bargain with Drake."

Todd said, "Just like our buddy here did last night," jabbing a thumb Paul's way.

Ignore it, Paul told himself.

"Never trust them," said Mona. "That doesn't mean you can't negotiate from a position of strength. Hurt his enemies and you bring something to the table as far as Drake's concerned. Besides, I know where to find Purcell. He's easier to hit than Drake."

All eyes tracked her now.

"Winking Dog Saloon," she said. "It doesn't open till the dinner hour. Bunch of them crash in an apartment over the place."

"We can't," Paul sputtered. "We can't get out of the motel. Look what happened to Duke Gates and the others when they tried leaving."

D.B. said, "They're expecting us to try to sneak out, not go on the attack. Duke and the Santanas got caught on the back roads. The trick is to stay public. Hit 'em where they're not expecting it."

"That's right," said Mona. "My van's big enough to hide several of you and it's a familiar sight around town. Marty wouldn't dare do anything to me in front of a town full of witnesses. Not until Purcell gets a whole lot stronger."

"I don't know," Paul said.

"Then don't go," Dunbar snapped.

Paul thought a moment. "Obviously they didn't cut every phone line in town."

"I doubt it," said D.B.

"This place where Purcell's at, he's got one—right?"

"I would guess so," said Mona.

"Then I'm in."

"Stay down," Mona muttered before stepping out of the van and quickly and quietly closing the door.

Kathy Lee wiggled over to the driver's seat and placed both hands on the wheel. Paul caught a quick glimpse of her worried eyes before she adjusted the rearview mirror for a straight shot behind her. There had been no time for rehearsals. No contingency plans for dealing with a police car squealing into the parking lot off Middle View and sealing the only route into and out of the alley behind the building. If that happened, Paul thought as he hugged the rough floorboard carpet with a sweating cheek, they were all dead. And so was his family.

He could hear Mona's muffled rapping on the door facing the parking lot entrance to the Dog. She'd make up some lame excuse and scuttle the raid if a daylighter answered.

217

Paul wished D.B. had taken personal charge of the raid, but they'd all agreed that their de facto leader was needed to hold the troops together at the Sundown. The unspoken thought was that D.B. was too valuable to lose if they didn't make it back.

Paul's breath hitched when the van's door rumbled open.

"Jesus, don't scare me like that," Jamey gasped. Tough to tell whether he was talking to Paul for the inadvertent hitch or to Mona for causing it.

"Everyone out," she said in a low, level voice.

Wordlessly, the three sweaty men scrambled out and stood blinking into the sun. Dunbar, looking sicker by the hour, held up a bulky blue duffel bag like an umbrella. Jamey Weeks carried a small, battered toolbox, while Paul's only load was fear. Mona led them around the corner of the building, exposing them to a trickle of traffic on Middle View Road.

They moved fast, staying close to the brick side of the Dog. Paul felt naked and vulnerable until they squeezed through the unlocked main entrance where they faced two locked interior doors. One was frosted glass, with a crudely painted German Shepherd that had an obscenely long tongue and one closed eye. The other, a heavy wooden door, painted chocolate brown like the foyer, had a hammered metal mailbox next to it and the number "101" over a peephole.

That was the door Mona stood behind. She rattled the knob just to be sure it wasn't going to be easier than they expected. It wasn't.

"How do you know they can't hear us?" Paul whispered.

"They're vampires," Mona replied.

"I know that, but—"

"My grandparents, my folks and my in-laws are vampires. I know what they're like when they're out."

Jamey, meanwhile, had withdrawn from his unwieldy toolbox a long, pointy metal device on the end of a wooden screwdriver handle. He'd been chosen for this mission for his unique skills with such delicate tools. He knelt on one knee, inserted his homemade device into the doorknob and twitched his wrist a few times. Paul heard a popping sound and the knob turned freely.

"Holy shit," Dunbar mumbled when the door started to swing open.

It caught at the end of a taut chain.

Jamey looked up at Paul and smiled peculiarly. He reached once more into his felonious toolbox and pulled out a pair of yellow-handled bolt cutters. Wishful thinking on Paul's part that a safety chain would stop them. Jamey snipped it slack even faster than he'd popped the knob lock, and cautiously pushed the door open.

His role completed, he stepped proudly aside and waited for

someone else to enter the darkness first.

Their B&E man's movement had left Paul in front. It was like in that ridiculous war comedy where Abbott and Costello are tricked into accepting a deadly mission because everyone else takes a step back when volunteers are called for.

Or was it Laurel and Hardy?

He couldn't do it, he thought as he stared into the shadows beyond. He was fifty-two years old and suddenly feeling every day of it. At the same time, he was nine and terrified to walk into the dark cellar alone.

He heard an impatient little snort behind him and Mona took the lead. With his face burning, he let her. Todd, with a disgusted sigh, followed her. Paul only squeezed in ahead of Jamey because he didn't want his back exposed.

They climbed a steep set of stairs, into total darkness. Paul's hands began acting as eyes, feeling blindly for walls and obstructions. The place smelled of dust and rancid chicken, beer and cigarettes and body odor. Flies buzzed and he could imagine other creatures slithering out of his way as they tiptoed over groaning floorboards.

"Jamey, shut the door behind you," Mona called out. Not loudly, but too loud, as far as Paul was concerned.

The door squealed shut, leaving them in darkness even more complete than before. No one had brought flashlights because Mona had told them they wouldn't be necessary. When the light suddenly snapped on, Paul and Todd grunted in breathless shock.

"It's alright," Mona soothed. "Worst thing the light's gonna do is make them stir a little."

"Yeah?" Jamey said, voice quaking. "They're such light sleepers, how come I'm here?"

Paul figured he couldn't have asked a better question himself.

They stood in a long hallway narrow enough for them to touch both border walls at once. There were two doorways cut into the left wall and the same number on the right. The first to the left was a large open area still in darkness. Directly across from it, Paul could see the standing shadows of stove, fridge and countertops. As they crept past, Paul's nostrils were assailed by the strong odor of a backed-up sewer or unflushed toiled. He moved quickly out of scent range.

Todd sneezed loudly and was hushed by the others. Even by Mona, who'd earlier announced their presence by turning on a fucking light. Paul felt a comparable tickle working its way up his dust-clogged sinuses.

"Two in here," Mona said. She'd entered the second room on the left and Paul could hear her patting down the wall for a light switch.

No, Paul wanted to warn her, but as he came up behind she found what she was looking for and flicked to life a single naked bulb on the ceiling. It did little more than toss shadows around, but that was enough to reveal the two squirming pink figures on the bed.

He was out of there. Paul backed up without looking and crashed into Jamey, who said in a strangled voice, "Hey, what the hell?"

"Paul, it's alright," Mona said, sounding nearly as agitated as he felt, but holding it together better. "They're asleep. It's just an involuntary response to the light."

"I'm experiencing a similar response to them," he muttered.

Heart thudding and black spots mushrooming in the corners of his vision, he chanced another peek at the nude couple, limbs intertwined on the bed. Not a bed, but a mattress set on the floor. The bedsheet had been pulled up on one corner to partially cover them, but they'd tossed it off.

Mona bent over the two. "Warren Lattimer, the bartender at the Dog," she said, straightening. "The girl with the cracked red toenail polish, I'm pretty sure it's Perry and Dot Farr's younger daughter. I had no idea. There hadn't been any rumors about *her*. She's all of sixteen," Mona said, shaking her head sadly.

The beer poster in the bedroom caught Paul's eye. Not the poster itself, but more the way it was taped high on the wall over the bed. The way it clung to the wall with multiple layers of masking tape when four small strips should have done the job.

Someone wanted to make damn sure it wouldn't come down. It firmly blocked out the room's only window.

Following his gaze, Mon said, "You need any more proof of what we're dealing with, you just tear that thing down."

Not likely. Paul couldn't stop wondering how he was going to do what had to be done. He followed the others down the long corridor and through the open doorway near the front of the apartment. Find it fast, he urged himself as the others ahead of him fumbled for a light source. He saw too much in the dark, too many still black lumps on the floor.

Body bags was his first impression when someone finally found a workable lamp on the floor by tripping over it. The naked bulb cast a Rorschach pattern of light and shadows that made it difficult to see where one vague shape left off and another began.

"Three, four of them," Mona said softly.

The room was still as death but for the harsh panting of four frightened daylighters. It was hotter than hell and twice as humid.

"Christ," Dunbar said, perching on the arm of a garage sale couch, about the only piece of furniture in the room. Paul stared at the oddly lumped shape of the cushions until it dawned on him that a figure lay beneath them.

Most of the yellow lamplight extended waist high and no higher. The papered walls, once a flocked pattern on white, were smudged colorless by fingerprints and darker matter. Paul felt heavy, damp air tickle his sweaty face, stirred by a slow-moving ceiling fan.

"They wouldn't risk opening a window," Mona said. "If a breeze fluffed up that shade, they'd be in trouble."

A bookcase in one corner held a CD player and a short stack of thrash metal CDs next to a tattered pile of men's magazines full of harsh pink shots. *Should have the Internet,* Paul couldn't help thinking. An empty six-pack of beer perched high atop the pile. Still attached to the plastic ring, it looked like the cans had been downed without being twisted free. Paul heard flies buzzing unseen at the front window, the faint tapping of their small bodies hitting the glass behind the one long shade.

"Looky here," Jamey said excitedly. He lifted a shotgun from the floor behind a stack of men's magazines. The stock had been crudely sawn. "Twelve gauge," he said, his foot accidentally kicking a pile of shells across the floor.

He broke the thing open and peeked into the twin barrels. "Gimme them," he said, taking the handful of shells Paul and Mona had collected from the floor. Jamey dropped a couple into the barrels and made a series of loud clacking sounds with the weapon before proclaiming himself, "Armed and dangerous."

"Easy," Mona murmured.

His sensitive stomach not appreciating the fact that it was Jamey Weeks covering him with a loaded sawed-off, Paul returned his attention to the shapes on the floor.

Despite the room's intense heat, one was burrowed under an open sleeping bag. Another had taken what he assumed to be the top sheet from the mattress in the bedroom while a third had slit open and taped together green plastic trash bags to wear as a shroud.

"Four for sure," Mona said after fearlessly peering into sleeping bag, garbage bag, sheet and under the couch cushions. And then: "Oh shit."

"What?" Paul's throat very nearly locked under his panic, his breath wheezing from him.

He could see Jamey Weeks inching toward the open doorway, captured shotgun sweeping the room. He seemed ready to bolt for daylight, and Paul was looking to be two steps behind him.

Mona swore again and repeated the process of examining each of the inert figures. Paul could see limbs switch as she briefly exposed them to what little light found its way into the room.

"He's not here."

Dunbar sprang off the arm of the couch, then braced his hands on his knees, panting as though rising too suddenly from a dead sleep. "What're you talking about?" he choked out.

She went through it all a third time. "He always sleeps here," she said. "Usually," she amended softly.

Dunbar grabbed her, squeezed her upper arms until she hiccuped a sound of pain and surprise. "Purcell's not here," he snarled. "You told us—"

Mona twisted free and stepped back. "Maybe the kitchen," she said, sounding like she didn't believe it herself.

"No one's there," said Jamey, who'd apparently looked while considering exiting the premises.

Obviously frustrated, Mona said, "There's more of them now than ever. That means more safe houses, more places to spend his days."

Dunbar made a peculiar hissing sound. He sat hard on the arm of the couch, as if exhausted by his own rage. "Now what?"

"We do it anyway," Mona replied.

Paul shook his head. "No way. All we'll do by killing off his friends is antagonize him."

"Too late to worry about that," Mona said. "Don't forget the busted locks and the stolen shotgun. Besides, they have...other ways. He'll know we've been here so we might as well accomplish something. At the very least, we cut down his forces."

Other ways? That didn't sound too comforting. Paul sank wearily to the unoccupied couch arm. What a picture he and Dunbar must make, flanking a sleeping vampire like a pair of worried bookends. Every hour, every minute, he was dragging himself deeper into an impossible nightmare. Darby and Tuck wouldn't leave his mind. The understanding as they'd reluctantly split up that morning was that she shouldn't expect to hear from him for awhile, but they'd forgotten to define "awhile." Picturing his wife cruising the streets in search of him, their young son strapped into the car seat behind her, made the adrenalin bite harder at his stomach lining, doubling him over.

He straightened with all of his remaining might and said, "Purcell. If he comes back and sees what we've—"

"Of course he'll see," Mona snapped, pacing the room. "We have to give him something to remember us by. Prove we can give as well as we take. Make for a few sleepless nights."

It was obvious she was making this up as she went along. After the initial shock of not finding her husband's killer, she'd recovered to the point of sounding like things were progressing exactly as planned. *Couldn't be better.* But was she letting her fury for Purcell, her need for vengeance, get the best of her? Of *them?*

Paul had another thought. "A phone," he said. "Dammit, they don't have a phone."

"Yes, they do." Jamey aimed his new shotgun out the door. "On a wall in the kitchen."

The plastic handset felt too warm against his chin and ear. It smelled of garlic. Paul kept it as far from his face as he could and still use it. He couldn't remember the number. When he closed his eyes and forced his mind to paw through familiar combinations, he saw nothing but the twitching figures hidden from the light.

He muttered a curse and called up directory assistance. The operator asked him what city and he said Detroit and gave her the name of the law firm. After a short, static-filled silence, a nearly genderless voice gave him the number and told him it could be dialed for him for a small additional charge.

What the hell. The vampires were paying.

"Freddie Brace, please," he said when the call went through.

"Hurry up. We got things to do," Mona said, stepping into the central hallway. She held a shiny new hatchet against her chest like some murderous mama in a redneck drive-in flick from the Seventies.

Things to do.

Hey, Freddie, can we make this quick? I have vampires to behead.

Diamond and Streisand were dueting on hold as the sweat trickled down Paul's cheeks. He was picking up the kitchen odors of bacon grease and day-old burgers on top of all that garlic, proof that at least some of the legends got it wrong.

"Freddie Brace," came the voice on the line.

Paul closed his eyes with relief. "Freddie, what kind of car are you driving?"

White noise. Paul was about to hang up and tell the others to run for it because the town was on to them when Freddie said, "Who is this?"

"It's Paul," he said, exasperated. "Answer my question. What're you driving?"

"I've got a Prius and a Grand Cherokee. My yin and my yang of green acceptance."

"Definitely the Grand Cherokee. We need the passenger room."

"We? Passengers?"

"I need you to come down to Babylon and take some people away. I'll give you directions."

"Hold on, I'm writing."

The confusion had left his lawyer's voice. He now sounded rock-solid, which is the reason Paul had called him in the first place. Paul gave him detailed directions to his home and told him it would take him at least an hour from the moment he got in his car. "Which is very, very soon, I hope."

"Don't worry. I'm heading out the door."

"Without telling anybody." The fewer involved, Paul felt, the better.

There was a pause before the voice on the line said, "Lawyer-client privilege?"

"Exactly. Can't wait to get your bill. One more thing. Can you first do a quick Internet search? I'm looking for a crime story out of Ithaca, New York sometime within the last several weeks. Vicious attack, multiple victims, plenty of blood. Classic tabloid sort of thing."

"Don't you ever pick up a newspaper or go online?"

"I've been a little busy and we don't get the Internet here."

"What year is it in your world?"

"Freddie, I've got no ti—"

"Okay, listen up. Three adults and two kids wiped out in a trailer park or something. Grisly enough for you? The woman was mutilated, they're saying she was pregnant. No suspects. It's a pretty big story, man. Hello?"

Paul stared at the wall. With the police all over it, why hadn't they traced the McConlons back to Babylon yet? Were the residents of the town so untethered to 21st century American life that they left no trail?

"Come on, Paul. Let's go."

It was Mona. He gave her a hand wave and paused, thinking. One part of him wanted to tell his lawyer to bring holy water, sharpened stakes and crucifixes (might as well forget the garlic). But he knew that was just popular culture. Or thought so, anyway. Besides, Freddie would also bring along a psychiatrist if he made that kind of request.

"That's it for now," he finally said. "Just get in your SUV and get here. Okay?"

Mona and Jamey were standing in the living room doorway, facing him. Waiting. Behind them, he could make out Todd's slumped form on the arm of the lumpy-cushioned couch.

"You're leaving?" Mona asked it with no expression on her face or in her voice.

"Not me. My wife and boy," he explained.

"Come on," she said, beckoning with a hatchet that still carried the bar code sticker from wherever it was purchased.

The world as he knew it seemed to be slowly flip-flopping, turning itself inside out. He walked, ramrod straight and graceful with terror, toward whatever awaited him in the room across the hall.

Jamey slapped Dunbar on the knee and said, "Hey!"

He jerked awake. How he could have nodded off at a time like this...

"Here," Mona said as they clustered around the inert vampires on the floor. She handed the hatchet to Paul.

"What?"

"You're stronger than me. You won't be able to take the head completely off with one whack, but it's important to at least cut through the vocal cords in the first swing."

Like she'd read up on dismantling vampires.

The hatchet felt cold and heavy in his trembling hands. This is *not* real, he said.

And what if it wasn't? What if he'd allowed himself to fall victim to some mass delusion, one person's vivid fancy sparking the imaginations of everyone else? He could see himself on death row, trying to explain to the chaplain how beheading five or six sleeping people had seemed to make such perfect sense at the time.

"I can't," he said. He looked at Jamey to his left, but the younger man backed away in speechless refusal.

"It would have been faster with the chainsaw," Mona said, "but too loud."

"I thought they couldn't hear anything when they're like this?" Jamey whispered.

"Well. Within reason."

Dunbar growled. "For being the expert, Mona, you don't know shit."

"Just because my folks are vampires doesn't mean I've got a lot of experience decapitating them," she replied hotly.

Paul pointed with the hatchet to the huddled figure in the sleeping bag. The one closest to their feet. "What if you're wrong?"

Mona stared at him. "Wrong?" She flipped back a section of sleeping bag with her shoe to reveal a man's head. He looked to be in his late twenties or so. Weak chin, high forehead, prematurely thinning brown hair. "Gary Leckner," she said, as if that explained everything.

Dunbar, rallying slightly, said, "He was one of them at the Dog on Friday night." He rubbed his shoulder, wincing.

"You need proof, do you?" Mona asked.

She moved to the next prone figure and toed aside the garbage bag shroud to expose a tangle of blond, greasy hair. He lay on his belly, one side of his gaunt, white face exposed. "Jason Penney, Purcell's best friend." Her lips curled in a grimace. "Watch this."

It was a large window with a single shade tied down to a radiator. She asked Jamey to hold the shade tightly while she untied the cord. "Don't let it get away from you," she warned.

She pulled the shade down slightly, just enough to release the locking mechanism, then took the cord from Jamey and let it slip slowly through her fingers.

As the shade gradually rose, Paul watched a razor-thin sliver of white light pop into existence on the bare floorboards and work its way toward the sleeping man. Paul's stomach crawled with fear, dread, revulsion and something even akin to pity as he watched the bar of light pull flush with and slowly overtake the unwashed blond hair. Penney flinched in his sleep as the razor line grew and moved steadily closer. He shuddered. He issued a nearly inaudible mewling sound from deep in the back of his throat. His eyelids twitched as though in deep REM sleep and dreaming whatever horrors a vampire dreams.

"Now watch this," Mona whispered.

Paul did, as repulsively fascinated as when he'd been a kid watching magnifying glass experiments on ants.

The white light crept steadily over the man's face, setting off a series of twitches and grimaces. The head flopped violently, Penney's face thudding against the floor as he tried to shake off the light and the heat in his sleep. Paul watched a thin wisp of smoke curl skyward as the mewling sound gained volume and pitch.

"Enough," he said hoarsely.

His limbs shaking so hard he could barely walk, he picked his way over the unconscious man—vampire—to take the shade cord from the motel owner and tie it down again. The pitiful cries had died down, but the thing twitched for several seconds more before drifting back to sleep. The sunlight had raised a red welt the size of a half dollar on the creature's cheek.

The scent of burned flesh singed the air.

"Give it to me," Dunbar rasped. He held out his hand and Paul gladly yielded the hatchet. Dunbar kicked more of the sleeping bag cloth away from the vampire Leckner and said, "I need more light."

Mona removed the shade from the room's only light source, tipped and aimed the lamp like a flashlight at their victim's throat. "Remember," she said, "try to cut through the vocal cords in the first swing."

Dunbar straightened. "Where are they?"

"In his throat, of course. I mean...I assume."

"So you don't know."

"I don't know. Just swing the fucker as hard as you can."

"Our expert," Dunbar muttered. He clutched the small ax in both hands and began to experiment with grips and stances.

Paul could see the handle darken with sweat where Dunbar's hands clenched it.

He turned away to study a stained section of wallpaper. The lamplight from the floor hit that wall in such a way as to cast a vivid and oversized shadowplay version of unfolding events. Paul watched the shadow axeman pitch back on one leg, raise both arms high above his head and hold the position for a dreadful period of stasis that gave Paul time to avert his gaze or close his eyes...but he could do neither.

When the blade came down, it made a soft, wet sound that ended in a brief, startled inhalation, as though its victim had time to gasp in wonder before the damage was done. Paul kept his eyes fixed on the wall as he heard the harsh breathing of Dunbar, Mona and Jamey—and probably himself.

Jamey grunted.

With a quick sideways glance, Paul saw the younger man on sentinel duty by the front window, his shotgun cradled. Though several feet removed from the murder in progress, speckles of blood dotted Jamey's face and clothing.

Paul wondered how he looked. He shifted, moved a step away from Dunbar's mad blade, but continued watching the wall where the shadowplay continued.

The ax fell again, the motion ending this time with a disconcerting crunch of metal against bone.

"Ah, Jesus," Jamey mumbled. It sounded like he'd be sick.

Paul heard liquid spurting, hitting floor and walls.

The prone shadow near the baseboard twitched. The hatchet man made a strangled sound in the back of his throat as he raised the blade for a third time and brought it down faster. Finally, the motion ended with the thud of metal biting floorboard and the unmistakable sound of a head rolling across the floor.

Dunbar's shadow remained hunched, all but motionless. Paul could hear his labored breathing. A steady, rhythmic drip.

"How's it going?" Paul asked hoarsely.

"How's it going?" Dunbar's gaze cut like a dagger. "You get the next one, Country Club," he snarled.

"I can't take this," said Jamey from his station by the window. He stared at hands splotched with a flying pattern of blood and gore.

Since he'd stood even closer than Jamey to the revolting act, Paul would be even more spattered by the messy death, but he couldn't bear to look.

"Here," Dunbar said as he bumped Paul's hip with the blunt edge of the blade.

He was supposed to take it. It was fair, but Paul kept imagining his wife and toddler son watching him decapitate a sleeping stranger.

"Here," Dunbar repeated, sharper this time.

"I can't take no more," Jamey said.

"We have to," Mona said thickly. "Paul, take the hatchet. It's your turn."

Paul, it's your turn. What his mother used to say when it was his week to do dishes. If Mom could see him now.

"I know a faster way."

Later, Paul would try to examine Jamey Weeks' words. *I know a faster way.* He'd hear Jamey in his sleep or at odd times and wonder why he hadn't acted sooner. Why he couldn't have predicted what was to follow. In those dreams or fantasies to come he'd see Jamey reach for the shade cord where he'd tied it to the radiator, Jamey always moving as slow as the action sequences in a Sam Peckinpah film. Paul always having time to stop him—or, if it was a particularly gruesome nightmare, to stare in frozen horror, knowing exactly what was to come.

But that wasn't the way it really happened.

I know a faster way.

A blur of movement. Jamey untying the cord, fingers flying.

Mona shouting, "No!"

Too late. The shade flying skyward.

And then, of course, all hell breaking loose.

Chapter Forty-Two

What happened next could never be retold with absolute certainty. Whenever Paul tried reviewing it, or when it plundered his sleep, the facts as well as the sequence of events would get snarled up. Or some details taking on greater significance in one nightmare, less in another.

Sometimes he'd recall the blood spraying the room like a fountain that began under Jamey's chin, while at other times it seeped.

But the way it really went down was like this. *Something* like this...

The shade shot upward with cartoonish speed and white-hot sunlight poured in, pierced the room like a brilliant death ray. Someone screamed: the body wrapped in a grimy bedsheet. It rolled across the floor, picking up speed like a cockroach in full retreat. The vampire Jason Penney howled. Still wrapped in garbage-bag plastic that seemed to be melting on his hot body, he—it?—scrabbled to his feet and stumbled for cover. He crashed into Dunbar in the suddenly too-small space and jarred loose the hatchet. Sent it skidding across the floor.

Mona yelped. She sidestepped the frenzied creature and stuck out a foot to upend it as Dunbar stuttered clumsily out of reach. The Sundowner lost his balance and fell into the garage sale couch with a thick arm dangling grotesquely under its cushion.

The vampire in the bedsheet proved to be another female, a girl with greasy black hair. Shrieking, she pawed the air with an arm that blistered as soon as it came in contact with the sunlight. Her damaged hand wrapped around the base of the lamp and she flung it.

The lamp struck Mona in the forehead, the bulb shattering with a hollow *pop* as it knocked the motel owner off her feet.

The cocooned Jason Penney lay writhing like a worm caught on pavement after the rainclouds had cleared. As the plastic bag melted onto his seething body, the thing rolled over the hatchet on the floor where Dunbar had dropped it. When it rolled away, the hatchet was gone. As if devoured. The creature rose with a cry that contained equal parts frenzied fury and agony. Shielding his face with a sizzling hand, Penney peeked between blistered fingers to take dead aim at Dunbar.

The Sundowner sat glassy-eyed on the couch he'd stumbled onto, seemingly oblivious to the hand that twitched convulsively from under the cushion between his legs.

"Todd! Look out!" Paul screamed.

He snapped out of it as Penney came at him, the bloody hatchet dangling at the end of one ashen arm. Leaping to his feet, Dunbar snatched up the cushion and held it to his chest like the world's least dependable shield.

His attention seemed immediately diverted by the wide shoulders, deep chest and thick, flailing arms he'd exposed by removing the cushion.

"Zeebe," Dunbar said. Dazed.

"Look out," Paul shouted.

Flinching, Todd resumed his defensive stance, cushion held high, just as Penney brought down the blade.

It cut through the fabric, spewing gray padding. The vampire's blade kept going, going all the way through the cushion and into Dunbar's cheek.

Paul's mind played a troubling trick as he watched, in shock, the vampire shave the side of the Sundowner's face. It seemed as though the inhuman growl, much like the unforgettable sounds he'd heard the night Judd Maxwell disappeared—seemed like it had come from Dunbar's side of the cushion.

A thin spray of blood jetted from Dunbar's face as he shoved cushion and vampire away. The creature Penney tripped over Mona Dexter's prostrate body and fell squarely in the middle of the bright rectangle of sunlight where he lay screaming and writhing convulsively.

Smoke poured from his body as though from a broken car radiator.

Until that moment, only two of the daylighters—Dunbar and Mona—had been directly involved in the claustrophobic battle. Jamey and Paul had remained frozen on the sidelines. But with Penney crumpled to the ground and the girl screaming, still tightly wound in her bedsheet, Jamey Weeks saw a chance to escape his trapped position by the window shade he'd so injudiciously raised.

With the shotgun clutched to his chest like a good-luck charm, he made a mad dash for open ground. Almost made it, too, but he slipped in the pool of blood and gore near Penney and the beheaded Gary Leckner.

He went down to one knee, eyes wild, as he studied the thrashing vampire on the floor next to him. In his panic to rise and get the hell out of there, Jamey slipped again, this time falling fully over the spasming creature. Jason Penney instinctively buried his teeth and swollen face into the man's neck and tore at his flesh like a pit bull taking down a poodle.

Jamey's blood had a cooling effect on the creature, hissing as it splashed over his overheated face. Penney hoisted Jamey's twitching body in a two-handed grip over his head as protection from the deadly rays.

Paul could no longer watch. He grabbed Mona, still stunned by her collision with the flying lamp, and whisked her to her feet. "Todd, fall back," he barked. "Get out of there."

Dragging Mona, he took two steps to his right and grabbed the shotgun next to Jamey's slashed body, and five shells that had fallen from the dead man's pocket.

Dunbar was holding the side of his face, but blood trickled freely between his fingers. He grunted from deep within his chest as his legs did a rubbery, vaudevillian shuffle. It looked to Paul like the wounded Sundowner might keel over in the next second.

Paul stuck the shotgun high under his free arm and grabbed Dunbar as he fell. He pulled and dragged the three of them toward the hallway.

As they passed the couch, a thick-fingered hand shot out from behind a hastily stacked tent of cushions to snag a section of Dunbar's T-shirt. Paul let go long enough to slam the vampire's hand with the stock of the sawed-off. It made a satisfying crunch and elicited a howl of pain as Paul yanked the bloodied Sundowner out of reach. Then he reversed the gun and let go with both barrels. A deafening roar, an explosion of couch guts and a scream of pain as acrid smoke filled the room.

"Fuck you, Zeebe," Dunbar said with the last of his foundering strength.

His knees buckled and he choked on the smoke. Paul leaned him against his hip and somehow hugged and tugged and dragged both barely surviving Sundowners down the narrow hall and out the apartment door while still clenching the red-hot shotgun under one arm.

"Wait here," he gasped, propping Todd and Mona against the wall at the head of the stairs before ducking back into the horror apartment.

Vampire snarls had turned to mewling cries that Paul tried to ignore. Holding his breath against the smoke, he grabbed the phone receiver in the kitchen and ripped the cord from the wall. He depressed the inside doorknob button that Jamey had popped open only minutes and a lifetime ago, then closed the door after him, locking it. Buying them a little time, he hoped.

Gulping for air, he examined the front of his clothing and beheld an even ghastlier sight than he'd imagined. He'd be arrested or shot on sight if anyone saw him on the streets—even in a more normal town—but he'd have to risk it.

Mona had slumped to one knee by the time he got back to the dark foyer. Dunbar stood at her side, as though at attention and unaware of her presence. Unaware of much of anything. The blood from the six-inch gash on his cheek had begun to coagulate, but Dunbar had a dazed, irretrievable air about him that worried Paul even more than the injury.

They'd have to hurry. Paul tucked the shotgun under Dunbar's arm and pushed and led the two down the stairs. He made his face a mask of bored unconcern as he pushed open the exterior door. Both wounded survivors gasped in panic at the sudden daylight.

Leaving them behind, Paul forced himself to saunter casually to the parking lot. He found the van behind the building where they'd left it, engine running and Kathy Lee behind the wheel. It seemed impossible how normal and unchanged it all seemed when the entire world had been shaken from its moors inside the bloody apartment.

He made the cranking motion he'd stolen from Ponytail Pete, and Kathy Lee rolled down the window. "What happened? I heard—" Her eyes popped when she got a good look at him. "Oh my God, you're covered in—"

"Pull up closer to the door," he ordered.

He slid open the van's door as she backed out of the alley and squeezed as close as possible to the side of the building. Todd and Mona seemed incrementally aware of their surroundings when he went back for them. They walked on their own, albeit shakily. As they climbed into the van, Mona exchanged seats with Kathy Lee. Todd and Paul crouched between the two rows of back seats, as before. They smuggled the still-smoldering shotgun into the floorspace between them.

"What about Jamey?" Kathy Lee wanted to know.

"Let's go."

His tone of voice must have answered her question. Paul regretted having to leave Jamey behind, but they simply didn't have the strength between all of them to carry him out—or anywhere to put him if they did.

"Head back to the motel first," he told Mona. He caught a brief glimpse of her forehead welt in the rearview mirror as she tried to shake the cobwebs loose. "We'll pack up the Dunbar kids and Kathy Lee's. They're going with my wife and son. After we get someone to patch up Todd's cheek we'll—"

"I'm okay."

Paul had been avoiding the sight of Dunbar's bloody face, but something made him glance at the man huddled on the floor near him. He wasn't sure what he was seeing, and the closer he looked the less sure he became.

Dunbar's shirt and pants were sticky with blood from a gash that had gone cheekbone deep, and the van was similarly smeared. Mona had tossed the injured man a room towel from the duffel bag Dunbar still carried over his shoulder, and he'd clamped it to his face. Now, as though to prove a point, he held the blood-soaked towel aside.

All that remained of the injury was a thin red line that looked plenty sore to the touch, but the bleeding had stopped.

Paul's lips smacked with a dry sound as they parted. He tore his glance from the scarred face, but his eyes returned, unable to look away.

"Guess I wasn't hurt as bad as I thought," Dunbar mumbled as he dabbed at his cheek.

"Guess not."

There was always a lot of blood with head wounds. That was common knowledge, wasn't it? Anyway, there'd been so much madness and mayhem in that dark apartment that it wasn't surprising if his mind had put the worse spin possible on the injury.

Nonetheless, another voice kept saying, *I saw what I saw.*

He turned toward the two women in the front seat, trying to remember what he'd been planning. "The daylighters aren't used to making decisions for themselves. That's why I think we can make it to the motel and out again as long as we do it with the sun up. I want all of you to grab your families and stuff your things in a few small bags. Take nothing that won't fit on the floor of the van, and hurry up about it."

He was amazed at how in control he sounded.

"I'm not going anywhere," Mona said.

"Sure you are. I want the women and children—"

"I don't care what you want," she snapped. "I've lived here all my life and I'm staying."

There'd be no room for argument. Paul sighed. "Then we'll leave you at the Sundown, but we still need your van."

"I'm staying, too," said Kathy Lee. "I can handle a gun as well as any of the boys."

"I know you can. That's why I want you to lead the way out. There are few people I'd trust more with Darby and Tuck. Besides, you've got your own kids to think about."

She made no reply for a long time. Finally she said, "So what do you have in mind?"

"No time," he said. "I'll explain it as we go along."

From this moment on, there wasn't room for a single mistake.

Chapter Forty-Three

The day had not gone well, to say the least, and now he had a swarm of loud, curious kids to deal with. Todd wedged himself into a tighter ball, burying his face between his arms and the base of the van's middle bench seat, but the sunlight pricked him like tiny arrows.

Pricked him like the paper clips being shot at him from the rear seat.

"Ouch, goddamn it," he snarled as one tiny bit of metal made contact.

"Sorry," said one of the Dwyer kids, but his fit of giggles robbed the urchin of all credibility.

Todd's cheek still hurt, but not like before. He'd sneaked a peek at the mirror in the room while Joy and the kids stuffed suitcases, and saw a scar that looked a week old. He'd given his wife an abbreviated version of events, a story that was horrifying even with most of the worst parts edited out.

"You did *that* today?" she'd asked, touching the dry welt.

He'd jerked away as though her touch pained him, but it hadn't. Not really. "Of course I did it today," he'd shot back. "When do you think I did it?"

She'd looked at his face funny after that.

Even worse than the cut itself had been the way the other Sundowners had looked at him as he sneaked his family out to safety. He'd taken only D.B. aside to explain the situation, but it was like everyone knew he was taking advantage of an opportunity only limited to a few.

Then there was that little problem of impending vampirehood.

"Daddy, does it hurt?"

He felt a burst of irritation as Crissie's little finger poked his cheek, but he stuffed the anger down inside himself, in the dark place where he stored everything he didn't want to take out in the light of day. He found his five-year-old's hand with one of his own and squeezed it.

"I'm okay, honey bear," he whispered, holding a finger to his lips. "We're hiding, remember? Keep your head down, Cris."

He'd spent plenty of restless nights in other people's homes. Times when they'd lost their apartment and friends or relatives had taken them in for days or weeks. But despite his ample experience worrying about what the morning would bring, even his bleakest moments hadn't prepared him for this. Joy and the three kids and him, hugging the floorboards in front of the middle seats of Mona Dexter's van while being assaulted in a rubber band and paper clip volley by Kathy Lee's two brats from their hiding place next to Highsmith, last row back. Kathy Lee drove, oblivious as usual to the commotion caused by her demonic offspring.

The nine of them could be shot, jailed or worse at any moment. That's what he'd brought upon his loved ones by taking the backroads to Detroit.

Todd squeezed Melanie's shoulder, then reached out to touch Little Todd. Joy took and held his hand until he pulled it away, as casually as possible, from the sun's bite.

Kathy Lee's kids giggled louder as another length of paper clip wire zinged past Todd's ear.

"What're you brats up to?" Kathy Lee drawled. Then, for the benefits of the adults stashed behind her, she added, "We're almost there."

The van made a couple more lazy turns, Kathy Lee doing all she could to convince anyone who might be watching that she was in no particular hurry.

Putting her behind the wheel was a risk they'd had to take, according to Highsmith. "Purcell's daylighters aren't real sharp and they're spread pretty thin," he'd said before they'd headed out of the Sundown. Word of the bloodbath in the apartment over the Winking Dog wouldn't get out until nightfall, the theory went. Since the daylighter cops guarding the front of the Sundown had seen Mona's van coming and going all day, they'd either not notice that Mona wasn't driving or not care. Even if they knew it was Kathy Lee in the driver's seat, they'd figure she wouldn't be going far without her kids—as long as the cops didn't spot them in hiding.

A whole lot of *ifs*, *probablys* and *hopefullys*.

Todd felt the van whine slightly as it took a sharp turn and a rise.

Kathy Lee murmured, "Heads down, heads down...okay. We're here."

No one said anything for several seconds. Not even Kathy Lee's own kids, never at a loss for words. Todd peeked cautiously out a window while maintaining a tight grip on the stolen twelve-gauge stashed under the seat.

The house stretched for the horizon, but soared high in the middle, a fairy tale structure of stone and timber and glass. And that was only the view from the back, the van idling where the long driveway ended at an attached garage that was larger and pricier than any house they'd ever called home.

"Daddy, is that a castle?" Crissie asked in an awe-filled whisper.

"No, honey, it ain't." Easy to say. Harder to believe.

235

House like that, you'd have more bathrooms than you could count. No waiting in lines for three poky kids to quit splashing in the tub. There'd be TVs everywhere—flat screens—and central air and rooms you didn't even know the names of. You'd go right through sunrooms and dens and family rooms and music rooms and libraries and playrooms. Go right through them and still have rooms waiting to be discovered. If that wasn't a fairytale...

Todd glanced at his wife. She, too, had risen to take in the view out the van windows, a dazzling smile playing in her eyes and on her lips as though the fairy tale castle had been built and placed there for her viewing pleasure. It was despair and a slow and untargeted anger that kept Todd from saying another word.

With a motorized whir, the overhead garage door came down and lights lit the three-stall garage. The concrete floor looked newly poured. The riding tractor off to one side cost more than Todd's last two cars. Tools hung from the walls over neatly stacked boxes. Damn if it didn't feel air-conditioned out here, even.

"Wait till I get the door open," said Highsmith as he slipped out of the van.

Todd watched him insert a key into the garage door and open it just an inch until a security chain stopped his progress.

"Darby!" he called out in a stage whisper.

Seconds later, the door opened and a young, trim and attractive blond had him in her embrace. Todd smirked as he tried picturing the woman with her arms around the old guy if he was a truck driver or drywall hanger.

Kathy Lee got out and rolled back the van's side door so her kids could jam their way past Todd. His kids followed, cautiously, like mice peering from a safe hole. Joy laid a cool hand on his neck on her way out and he offered her a grim, unfelt smile. Clutching the stolen shotgun, he came out last.

Trailing the others through the garage door, Todd found himself in a pitched, high-ceilinged stone and timber kitchen with gleaming copper pans and an array of stainless steel appliances. The sun lasered down through a skylight, its awful power unfiltered by a row of hanging ferns.

Todd bit off a scream. His flesh stinging as though immersed in acid, he tripped past his kids as inconspicuously as possible and took a spot against the room's best-shaded wall. Only when his breathing evened out again could he take in his surroundings.

By an arched doorway that led to a dining room with too many windows, the bubble blond Darby Highsmith stood watching him, a young boy pressed tightly against her.

"Todd, Joy, Kathy Lee..." said Highsmith. "Meet my wife, Darby."

Todd nodded and mumbled something. He felt awkward, standing there with a shotgun like some goddamn toothless hillbilly.

"My husband will take that if you'd like," said the cheerleader, nodding at the weapon.

"Oh. Yeah." Todd handed it over and it disappeared into another room, one presumably more child-proof than the kitchen.

When Highsmith returned, he flitted from window to window in the dining room and beyond. The house went on forever, Highsmith's footsteps echoing and fading and rising with his progress.

"Coffee or something?" Darby's voice was high and feminine, a perfect match for her petite form, but deceptively firm. "Something for the kids, maybe." She nodded at the five youngsters. Even Kathy Lee's kids looked quietly intimidated in the soaring structure.

Todd watched his own for reactions. They wore expressions that were too old, too distrustful and experienced with danger to be as young as they were. They looked pale and pinched, nothing like the golden-toned toddler standing so self-assured in front of his mother.

Joy answered for all of the Dunbars with a barely audible murmur. "Thank you, ma'am. We haven't eaten," she said timidly. She looked big and unkempt in the same room with the cheerleader.

Darby responded with a gasp of sympathy and a burst of activity. She began pulling loaves of bread and crackers and cheese and fruit and lunchmeat from the vastness of her cupboards and refrigerator.

"Help me, Joy. Kathy Lee. We'll make sandwiches," she said before the three women fell to the task.

Later, Highsmith's wife begged them to eat more. She was wearing short shorts and now she rubbed her hands along her naked thighs, the skin so shapely that Todd met the movement with an angry blush. She tilted her head toward the doorway through which her husband had departed twenty minutes before.

"He's expecting visitors," she said when she noticed Todd tracking her gaze.

She dropped both hands tenderly to her young son's shoulders, a gesture that encouraged Joy to do likewise with Crissie and Little Todd. Even Kathy Lee made a half-hearted attempt to track down her two and yank them closer.

The richly carpeted footfalls were so muffled that Todd didn't hear Highsmith's approach until he spoke.

"He's pulling in the driveway," he said as he strode into the kitchen. "But there's someone with him." That last part didn't sound like good news.

Highsmith moved to a window over the sink where Todd looked over his shoulder for as long as he could stand the sunlight. A navy blue SUV glided to a halt behind the van and both of the ample

237

vehicle's front doors opened at the same time.

Highsmith squinted. "Who the hell...?" he said in a voice so full of wonder that Todd had to lean closer to the glass, shielding his eyes with an instantly sunburned forearm, to see what was happening.

The driver was a black guy in his forties, maybe. Slightly shorter than average and on the soft side. He spun in a slow circle to take in the house, the yard, and finally his passenger as she emerged from the vehicle and rounded the front of it and came up behind him.

Highsmith made a sound deep in his throat. "Wait here," he said to no one in particular before rushing out the door.

Todd turned on a sink tap to cool the sun's sting from his wrists and arms while watching the confrontation.

The young woman struck a casual pose against the side of the Grand Cherokee, her face locked in a smile that more closely resembled a grimace. She was tall, slender and tanned golden. Her sandy blond hair looked expensively tousled so that she had to keep removing strands of it from her eyes.

"Interesting," Todd murmured.

Paul absently touched the black guy's elbow, but his head was angled toward the hot young chick.

"What have we here, a little competition for the cheerleader?" Todd asked himself.

"What's that, hon?" Joy asked.

"Nothing."

He shut off the tap and bathed his face in the water on his hands. It helped, but only a little. He inched closer to the back screen door, stepping very carefully around the sunbeam in the middle of the room.

"Todd, what are you doing?" Joy froze in the act of cleaning up the kids' mess. "Don't you listen in on them."

"I'm not," he said, waving her off.

From the doorway, he saw nothing but the branches of the young oaks, but he could hear conversation distinctly enough.

"It was my decision, Dad," the young woman was saying in a strong, ringing voice. "I told Freddie he could either give me a ride or I'd try to find your place on my own and probably end up lost."

Dad, Todd thought, vaguely disappointed.

Highsmith said, "Let's get in the house."

Todd skittered away from the door, yelping sharply as the sunbeam slashed a patch of exposed wrist.

Highsmith, holding the screen door for his daughter, squeezed her shoulders as she walked in ahead of him. He said, "Honey, don't get me wrong. I love seeing you, but now isn't...it's dangerous."

"That's why I'm here," she said.

Up close, she looked about the same age as the old guy's wife.

Interesting development.

"I didn't understand a thing Freddie was saying, but I figured you needed more help than you'd ever ask me for. Whatever it is, Dad, you've got two lawyers from one of the most powerful law firms in Detroit at your service."

Highsmith chuckled and Todd did, too. In both cases, it sounded forced.

"Well, you might as well meet everyone," Highsmith said. "Before I get into my story I want you both to note that they all seem at least as sane as Freddie, here. That's important because you'll question our mental health by the time I'm through."

Chapter Forty-Four

First Highsmith led a parade of kids and trailing adults to a finished basement room chock full of video games and old-fashioned penny arcades. There was a big-screen television on one wall and shelves jammed with kids' books and DVDs on another. He found an age-appropriate movie for all of the kids and showed them how to operate several of the games.

"That ought to hold them," he said as he took the adults and his young son back upstairs and into a sun-drenched room with couches and plush chairs where Todd had to work hard to find a shadowy corner.

Then Highsmith set off another hurried round of introductions. Connie Highsmith, Todd noticed, seemed to keep her distance from the young wife, who she apparently already knew, and to devote most of her smiles and attention to the toddler, who'd be her half-brother. After his initial shyness, the kid sat on her lap.

"Alright," Highsmith started, once everyone was settled and introduced. "We have an unusual situation here and not much time to explain it."

Unusual situation. Understatement of the day.

Their host went into an impossibly brief summary of the last several days, but even this cobbled together version of events drew the wide-eyed attention of the two newcomers.

And yet they hardly looked convinced. If the persuasive Highsmith couldn't even win over family and friend, Todd was thinking, how the hell did they hope to alert the outside world?

"Dad, you've got to be—I don't know—mistaken," said Connie.

Highsmith grimly shook his head. "Honey, we've looked at this a thousand ways. Whatever you want to call these people, they're dangerous. Trust me."

"Well, whatever's going on," the lawyer friend said, "job one is to get everyone out of here. We'll need more than my Grand Cherokee. If we can also use that minivan parked in front of—"

"I'm not going," said Paul, his quiet words drawing shocked silence all around.

Darby stood and took a couple nimble steps to her husband's side. "What do you mean, Paul?"

He gave his young wife a sad smile. "Darby, you heard what Drake said. That he'd find us wherever we went. I believe him. If I don't handle it right here, right now, we'll always be running. And I'm too old and easily frightened for that."

"But we've got him," she cried. "I thought we decided—"

"It's not enough," Paul replied. "We need more, and I know just how to do it."

Huh? Todd felt lost. *They had him?* What did that mean?

"Apparently you haven't told us everything, Paul," the lawyer said, pretty much echoing Todd's thoughts.

"There's no time," Highsmith replied.

Darby looked like she had another argument in mind, but Todd watched it dribble from her face.

"Well this is crazy," Connie Highsmith said. "Vampires, conspiracies, dead people, fleeing town before dark."

"I was there," her father told her firmly. "So were these other people." He swept the room with a hand gesture. "Either it all happened like I said it did, or we're all lying for unfathomable reasons."

Connie took the Sundowners in without looking at anyone directly. "Or...I don't know. You're all somehow imagining..." She let it trail off as if unable to convince even herself.

Freddie Brace nodded. "Mass hypnosis. Like seeing the sun dance in the sky while the Blessed Virgin visits thousands."

"Christ, Freddie," Highsmith said.

The lawyer waved him off. "Hear me out. I'm not saying that's the explanation. It's too pat, too flippant to ever sell to a jury. Generally speaking, if someone I know and trust tells me he saw pink elephants in tutus crooning Perry Como tunes, and I'm convinced he's not emotionally or chemically unbalanced—or pulling my leg—I'm going to think that there's something damn strange and interesting going on. If it's not a singing elephant in a tutu it's... something."

"Then you sort of believe me?" Paul said in amazement.

"'Sort of' being the operative phrase for now." Freddie shrugged. "You're too smart to be duped and I know you're not lying. Also seems unlikely I've been dragged to the sticks to get punked. . So I'm staying here with you until I see those crooning, tutu-wearing elephants for myself."

"I wouldn't recommend it," Highsmith said.

"You didn't. Now let's get everyone out of here. If I remember my Dracula movies, they have to be gone before sundown."

"Forget the movies," Kathy Lee said. "The way things really are is more dangerous than anything you ever seen at the theater. In many ways, those things are more human than my own kids."

"But the sun really does hold them off," said Joy. "That's why we're relatively safe for now."

Then she described the attack at the apartment over the Winking Dog as Todd had explained it to her. She told how Jamey Weeks had been killed as a result of exposing the sleeping vampires to sunlight. One of the stories Highsmith had neglected to tell, maybe in deference to all the women present.

At least Jamey's death had been fast and final, Todd thought. He wouldn't be in the process of making the transition from human to something far worse. Todd felt his heart hammering and knew he had to refocus his thoughts. He tuned back in to the conversation.

Highsmith was giving orders, a role that seemed to suit him. They were to pile into the Grand Cherokee and Mona's Dodge minivan. Todd would drive the Cherokee with his family aboard while Kathy Lee brought up the rear in the van with Darby, Connie, Tuck and her own awful twosome. Highsmith had found a Mapquest map he'd printed out before moving to the remote community—back when he had Internet access like the rest of America. He'd highlighted a path that would keep them off of what passed for main roads in this stretch of woods. As small as the town police force was, it was unlikely they'd have the chosen route covered. Or at least that was the theory of the moment.

Highsmith turned to his wife at one point and told her to not forget the memory card.

"What memory card?" Connie Highsmith asked the question, but it could just as easily have been Todd.

"Not now, honey. Darby will explain it in the car." Highsmith turned to his wife. "Just remember to call at precisely nine o'clock."

While everyone else in the room listened with blank expressions, Highsmith made Darby repeat a local phone number that Todd didn't recognize. Under no circumstances, his wife and daughter were told, were they to tell him where they were calling from. But wherever they touched down, they were to find a wireless signal and Darby was to check for email.

"I might have to find a Starbucks in the next town, but I'll find online access somehow," Highsmith said. "Later."

Darby just kept impatiently nodding—she'd heard this all before— while her eyes flitted from window to window as the sun grew less intense. Made Todd feel a little better, at least.

It was getting more difficult to follow all of this as his limbs grew wearier, his eyelids heavier. Highsmith prattled on and on.

"Honey, use credit and debits cards and take ATM cash withdrawals for the first twenty-four hours only. Then cut up all of your plastic. You should be able to use Connie's credit cards longer since it'll take them awhile to trace her. Don't stay with relatives or obvious friends, and keep moving. That's the most important thing," he said. "Keep moving."

Highsmith made his wife repeat the local phone number again and reminded her to place it from a throwaway cell phone at exactly nine that next morning. If Paul didn't answer by the end of the third ring, they were to hang up and toss the phone.

At a break in the action, Todd glanced at his watch. It was nearly 7:20, still time remaining till dark. Too much time, he thought, his flesh still tender from the midday sun.

"One more thing," he said, rising painfully to his feet. His shoulder throbbed with the movement. "I won't be going."

There. He'd said it. It wasn't so bad. Even Joy just stared at him with a distracted look that contained not a trace of alarm. Maybe it would go over a lot better than expected.

"You mean you're not ready yet, hon? What? You've gotta go to the bathroom?"

Or maybe not.

"I gotta be here," he said.

"No you don't," Highsmith barked. "You've got three kids and a wife depending on you."

"You got a wife and kid here, too," Todd replied. "Two of them," he corrected himself.

Joy got in his face with her husky body like she wanted to tackle him. She probably did. He took a couple backward steps with her in his arms, and pressed her tightly To his chest.

"You have to listen to me," he whispered, embarrassed at their public display. "I'm staying for reasons you can't even guess. I'll be careful, but you gotta believe I know what I'm doing."

He could feel her head shake from side to side as she murmured "No, no, no…" into his chest. He burrowed deeply into her, unable to make eye contact for fear of losing it. It was worse than when Chaplin's teeth sunk into his shoulder. Worse even than that godawful moment when he knew he'd been infected and there was probably no cure.

But if there did exist an antidote of some kind, he would only find it here. That much he knew. And for that possibility he had to stay strong.

And so they left him: Melanie and Crissie and Little Todd. The two younger kids were still sobbing quietly as they were packed into the Grand Cherokee, Connie Highsmith behind the wheel. Melanie's tears had ended, but she hid her red face from him. He wanted to pull her to his lap like when she was a little girl and explain everything. Make her see how he had to do what he was doing.

He said nothing. He turned to his wife, sharing the ample shade under the backyard oaks. "Last chance," he said quietly. "I wish you'd go—"

"I'll see my kids soon," Joy said, smiling through her tears. "We both will. Kathy Lee and Connie will take good care of them until we

243

pick them up together. That's what I promised Melanie, and it's a promise I'm going to keep. We both are."

Todd thought of Jermaine and Tonya Whittock, their kids packed away in Detroit, and despair squeezed his chest. As Joy suddenly ran to the big SUV and reached in to hug her crying children one last time, he considered stepping into the last of the sunlight and shoving her into the van with them, slamming the door and waving the vehicles out of this godforsaken town.

Thought about it, but then saw the grim set of Joy's mouth as she returned to him and knew she'd never give him up that easily.

"We're losing sunlight," Highsmith called out to the drivers. "Hurry up and get out of here."

From windows inside the huge home, Todd watched his escaping family until the minivan and SUV disappeared from view. His skin tingled as though he'd fallen asleep under a heat lamp. Wrapping one arm tightly around Joy, he could feel her shoulders heaving with the force of her silent tears.

A nap. That's what he needed.

Chapter Forty-Five

He was up and out, padding silently through the dark room. Too silently, too quickly, the room looking not nearly as dark as it should. He was weightless and now look at this: he was floating.

He was dead.

No, he was dreaming. Had to be, but it didn't feel like that, either. And then he spotted the still figure on the bed and went over to investigate.

Uh-oh. Bad news here. It was *him*, that still figure. Not dead. Just sleeping, the naked chest expanding and contracting with easy regularity, the blood-spotted bandage on his shoulder, the sheets tangled around his legs. He—the *he* on the bed—wore the same pair of cotton boxers he'd put on that morning.

But there was no time for contemplating the sleeping *him* on the bed. He shot right out of the room, right through the closed door. A dream state with benefits.

Voices down the hall. The hushed conversation of at least two men. He drifted toward the sound, transported by his dream's mysterious means of locomotion through walls and doors until he found himself pausing briefly. He was high on the ceiling over a balcony railing where he overlooked two seated figures.

Paul Highsmith on a leather lounger and his lawyer friend on the couch. They sat hunched, staring at one another, only feeble lamplight between them.

"They'll make it," the lawyer was saying.

"We won't know until tomorrow," came the glum reply. "I don't know, Freddie."

It was the two-story family room of the Highsmith room. A carving knife and tennis racket sat on the glasstop table between the two men.

Perfect. If the vampires broke in, they could volley the things to death.

Freddie had added a pair of wire rim specs to his wardrobe since Todd had last seen him, an accessory that Todd must have added in his dream state. But what if, upon awakening, he was to ask Freddie if he owned a pair of wire rim glasses and Freddie said he did?

What then?

No time to think about it. He was on the move again, pulled from the room like a storm cloud. From another part of the huge home he observed Joy propped in a chair, a thin blanket tucked around her. She was in an upstairs room, staring at a large-screen television with the sound turned down. Todd called her name, but she didn't stir.

Then the dream took him out of the Highsmith home. It was still early evening, a shaft of light just dying in the west. As it did, the night came alive before him. He could smell the late-season lilacs, hear acorns falling from the oaks swaying in the slightest breeze. Crickets screamed, moths fluttered. He could feel their wings beating the cooling air, hear them touch down and even smell their dusty odor. He could see and hear and smell the night itself as if it was a different thing altogether from day and he'd know the difference even with his eyes closed. Owls glared, snakes slithered, bats fluttered in random flight patterns and red-eyed rats dragged their heavy tails through the grass. Mice and shrews and rabbits and nightcrawlers hugged the ground, their instincts honed to survival mode.

It was a deadly stew of nature out there, and Todd loved it.

He moved faster, whizzing seven feet off the ground. His eyes rose to the dim moonlight overhead, and he felt more powerful than that weak orbiting satellite. He chuckled soundlessly.

Yes, it was a dream, but one of such vivid detail that it frightened him when he thought about it, so he didn't. He let himself go, the cool night air soothing his sweaty flesh, caressing his bandaged shoulder.

What flesh? What shoulder? He was nothing, and that wasn't a bad thing. He was a dream wisp, an abstraction of existence. It was what he'd always wanted to be but hadn't known it until now. He let his imaginary body drift higher to follow the tree-lined street out front of the Highsmith home.

He floated over the residential streets, beyond the downtown and onto the industrial parkway with its sheet-metal buildings on both sides of Sennett Street and the untraveled roads beyond, and he kept moving. He flew faster and higher, until the treetops were green puffs under the vague moonlight.

And now he'd left the town behind and was swooping down upon winking taillights, and he knew immediately whose he followed. It looked at first as though the two vehicles traveled bumper to bumper until he saw that his perspective was off and that a hundred yards separated them. But the trailing vehicle was closing in fast.

Good, he thought. Hurry up and fall in behind Kathy Lee. She was the one with the twelve-gauge, so she shouldn't allow such a gap between her Explorer and the Grand Cherokee ahead of her.

Ford Explorer.

Todd put his mind on rewind and saw the two vehicles reversing down the Highsmith driveway. Connie Highsmith and his own kids in the navy Grand Cherokee and the noisy Dwyer clan bringing up the rear in Mona Dexter's maroon Dodge minivan.

Maroon minivan.

Not a dark green Ford Explorer. Not even close.

Todd somehow strong-armed his hijacked consciousness to move closer above the Explorer so he could peer into the driver's seat. Voluntary movement was as difficult as steering a falling feather or sustaining an erection after too many Johnny Walkers, but by focusing sharply he could make his formless self move clumsily closer to the trailing vehicle.

Barry! The young daylighter cop who followed Marty McConlon around like a duckling trailing its mother. That's who was behind the wheel. But why, Todd wondered, would he be dreaming of the young cop closing in on his family in the dead of night?

And where the hell was Kathy Lee?

The glorious new freedom he'd seemed to possess just moments before felt like a cage now. His consciousness was a kite drifting wherever the damn wind took it. He had to get to the Grand Cherokee, get a warning out to his family.

Just wake up. He was trapped in a horrible dream, that's all. If he could pinch himself, thrash, open his eyes, it would end.

Better be soon. The Explorer was picking up even more speed. He caught a wink of light in the car's interior. Barry, the driver, grinning like a maniac as his foot crunched the gas pedal. Next to him, moonlight glinting off a long barrel. More moonlight in the backseat: two more long gun barrels.

Jesus. Why had they waited till nearly dusk before sending the women and kids out? Secluded back road in the middle of the night. Great idea, Highsmith.

Todd screamed with nonexistent mouth; nonexistent vocal cords. A silent scream of paralytic panic as the green Explorer with its cargo of death drew closer.

As his consciousness flitted back to the SUV holding his family—now he could see his own kids dozing in the back—he almost missed the third vehicle.

His attention returned to the Ford Explorer, the grinning men, and the maroon minivan that raced to catch up and pull parallel.

The passenger window of the minivan rolled down electronically. Todd could see Kathy Lee steering with one hand, holding something with another.

"Get down, kids," she shouted.

The men in the Explorer slowly turned their attention to the van, as if seeing it for the first time. Then came an earth-shattering explosion of glass and metal and flesh and bone obliterated by the twin-barrel roar of shotgun lead.

"Everyone alright?" she shouted as the van sped up and drifted into the lane formerly inhabited by the Explorer which had, by now,

247

plowed headlong into a century-old elm on the shoulder of the road.

The question was followed by the hoots and cheers of her hellion kids.

Jesus, you don't mess with Kathy Lee Dwyer even in your dreams.

Todd made a ferocious attempt to psychically pull himself into the Grand Cherokee with his wife and kids, and nearly made it before feeling himself snapping like an over-extended rubber band, in a return trip to Babylon.

He flew past cars and foot traffic. He crossed the tasteful residential streets of Crenshaw, Tolliver, Drake, Appleby, Price, then whizzed across Middle View and flew higher over the nameless woods and the narrow, meandering creek so full of its own distinct nightlife.

He hovered low over the ravine alongside the Sundown Motel, where he heard voices. Whispers. Giggles.

He sniffed the air and found the heavy, male scent of sweat. A figure crouched ahead and just below him. The figure turned, ball cap pulled low over dark eyes. The blue-whiskered man pointed, gestured for someone to sweep to the right.

It was Jim Zeebe who responded to Purcell's command, the garage owner crashing out of the woods and ambling off.

"We ready?" Jason Penney whispered.

The man with the stringy blond hair and taunting voice stood shockingly close, but it didn't matter. They couldn't see him. The vampire's pale face looked virtually unmarked, the effects of the afternoon tangle with daylight nearly gone.

"At the signal," Purcell muttered. "Now get outta here."

Even the insects seemed to whisper. To wait.

With a flurry of mental effort, Todd lifted up and away for a bird's eye view of the woods and the motel sitting high with nearly every light blazing. He saw half a dozen figures patrolling the grounds, armed with guns, ball bats, kitchen knives.

Todd's stomach twisted. He tried warning them in his never-ending dream, tried making his presence known in some way, but couldn't. He wasn't so much a kite as a baby bird trying out its wings for the first time, unsure of what he could and couldn't do.

But while he had less than ideal command of his presence, his senses were fully attuned. He could hear bushes rustling, twigs snapping underfoot and the stage whispers of the night creatures as they climbed out of the ravine and approached their target. How could the Sundown sentinels be so dead?

"Now!" Purcell ordered in a thick whisper, and all pretense of stealth was gone.

Todd watched, hovering helplessly overhead. He listened to the grunts of young vampires as they swarmed the outer perimeter of the building. Giggling as they drew closer to the first sentry, stationed at the cracked pavement surrounding the stagnant swimming pool. It was a game to them, Todd realized as he screamed out a warning which only his mind picked up.

"They're here," the lone sentinel cried.

Todd recognized the voice immediately.

A gun barked, a vampire fell. More gunfire, more giggles, and another night creature toppled. Two more shots by the sentry, but wild, panicky shots that plowed earth as at least three of the vampires fell on the shooter.

One of the attackers, Zeebe, wore a bullet-tattered and blood-soaked shirt. The other two elbowed the older man aside for a taste, but he growled through a mouthful of flesh and gore and the others backed off slightly.

Noooo...

Todd picked up other nightmarish sounds, the confused, alarmed cries of Sundowners, in the most lucid dream he'd ever experienced. Another shot rang out and Zeebe fell over again, drawing fresh peals of laughter from his inhuman friends.

"Not again," one of the creatures tittered while Purcell grabbed hold of the dazed mechanic and said, "Time to move, boys."

"Teach 'em to fuck with us," Jason Penney snarled as they swept the open field and slipped back down the ravine.

"Let 'em think about that," Purcell said.

"Shit, that last one stung a little," Zeebe said as he dragged himself through the underbrush.

The vampires hooted, slapping palms as they smashed through the night.

Something crawled across the ceiling. A centipede or whatever else might have a hundred fuzzy legs. Todd watched its stop-jerk progress and wondered how it could travel upside down like that without the blood rushing to its head. That made him wonder whether or not insects even had blood, and that mundane thought made him realize he was awake.

He blinked. Made a fist and drew a breath. Felt his fingers meet his palm, his lungs expand, the mattress against his back. He knew he had his body back. He'd finally returned from wherever it was he'd been.

The door snickered open and Joy tiptoed in. Seeing him awake, she sat on his bed, her eyes dark, their corners lined with worry.

"What time is it?" he croaked, noticing it was still dark.

He'd slipped upstairs and into a spare bedroom for what he

thought was just a nap soon after the van and SUV pulled out.

She didn't answer.

He had much to tell her. First he must explain the condition he was in and find a way to convince her it had its advantages.

He knew by now he'd dreamed no dream. And that Tonya Whittock would never see her children.

Todd reached for his wife's hand and started to tell her all this, but she spoke first.

"Honey," she said, "you better get out here. There's a bunch of those things outside and they're trying to get in."

Chapter Forty-Six

"I checked it. It's locked," the lawyer shouted from somewhere toward the back of the massive home.

"How about the windows?" Highsmith asked from the living room.

"Locked, too. You think the glass will hold?"

Highsmith shrugged as he stepped into the foyer. "It's not bulletproof."

The shrug couldn't be seen by his friend, but Todd saw it from the second-floor balcony railing. He watched Highsmith prowl through the foyer and family room with a tennis racket gripped like a club. If that's the best they could do for weapons, they were screwed.

Walking felt funny to Todd as he shuffled along the railing. It seemed a laborious way of getting around, the constant tangle with gravity. The carpet felt rough and ticklish against his bare feet. He cleared his throat as he descended the staircase, but still managed to startle the homeowner. Highsmith wheeled and drew back the racket.

"Easy, it's me. What's happening?"

"It's alright," Highsmith replied, as though Todd were the one acting highstrung. "It's the old folks under Drake. They probably don't even know what happened at the Winking Dog. I saw John Tolliver in the crowd out there. I think this is his thing and he just wants to scare us."

It seemed to be working, Todd thought. Highsmith's eyes were wide, his words of comfort fast, jerky, breathless. He was in constant motion, his eyes flicking to the black windows while his tennis racket hand fanned the air.

Freddie Brace joined them. "Umm." He flicked a thumb over his shoulder, a strange, set expression on his face. "There's someone at the door for you."

Highsmith stared at his friend. "For me?" he asked stupidly.

Freddie shrugged. "It's your house."

Todd found an attractive middle-aged woman waiting for them at the back door. Highsmith reluctantly let her into the kitchen and swiftly shut and locked the door behind her. She stood by a built-in desk against a wall. She met each of the three men with a dazzling smile and said, "Now isn't this a fun surprise?"

She nudged a stool with a sandaled foot and sat. "You know, Paul, all this is really more hassle than it's worth." The smile never leaving her lavender eyes.

Highsmith put his weight on the work island in the middle of the sprawling kitchen. When his friend extended an arm and a hesitant smile to the woman, Highsmith blocked the handshake with the tennis racket.

"Easy, Fred," he said softly.

"Honestly," the woman said, her eyes glittering. "Why would you be such a crank, Paul? I'm only being friendly."

She peeked over Highsmith's shoulder. "Hi, I'm Savannah Easton," she said to Todd. "I got Paul and his lovely family this home. Nice, isn't it? A steal at the price. Right, Paul?"

"You're dead," Highsmith said.

She slipped off the stool with a bemused expression and tapped her foot repeatedly on the floor. "Do I sound like a ghost, Paul?"

"Worse than that."

The woman laughed. It had the lusty tinkle of someone who enjoyed a cigarette and a drink, a naughty remark and the occasional night out. It wasn't a vampire's laugh at all, but Todd wasn't fooled.

"Stay away," he murmured, once more drawing her attention.

"I never did get your name," she said coolly.

He grinned. Couldn't help it. Just a go-for-broke response that he couldn't have held back any more than the words that he knew were going to be coming from him. "I'm one of you." He heard Highsmith suck in his breath in shock and fear and that made it all worth it. "So I know all about you sick fucks. For instance, I know that Purcell's clan just attacked the Sundown a few minutes ago and killed one of them."

He heard a gasp from behind him, but didn't turn to see. He already knew who'd made the sound.

"You must be the lovely wife," said the vampire, looking beyond him.

When had Joy entered the room? Todd kept his glance straight ahead as his eyes glistened with burning tears. He hadn't wanted her to find out like this, although he hadn't come up with a better place and time.

He cleared his throat and brought his mind around again to the thing in the kitchen. "Go tell Drake he's up against one of his own kind now and I'm twice as pissed as Purcell."

Her lavender eyes flitted to each of the four people in the room with her. "Oh, sweetie, you didn't know," she said to Joy, the trickle of a smile contrasting with the pity in her voice and eyes. Then she shifted eye contact. "I came to deliver a message, Paul."

Highsmith started and stopped. It seemed to take him some time to find his voice. Finally he got out, "Hurry up. And then leave."

"You can't control this situation. Miles is in charge, and he's always two steps ahead of you, Paul. Don't try to change what can't be changed. Get out and get on with your life and don't look back." She gave him her warmest smile, then turned her attention once more to Todd. "Ah, the places you'll go."

"Get out of here," he said, ending it in a predatory growl that he hadn't expected.

"Certainly," she said, and then eyed Joy one last time. "Obviously the two of you have much to discuss."

Todd could feel the focus of the room shift to him as soon as Savannah Easton was gone and the door had been relocked. He could hear Joy's harsh breathing and a silence so complete from the two men it was almost in itself deafening.

He turned to Joy, his arms opening for her, but she stayed where she was.

"I suspected," she said. "But..."

Todd remembered how he'd spent the day dodging sunlight, and the troubled glances he'd gotten from Mona Dexter and Kathy Lee. He wondered if he'd actually fooled anyone.

Joy crossed the room and hugged him tight to her. "We'll handle it," she said. "Together."

He felt a single tear slip from his eye, follow the contour of his nose and fall into his wife's hair.

She steered him into the family room where he was joined by Highsmith and Brace. He told them everything. Left nothing out. When he got to the part about his consciousness being able to float away, Highsmith frowned.

"That's what Savannah meant about Drake always being two steps ahead of us. But if that's the case, how were we able to take the vampires by surprise this afternoon over the Winking Dog? Why didn't they know we were coming?"

Todd licked his dry lips. "It wasn't much different for me," he said. "I saw my family about to get attacked out on the highway, but I couldn't do a damn thing about it but watch. I think they're virtually paralyzed while they sleep. They see—but can't act. The only reason I came out of it before dawn right now is that I'm still in the..." he shrugged.

"Transitional phase," Highsmith murmured.

"Yeah. Whatever."

Highsmith's face blanched when told of the highway ambush. Todd also described how the Sundown had been attacked again, this time by Purcell's crowd, and how Tonya Whittock had been killed.

"I couldn't warn her either," he said dejectedly.

Then Highsmith told the Dunbars what he and Freddie were up to. He did it by whispering and by scribbling notes that were quickly burned with Todd's cigarette lighter—just in case they were being

253

eavesdropped upon by the unseen.

It was suicidal, Todd thought of the plan. But the most terrifying thought of all was that what Highsmith proposed was the most sensible plan they had.

Chapter Forty-Seven

"The best time to travel," said Paul, "is just before dawn."

He'd used that line for the first time in hushed conversation with Darby, after his night-long meeting with the vampire Drake. Then again to Todd and the others after their visit by Savannah Easton.

The best time to travel is just before dawn. Trying to convince himself, is what it sounded like to his own ears.

"You got the stuff?" Freddie asked. Also not for the first time.

Paul shrugged, but to bring attention to the black backpack riding between his shoulder blades.

"Well then?" Freddie stood, slightly stooped, a knife grip ridiculously sticking out of the front of his pants. The lawyer had fashioned a sort of sheath from a checkered dish towel, apparently so he wouldn't castrate himself. He seemed impatient to begin their horrible little adventure, but came across as nervous, fidgety.

"Four more minutes," said Dunbar, glaring at his leather watchband from his position on the staircase. Joy sat beside him, stroking the back of his neck as if her plump hands could draw out the worse-than-fatal disease coursing through his bloodstream.

Dunbar's face was totally devoid of the terrible slashing injury to his cheek from the day before.

With the Internet out of his life, Paul had gotten reacquainted with newspapers. From yesterday's local edition he'd found that the sun was due to rise at six fifty-eight today, and figured that the safest time to start out on their risky mission was about ten minutes before dawn. His working theory was that the vampires would be off the streets by then since they couldn't afford to cut it too sharp. Purcell's daylighters, on the other hand, wouldn't be up yet. He hoped.

Thus, their window of opportunity opened in about four minutes.

"Question," Freddie said. He absently rested a hand on the wooden hilt sticking out of his waistband. "Is dawn defined as when the top of the sun pops into view, or does it actually have to be light out?"

Paul rolled his eyes, said, "Let's do it." Sounding unbelievably macho. Hell, he almost fooled himself.

He took in the Dunbars, still perched on Paul's stairs. "We'll be heading out now," he said. "You're welcome to stay here, you know."

Todd stared at Paul for several seconds as his wife's fingers drummed the back of his shoulder. "We need to borrow a car."

"Take the Lexus. The keys are on the counter by the kitchen door.

Todd gave him a small, tired smile. "A Lexus. I'm finally moving up in the world."

No one even tried to laugh. The silence felt more sad than fearful.

Paul squatted to get on eye level with the couple on the stairs. "If anyone knows a cure," he said, "it's Drake."

Todd waved a hand as if dismissing hope. He'd argued earlier against the plan. "We'll talk about it later. You sure you don't need my help?"

"Even two's too many," Paul replied. "That's what I tried telling Freddie, but he wouldn't listen."

"Just wait till you get my bill," said the lawyer.

Paul had a hard time admitting it to himself, but he was thankful that his friend had insisted on going along. As the time drew nearer, more doubts had arisen. Could he actually *do* what had to be done?

He stood and took in Freddie. His gray windbreaker looked stiff, his jeans too blue and sharply creased, like he'd just bought the outfit to look appropriately attired for hunting vampires in the sticks. Then there was the hand towel-sheathed steak knife sticking out of his pants.

"Okay, Van Helsing," Freddie said. "Your Jonathan Harker awaits."

Paul was glad he'd worn a jacket. It was autumn out there, the early morning air crisp and clean. They moved like cockroaches down the street, avoiding the pools of light thrown by street lamps and lit front porches. Paul tightened every time a dog barked and he avoided glancing up at a sky already purple and gray with the first hint of dawn.

What if his theory was wrong? Their window of opportunity one-way glass with Freddie and him on the wrong side of it. His mind kept replaying the gory scene from the apartment over the Winking Dog, the room running red with Jamey Weeks' blood.

He shuddered, walked faster.

"Hold up," Freddie wheezed. "I'm a semi-reformed smoker."

That troubled him, too, the fact that his friend insisted on playing it for laughs like he was in some sort of movie instead of reality life or death. He wasn't even sure Freddie believed Paul's version of events. It sounded at times like he was only humoring him. That could get them both in trouble.

Paul waved for complete silence as they hit Middle View. His backpack felt like it was already raising welts on his shoulders, and they still had blocks to go.

Crenshaw was the easternmost of six streets that made up Babylon's preferred neighborhood. The street they needed—Drake, naturally—was two blocks away. They all ended in cul-de-sacs, only Middle View intersecting all six. Rather than risk discovery by dogs and early risers—or retiring vampires, for that matter—they had to head up Middle View, hang a left and cut back down Drake. Judging by the address, the house they sought should be nearly parallel with Paul's own.

Opportunity's window seemed to have remained open so far. The shops and businesses catering to the night trade were as dark and shuttered as the daylight businesses that were still hours from opening. Their footsteps echoing ominously, they scampered for storefront cover whenever they saw a shadow they didn't like in the pre-dawn light.

Drake was an older street than Crenshaw, its tall century homes sitting behind massive trees on lawns steeped in acorns. Here, too, most of the windows were dark, unlit.

Paul kept tight hold of a torn scrap of paper with the number he'd already memorized: the vampire's street address. He'd plotted aloud a few complicated tricks for securing the information without use of the Internet. There were ways, he'd told Darby, nodding wisely.

"Have you tried the phone book?" she'd asked.

He'd given her a patient chuckle. "Vampires don't exactly list themselves, Darb." But he'd sneaked a peak anyway and found a Miles Drake residing at 532 Drake Avenue.

"That one," he whispered now, clutching his friend's arm and pointing out a house with lights burning in first-floor windows.

It stood three stories high, a light-colored clapboard colonial with dark shutters, an attached garage to one side and a porch that wrapped around a corner. The porch invited guests with wicker furniture that wore striped cushions. There were flowers spilling from window boxes and clay pots set on the steps.

Every effort had been made to tame the front yard of its green overgrowth. Beds of petunias and violets and prickly rosebushes had been planted, and wood chips spread where too much shade from the ancient giant oaks had thinned the grass. Pine trees immense with age patrolled the property's back and side perimeter.

"It's nice," Freddie said, as if surprised after all he'd heard.

Despite the gardening touches, the cumulative effect was of wilderness winning the struggle. The two men chose a nest of needles under one of the side yard's towering pines to watch the sun rise behind them. Paul gingerly extricated the backpack from his tender shoulders and laid it carefully on the soft ground between them.

"What do you think?" Freddie asked, whispering.

Paul knew he was talking about the handful of lit windows they'd both seen before the sun's orange glare hit them.

"It's the daughter, I'm pretty sure," said Paul. "She should be taking off for work soon."

"How do you know she lives with him?"

Paul had to proceed carefully here. "I don't, but where else could she live? The phone book lists five Drakes, but no 'Tabitha' or 'T.' She wasn't wearing a wedding ring and everything about her screams lifelong spinster. Small town like this, what's the point in having an unlisted number? And Miles Drake must rely on trusted daylighters to care for him and watch his back. He brought Miss Congeniality along when he called on me. She seems like a virtual servant of the old man, so she's the logical choice of house partner."

Or at least it sounded good as it was coming out of his mouth.

Freddie took his time with it. "But if the daughter works conventional hours, she can't be of much use to him during the day. How do you know he doesn't have someone else sitting up with him while he sleeps?"

Paul didn't like the question. He shifted, dug a deeper trench for himself in the loose, rich soil and needles under the tree. He tugged out his cell phone—at least its digital timepiece still worked—and reported the time to be eleven after seven.

"I don't know everything for a fact," he finally admitted. "But it seems to me by recent events that their survival skills have dulled after a century of peace and harmony. Not that they're not still deadly, but I think they've missed a trick or two. Drake might continue to live with a daylighter, but more out of habit and an expectation of being served than any real need. I don't think he thinks he needs round-the-clock protection."

A squirrel chattered crankily at them from high overhead.

"Everyone around here is like that," he continued. "They feel too safe, too smug. For instance, I haven't seen a single home security system. They don't worry about burglars because in Babylon, *they're* the badasses. Or used to be. Who's gonna mess with them?"

Freddie cleared his throat. "That was going to be my next question. How are we going to break in? You think they're going to just leave the door open for us?" He paused, then said, "I just realized, I experienced my low point as an attorney when I uttered the sentence, 'How are we going to break in?'"

Paul laughed quietly with him, then said, "It might not be easy. We might have to break a window in back or something."

Freddie gave him a nervous look. "So you haven't given that part much thought." He got no response. After a moment, he said, "Guess we'll know soon enough if there's someone with him. And how soundly vampires sleep. Soon as we break the window glass."

"Don't worry. They're groggy during daylight hours. I don't think there'll be anyone else there, and I doubt that Drake will do more than toss and turn."

Paul wondered if he would have made an investment for a client with as little solid research as he'd put into his current venture. Then he had to admit to himself that he'd done just that. Many times.

Freddie chuckled. "You ever think you'd be doing something like this?"

It was a welcome interruption. "What do you think?"

That conversational thread had nowhere to go, so they lay there in silence and their own thoughts. Paul couldn't shake the feeling that Miles Drake might be watching them right now. Or at least that his...spirit...for lack of a better word, hovered invisibly overhead.

Forget it, he told himself. That would either be a factor in what they were going to do, or it wouldn't.

But what he couldn't forget was what Todd Dunbar had told him earlier about "seeing" Tonya Whittock being slaughtered by Purcell's crew. Paul had instinctively accepted the morbid news, maybe because he needed to believe the rest of Todd's vision—that Darby and Connie had escaped the daylighters. That his wife and son and daughter were alive and safe.

But he couldn't shake his guilt about Tonya. He hadn't even thought about including her in the caravan leaving Babylon. He could defend himself as having used cold, rational sense. They couldn't save everyone without a convoy drawing the attention of even the town's most witless cop, but that didn't make him feel any better now. Every decision he'd made had repercussions, and he seemed not to have properly thought through the ramifications of any of his actions.

Much like he'd conducted his professional life, but with astronomically higher stakes.

World, slow down, he thought. If he started doubting himself now, he was lost. He and a whole lot of other people.

"Sun's all the way up," Freddie said.

Paul burrowed deeper still into his dirt and pine needle nest and glanced at the street a hundred yards away. "Think anyone can see us?"

Freddie shook his head, pine needles falling from his hair. "No, but we'll know for sure in the next few minutes," he said, grinning.

"We might be walking into a trap," Paul admitted reluctantly.

"Yeah, I already thought about that." Freddie said after half a minute.

It made Paul wonder what the other man was doing with him if his thoughts ran in that direction.

"However," said Freddie after another long moment, "I remember what you said happened when you and Todd and the others hit the apartment over the saloon."

"You mean when Jamey Weeks was killed?" Paul asked, bitterly.

259

Yet another victim of his miscalculations.

"Yeah, but not that part. That part about how you took them by surprise. They weren't exactly laying in wait for you."

Paul thought for a moment, his heart rate kicking up. "We planned that attack during the day. And according to Todd, his floating consciousness didn't take off until after sundown."

"The women made it out okay. It sure would have been easier taking them out while they were still in town. The daylighters didn't get any help from mind-ghost Drake...whatever you want to call it. The cops got a late start and simply caught up with them on a remote highway."

Paul smiled. "Daylighters. You're picking up the language."

Freddie rolled his eyes. But he was making sense. It seemed likely that the vampires could only train their minds to float like that during their active hours—after nightfall or just before awakening. A narrow window. If they were right about that, it would mean that it was unlikely that they'd fall into a trap in the next hour or so.

Unlikely. Not impossible.

"It's like my profession," Freddie was saying. "You learn everything you can about your client and his enemies. You learn to speak the language and even think like those you're up against."

"These things, they're not clients or opposing legal counsel, and this is not a game," Paul warned his Machiavellian friend. "You lose sight of that and you're dead."

Freddie brushed pine needles from his tight scalp. They were both starting to sweat a little now as the temperature rose. The workweek had begun, traffic trickling out of the long driveways up and down the block. Now they were exchanging one set of risks for another. The vampires were all beddy-bye, but everyone else was stirring. Dawn had broken. Paul felt exposed, he and Freddie ridiculously hunkered down under a pine tree like kids playing cowboys and Indians.

Freddie groaned. "Man, these needles are killing me."

"Me, too." Paul shifted until he found more loose soil than dry needle-nose needles and used his arms as a pillow.

"There she goes."

Paul blinked. He knew by the sludgy response time of his thought-processing skills that he'd briefly fallen asleep. For seconds, maybe. Minutes? Adding to his general confusion was the odd buzzing sound he heard in the distance.

"What time...?" he asked groggily. Not sure why it mattered.

"You've been out about forty-five minutes," Freddie said. "Wait for my signal."

Forty-five minutes?

Paul's accomplice was on his feet. Freddie slipped from under the trees, half walking, half running in a crouch, following the treeline toward the back of the house.

Paul could only think, *What the...?*

Time was moving too quickly. His heart hammered like when the phone rings in the middle of the night. He looked for danger everywhere: on the street out front, from the neighbor's yard and coming at him from the lush lawn out front. Then he saw the garage door inching upward and began to understand.

It was the source of the droning sound he'd heard upon awakening: the automatic garage door opener doing its thing.

Paul eyed the route Freddie had taken toward the garage. He would have stayed in the shadows until he could sidle up to the attached garage on the near wing of the home without being seen.

And there he was.

Paul watched his friend grin and wave as the unwieldy door took its time grinding to its upper extremity. Paul scanned the street out front in the fear that the door was lifting for someone entering rather than leaving, but he saw no one. A moment later, a long gray Buick inched out amid the low rumble of its big, tuned engine.

Freddie stood at a rear corner of the garage, beside a tall, flowering bush on the near side of the driveway as it turned and cut horizontally to the twin overhead doors. Still grinning, he only stepped back, behind the leafy bush, when the car was most of the way out. Still, he was only partially concealed, no more than four feet from the passenger side of the car.

Paul stopped breathing. He silently cursed his friend as he watched the woman back out. Yes, it was Tabitha Drake, her body twisted away from Freddie so she could look over her shoulder as she reversed out.

The Buick took maybe an hour and a half to creep down the drive. Seemed that long. Paul watched, horrified, as Freddie stepped out from behind the flowering bush and took his time sauntering into the garage the land-yacht Buick had barely cleared. If Tabitha Drake had used her rearview mirror rather than turning her whole body, she'd have seen him.

"But she didn't," Paul told himself with a quick, tension-draining laugh.

Freddie had disappeared into the garage and safely stowed himself away by the time the door began its slow descent. The Buick backed into the street and nosed out of view.

Paul stared at the lowered overhead door before remembering to breathe again. He came painfully to his feet, his stiffened muscles protesting. He glanced up and down the street before returning his attention to the silent garage.

The Drake property looked well protected from prying eyes, the perimeter evergreens thick and tall on both sides. He took a slow, casual stroll to the garage. Here, he could be spotted at a certain angle from the street and sidewalk out front. Paul could only hope that the hour wasn't right for curious passersby or that his movement looked so blatant as to be beyond suspicion.

He stared at the garage door. Waited. Knocked softly. The tentative sort of sound when it's presumed someone might be sleeping.

And someone might be.

He jumped at the sound, a faint hum that built into a low rumble as gear teeth found purchase and began to hoist the door on its track. Paul stepped back, ready for a quick exit if anything unexpected came out.

Behind the rising door, he saw a pair of sneaker-clad feet...creased jean legs...hips...torso...windbreaker...

"Ta dum." Freddie stood in the center of the garage, arms spread like a victorious magician. "What do you think, man?"

He flicked a wall switch and Paul ducked under as the door started its slow descent.

"Okay, now what?" Paul rasped once they'd locked themselves in.

A mile-long Lincoln occupied the other stall, a John Deere riding mower along one wall. Yard tools hung from wall brackets. The floor was swept and clutter-free.

"You tell me. This is your show."

"My plan," Paul said, "was to break a window."

"That's one way," said Freddie. "Mine, it's in and out and we leave everybody guessing. They think we're magic, can get in any time we want. Locks can't hold us, can't stop us."

He was right. Paul mumbled an apology, but couldn't stop himself from adding, "Course, your way goes in the crapper if that door's locked."

They stared at the heavy wooden door between the garage and the house.

"Would you lock it if you had an electric garage door in front of it?" Freddie asked.

"It's not what I'd do that matters."

They stared at the door some more. Freddie snickered.

Paul turned. "What the...?"

"You're about as eager to see what's waiting for us in there as I am."

That reminded Paul of the nearly empty backpack he'd lugged around for so long he'd nearly forgotten about it. He shrugged it off, lowered it to the concrete floor and unfastened the zipper. There were two objects in there, both swaddled in towels. He took out the larger object and carefully unwrapped it.

The two wordlessly examined the hatchet, first one and then the other hefting it, testing its one-handed grip.

Freddie said, "Is this the hatchet—?

"From yesterday? No."

"Can I carry it?"

Paul nodded. "Yeah, sure. Means you have to be the first one in." He hauled the backpack, even lighter now, back over his shoulder. "Ready?"

Freddie's face tightened as Paul filed in behind him in front of the door. Freddie turned the knob.

Something on the other side pushed back.

Chapter Forty-Eight

It was turning into a bad morning even before the red and blue light lit up Todd's rearview, reminding him all over again of that first time. Good ol' Marty McConlon, he was nothing if not persistent.

Todd had climbed behind the wheel out of habit. He always drove, Joy's job to keep the kids in back from starting fires or causing internal bleeding. Only this morning there were no kids to corral. Too much silence back there.

"Honey, we did the right thing," he'd told Joy earlier, at the Highsmith mansion, his head pounding and nerves frayed.

It felt like he was hungover and over-caffeinated at the same time. And that was with the sun barely up. Should be interesting by midday.

He'd found a pair of sunglasses to keep the early morning rays out of his eyes and a fancy dress shirt of Highsmith's with long sleeves and a collar he could button to the throat. Something, at least.

Joy had halfheartedly agreed that sending the kids away had made sense, as much as it hurt.

"I wish you'd gone with them," Todd told her as they held hands at the breakfast table while, in the next room, Highsmith and his lawyer pal went over their crazy schemes again.

They'd held hands a lot lately. To Todd, it felt like they were clinging to each other for dear life.

She'd fiddled with a stainless steel napkin dispenser while replying. "I told you, if you stay, I stay."

He'd never seen her so firm. So hard to deal with—but in a good way.

"Does it make any difference now that you know why I can't leave?"

She shook her head unhesitatingly, eyes still fixed on a vintage napkin dispenser that probably cost a fortune just to give their million-dollar kitchen the look of a common diner. The sort of place Todd looked for out of desperate necessity when job-hunting with the family—and which Mr. Paul Highlife had never had cause to enter.

"No," she said. "None."

Besides, the cure to what ailed him was right here in the town if it was anywhere, he told her, trying to assure himself as much as her. It kept coming back to that. But she kept not making eye contact. He said, "It's not like we can just waltz into some big-city hospital and say, 'I'm turning into a vampire. Can you give me a shot or something?' It's not like there's a vaccine, Joy."

He'd tried to keep it light, but he could hear steel creeping into his voice. Sarcasm, not humor. He squeezed her hand, a gesture as close to an apology as he could muster.

"I'm glad you didn't go," he told her then, and meant it.

The Highsmith's garage had felt so invitingly cool and dark that he'd wanted to just stay there, curl up, get himself forty winks. Instead, he'd grit his teeth—literally—and made himself exchange cool shelter for sinister sunlight.

The Lexus had too many buttons and knobs. Everything was electrical, simple tasks like adjusting the seats and outside mirrors and rolling down the windows turning into comedy routines with the wipers dry-wiping the windshield and a blast of hot air hitting him in the crotch. Not to mention the search for the garage door remote, which he eventually found on the visor. He cursed the car, cursed the town, the Highsmiths and everything else that came to mind while Joy, next to him, wore an expression that was about four seconds from tears.

Todd knew it was the deafening silence from the backseat affecting both of them. Little Todd should be giggling over silly Daddy and the wacky windshield wipers while Melanie and Crissie fight over whose turn it was to sit by the window.

Todd clutched Joy's hand as they rolled out of the drive and headed down the street. They got as far as Middle View, no traffic in sight and a clear shot to where they had to be, when he said, as calmly as he could, "Maybe I should pull over for a few minutes." Like they'd been driving half the day.

"You be more comfortable in back, hon?" Joy said, watching his face carefully.

Hell, he'd be more comfortable in the trunk, but he wasn't going to tell her that. He fiddled with the sun visor. Like trying to stop an elephant with a flyswatter, but it gave his hand something to do.

A second later he said, "I think I'm going to be sick."

The tires screeched—the rich guy's tires, so he took a tiny measure of satisfaction in taking off a layer of rubber—as he hung a hard left across two empty lanes and barreled into a parking lot. Pizza Cavern, the sign said.

A cavern. Exactly what he needed.

The restaurant hadn't opened yet, but a stand of willow trees offered a little life-saving shade in the back of the lot. There were a couple picnic tables back there in a dirt patch island in a field of weeds. Todd briefly wondered about people who'd picnic in a Pizza Cavern parking lot.

The shade cooled him down a little, made his lungs quit pumping fire. He chuckled, keeping the situation as light as possible. "Just let me rest a little. I figure we'll make the Sundown by Thursday."

He closed his eyes, let the slight morning breeze chill the film of sweat on his face. He crossed his arms over his chest and slumped low in his seat.

His mind's eyes saw the way Denver and Jermaine had looked at him just before he'd sneaked his family out of the motel. Taking everyone would have advertised the fact that they were escaping, he told himself. But he punished himself with a mental image of Tonya Whittock, her wide hips, nervous smile and three motherless kids.

Shit.

"Honey?"

Maybe he'd said it out loud. But it wasn't that, he saw when he caught her looking out the back window and tracked the cop car in the rearview.

"Uh oh," he breathed.

Marty McConlon stepped out of the cruiser he'd slid up right behind them. He wore a big-ass grin as he approached the car. While reluctantly powering down the window, Todd noticed the cop was a solo act today. Looked like Barry had pulled a no-show.

"Hey, how you folks doing? Everything alright here?"

Todd nodded. "Yeah, fine." Just as casual.

The soft cop stood behind the driver's door and about four feet back, evidently not trusting the Dunbars any more than they did him. "You on your way to work and decide a pepperoni and double cheese might hit the spot?"

Todd's hand in his lap strayed slowly to the kitchen knife stuck into his waistband, under his shirt. "We're not going to work today. Like we told you before."

"Oh, that's right," said McConlon, sounding genuinely interested.

The Lexus swayed slightly as the cop leaned his weight on the hood.

"Yeah, I remember now. That's when I asked you and your buddies at the Sundown real nice-like to hand over your guns. You the one telling me to go ahead and try to take yours if I wanted it so bad? All the confusion yesterday morning, I can't remember."

Todd kept both hands fixed to the steering wheel and his eyes out the windshield. He wasn't going to give the cop any excuses. Not just yet anyway. Out of the corner of an eye, he could see the soft belly up to his window twisting, shifting.

McConlon said, "Funny you driving this car. I mean, I get you this great job, you only punch in—what, once? Twice?—and make enough money to buy yourself a Lexus. God bless America, right?"

The sun was doing something funny. It had found an opening in the willow tree shroud and now it was making Todd's skin tingle like before. It felt red and raw, the rivulets of sweat not cooling the flesh in the least.

Joy leaned over and said, "My husband's not feeling well. That's why we pulled over."

Todd could hear the cop's labored breathing on the back of his neck as he bent in for a better look.

"Hey," he said cheerfully, "you really do look sick. What, you order bad anchovies on one of those *Pizza Cavern* pies?"

Todd's grip on the wheel tightened.

McConlon took a step forward to stand alongside Todd, and then a step away. So he'd drawn even with him, but was more than a knife swipe out of range.

"Maybe I'll have better luck this time asking you to turn over your weapons. Then I got some questions concerning your whereabouts yesterday afternoon. And while I'm at it, I might as well ask to see your registration for the Lexus."

Todd still had the shotgun, but he'd stashed it in the trunk. He didn't know what the state penalty was for driving around with a loaded sawed-off next to him, but he hadn't wanted to chance it.

He shook his head. "I'm not carrying a weapon."

From the corner of his eye, he could see one of the cop's hands resting on the butt of his nine.

Conversationally, McConlon said, "I could take that as a refusal to give it up. Anything could happen if I think you're going for a gun."

Todd thought about Duke Gates, caught on a back road by Marty McConlon. With the Santana family and others. He swung his head almost lazily up toward the cop, making eye contact for the first time. Letting the sun burn him raw. "Bet you carry a throw-away for just such emergencies," he said. Grinning through the fire.

"Honey?" From Joy, who knew her husband better than anyone. Knew he'd go for broke if he knew he was broke anyway.

Marty gave him a blue-eyed smile. "You mean like I'd pop you, then drop an unregistered gun in your lap? What kinda cop would I be?"

Todd said "Nah, I don't think it would go down like that. Not exactly." He flicked a glance out the rearview at a car or two drifting by. "It's daylight, a little traffic on the street. And then there's Joy here. Be hard enough convincing Drake you had to kill me. Add a potentially hostile witness you gotta make dead, now you have to come up with a story that really strains the imagination. We *both* drew on you?"

McConlon took a small step forward. Just about close enough.

"Drake," the cop said, snickering. "Yesterday's news. You ever hear of the title, Chairman Emeritus? He sits on a corporate board."

Todd shook his head. "I don't get the *Wall Street Journal.*" Meaning it in more ways than one.

McConlon laughed. "I guess I was fooled by your new car. Anyway, old bigwig, he can't find the executive washroom anymore, so they give him a title. Chairman Emeritus, or some such. Means jack shit. Means he no longer remembers to zip up when he's done, but it's a title of respect. He gets to keep reporting to work in the morning if he wants to, keeps a bigger office than he needs and the secretaries call him 'sir.' You see where I'm going with this, Todd?"

He did, but he didn't give the cop the satisfaction.

"That's what I told that pissant department store owner who thought his shit didn't stink. Couldn't believe how we had to strong-arm him to get one lousy job out of him, then he refused to continue to cooperate when that job needed..." he grinned, "...filling again. And look how things turned out. Did his buddy Drake save him? Those old fucks couldn't even handle a simple surprise attack against a bunch of bums in a day-rate motel."

The cop set his elbows on the window frame and leaned in. No longer so cautious.

"That's right. I know all about it. Darwin Dukey Gates got quite chatty toward the end. Figuring, I suppose, it'd help his cause."

After the jolt of fear had spent itself, Todd remembered that Gates and the Santanas had been taken care of in a desolate patch of highway. Not in the middle of town with the sun shining. Not that many of the good citizens of Babylon, Michigan would report the sounds of gunfire.

"Bottom line, you don't have any protection, Dunbar. Step out of the car and—"

Todd was ahead of him. He'd already thrown open the door, bumping the lawman aside, and was climbing out of the Lexus. The knife spilled out of his waistband and fell harmlessly to the ground. McConlon went for his gun. He looked scared, but he had the nine leveled at Todd's chest in a two-hand stance, the barrel only wavering slightly.

Todd's sudden response had played out a whole lot more dramatically in his mind. In reality, the sunlight hit him like a Taser, wobbling him until he thought the most aggressive thing he was going to do was puke on the cop's shiny black shoes.

McConlon, maybe sensing the same, took a step back. He barked an order Todd didn't clearly hear.

"Fuck you," Todd rasped, the searing sun making his legs go rubbery.

Joy called out his name. Hearing it as if from a great distance in time and space, he ignored her, tried to focus on the cop who seemed to be spitting out more commands.

"If you're not afraid of Drake, shoot me right now, asshole," Todd choked out.

He reeled, awaiting a bullet and oblivion. Easy to be brave when life itself held so much more terror than death.

"Might be an idea," said McConlon.

The cop's eyes flitted to the street at the top of the deep parking lot. Judging the likelihood of witnesses.

Wracked by a lightning bolt of pain that flash-burned his insides, Todd grabbed the door of the Lexus and doubled over. His skin was on fire. He was going to faint, collapse, and then die like a worm caught high and dry after a rainstorm.

"Leave him alone, he's sick," said Joy, jumping out of the passenger seat and jogging around the Lexus to join him. "You shoot him, you shoot me," she said simply.

Todd raised his head and saw McConlon waving his firearm from one Dunbar to the other. He nudged his wife aside, out of the immediate line of fire.

Jaw clenched tight, he said, "What the hell is it you think I got the matter with me, Marty? Can't you figure it out? Don't you recognize the symptoms?"

He licked hot sweat from his lips and felt it trickle through his hair and into his ears. It dripped from his nose, spattering the pavement like fat, salty raindrops. "Go ahead, motherfucker. But you better take off my head afterward or I'm coming for you."

The cop backed up, onto the patch of weeds. Nearly tripped over a picnic table leg.

"If you do score a direct hit, you got Drake coming for you. But that's right—you're not afraid of that old man. Can't even find the washroom. I almost forgot."

The cop's gun hand wavered. He flicked his gaze left and right, as though hoping that comment hadn't been overheard. "No. That can't be."

"Drake converted me himself," Todd said, a go-for-broke lie.

It didn't make much sense if McConlon stopped to think about it, but Todd bet he wouldn't. Not if he and Joy gave him no time to do so. He motioned for her to help him into the passenger seat and told her she'd have to drive.

"We're leaving," he said over his shoulder, voice cracking like the rest of him.

The cop obviously didn't know what to do. It was like what Highsmith had said yesterday: the town's daylighters had been mindless followers for so long they'd lost the ability to think for themselves. So Marty McConlon stood there waving his police-issue nine at them as Joy clumsily reversed the unfamiliar car and got its nose pointing toward the street.

"What now?" she asked, casting nervous glances at the gunman in her mirror.

That was easy. The cop would either holster his weapon or empty its clip into the rear window. Could go either way.

"Just drive."

Todd slumped low in the seat, trying to escape the sun more than McConlon's aim. They took a right on Middle View, Joy flicking one more glance in the mirror as they did so.

"He's just standing there," she said. "Still holding that gun."

No bullets flying. Yet.

Chapter Forty-Nine

"Humidity," Paul murmured. "The door's just hung up on the floor."

"Oh...yeah." Freddie giggled.

Paul recognized the quiet laughter as Freddie's way of venting terror. He wondered if his friend had been as close to cardiac arrest as he himself had felt when that door had seemingly pushed back when Freddie turned the knob and started to slowly swing it open. Probably.

Now the lawyer gave it a bit of a shoulder and the door popped open. Both men froze at the sight before them.

"It's too sunny," Paul whispered.

Not at all what he was expecting. It *felt* empty as the men began the slow walk-through. But way too light and airy. The place in no way resembled the picture Paul had drawn in his mind, probably after watching too many late-night movies. He'd expected grime, dust and clutter, a la *Texas Chainsaw Massacre*. That, or a drafty Transylvanian castle, all black shadows, velvet drapes, damp dungeons. Instead, they wandered through a cheerful albeit tired-looking colonial. The wallpaper looked dingy and forgettable, as did the furnishings, but the house was clean and relatively tidy.

"Books everywhere," Paul murmured as he followed his hatchet-wielding friend from room to room.

Magazines and newspapers were scattered across many of the flat surfaces and piled in corners. *Time. Newsweek.* Books jammed in bookcases and stacked three or four deep on the floor. Popular novels, pop histories, coffee table art books. Nothing dedicated to ancient deities or spellcasting.

There was an out-of-fashion nineteen-inch television in one room with a DVD player and a collection of recent movies with stickers identifying them as rentals from the local library. No porn or slasher flicks. It all looked just so...normal.

"You sure we broke into the right house?" Freddie whispered, their thoughts aligned.

"Come on. We've got to find him," Paul said. They stood at the foot of the steep stairwell in the black stone entry foyer. "Let's go."

Freddie halted him by touching his chest with the broad side of the hatchet.

"You realize," he said, the sound barely escaping his throat, "that we're just putting off the inevitable. He's not up there. He's in the basement."

Sure. Paul had known that all along, but had decided to ignore the fact for now. Start elsewhere, with the cheery kitchen, the sun-drenched, book-strewn living room, the den that looked like everyone else's. Then try the bedrooms upstairs. It can't hurt.

But they knew.

Fifteen minutes later, they found that at least the light worked. Not like in the movies where the heroes would click, click the wall switch at the top of the basement stairs and find the bulb was dead—surprise, surprise—and that they had to traipse to the vampire's lair in the pitch dark.

Paul in the lead, they crept down the brightly lit wooden slats, Freddie gripping Paul's arm and resting the broad end of the hatchet on his shoulder.

The creaky stairs ended at a large, unlit room as dark and musty as Paul's imagination had painted it. Freddie pulled the hanging cord of a wobbly bulb that threw down a smeary wash of light. Paul could see a concrete floor that was chipped and cracked. It rose in little hills as though poured over a stormy lake. The room smelled of turpentine and bleach and other strong chemicals, and of dust and age.

We're trapped down here, Paul thought. Screwed if someone came to block the top of the stairs.

Freddie waved the hatchet at a washer and dryer, at a paint-splattered sink, a rotary-dial telephone attached to one wall.

Paul pointed to a high hump in dirty laundry piled on the floor.

"You think?" said Freddie.

Paul edged closer, meaning to nudge the pile with his toe, but his muscles locked up and his foot refused to raise. Instead, he dragged it toward the lump, imagining a withered hand whipping out and grabbing his ankle.

Paul blinked, mildly surprised that it didn't happen that way. That the lump remained sentient as his foot snagged it. He toed clothing away until nothing remained of the pile but more clothing, and only then did he let loose a breath he'd forgotten he was holding. It made a small sound, like air escaping an untied balloon.

"The door," Freddie whispered, laying a hand lightly on his shoulder.

Against a cinderblock wall on the other side of the dank room was an unpainted wooden door sealed flush with the rough wall. It might gain entrance to a storage room, a workshop, rec room...anything.

But it wouldn't be any of those things.

Paul knew.

Having practiced their procedure on some half-dozen closed doors in upstairs bedrooms, cluttered closets, a bathroom and elsewhere

272

throughout the house, they knew exactly what to do. Paul would press his back to the wall by the frame, take a firm grip on the knob, turn it as quickly and silently as possible and push the door open. Freddie, stationed near the hinge side and holding the hatchet in a two-handed grip, would get to charge in first.

But this one was different. This was the real deal, they both knew. Paul could read it on Freddie's face as they stared each other down.

Paul made a throat-clearing sound. When he spoke, it was low volume, but not a whisper. Why bother? Either they were already expected on the other side, or they weren't. "When you're ready," he said.

Freddie nodded, absently scraping his whiskers with the back of the blade.

"Me first." That was a break from the standard routine, but it felt like something Paul had to say. His house, his godforsaken community, his decision to move here.

Freddie didn't fight him for the honor.

Chapter Fifty

Ponytail Pete obviously loved his assignment. He had the Rambo thing going with a red bandanna tied to his forehead, Judd's taped baseball bat slung in a homemade sling on his back and Denver's 30-.30 deer rifle cradled in his arms.

"Nice," Todd murmured as Pete helped Joy drag him out of the Lexus.

"Where you hit?" the snaggle-toothed driveway sentry asked, his voice sounding hazy, as though coming at him from far away. "They catch you guys, those bastards down by the road? We thought you left us yesterday, man, but Mona tole us you'd be back. You should see what they done to us last night. Poor Tonya dead and Jermaine near crazy. Say, you dint bring any food back, didja? We're running low."

The single squad car at the foot of the motel drive had left them alone. Maybe Marty had radioed ahead to make sure the Dunbars were ignored. Or the cops were just too afraid to act without orders. Likelier still, the Sundown was like one of those roach traps that lets you in without a problem. It's getting out that's the bitch.

Todd heard Joy from miles and miles away saying no, everything's fine. Just help me get him in and put him to bed.

"But what happened?" Pete was asking as he tugged on Todd's sluggish body.

Or maybe it was someone else doing the tugging. It was hard to say, all stimuli fading so fast. His last thoughts before his brain turned off the lights were about how his Sundown friends would react when they found out the truth. Maybe he'd wake up with an ash stake through his heart.

The robbery itself was no problem whatsoever. Just two guys at work and a single customer, a house painter buying solvents. The locals took one look at all the guns pointed their way and got instantly cooperative.

Nope, no objection at all to you boys loading up as many hatchets and chainsaws and fuel drums as you can carry. Hey, we'll even help you pack up your car. Don't have one? Why don't you take the Chevy pickup parked right outside?

Well, maybe not as cooperative as that, but close. The gunmen added flashlights and lanterns, batteries and walkie-talkies to their shopping list, even bags of trail mix on display by the cash register.

The gas station on Third and Main View, same way, but only after

D.B., Denver and Jermaine had locked the hardware store people in the basement and cut the phone lines and told them to count real slow to five hundred before coming up.

Things didn't get complicated till the men in the gas station figured out that the Sundowners needed the fuel pumps turned on, but weren't going to submit credit cards for payment. They didn't take well to that, but Jermaine waved that Smith & Wesson of his and everyone went running for cover.

D.B. was keeping everyone cool, especially Jermaine, who looked grim and half spent. D.B. hadn't even wanted the new widower going along on the raid, but what could he do? There was no stopping the guy.

Then someone said, "Hey, I think he's coming around."

Then someone else goes: "The sun's not even down yet."

And Joy goes, "Well, you know, he's not a full-fledged vampire yet, so I guess he don't follow all the rules."

Todd in his sorry-ass in-between state thinking, Jesus Christ, you can*not* keep that woman quiet.

Todd closed his eyes and opened them again, but no, it wasn't just a bad dream. D.B. was still there, his pink grinning face all of a foot from his own. The room was dark and stuffy, shades drawn, curtains pulled.

Todd licked his lips, his mouth so dry it felt like he'd swallowed sand. From somewhere beyond D.B.'s big pink face, Mona Dexter was saying, "Sorry about the lack of air conditioning, but they cut the power toward morning."

Not that he'd experienced a working window unit since they'd gotten there, but the guest room of Mona Dexter's usually icy apartment felt even stuffier than the Dunbar family's old rooms.

Joy came into view, sat on the bed and squeezed Todd's hand. "It's okay, honey. D.B. and Mona know what happened."

"We don't hold it against you," D.B. offered.

"Who else?" Todd's voice sounded rusty to his own ears, like he hadn't used it for a half-century or so.

"Well, Carl," Joy admitted. "And he might have mentioned something to Jermaine, thinking he might enjoy someone else's bad news. You know, so he don't think he's the only one suffering."

"Glad I could help," Todd grumped. "Then what happened?"

D.B. frowned. "What do you mean?"

"You slipped out of here through the woods to avoid the cops at the end of the drive, stole a pickup and stuck up the hardware store and gas station. What then?"

The group surrounding him stared, wide-eyed.

"Musta heard us talking," D.B. said.

Once again, Todd had felt himself rising, floating out of his bed and joining the others as an observer. The scene felt disjointed, scenes jumbled and surreal gaps of action missing. Like someone put behind the wheel of a car for the first time and told to take off.

"That must be it," he said.

He took his first good look around the intensely feminine room. Joy sat on the bed next to him, holding one of his hands in both of hers over the lacy spread. Mona Dexter rocked gently in a rose-painted rocker in one corner while D.B. hovered overhead like a big pink jack o'lantern.

"Water," Todd croaked.

He felt numb with weariness. He downed the glass passed to him from his wife as he felt the others studying him with concern. Wondering what a vampire looked like up close. Maybe gauging the odds of him ripping their throats out if they strayed too close.

Frankly, he was working himself into enough of a simmering piss fit to consider the same odds.

D.B. said, "Well, picking up where we left off..."

It was a part of the story that had come in to him particularly hazily, so he listened carefully.

The three men—D.B., Jermaine and Denver—had squealed out of the gas station in the stolen pickup, Jermaine waving his .38 like a black Dillinger. As they hit the 'S' curve where Main View became Pleasant Run, Denver poked his scoped deer rifle out the passenger window.

"We had to assume the squad car that had been parked at the foot of the Sundown most of the day would still be there, the cops alerted by radio," said D.B.

But if the radio had been on, the two cops, not much more than boys, hadn't been listening. One lay sprawled on the car hood with his shirt unbuttoned, taking in the afternoon rays. The other had just found a tree for relieving his full bladder. They scattered as the pickup came roaring at them, Jermaine and Denver riddling the cruiser just for the mean hell of it.

Yes, thought Todd. He remembered this part. Sort of. But the images came back to him like the parts of a movie glimpsed while in the process of nodding off on the couch. You have to rewind it some the next day to make it all make sense.

"They fired a couple wild shots at us, I think, but didn't try coming after us."

"They won't," Todd said. He was fading fast. He moved his numbed fingers over his wife's hand just to try to get feeling back into them. "Purcell's daylighters are after immortality, or as close to it as they can get." He had to struggle for every word, his mind as tired as his body. "But that don't mean shit if they get killed before they can get it. That's why they won't take any chances they don't have to take. And they sure won't call for outside assistance. But watch out for them. They're..."

Sneaky, he meant to say. But the merciful blackness set in and took him once more out of the agony of daylight before he could get the warning out.

Chapter Fifty-One

There was no sudden movement as they crept into the small room. No charging, hissing vampires. It was a tidy rectangle, a windowless space that might have once been a wine cellar. With only the light from the larger basement room behind them, it was hard to see much detail. Paul's roving hand snagged the cold, musty wall just inside the doorway and crawled along it until he found the switch he was fervently hoping would be there.

It was wired to a small lamp sitting on a nightstand behind one of the room's two single beds. A lamp whose smudgy yellow shade seemed to capture most of the bulb's glow, but enough escaped to show Paul more than he wanted to see.

He heard Freddie suck in his breath behind him. He waited, really needing a wisecrack that never came. Holding the hatchet as far out in front of him as his arm would allow, the lawyer jerkily backed out of the small room, looking like he could bolt for the stairs at any moment. Paul was right with him.

He said, "Freddie," trying to steel his own nerves as well of those of his friend.

His voice rang out too sharply in the heavy silence. It bounced from wall to wall, eliminating whatever element of surprise they'd somehow managed to keep, but caused no movement of either sheeted figure in the space whose doorway they precariously blocked.

Paul gently pulled his friend back into the small room.

"Jesus," Freddie whispered. It sounded as much like a prayer as an exclamation.

Paul read plenty into that single word. Freddie had accompanied him on a lark. Never really believing in vampires, for God's sake, but possessing enough of an imagination to be frightened at all the right moments. Until now, the fear was that of kids too old to believe in ghosts even while telling ghost stories at night.

Now it was the real deal.

Paul jumped nearly as high as Freddie at the piercing shriek that bounced from wall to wall. Freddie spun in circles, waving the hatchet wildly. At Paul, at the beds, at the sheeted figures, the doorway and everything beyond.

"Easy, Freddie, it's just the telephone," Paul gasped, only fully realizing the fact as he said it.

He tore his cell phone out of his pocket, but only to use its digital timepiece.

"Darby," he said as the sound tore through the darkness a second time. "Just like we planned."

In all the suspense and drama he'd forgotten all about her scheduled nine o'clock phone call. Since cell phones were so undependable, she'd taken the Drake home phone number with her so she could call him here to tell him she was safe.

Paul backed once more out of the small room and eyed the rotary dial phone on the wall of the larger space. Evidently the thing actually worked.

"What if it's not her?" Freddie asked as Paul moved toward it.

He stood stock still. It seemed like he, Darby and Freddie had thought of everything. For instance, if she heard a stranger's voice when she called she was to ask for someone else, apologize for the wrong number and get the hell out of whatever rest stop they were at. And even if Paul did answer, she was not, under any circumstance, to tell him where they were.

All of those sensible precautions but they'd never thought to devise a way for him to safely answer in Drake's house. Presumably, anyone who knew the family would know that Miles was "indisposed" during daylight hours—but what if it was someone expecting Tabitha to be available? How long would it take for word to get around the tiny town that a stranger had picked up the Drakes' line?

"You gonna get it?" Freddie said after the third stomach-twisting ring.

They should have devised a code: ring twice, hang up, three more rings, pick up. Whatever.

Four rings.

"Do it," Freddie hissed. "For chrissake, you're waking them up." The lawyer, eyes wide, nodded toward the sheets twitching in both narrow beds.

Paul moved to the larger room and pulled the receiver off the hook. "Yeah. Hello?" he said before he could overthink it.

"My God, you did it."

It was Darby. Paul closed his eyes in relief. It felt like every muscle in his body slackened. He let himself sag against the cold, damp wall.

"Paul? Paul?"

"Yes, honey, I'm here. You're at a pay phone, right? Don't tell me where, but you're going to immediately leave the location when you hang up, right?"

She told him that everything was fine and that she knew what to do, and asked him how he was doing.

Paul chuckled, a sound that slipped off the basement walls. "Well, we got in the house. As you know. The…things…are in the basement, and we were just about to—"

279

"Things? As in, plural?"

"Come on, Paul. Hurry up," Freddie whispered hoarsely.

Paul waved him off. "Two of them. We're not sure which two yet. We just got started. But tell me what happened last night."

Musty. The place smelled like his nightmare concept of a tomb. Paul tried stretching the cord as far as it could go, but couldn't get enough flex to check out the sheeted figures Freddie was watching in wide-eyed repugnance from the relative safety of the doorway.

Meanwhile, the story poured forth from Darby like she'd been waiting for him to ask. She was telling him as though for the first time, but it sounded a little like a summary of a film he'd forgotten having long ago seen. New...and yet maddeningly familiar. It took several seconds before it dawned on him that she was telling him the up-close-and-personal account Todd Dunbar had earlier relayed from a psychic distance.

Darby's voice expressed all the terror that had been missing in the tale previously. He could now feel what it felt like to be stalked by a silent van on a desolate road in the middle of the night. Gunshots, bullet holes, shattered glass, crumpled metal, screams, flames, hysterical children.

"I'm sorry," he whispered when she'd finished and he could hear the tears clogging her throat.

They listened to each other breathing on the line until Freddie interrupted with, "Um, Paul? They keep...moving."

He told Darby he loved her and she said the same and he told her to be safe and to keep their son and his daughter well.

As he cradled the phone, he turned to see Freddie holding the Canon in the palm of one hand.

"I think we should hurry, man," he said.

Meaning it was time to unwrap those things. Paul stood in the doorway of the smaller room for a closer look. One narrow bed lined up against each parallel wall, with maybe four feet of walking space between. There was a single nightstand with a single lamp filling up that common area, a rag rug underfoot so the sleepers wouldn't have to wake up to cold feet on bare concrete. The walls had been whitewashed in a bleak attempt at brightening the place.

"Now what?"

"Turn it on."

Paul had given his friend a brief lesson in operating the camera in video mode. Still, Freddie looked and acted like he'd never seen a digital camera before. He struggled with buttons, toggle switches, the zoom setting, the record button and viewfinder.

"What if the batteries—?"

"They're fully charged," Paul snapped. "I handled it overnight. Just point and shoot."

"Nothing to shoot." Freddie looked up at him. "Yet."

Paul's cue. He stared at the two wrapped lumps. The sheet on the left twitched. An elbow, maybe. Looking closer, he could see both sheets inflating and deflating where mouths would be.

"When you get a red "Rec" icon in your monitor, you're recording," he said.

"I figured that out already. Quit stalling."

They looked like a pair of mummies. Paul inched closer to the one on—flip a coin—the left and took hold of the sheet. It was warm with body heat. Paul pulled his hand away and wiped it off on his shirt.

"Come on," said Freddie, barely breathing.

"You getting this?" He sure as hell didn't want to have to do it again.

Freddie didn't even dignify it with a response.

Paul started to rip the sheet away in one fluid motion, like an amateur magician doing the old tablecloth trick. Started to, but caught himself. Bad plan if it disturbed the thing's sleep. He remembered with a shudder poor Jamey Weeks letting that shade fly.

He moved through it cautiously. Slowly peeled back the sheet, the camera soundlessly documenting. At least it better be.

He picked up his pace, revealing a head of hair not as white as Drake's, and less of it. The head rounder, the skin more wrinkled but less mottled. He pealed back more. The inverted smile, the forehead creased in a sleeping scowl against the lamplight...

John Tolliver.

The eyes were going to fly open, the irises hard and brown and knowing, and he'd be captured by the vampire's hypnotic glare.

Paul stepped way. "Wrong one. Turn it off."

"So that's it,"Freddie said, lowering the camera. "I guess I thought it'd be more..."

He didn't finish it, but the unspoken word *dramatic* hung in the air.

You want drama, you should have been with us yesterday, Paul thought.

He went to work on the other bedded figure, faster this time. "You getting this?" he asked over his shoulder.

"Yep."

"Come closer. I mean, zoom in. Remember how?"

Paul sat next to the prone figure, his face nervously posed no more than a couple feet from the other's. The thing had the pallor of putty. His face looked dry and chalky to the touch, the lips with barely more color than the cheeks.

"We're getting a close-up, Drake," he murmured. He had to

concentrate to steer the fear from his voice.

He even managed a small, tight smile. "You're gonna be a big star, Miles Drake," he said, speaking loud enough to be picked up by the camera's microphone. "Think back to Sunday night, when your cronies attacked the Sundown while you gave me more than a century of background. Everything, Drake. Dear homicidal Frederick Darrow and that sweet daughter of yours. And the murder of Frank Dexter? But I think the highlight of the long evening was how your vampire buddies wiped out the Jeff McConlon family in Ithaca, New York."

The vampire's mouth twitched. Just reflex action, Paul told himself. He had to believe that.

He cleared his throat. God, it was hard sounding calm and self-assured when his stomach roiled, when his skin ran slick with sweat on a cool morning in a cool basement.

"Quite an earful, Drake, but who'd believe such a bizarre story if I went to the police? No one. That's why you were unconcerned about giving me every last detail. That and the fact that you had to keep me busy while John here and your old friend Chaplin and the others attacked the Sundown."

He could feel his anger growing as he chatted on. He leaned even closer so Freddie could catch him in close frame with the putty-skinned vampire.

"Get ready for this, Drake. Darby and I ran video and audio the whole evening."

That was the hardest part, having to implicate his wife. But it was necessary to lend credence to his story, so Drake would know he wasn't bluffing. Paul briefly explained how she'd caught him on videocam from the second floor balcony and how they'd rigged a second camera in a bookcase and a digital recorder between the cushion and his easy chair.

"We got two video angles and an audio file out of it, Drake," he told the sleeping creature. "Now Darby's long gone and even I have no idea where she is. But what I do know is that she found a coffee shop or a library somewhere along the way—an anonymous place where she could download the files and send them as email attachments to various addresses."

Paul thought he saw REM activity under the vampire's nearly translucent lids, and he moved his head away.

"She stored them online somewhere and sent retrieval directions to various people. Maybe to friends, lawyers, old classmates. Even I don't know because I told her not to tell me. She told the recipients to only take action if she disappears, at which point they're to send the files to police agencies and media."

He forced himself to smile confidently for the camera.

"You'll try to recall exactly what you told me the other night and wonder how much of it is prosecutable. You'll also figure that the police will dismiss it as nothing more than the ravings of an elderly man—and you might be right. But I'll bet you gave me details of the McConlon killings that weren't released to the public. The way you tore into the pregnant woman's abdomen for the fetus, for instance. That sounds like the sort of thing that isn't graphically shared even today. And consider this, Drake."

Paul moved in closer again, his fear of the sleeping creature at its lowest point since they'd broken in.

"At the very least, the police will visit Babylon to investigate. Not to mention the tabloid journalists with camera crews. Darby added her own narrative to the digital files, Drake. With lots of names. The cops will want to know what happened to the Highsmiths, the Dunbars, Don Brandon and the rest. And what will your people think when outsiders start tearing this town apart? What if the police demand an interview with you and others of your kind at, say, high noon? When the reporters knock on your door, middle of the day?"

He pulled away again, but stayed close enough to make camera frame. This was the part he found hardest to deliver. "But your secrets are safe with us, Drake. The only way we'll give you up is if our lives are in danger."

Freddie murmured, "It's getting late."

Paul nodded and returned his attention to the vampire. "Think what we could do to you and Tolliver right now, Drake. We had no problem breaking in, no problem getting to you. But we let you live because we need you as much as you need us. We can't move all of the Sundowners out without attracting unwanted attention from your daylighters, so we need you to do what you want to do anyway. Take on Purcell."

On camera, he sounded so much more confident than he felt. He forced himself to once again move in close to that mottled, ancient skin. He caught a whiff like the long-term storage scent of old clothing.

"You've got a precarious hold on things around here, Drake. Some of the younger generation thinks you're a joke. Think about what happens to your reputation if the authorities move in because you said too much and it all got caught for the cameras."

While filming, Freddie had been removing one of the final items from the backpack. Now he opened Paul's laptop, attached the cables and they quickly connected camera to computer and transferred this latest video file to the hard drive.

Paul, meanwhile, took the memory card out of his camera and stared at it.

"What?" Freddie asked.

"I'm not even sure he'll know what this is," he said.

"Then leave the whole camera. Even he'll be able to figure that out."

Paul re-inserted the memory card and left the Canon on the vampire's pillow.

"You wake up with a camera by your head that wasn't there when you went night-night," said Freddie, "you get curious enough to play it. Don't you think?"

To be on the safe side, Paul scrawled some basic usage instruction on the back of a dog-eared business card he found in his wallet and left it with the camera.

Chapter Fifty-Two

Many transvestites are practicing heterosexuals. Some, in fact, have more practice at it than a lot of men who can stay out of their wives' underwear drawers. Furthermore, cross dressers come in tall, short, fat, slim, hunky and frail packages, and as far as jobs go they run the gamut from construction workers to male models to chemical engineers. And the women who stay with them! Positively gorgeous, some of them, the kind you'd never get a shot at if you had a deep voice and five o'clock shadow.

"It's unreal, man."

Freddie's words every time he'd come rushing back to Paul at commercial breaks from whatever daytime television show he was watching. "This is wild. Hell, some of those guys are so pretty *I'd* date them. Can you imagine how memorable your first time would be?"

Freddie was in denial again, and not only regarding his sexual orientation. He'd spent most of the remainder of the morning and early afternoon in brooding silence. Like a lawyer considering his options. Toward midday he'd found the remote and the flat-screen in an upstairs den and kept checking in with Paul in his and Darby's bedroom where he was trying to make up for his lost sleep and convince Freddie to do the same.

The night to come would be more memorable than the most shocking *Springer* show ever recorded, he reminded the lawyer. Freddie had just waved him off and gone back to the den.

Not that Paul was handling the situation much better. His nerves had frayed as the late morning light gave way to the afternoon angle of the sun. It was a down time in their planning, and in many ways that was worse than being in the same tiny basement room with the vampire. Too much time meant too much time for thought.

When he dozed for a few minutes at a time, Drake haunted him. *"You learned nothing from the McConlon family experiences,"* the dream-vampire said with a sour expression, snapping Paul instantly awake from one brief doze.

The hours crept by, but late afternoon eventually gave way to twilight. Toward dusk he felt he'd gotten so good at observing his bedroom's play of sun and shadows that he could tell the time without a timepiece. Just examine the colors: soft yellows muting to goldenrod before the grays and purples moved in, one horizontal shaft of pink fighting for survival on the horizon.

"It's time."

He mouthed the words, but didn't move off the bed where he lay on his back, his head propped in his hands. His body and limbs felt too heavy to support movement. His paralytic fear had left him weak but seemingly calm with dread as he watched the color drain from the sky outside and convinced himself that he wasn't stalling; he was giving the master vampire time to find and play his leave-behind message.

He'd never felt such a weighty sense of impending doom. Everything he saw or heard or smelled made him wonder if this would be his last experience with that object or sensation.

A good deal of his bleak outlook could be traced to separation from Darby and Tuck. What had he been thinking, putting them in such danger? His mind ran over a million alternatives to the plan they'd so carefully worked out, but, if he was being honest with himself, none sounded any better than what they'd chosen.

He knew and trusted one thing: there was no security anywhere unless they won it for themselves.

The television was playing too loudly in the den, some cable-produced sitcom without a single familiar face. Either television was getting more niched and obscure...or he was getting older.

"I'm going, now. Lock up after me," he told the man sacked out on the couch.

Freddie jumped to his feet, wobbly from the sudden transition from sleep state to relative wakefulness. He found the remote and killed the TV. "You mean *we're* going. Right?"

Paul paused. He already felt bleak, weighty guilt about his wife and daughter, his young son, his ex-wife Meredith, his two other daughters, Tonya Whittock and all of his former clients. He wasn't crazy to see the list growing. "You know you don't have to," he said.

"You kidding? How many people you know have ever been on an adventure like this?"

There was nothing funny about it. Paul didn't try to hide his grim outlook. "Tonight won't go well, Freddie. Purcell's faction will be steamed up about what went down yesterday and Drake will be less than thrilled when he plays back the camera."

"Should be memorable. Let's get going."

Paul swallowed hard. He found his car keys and said, "You've been warned."

Safely locked into Darby's sporty Jeep, but before buckling, Paul craned his neck into the darkness behind him.

He let out a breath. "I can't believe I did that. Looking for monsters in the backseat. This is going to be one memorable evening."

"What I've been saying all along."

They drove up Crenshaw and onto Middle View in silence, but as they cruised past the Drake Municipal Complex, Freddie said, "I guess if they were going to do anything they'd do it now. Before we get to the motel."

Paul shook his head. "I think we're still a little hands-off. At least until they figure us out."

Hopeful thinking more than anything. At some point, Paul knew, one faction or the other would decide he was more trouble than he was worth. His only hope was that the video would freeze up the old-timers and their allies long enough for Paul and Freddie to slip through. And that Purcell still retained enough fear of Drake to ignore the two of them for now.

Feeble hope, but he needed whatever strength he could pull out of the air.

"More young people than I was expecting," Freddie murmured.

He was right. Over the course of the last few days the average age of the town's afterhours population had dropped noticeably. Not that each and every one of them would be a vampire, but he had the distinct impression that most daylighters liked to keep their doors locked and shades pulled when the sun went down. Just in case.

At least that had been the case before Purcell went to work convincing them there was no reason to wait.

He hung a left onto Second and winced in the morbid expectation of bullets shattering the glass. Bungalows and wood-frame homes in need of paint, the residential monotony was broken by a hair salon with a self-painted window sign and a concrete bunker of a structure that seemed to be offering discount auto glass. Half as many streetlights lined the street around here as had been present in the wealthy area of town and many of those were unlit.

Even in progressive vampire societies, it would seem, some were more equal than others.

No whizzing bullets so far, but Paul couldn't relax the tension he felt in his jaws and in the muscles just under the flesh of his face. Signaling carefully, he made a right onto Main View.

"If Drake's seen the camera by now, he'll make sure no one touches us."

"*If* he can figure out how to playback the video," said Freddie. "*If* your argument convinces him to hold up. *If* everyone in town still listens to him. And *if* I don't die of a massive coronary in the next few minutes."

Paul chanced a quick glance at his friend. Freddie sat there as seemingly calm as he'd been while watching his afternoon television. Which is exactly why he'd wanted the man in his corner if he was ever indicted for financial malfeasance.

Paul hoped he was holding his own fear in check as his eyes snapped to a rearview mirror filled with headlight beams. At the next red light, he forced his attention to stay riveted out the windshield and to barely see the green pickup with chugging engine in the next lane that filled his peripheral vision. He could just make out a male figure behind the wheel while something from a hair band he could almost name screeched on the radio.

If he spied a gun extending from that open window, he'd have little time to react. He almost stomped the gas and ran the light, but a cluster of old vampires ambling through at the crosswalk stopped him.

"Some of Purcell's?" Freddie asked, meaning the pickup he hadn't even seemed to glance at.

Paul nodded. "I think so." He powered up the windows as if the glass was bulletproof, and flicked on the air conditioner as they rolled through the green light.

"Maybe you should get your head down," he said quietly.

They were coming to the most critical part of the trip, the long, steep drive of the Sundown Motel. As they drew closer, Paul could see the police cruiser parked at the foot of it. Less than a hundred yards from the motel. If they were lucky, the young cops sitting in it in sunglasses and poker faces would have gotten a radio dispatch from Bill Sandy immediately after the police chief had been contacted by Miles Drake.

Or not.

Freddie ignored him and studied the scene as they coasted slowly past. "What are those? Bullet holes?"

Sure looked like it. At least a half dozen stitched the side of the parked squad car.

"Don't ask," Paul said.

He took a stuttering breath and waited for something to happen. It was a mild September early evening, but hot and stuffy in the car, even with the air conditioner.

"You got a knife, right?" Paul asked.

"Yeah."

"Good. It might slow them down some if we run into trouble, but I doubt it."

"Keep talking. You're doing wonders for my morale."

Paul took the turn without slowing considerably. The tires wailed and they came sickeningly close to fishtailing into the parked cruiser. He gave it more gas up the driveway, the two of them sunk down in their seats like lowriders.

Freddie said, "You worked out a signal with the others, right? So they'll know we're the good guys and not blow us to shit?"

Paul flicked his headlights twice, a code he made up on the spot.

"It's not like I do this for a living," he grumbled.

"Great. Now we got crossfire to worry about."

No bullets flew, but it was a less than comforting sight that greeted them halfway up the drive.

"Who is that?" Freddie asked unsteadily.

Paul squinted to see around the flashlight beam coming out of the darkness, straight at them.

"They call him Ponytail Pete, I think."

"Oh, Christ."

Paul braked and lowered the Jeep's window.

He looked like a scrawny Rambo, his long hair held in place with a doo rag. He carried a black baseball bat in a homemade sling on his back and three liquid-filled beer bottles cinched together with rope at his waist. A chainsaw was gripped in one hand and balanced on a bony shoulder while his other paw was occupied with the flashlight he shone in Paul's eyes.

"Hey," said the skinny warrior.

Paul wasn't sure how to respond, but he didn't have to. Mona Dexter came flying into view behind another bobbing light beam.

"They're okay, Pete. Thanks."

Ponytail Pete grunted as if disappointed at being uninvited to fire up a Molotov cocktail or rip the cord on the damn chainsaw.

"You've got some very interesting friends," Freddie muttered.

"Leave your car," Mona told them. "The guys'll take care of it."

She swung her light toward where the top of the driveway had been barricaded by rusted cars and trucks. Denver and D.B. were couched by Mona's minivan, siphoning gasoline into a bottle.

"We just got a message from one of the old vamps," Mona said tersely. "Miles Drake is on his way."

Chapter Fifty-Three

They met in the motel owner's stifling apartment to discuss how they'd receive the master vampire.

With the power gone, her big air conditioning unit in the dining room only clogged a window that could have otherwise been opened. Other sashes were open, though, and the ominous scent of gasoline hung in the air along with the screeching of night insects and the quiet, tense murmur of male voices preparing for the worse. The inside smelled like a spicy gift shop, all the scented candles glowing around them. Mona sat at her dining room table fanning herself with a rolled newspaper.

In the white glow of the candles and battery-powered camping lanterns, faces glowed ghastly with tension. Freddie had claimed a window seat, and was monitoring activity on the front grounds and the pool area while he listened in to the discussion in the room.

"The flashlight signal will be for Drake's benefit," D.B. said. "Pete's actual first warning will be by walkie-talkie, but I want them to see we've got an early warning system."

Impressive, thought Paul. The man given the responsibility of leading the motley crew seemed to know what he was doing. He remained in constant motion while reviewing the plan, coming across as calm but energetic, holster pressed against his hip.

"It'll be his daughter driving his big old gray Lincoln," Mona said.

"Are we inviting him in here or talking to him outside?" Freddie asked.

The room pondered the question. A tough choice of options, none good.

Paul said, "If we stay outside, we could get hit by snipers, rats, whatever they throw at us. I think we've got to bring him in here."

D.B. said, "Definitely inside."

"Let's hope he agrees to that," Mona said. "He might not trust us enough."

"Doesn't trust *us*," D.B. snorted.

"Who's going to be where?" Paul asked.

D.B. held up a finger, as though to hold off the question, then slipped out of the room. When he returned, it was with a single sheet of lined notebook paper.

"I made a map," he said, taking a seat next to Mona.

As D.B. moved one of the lanterns closer to his work, Paul could hear the low-level static of a momentarily forgotten walkie-talkie playing in the background.

Together, they stared at a crude pencil drawing of the motel and grounds. A rectangle within a rectangle indicated the front lawn and pool, with squiggles for the ravine and tree line out back. The driveway and parking lot and the road out front were similarly demarcated. 'X's obviously represented the last known location of police cars, and initials stood for posted Sundowners.

D.B. stabbed a finger as his drawing. "The drive is fully barricaded with two rows of cars and trucks. We got Ponytail Pete ("PP") roaming the front grounds with a two-way and flashlight."

"A big ole bat and gas bombs, too," Freddie said.

"He flicks the light every few minutes so we know he's okay," D.B. continued. He pointed out "JW," another set of initials. "Jermaine's on the upstairs balcony with the two-way, watching Pete and the front grounds. Denver, too. If they don't see that flashlight flicker, we hear from them. We got Carl in back, keeping an eye on the ravine. He's got a radio, too."

Paul tapped the map at that last location. "That's where we need more people. When the attack comes, it comes from the ravine. Less open ground to cross."

"I'll go," Freddie said.

D.B. turned to him. "You don't have to leave the premises. Take an upstairs room. They've each got a window facing the back. If the action comes from the other way, you can swing onto the front balcony and support Jermaine's sector."

Sector, Paul thought. Things getting more surreal as the night lengthened.

D.B. returned his attention to the creased drawing. "The rest of us are more or less stationary here. Mona mans our command center. She passes messages back and forth to Carl, Jermaine and Pete. Paul, you and I will go wherever we're needed most."

Leaving two gaping holes in his defenses.

"What about Todd and Joy?" Paul asked.

D.B. took his time refolding his map. He went to great pains to rub it flat against the tabletop. "I didn't forget," he said. "They're in a second-floor room, sleeping. Jermaine's guarding their doors from his balcony sentry post."

"Is he guarding the Dunbars?" Paul asked. "Or guarding us from them?"

D.B.'s hand pressed new creases into his map. When he looked up, his face was white in the lantern glow. "We know nothing about Todd's...condition," he said.

The others looked away. Paul wanted to offer the Dunbars a level of support, but he couldn't find the words. He hated to admit it, but

291

the Sundowners were right to be cautious.

A squawk of static interrupted his thoughts. Through a field of white noise, they could hear Ponytail Pete saying, "He's coming. Big gray Lincoln, and he ain't alone. Whole shitload of 'em coming up the drive."

Seconds later, they got a similar report from Jermaine up on the balcony: driver and several passengers.

Staying away from the windows, Paul, D.B., Mona and Freddie crawled to the tiny, adjoining room that served as the motel's office. From the glass entrance they spied the big Lincoln pull under the carport and idle for several minutes.

"What're they doing? What're they up to?" Mona asked of the motionless vehicle and its flickers of shadowy movement within.

"They're going to take their time," Paul said. "They know exactly what that's doing to us."

As all four car doors were flung open at once, Ponytail Pete's voice crackled on the two-way. "What do you want me to do?"

They all seemed locked in indecision until D.B. grabbed the radio from the table and said, "Let them in."

Not that the four were awaiting an invitation. From the vertical slit of a pair of closed drapes, Paul watched Miles and Tabitha Drake, Olan Buck and Bill Sandy plod toward the office door. He mopped his face and prepared to meet the vampire.

Chapter Fifty-Four

Miles Drake's ramrod stature and taciturn nature filled the apartment even before the others filed in behind him. For one brief moment, Paul and the vampire stood alone, facing each other.

"You certainly have set an unalterable course of action," said Drake.

Paul felt dizzy. He lowered himself carefully into a living room chair, his scalp itching with the intensity of his fear.

Drake sank into the couch and sat alone. He draped both arms over the back in a crucifixion pose, his eyes still fixed on Paul. The others wore expressions that couldn't be read as they found seating or standing room against a wall.

Bill Sandy's gun jutting from the holster snuggled under his impressive swath of belly got Paul wondering whether disarmament should have been a precondition. Too late now, he thought as he combed his fingers through his tense scalp.

In his cheap blue dress slacks, white short-sleeved shirt and twisted tie, the master vampire more closely resembled a Jehovah's witness or mailroom supervisor than the master of some sinister and deathless clan. But the room respected him despite his attire. It waited for him to speak, but his dark eyes first fastened on each in turn. They lingered over Freddie. The vampire opened his mouth just as Mona's two-way belched static and he whipped his eyes to the source of the offending noise.

A million thoughts seemed to flash through his mind as his eyes focused on the sound source. His nostrils flared and cheeks pinked. "*You* called *me*," he finally said to the room at large.

Now everyone's attention fixed on Paul as he struggled for a start. But the vampire spoke first.

"I believe I can smell your fear, little man," he said, fixing his dark gaze on Paul. "You sit there helplessly riveted to your chair, knowing you must take action. It's an uncomfortable sensation, isn't it?"

Paul worked his tongue loose from the roof of his mouth. "I've already taken action," he said.

"Yes, you have." The vampire leaned forward, dropping his hands to his knees as he'd done in the Highsmith home.

Paul's jaws locked. He could feel his courage melting under the hard glare, but D.B. saved him.

"What matters, Mr. Drake," said the Sundown leader, "is that you're here tonight and we can all help each other."

"I hardly see how that's the case," said Olan Buck as he shot out of a straight-back chair dragged in from the dining room. "I can't figure how it can possibly be in our best interest—"

The master vampire held up a hand that instantly granted him the silence he desired. "Let them talk."

The town mayor slumped back to his seat with an exasperated little sigh.

Drake flicked a hand at D.B. as though brushing away a fly. "But not you. I want to hear it from my friend Paul."

His mottled pink face swung back and the vampire smiled for the first time that evening. Smiled in a way that made Paul appreciate the coffee table between them.

"Paul and I have a special bond," the vampire explained. "I exposed my soul to him, so he knows more about me than my various wives through the ages. He's stood over me while I've slept. That's how close we are. So speak your mind, Paul. Please, be as brave and frank as you were while addressing me earlier today through your sly camera lens."

Playing with him like that.

Paul had so much to say, so much on his mind, but where were his words now? He could feel the others watching. Waiting. Wondering if he'd save them or trigger their destruction.

"We have you," he finally said, struggling to keep it simple.

Three brief words, but Paul's audacity gave him strength. He found, and this time held, the vampire's gaze. Held it long enough to watch the cruel smile fade. Paul rose to his feet, made himself step around the coffee table and stand directly over the incredibly old man who sat alone, spread out comfortably while others stood.

Chief Sandy moved as though to intervene, but a flap of the vampire's hand held him back.

"All Darby and I did was let you talk, something you were eager to do." Paul bent slightly as though unafraid to draw closer. "We let you ramble on all you wanted about murder and mutilation. You tried so hard to frighten us that you gave a full and explicit confession. You're so much smarter than we mere mortals that you never saw a need for caution."

Paul drew even nearer. The vampire could have ripped open his throat if he wanted—and Paul was sure that he wanted.

He said, "You underestimated us, Drake. Now you have to deal with us."

He could hear the vampire breathing, the air whistling from his nostrils. Could see the fine nose hairs bristling with every expulsion. Feeling the hidden reservoirs of hatred emanating from the vampire like heat, Paul backed away, returning at feigned leisure to his own seat.

294

And waited.

Breaking a dreadful silence, the vampire said, "Don't gloat, Paul. It tends to rally the other team."

"If I wanted to gloat I'd think about Purcell getting a copy of the audio and video files we produced."

The vampire's face darkened.

He was going too far, but picturing the Dunbars alone in the dark, trying to save something of their relationship, spurred him on. "I can imagine Purcell playing our files to townspeople still on the fence, then asking them how they feel about continuing to follow an old man who's obviously lost it. A man so senile that he could be tricked into sharing his story—their story—with the world."

A silence like death, until Olan Buck scuffed his feet on the carpet for attention. "See here, young man. It's counterproductive to be throwing threats and insults around. Let's coolly and rationally discuss the situation at hand."

A big change in demeanor for the surly mayor. Paul didn't mind the reference to "young man," either.

Voices carried in the open window on a breeze that smelled like rain. Ponytail Pete called up a greeting to Jermaine on the balcony overhead—sounded like he was bored—and got a grunt in return. D.B. quietly left the room, hopefully to chase Pete back into the yard.

Paul said, "We could be attacked any moment by Purcell and his followers. But as you can see, we're ready."

That got a roar of laughter from Drake, and even Buck gave up an appreciative smirk.

"You're ready, huh," said the master vampire.

"You could stop them," Paul said.

"Stop them," Bill Sandy snorted.

His derision drew glances from the vampires that withered the head cop. He was a beaten man.

Drake returned his attention to Paul and shook his head. "You take me too lightly, yet at the same time overestimate my strength."

A burst of radio squawk caused Drake to whip his attention once more to the two-way on the table.

It was Carl, reporting in. "Nothing so far. Over."

Mona snatched the radio and murmured into it while disappearing into the kitchen for privacy.

Now Paul and Freddie alone shared the room with the two vampires, the town's ineffective but armed police chief and the ashamedly human Tabitha Drake.

"You should have left quickly and quietly, as commanded," Drake said. "We meant you no harm. We wished only to carry on in peace with our century-old way of life."

"Meant no harm?" Paul shot back. "How do you explain having the Sundown attacked while smoking the peace pipe with me?"

The vampire glared. "You mean the night your wife secretly recorded my every confidential word?"

Paul sat back. *Touché.* "So neither of us trusts the other."

"Oh, I trust you, Paul," said the vampire with a soft smile. "I trust you because you and your kind have no heart for intrigue as we know it. Of course, we've had more than a hundred years to hone that skill."

"I'd be careful," said D.B., strolling in from the lobby, obviously having overheard at least some of the conversation. "Your friend Chaplin thought we'd be a cakewalk, too. Don't take us lightly, Drake."

The vampire's eyes flashed. "I'd never do that. I haven't much confidence in the intelligence of my friends, but I do respect the cunning of my enemies. Now stay out of this, daylighter. I was talking with Paul."

Miles Drake brushed at his nose with a long finger and thumb, seemingly lost in reflection before rallying.

"Since it keeps coming up in conversation, I'll explain the reasoning behind my attack that night. I felt, Paul, that you were being held back by your misguided loyalty to the riffraff here." The vampire took in his surroundings with another wave of his hand. "I knew that you found it impossible to leave as long as they needed saving."

"So you were going to slaughter us just to make the Highsmiths' decision to leave easier?" D.B.'s voice was filled with disgust.

Paul could see shards of white forming and breaking in the vampire's irises.

"Again. I was speaking to Paul."

Mona, having returned from the kitchen with the two-way no longer squawking, laughed abruptly. "Expect only cold-blooded logic from these things."

Drake twisted to confront her, his face already clogged with fury. "That's right, Mona. We live by a coldly logical code that says you don't consort with outsiders and you certainly don't share the community's secrets with them."

"All the more reason my video and audio files could be eye-openers," Paul contributed.

Drake's face changed, his mouth and cheeks seeming to momentarily sag. "Yes," he said. "If they're ever seen."

Paul said, "I'm going to assume that's not a threat. I'll interpret it as a statement of your willingness to work with us to see that there's no reason for them to be released."

The vampire carefully examined a finger held close to his face. He found a yellow nail to nibble. "I suppose that if your wife doesn't hear from you on a predetermined basis, your illegally obtained tapes—or files, as I guess they're now called—will be turned over to specific sources in a pre-specified manner."

"You got my message," Paul replied. "Those sources include media outlets that aren't going to care how they were obtained. Your little town will be all over the Internet, which means all over the world. Then the police show up." Paul glanced briefly at Chief Sandy. "I mean the *real* police."

The chief winced, but Drake showed no reaction.

Paul risked a glance at his watch. It was a quarter to eleven. "You don't have much time to think about it," he said. "Yesterday afternoon, we broke into Purcell's safe house and killed one of his most trusted friends."

"We know," said Mayor Buck.

"That evening," Paul continued, "one of ours broadsided and probably killed a cop, one of Purcell's daylighters who was trailing them."

"Barry Cook and his cronies," Chief Sandy muttered. "Good riddance."

"Earlier today," Paul said, "some of ours took on the town like the James Gang. I think Purcell's had enough. Their little skirmishes haven't accomplished anything, and patience isn't a virtue. I think they'll soon hit us with everything they've got. Probably tonight."

"Haven't accomplished anything," D.B. said, "except killing Tonya Whittock and converting Todd Dunbar."

Tabitha Drake gasped, her first visible reaction to a word spoken all evening. Her father's mouth fell open to expose his stubs of yellowing teeth.

They hadn't known. Dunbar's conversion was an advantage they should have kept in their hip pockets. Now Paul had to make the best of it. "That's right. We've got one of your own kind with us."

"You're lying," Tabitha hissed.

Paul ignored her. He eyed her father for a reaction.

"That's not possible," Miles Drake rumbled. "Who'd convert one of *them*?"

"It was an accident," Mona said. "Chaplin bit him before he died."

"Impossible. The process only occurs following careful placement of the teeth along a major artery," Drake snarled, suddenly the Miss Manners of bloodsuckers. "James would have been trying to tear his fucking head off, not convert him."

"I once heard about this guy," D.B. said conversationally. "True story. He's despondent, suicidal. He takes a gun, points it at his own head, pulls the trigger. End of story, right? Oh, and the gun's loaded. Only instead of painting the walls with brain matter, the bullet takes off something, a tumor or dead patch, whatever it was making him

297

crazy. He wakes up in the hospital, hell of a headache, I'm sure, but otherwise fine. No more depression. Moral of the story?" D.B. leaned against the wall, spread his arms and grinned. "Shit happens."

The room met the story with blank faces or obvious annoyance.

"However it happened doesn't matter," Paul said, trying to get them back on track. "Dunbar doesn't want to be in his condition any more than you want him there. So how do we do it? How do we cure him?"

The vampire stared him down before relaxing into a yellow-toothed grin. "Paul, I just get to thinking you have all the answers, and then something comes up that reminds me you're a blind man stumbling in the dark. You represent all the other blind people, though, and you carry out your responsibilities so professionally, so smoothly that I tend to forget."

"Meaning what?"

"There's no 'cure,' as you call it. Which is a little insulting with its suggestion that your man's condition is so disagreeable that an antidote must be found. I guess I'm feeling a little like a puff hearing of a *treatment* for his sexual disorder. But to the point, there's no returning home. Think about that the next time you want to go nose to nose with us, Paul."

"That cuts both ways," he replied.

The thought occupying his attention now was how he was going to tell Joy Dunbar that she'd never get her husband back. He pounded the chair arm in sudden rage, making everyone but Miles Drake jump in alarm.

"Go ahead," Paul said. "Wipe us out, wipe this whole motel from the face of the earth."

"Um, Paul?" said Freddie.

Paul stood and moved in closer to the master vampire. Drake didn't move a muscle. "Come on, Miles. We ignorant humans are stupid and fragile. You have all the answers. So let's boogie. D.B. here," he said, pointing vaguely to the other man holding up one wall, "has a .38 under his shirt. I say the word, he plugs you right between the eyes. That keeps you down long enough for us to take off your head with a chainsaw...which we also have on hand."

Out of the corner of his eye he could see Chief Sandy's hand drop slowly to his gun butt. Paul turned his fiery gaze on him.

"You're a daylighter, Chief, so it wouldn't even require that extra chainsaw step."

All movement stopped.

"But don't worry," Paul continued, softer now. "I'm not going to do that."

"I wasn't worrying," Drake said. He sat loose-limbed, his face mottled marble in the sickly white glow of a battery-powered lantern and a few flickering candles. "A gun battle in a small space like this, survival's a bad bet for everyone." He let a slight smile play on his bloodless lips. "You're a successful investment banker, Paul. I'm sure you don't take dangerous risks. Do you?"

Paul had to refocus, distracted as he was by the burn of embarrassment he felt rising up his cheeks. After a moment he said simply, "Deal with us or let's all destroy each other. Your call."

He was panting for breath by then, his fear and fury used up. He fell back into his chair and waited for his vision to clear.

The room fell deathly silent.

It was time to offer a more viable alternative to the blood and rage scenario he'd drawn. Paul brought both hands up in a vaguely supplicant gesture. "Look, Drake. Our fight's with Purcell, not you. Not that I trust you any more than him—I'm being honest here—but your faction's more rational and less bloodthirsty. If you want to put a purely cynical slant to what I'm saying, you're easier to blackmail because you're not bent on self-destruction like he is. You want to protect the town and continue your ways. He doesn't give a shit. So let's help each other."

It was all he had. It worked...or it didn't.

The vampire brushed his fingers together in a gesture Paul couldn't interpret. "As I told you before, Purcell and his followers don't even listen to me. He's young, I'm old."

Bill Sandy muttered, "Goddamn McConlon, but what can I do," a comment that drew a dark look from the master vampire.

Paul resisted the impulse to pace the room. Darby, Connie and Tuck were out there somewhere in the night. There might still be headlights following them, waiting for them to check in somewhere for the night. Or they were already sleeping behind flimsy motel locks...

No.

Calmly, he said, "That doesn't sound like the Miles Drake I met the other night. The man who escaped hostile crowds in Buffalo, Chicago, Louisiana. *He* wouldn't allow himself to be defeated this easily."

"Don't try your transparent head games on me. I was around long before pop psychology was invented."

Paul leaned forward, gripped the armrests so that his fingers whitened. "Drake, it's not us who are disturbing your way of life. They are. They think they're so clever, picking loners off the road for future 'harvesting.' But people are too connected these days. You can't even keep cell phones and the Internet out of here for much longer. Eventually someone will come looking for one of us. For all of us. Then what happens to your town?"

It was hard to tell from the vampire's granite expression whether he was getting through, but Paul's words had had an obvious effect on the others. He held a mesmerized audience of friend and foe.

He tracked periodic bursts of radio static. He heard the crunch of footsteps on the pavement outside the window and prayed it was Ponytail Pete. A finger of sweat tickled the back of his neck. He fought off another urge to peek at his watch and made himself forget all else.

Wait for the vampire to speak.

Drake slid both long arms to his sides and used them to hoist himself forward and off the couch with an old man's grimace. His daughter, Olan Buck and Bill Sandy instantly surrounded him.

Drake said, "There's much to think about."

Paul added, "And very little time."

"Nonetheless."

The ancient vampire walked steadily to the door, his small entourage at his heels.

Paul followed them through the small lobby and to the glass door beyond. He almost grabbed Drake's arm, but thought better of it. Instead, he asked him to wait while he propped the door open with his back and faced the vampire.

"They're coming tonight, aren't they?" he murmured, already aware of how exposed he might be, but thankful for the power cut. Hopefully, he was only a shadow out there.

The vampire seemed to contemplate the question, though he must have already formed an opinion. Playing with them, Paul thought.

"Tonight, I imagine," Drake said.

As professionally as a doctor verifying the malignancy of a mark on a scan.

"You'll get back to me." Paul hoped he didn't sound as desperate as he felt.

"There's much to think about," the vampire said while examining the ample darkness beyond the Sundown Motel.

Chapter Fifty-Five

He awoke to beautiful darkness.

It was exhilarating, like coming out of a deep, satisfying sleep with a hard-on and a willing partner. Better, even. He could feel the warmth of her body next to him, could feel the steady pounding of her pulse. That loud rhythm is what had awakened him from a sleep that wasn't sleep at all. It was more than sleep. More fulfilling, more enriching.

He sniffed the air between him and the prone figure beside him: sweat, shampoo, lipstick, the powdery scent of her deodorant. But none of these was as pleasing to him as the iron scent of the purple blood streaming through her veins.

He shifted slightly and she murmured and he froze. He stared up at the ceiling and let his mind replay, as a distraction, the scene laid out to him in his trance state of moments before.

They were gathering in the woods, snapping beer can tabs and hiding the glow of cigarette embers behind hands anxious for battle.

They're out there, he thought, his own excitement building, his own hands and teeth and strong legs as ready as theirs. But still he heard the steady, rhythmic twitch at the throat of the woman—his wife—still asleep next to him.

He watched her, practically hypnotized, his nostrils flaring in an effort to take in more of that coppery highway. He slid closer to see more, smell more.

She moved in her sleep, uttered a sound, maybe his name, and he recoiled as if struck.

Joy. He had to remember that. It wasn't a woman next to him, it was Joy. It was his wife's blood pounding so loudly in his ears. He moved quickly, quietly, slipping out of bed and pulling on a pair of jeans he hadn't even remembered removing before drifting off earlier that day.

In the daylight.

Joy must have undressed him in that unfamiliar room.

Joy, his wife. He had to remember that.

He moved to the door with the quick efficiency of a wolf. He hesitated long enough to give his brain a chance to catch up, to tell him where he was. Then it came to him. He faintly remembered bits and pieces of being half-dragged to the second-floor room.

He took tight hold of the doorknob and turned it slowly. Joy stirred as it creaked open on dry hinges, but she didn't awaken. Todd knew who'd be out there on the balcony, and then he remembered how he knew. He'd left his body again, and had seen like before. Which is how he knew about the vampires gathering in the woods.

He poked his head out. Saw no one. Allowing the door to open just enough for him to squeeze through, he shut it softly after him. He crouched, waiting, listening, sniffing the humid night air.

Every sense felt sharply attuned, an orgy of sensation hitting him. It smelled like rain and cigarettes, and now he could see and smell the faint glow of lit tobacco in the front yard just beyond the balcony rail. He listened for movement and heard only crickets and the occasional drone of faraway traffic from somewhere safely far from Babylon.

God, to be back out there, eating up the miles on the highway. Even in his for-shit Olds. To have Joy in the seat next to him and Melanie, Crissie and Little Todd whining in back.

His eyes burned, causing him to wonder if vampires cried. Maybe there was hope for him yet.

He took two cautious steps, making the floor of the metal balcony groan. Two more steps to the exterior stairwell, and that's when the voice got him.

"Hold it!" it said in a harsh whisper.

He straightened. Said "Jermaine, it's me."

Taken by surprise by the first daylighter to stumble his way. So much for his ferociously attuned senses and invincibility.

"Yeah, it's you," Jermaine said.

But he didn't lower his Smith & Wesson. He aimed a flashlight beam in Todd's face.

"Turn that thing off. They'll see it from the woods."

Jermaine's eyes did a quick dance to what he could see of the motel's perimeters. He killed the light, but still held the handgun at chest level. Still kept his distance. There was a beer bottle tucked in his waistband with a cloth stopper and a scent that was nothing like beer.

Todd said, "I gotta go, man. Just for awhile. I'll be back."

Jermaine's eye flicked to the door of the room Todd had exited. He was surprised at how clearly he could read the gunman's face despite the near absence of light.

"Is Joy...?"

"She's still in there. Sleeping."

"I don't know," Jermaine said.

"Keep it down. You'll bring Denver on the run."

As the words left his mouth, it occurred to Todd that he knew exactly where Denver Dugan was posted. While his mind had literally wandered the premises in his sleep, he'd "seen" the older man sprawled on a cheap vinyl chair with his deer rifle in his lap, guarding a back window three or four rooms down from where the Dunbars had slept.

In a more placating tone, Jermaine said, "Todd, I don't know if you should—"

He put a finger to his lips and gestured for Jermaine to follow him to the nearest empty room. All of the unoccupied doors upstairs and down had been left unlocked for quick access.

With Jermaine reluctantly following, Todd entered the dark room and drew the drapes closed for an even darker shade of void. The other man angled his flashlight on a dresser with the beam pointed Todd's way. Like he needed to be kept in sight.

Todd sat on the bed and motioned for Jermaine to take the desk chair.

Jermaine came closer, but remained on his feet. He'd turned the barrel of his gun away from Todd's chest—but not by much. Todd now knew that the gunman's purpose for being stationed on the balcony was as much to keep an eye on him as it was to guard against outside attack.

"I'm sorry about Tonya," Todd said, and found it to be true.

Jermaine looked away, stared at a wall lost to the darkness. "When y'all sent the women and children off, you didn't even offer to take her."

"I know," Todd said.

Not much else to say. He wondered if Jermaine's mind was playing with reasons she'd been left behind, but he'd be wrong. Todd moved his face slightly from the center of the flashlight beam. He thought, *Do vampires feel guilt?* He said, "I'm going to get them, Jermaine. For Tonya. For all of us."

The man's face went hard. He gestured out the window with his gun. "Them?" And let a breath out.

"I'm not one of them, if that's what you're thinking."

Jermaine's face remained unconvinced in the splotchy light. He said, "We gotta tell D.B."

"Okay. But do it five minutes after I'm gone."

Jermaine's glare didn't fade. Todd waited. He edged closer to the foot of the bed, farther into the shadows and closer to Jermaine's gun if he had to make that move.

Jermaine seemed to read him. He backed off, found the doorknob behind him by sense of feel.

Then: "Five minutes. Hope I'm not doing the wrong thing."

No guarantees there, Todd thought. Even he didn't know.

Chapter Fifty-Six

Carl Haggerty patrolled the back of the motel in just enough of a soft, steady mist to cool the night air. Todd hugged the side of the building, waiting, studying the scene. Maybe two minutes of Jermaine's five-minute guarantee remained.

He could almost hear the clock ticking.

Carl finally moved far enough away for Todd to take that long, low-to-the-ground walk and finally slide down the slippery ravine. When he'd "seen" them in the woods earlier, the vampires had been far enough from the motel to whisper and light cigarettes under pine trees without threat of discovery. They hadn't seemed in a hurry, and it wasn't even midnight yet. They wouldn't attack until they figured most of the Sundowners were drunk or fast asleep, probably in the wee hours.

At least Todd could hope it shaped up that way.

He broke into a run on level ground, snapped a branch underfoot and heard someone topside crying out. Sounded like Paul Highsmith, then Carl taking up the call. The alarm had been sounded.

A beam of light hit a tree to Todd's left, moving him quicker through the brush. More Sundowners took up the call.

He wove expertly around sycamores and pines and splashed lightly across the shallow creek bed and kicked up pebbles glistening in the mist that tried to upend him with their slippery smoothness, but his senses were too sharp, too alert. Further out, the dark land rose again, steeply, before flattening and heading toward town. His feet bogged down in soft mud and almost caught on exposed roots, but he could see well enough to skirt most peril. Even the tree toads and the bright-eyed rats that marked his path.

The steep hill didn't slow him down or bother his nicotine-clogged lungs as it should have. Teased by the frenzying scent of warm blood seemingly everywhere, his steps became easier, swifter, drawing him closer to town. He bent and let his powerful legs negotiate the quietest routes around fallen limbs and last year's slick brown leaf rot.

In a clearing two hundred yards from the motel, a shadowy figure sat alone on a tree stump. Todd spotted him immediately.

He came to a standstill, then calmly moved in. From twenty feet away, the mingled scents of tobacco, cheap cologne and sweaty fear grew overpowering.

"Marty, I can't find no one and it's not my fault. Over."

Todd relaxed his stiffening muscles as he watched and waited behind a lightning-scarred elm. From the radio held close to the seated man's mouth came the response.

"Dammit, Ernie, why can't you keep up? Where you at now? Fucking over."

Marty McConlon's crackling voice was devoid of any pretense of joviality.

"I'm no boy scout, Marty. How the hell do I know where I am?" Ernie whined. It was the cop with the prematurely gray hair and bushy mustache. The one who'd slammed D.B. and him against the post office wall the night they got Judd Maxwell. "Shit, I'm in the woods," the mustached cop continued. "Just...woods. Not far from where we split up, I guess. Over."

"So you haven't made the ravine yet, have you?" McConlon erupted. "You'll never catch up in time. Penney and Zeebe and the others are almost ready to climb it."

Todd reeled as though he'd been hit. He'd missed them, the vampires having apparently advanced from farther east or west of where he'd dropped into the ravine, so their paths had never crossed. There was no time now to double back and confront them before they mounted the attack.

He'd never expected it to happen this early, this fast. Sick with dread, he kept listening. The gist of the mostly one-sided conversation was that Ernie might as well come back and join Marty on Buck Avenue. They'd come in together from the front, in the second wave.

Todd pulled himself into a tight ball of despondency. The Sundowners were too few and stretched too thin to repulse what sounded like a well planned attack from multiple positions.

Ernie the cop made glum plans to meet his boss, then signed off.

"Asshole," he mumbled when it was safe to do so. Then: "Hey, man. Who's that? Who's there?"

It went unanswered. Todd Dunbar leaped and sank his teeth into the tender jugular flesh and sprayed the cop's tree stump red.

Panting heavily, his stomach and mind engorged with blood, Todd slumped to the ground. His senses buzzed. Pink rainwater dripped from his face and fell onto his lap. Thrill of the kill. It took all of his willpower to ignore the torn cop at his feet and focus on his next step.

He grabbed the corpse's holstered nine millimeter, at first to fire warning shots, but thought better of it. It might make D.B. and the others concentrate too much on the rear of the motel, leaving them exposed to attack coming right up the front driveway.

Even in the act of reaching for dead Ernie's portable radio, he reconsidered. Purcell would be monitoring his frequency and he didn't know how to switch frequencies to one the Sundowners could pick up.

He'd be likelier to give himself away to the vampires.

He ditched the radio, kept the gun.

Now what? His original goal had been to do what he'd already done. To make bloody contact with the enemy and thin their ranks. He could retrace his steps back down and up the ravine and maybe run into several more of them.

Or end up getting shot by Carl and the others, mistaken for Purcell's people. Even if that didn't prove fatal, he bet that bullets hurt.

Buck Avenue.

He remembered an early evening stroll through Babylon with Joy during their very brief period of optimism. Their luck had finally turned. With him about to start work at the box factory and her with good prospects for employment, it was looking like they might finally have a little money for the first time in their lives. They could actually fantasize about being able to rent a modest home on this tidy street of old bungalows with well-kept lawns and fenced-in backyards.

He grinned a wet, ghastly grin. That's what he'd do. He'd pay a surprise visit to old Marty McConlon on Buck Avenue. He knew he could find the friendly cop even in the dark.

Especially in the dark.

Chapter Fifty-Seven

Freddie sat in the white glow of a toppled flashlight, fiddling with a long knife from Paul's butcher block they'd brought with them earlier in the day.

Was that right? Paul thought. Was it still Monday, less than a full day since they'd slipped from the house to audaciously record the sleeping vampires?

The mist held his attention at the window, but the stench of gasoline kept intruding. He glanced at his cell phone time readout even before Freddie said, "What time is it now?"

"Fifth time you've asked in the last hour."

"Fifth time you've looked. It's your looking that leads to my asking. So what time is it?"

Paul sighed. You couldn't argue with a lawyer. "Eleven twenty-eight."

"You could have said eleven-thirty and it would have been close enough."

Freddie was talking too much because he was scared. Paul understood that, but it didn't make it any easier to listen to. He yawned.

"You can sack out if you want," said Freddie. "I'll wake you in an hour."

"It's tempting. But I think whatever happens, it'll happen soon."

Freddie, perched on the shaky desk chair, and Paul, sitting up on the bed he'd dragged over by the back window, guarded front and back views from an upstairs room. Their only firepower came from a half-dozen gasoline-filled beer bottles with torn pillowcase fuses. Their sole flashlight lay on its side and threw a wide, feeble silhouette of light, enough to dispel a little of the darkness without making them much of a target from outside. Paul, also in possession of the unused hatchet, tried picturing himself leading a charge, the blade swinging wildly, a flaming Molotov cocktail also in his grasp, blood in his eye.

Yeah, right.

Freddie said, "So what's with Connie and you?"

Nowhere Paul wanted to be. He said, "What's *what?*"

Freddie tapped his knife maddeningly on the desk. "She demanded that she come with me because she loves you, make no mistake about that. But the ride up here was a little uncomfortable. A little awkward, maybe, when the subject switched to you."

Paul and Meredith had raised the kids to honor a strict but

sensible moral code. Trust, honor, loyalty, integrity. These were all hard, black and white concepts without much room for ambiguity. And yet, as he'd found while his marriage foundered and he'd taken to long lunch breaks with the young, attractive and personable Darby Kinston, life consisted of gray area.

Or maybe he was the one acting like a lawyer, now. Parsing morality itself.

As divorce became more than a fantasy and he suddenly had custodial support, three daughters to put through college and law school and a fourth child on the way, he'd found that it was not a good time to hear bad news about his financial foundation. Especially not from a final-year law student in the compliance department of Anchor/Tatum who just happened to be related to him and pissed off about the direction her father's life was taking.

Connie had tried to warn him that certain transactions looked fishy, the yields too good to be true in a souring economy.

So what if he couldn't compute the numbers to justify his returns? It was a feeder fund, so that was the responsibility of its principal. And who'd complain if it looked like they were making too much money?

"Dad, these returns are so much higher than the market and they have been for years. I've also found SEC complaints about slow settlements."

"Complaints, honey. That's not the same as a formal investigation," he'd told her.

"Dad, I know the difference," she'd shot back.

But what *did* she know? She wasn't an accountant. She hadn't even passed her bar at that point, and she already had a chip on her shoulder on her mother's behalf. So of course she saw nothing good about the way her father conducted business.

"It's complicated," he told Freddie after a long silence.

Freddie let his blade clunk into the desktop. "It's all complicated. Your life. Mine. Miles Drake's. No one's turns out like you think it's going to."

Drake. Now there was a man who accepted the gray areas in his life. Paul stared out the back window at the red cigarette wink that represented Carl, patrolling the open field. He'd advanced fairly close to the ravine. Paul hoped he didn't get too close to the drop-off.

Freddie said, "What do you think's happened to Dunbar?"

Paul shook his head. After Jermaine had alerted them to the fact that he'd slipped out—even admitting he'd given Todd a brief headstart—Paul and the others had tried calling him back. Joy was okay, though. Still groggily sleeping. Unscathed by the man who'd slept next to her.

Paul said, "Maybe it's just like Jermaine said and he's going after

Purcell and the others."

Or to join up and tell the vampires everything he knew about the Sundown defenses.

With the screen off the window and sashes raised, he could hear crickets shrilly calling out for love even in the rain. He picked up Mona's crackly voice on someone's two-way radio, and then Carl's response.

But there was something funny about that response. Paul heard it coming as though in stereo, both through the radio and the voice itself. Which shouldn't have been the case if Carl had wandered as far off as Paul had thought.

He grabbed the flashlight and arced its beam into the backyard.

There. Carl.

Stationed in the center of the yard and wheeling to face the beam pointing him out. Not eighty yards further upfield, near the ravine where Paul had seen the red ember glow.

Or what he'd took to be a cigarette glow.

"Aw, shit," he said softly. Then louder as the full impact hit home. *"Aw, shit!"*

Chapter Fifty-Eight

Paul's cry alerted Carl just as the red eyes charged him.

The mattress bounced as Freddie plopped next to him at the window, shouting "What? What? What is it?"

Paul zeroed in with the flashlight beam again, picking up Carl flailing away, beating the rat off with a tree branch and muttering curses. Off the spotlight, Paul could see more red eyes climbing out of the ravine and charging, maybe a half dozen pairs or more.

"Get inside," Freddie screamed into the night.

Paul grabbed a radio from the desk, stabbed a button and blurted, "They're coming from the woods."

He wasn't sure anyone was monitoring the call or even if he'd used the right channel, but it would have to do.

Loud thrashing from below. Again he aimed his flashlight beam on the night scene out that back window. Carl was holding his own against the one savage rodent and the others hadn't overtaken him yet. From the tree line where the land dropped off, he saw bushes bent as shadowy shapes much heavier than rats thrashed upward. Paul's beam caught a white hand gripping a patch of weeds at the edge of the ravine, and a human body lifting itself topside.

"To your right!" Freddie helplessly warned the Sundowner in the open.+

Carl stopped beating at the vicious rat long enough to take in the larger shape crawling to its feet. The ember at the end of Carl's tightly clenched cigarette grew brighter as he pulled a beer bottle toward his face and lit the cloth fuse. From a quick windup, he flung the homemade bomb. It hit the vampire too soon, before the flame had discovered the fumes. It fizzled and died in the now steady rain.

The vampire had been caught by surprise, though, and he threw himself over the ravine's edge as the bottle bounced helplessly off his elbow.

"He'll be back," Paul muttered.

Three more human shapes bound from the ravine as the door swung open behind them and got backstopped by the wall. Paul and Freddie wheeled to confront whatever was coming at them, a voice saying, "Easy, easy. It's me."

Big Denver Dugan stood in the doorway with his rifle on his hip and a look on his face like he'd seen it all before. He crossed the room, grabbed the bed the two men were perched on, and flung it aside.

Freddie and Paul toppled to the floor in an indignant heap and crawled to join the big man at the window.

Denver, who had his rifle barrel poked out and the scope up to his eye, got the bolt action flying. Squeezed off a muffled bark of a round. Expelled a shell with a flick of the bolt and fired twice more, knocking down all three charging vampires.

"Holy shit," Freddie muttered, obviously impressed.

Two more shadowy figures sprang topside. Paul tracked them with his flashlight beam for the benefit of the Sundowner struggling on the ground. While kicking at rats slashing at his ankles, Carl swung a tree limb at one of the charging vampires, thumping him in the ribs and sending him sprawling.

The second one was smaller than the first. The Craven boy Drake had told him about, Paul realized as the young night creature dodged a blow and snapped the air with his teeth.

Carl backed up, still swinging. Denver elbowed himself more room at the window and began steadily pinging lead into the rain. Mud divots flew.

"Noooo," a voice screamed, a bloodcurdling sound.

And now a teenage girl—Patty Craven, Paul decided—charged to the aid of her kid brother.

"Keerist," Denver said softly.

He targeted the girl, but missed. She charged like a wide receiver, running patterns, her dark hair flying wet behind her. She grabbed her brother just as one of Denver's .22s found its mark.

The Craven siblings fell. Paul winced at the sight of the two bullet-torn bodies, but that was before they rolled and rose to groggy seated positions.

Three more shadows disentangled from the vegetation at the ravine's edge.

The boy and his sister regained their footing.

"Hit them in the heart," Paul advised.

"Try it sometime," Denver replied as he twisted, pushed and pulled the bolt and squeezed off two more rounds. The second, time, all that could be heard was a metallic *clack*.

The old guy cursed. He tossed aside the long-barreled weapon and backed up to the middle of the motel room as he pawed at his clothing.

"Hope I got a cigarette," he said before finding one.

Paul swung his flashlight at every shadow that moved out there. Carl was swinging away with his tree stump, screaming "Someone do something" as he made a slow retreat to one of the lower floor windows.

He'd raised a screen beforehand for just such an emergency escape, but Paul saw that he'd never be able to wiggle through the small opening and into the relative safety of a room without exposing his back.

One bite was all it took.

Downed shadows on the field were clambering to their feet, and more climbed out of the ravine. One of the newcomers had flowing blond hair that instantly identified him at Jason Penney.

The air rushed out of Paul's lungs with the force of a hiccup as he was suddenly knocked aside. Freddie, next to him, sprawled in similar upended fashion as Denver cleared even more room at the window.

"Take this, you bastards," he shouted before dropping the flaming bottle into the night.

Paul got back to the window just in time to see it shatter, splashing gasoline all over the Craven boy and giving Carl time to duck into the first-floor room.

The young vampire looked up, his eyes gleaming with white-hot hunger.

No explosion. No eruption of fire. Not like in the movies at all.

"Son of a bitch," said Denver.

He filled his lungs with cigarette smoke, turning half the remaining butt to ember. He removed it from between his lips, stared at it for half a second, then flung it out the window.

Patty Craven screamed even louder than her little brother as his drenched clothing erupted in flames. The boy ran, a fireball, a beautiful streaking meteor of light and anguish.

Denver already had another smoke fired up. He used it to light another pillowcase fuse. He tossed the bottle farther out the window than the first one. It missed the roving shadow, but smashed on the ground in front of its feet, lighting the vampire's ankles. The flames grew as the creature made every effort to outrun it.

Freddie grabbed Denver's cigarette from his mouth and jammed it between his own lips. It crackled as he inhaled, and the ember grew. Beginner's luck, his first flaming missile taking out two of the night creatures.

Jason Penney's face turned skyward, contorted in agony and fury as his clothing blackened and drew tight around him. The vampire fell and rolled. Still smoldering in the rain, he crawled to the ravine lip and let gravity pull him from view.

But not before throwing Paul a glare of rage and pain that made him shudder.

"Listen," said Freddie.

All three froze in position. Paul could hear Carl slamming the window and stomping around in the room directly beneath them. Under that sequence of sounds, he heard the deep rumble of an engine of impressive size. He felt it in his feet as the motel trembled. They heard D.B. throwing out orders, his voice without its usual tight control.

"Everyone back, dammit," he shouted. "Jermaine, pick 'em off!"

"Stay here," Paul ordered the others before bolting from the room.

"Sweet Jesus," he heard Jermaine cry out.

He was crouched behind a metal balcony rail, his Smith & Wesson pointed at the night sky. The gun in his hand looked forgotten, useless.

Which it was, Paul admitted. Might as well have been a magnet-tipped dart against the monstrous vehicle roaring straight at the cars barricading the top of the driveway.

Paul fell back into the motel room he'd vacated just as he heard the other two crying out and flinging themselves to the floor. What buzzed past his face sounded like a hornet before it whacked a wall and buried itself into plaster that turned instantly to dust. The flashlight fell and threw wild, rolling patterns of light and shadow at the wall and ceiling.

In the next moment, more bullets zinged through the air and punched holes in the plaster, shattered the mirror and turned the cheap wall art to splinters. Outside, metal squealed and crashed against metal, glass broke and voices carried.

As the flashlight continued its wild movement, Paul caught sight of both scared men, gasping in pain and confusion, both covered in blood.

"Freddie, Denver. Talk to me," Paul said.

While shouting in their faces, he tried ignoring the other sounds, the barking of gunfire and the *whump* of gasoline bombs he could feel in his heart. Men screaming orders and squealing in pain from the front of the motel. Trying not to lose focus, he grabbed fist holds of clothing and dragged both men away from the window and propped them against a safer wall.

If there was such a thing.

All the while, he shouted at them, demanded that they speak to him, tell him who was hit and where.

"Will you shut the fuck up?" a voice sputtered.

Freddie coughed like a man pulled almost too late from deep water. He wiped a smear of blood from his fingers onto the front of his shirt. Examining it curiously, he said, "Must be Denver's. I'm okay, I think."

"Bastards shot us," Denver growled, stating the obvious. His eyelids fluttered, but couldn't stay open. "Shit," he said, a hand roving to the dark blood trickling down the side of his face. "I think they blew my brains out."

Paul following the weak, yellow glow to his flashlight, which had toppled and found cover under the bed. He spilled light on Denver's face. There was blood in his hair, on one cheek, and on his shoulder, and it dripped down one massive arm.

"You're okay," he said finally.

"No I'm not," Denver argued. He pawed his face and held up a finger covered with bloody shards and grit. "Bone and brain matter," he said resignedly.

"Window glass," said Paul. "You got hit somewhere by flying window glass. Where does it hurt?"

The wounded man let fly with an impressive string of oaths, ending in "*It hurts goddamn everywhere!*"

"Freddie, stay with him," Paul ordered.

"You think of fangs and cloaks and bats and hypnotic stare-downs," said Freddie. "You don't think of guns. What's going on out there, Paul?"

"That's what I'm going to find out."

He crawled out the door and onto the balcony. A hand grabbed his ankle and he yelped in panic.

"It's me, it's me," said Joy Dunbar, crawling up behind him. "Where's Todd? I woke up and he was gone."

"Stay here," he said, pointing her toward the room he'd just exited.

With Freddie and Denver in there, it was as safe as anywhere. But she ignored him.

I've got to find him," she said.

Paul tried to grab her, but she broke from his grasp and slithered down the balcony stairs on her ass.

As he peered over the rail, the rain beating the back of his head felt like yet another enemy. His first reaction to what he saw out there was to pray very loud and very fast and very earnestly for assistance he knew would never arrive in time.

Chapter Fifty-Nine

He found Marty McConlon at the end of his nose.

The mist had turned to a drizzle with hints of a hard rain to follow, but it didn't dampen Todd's new scent sense. Rocks, soil, pine needles, moss and even the smallest of crawlies all assailed him with their overpoweringly distinct odors. Todd had discovered a sensation as delightfully alien as the ability to see through walls.

The most appealing scent was that of Marty McConlon's warm blood. Todd found the pudgy officer standing in the open driver's door of his cruiser at the cul de sac that Buck Avenue became as it sideswiped the woods. The cop looked frozen in the act of stepping into the squad car, distracted by the thrashing of Todd making his way out of the underbrush.

"Ernie, that you?"

Todd skidded to a stop some thirty feet from the cop. He could clearly see McConlon squinting his way in the night rain.

Five running steps and he'd be there, but McConlon might still have time to throw himself into the car and lock the door. Then there was that fleshy hand of his wrapped around the black grip of the nine in his holster.

"Ernie?" Again, sharper this time.

"Uh huh," Todd grunted.

He could hear frantic voices in the distance, gunshots, squealing tires and heavy-metal collision. Todd took a couple unhurried steps to the vehicle.

"Hurry up, asshole, it's happening." The cop was looking away now, his concentration on the unseen action to the west.

Todd grinned as the cop's hand slid from the butt of his gun. He moved in, taking his time now, slow but steady. Two steps to go and he felt a beastly growl working its way up his throat as he bared his teeth.

He looked fat and happy, the cop who'd pulled him over and brought him and his family into this town, but his instincts were razor sharp. The gun was out of the holster even before Todd broke skin.

The bullet punched him in the belly, sent him reeling, crashing to the pavement. It sounded, even this close, less like a gunpowder explosion and more like the irritating noise made in popping a brown paper bag. Felt nothing like it was supposed to either, Todd observed as the rain pelted his upturned face.

How'd he end up horizontal like that? The clouds against the black sky looked unexpectedly white and shapely. He stared at them and at the rain shooting straight at him at an interesting angle. He'd never been under a rainstorm before. Not like this, looking up.

It wasn't supposed to hurt. The bullet, not the rain. He'd heard enough stories about people not even knowing they'd been shot and having to learn about it from others. He knew a guy who'd been shot in the head while sleeping, a stray bullet coming through his bedroom window. He'd only figured it out the next day in the emergency room where he went with a headache that just wouldn't quit.

That's not how it was for him, though.

It burned like hell, and right away. Right there in the pit of his stomach. He couldn't breathe. Couldn't think. Gut shot. The worst kind. His belly burning like that, bleeding internally. How come he felt so cold? Colder than the rain on his face. His teeth chattered as his limbs went numb and heavy like frostbite.

Chapter Sixty

A flicker of motion in the corner of his vision. The cop who'd quick-drawn his holstered gun like no one's business. From his position, sprawled on the soft ground, Todd saw a pair of wet, shiny black shoes coming his way, Marty McConlon taking his time about it. Still cautious, but now close enough for Todd to hear his raspy breathing.

"Dunbar," the cop said. Said it to himself. Hard to say if the word registered recognition or surprise.

Todd's eyes flew open, his hand shot out and grabbed an ankle above one of those wet, shiny black shoes. It was only as he was starting to bring the cop down that he noticed McConlon hadn't re-holstered the nine. Its barrel pointed at Todd's face. He let go of the ankle with one hand and blocked his face with a forearm as the gun boomed. Much closer this time, much louder.

In his mind, anyway, Todd could actually see the 110-grain bullet leaving the polymer barrel, passing all the way through forearm flesh, smashing bones and playing havoc with tough tendons and muscle tissue before continuing into his face, where it shattered jawbone and teeth easy as a bowling ball rolling into glass figurines.

Every nerve cell registered agony. He made a bubbly hitch of a sound nearly lost in the blood and bone grit and tooth enamel filling his windpipe. He retched, a powerful constriction of the muscles of his throat and mouth that burbled from him, not nearly as loud in the air as it was in his mind. His brain launched multiple electrical impulse reports, none of them good.

His body twisted involuntarily when two hundred pounds of law enforcement officer landed on him, the end result of Todd's having pulled at his ankle as he had. Somehow, his pain-clenched hands found by accident the cop's throat.

The gun was still in play, a critically important consideration after the first two jolts to the system. He let one hand slip free of McConlon's throat to grab the cop's gun hand so that the third shot, when it came, hit the wet sky somewhere. Todd pulled the shooter by his throat, brought the cop's face closer to his own, reveling in his bleat of terror.

Todd's mouth opened, his teeth anticipating.

"Noooo," McConlon screamed, the plea shifting abruptly into a moist gurgle.

Todd's mind blanked as the warm fluid washed over him, the gurgles turning to airless little gasps.

It was quickly over. The vampire Dunbar's shirt clung to him, heavy with blood and rain. His jaw throbbed. He felt and could partially see gunpowder-charred slices of his own skin hanging from his face. He reached again to tear at flesh already growing cold, but was interrupted by a crash of static. Todd rolled to one side, ready to greet new danger with a snarl of red teeth.

He saw only the fallen radio, a duplicate of the one he'd left with the earthly remains of cop Ernie.

"We got footholds on the front and back, McConlon. Where the hell are your boys?" the voice roughly demanded.

He knew that voice.

Todd stared dully at the radio before breaking into a pain-wracked grin. God, it hurt. He picked up the radio, his palms so slick he could barely keep a grip. He thumbed a button and held it close to his mouth, making his voice muffled and indistinct.

"Where you at, Zeebe?" He took his thumb off the button and waited out the static. He'd forgotten to say "Over," and wondered if that misstep would trip him up.

"McConlon? Goddamn it, where the hell you think I am? I'm at the foot of the ravine in back of the motel. We're taking potshots and gasoline bombs down here. Your people gonna back us up, or what?"

Todd fought through the pain with a wide smile. His tongue probed the places where only mush gums and sharp splinters had remained moments before. He could feel his jawbone realigning and baby teeth coming in.

It was great to be alive.

Thumbing the button, he said, "Wait for me, Jim. I'll be right there."

"Damn right you will," Zeebe growled. He said other things, too, but Todd wasn't listening.

Groaning and moving slowly, he dropped the two-way, stuffed McConlon's gun in his waistband and set out to find his car mechanic.

Chapter Sixty-One

The thing kept coming, roaring up the long driveway, barreling through the first line of defense and heading straight for the Sundowners' second junk metal barricade.

Jermaine Whittock, crouched next to Paul on the balcony, said "Holy Jesus" in a way that sounded honestly reverential. Freddie and Denver came up behind and joined them, Denver with a red-stained pillowcase wrapped tightly over the fleshiest part of his arm. Half of his face was bloody and still sparkled with glass from the window, but the rain was washing away the worst of it.

Paul closed his eyes a moment before impact, so he didn't see the town's blood donor vehicle, one Molotov-targeted tire aflame, slam into the second car blockade. He heard it though, the screech of metal and the compacted explosion of gas tanks going up. His eyes popped open in time to see a tower of fire consuming the night air. He watched Ponytail Pete scurry out from wherever he'd been hiding, hoist the chainsaw from his back and tear across the yard.

Almost made it, too. But then the blood bus veered sharply, squealed through torn metal and churned him under its wheels. Denver made a sound like he was about to be sick, but there was no time. The huge, battered vehicle was still coming.

The four men on the balcony remained locked in place, Paul certain that the thing had to slow down, had to stop eventually. Only it didn't.

"Uh oh," Denver said, pretty much summing up the situation.

It hit the front of the motel with a sound that was even more deafening than when it had taken out that second blockade. It jackknifed, the backside twisting violently so that men and a handful of women inside it got launched out the doors and shattered windows, some landing in one of the gas tank bonfires.

They got up again, most of them, and ran screaming, fanning the flames that followed.

Paul watched, mesmerized, unable to even think of saving himself as the huge inflamed vehicle turned the balcony railings to twists and jags of metal. He felt gravity make an interesting move, pitching him forward, up and over the disappearing railing. He landed on his shoulder on the blood vehicle's long expanse of hot flat hood, and felt the hatchet in his waistband bite into his flesh near a hipbone.

Painful as that was, it was nothing compared to how it felt a second later when a large body landed on his back and his vertebrae shifted to accommodate the load.

He grunted, rolled sideways and shrugged Jermaine off. Still in motion, Jermaine crawled toward the Smith & Wesson Model 15 Combat Masterpiece that had skittered away upon impact.

Paul let his eyes retrace the route of their fall and found Denver Dugan still clinging from the broken balcony with his one good arm. For another moment or two. Then the big man fell. He hit the back of the vehicle that had snagged the other two and slammed to the soft ground.

Paul groped under his shirt and brought out the small ax, its sharp edge tipped with a sheen of his own blood. Wincing, he felt around under there, traced a two-inch gash and extracted more wetness on his fingertips. Not much more, he convinced himself.

"Look out, man," Jermaine muttered.

Having struggled to his knees, Jermaine gripped the .38 he'd retrieved and aimed it in a two-handed stance at the dark-haired figure muscling itself onto the flat top of the big bus with them. Paul winced in expectation of the shot, but soon understood why Jermaine stood stock-still with the gun still leveled.

Up close, Patty Craven looked barely out of high school. Her hair, dyed jet black with streaks of red, looked rebelliously self-cut with dull scissors. Nevertheless, her efforts couldn't quite hide her pale natural beauty. It would be impossible to blow that innocent face away with a gun.

As her eyes danced back and forth between the two wide-eyed men, Paul could hear the sounds of the panicky and dying. The night sky lit up with the occasional spark of a gasoline bomb or the steady flare-up of ruptured fuel tanks. Shots were fired continuously, and D.B. was shouting, "Quick, someone give me a loaded gun."

Soon, he knew, they'd be out of ammunition, and then it would all be over.

"My brother," the girl said, crouching.

Then she screeched, nothing human to it, and that must have been the same thought Jermaine had, for the revolver in his band barked once, nearly taking off the side of her head. Her body whipped around. She stumbled and nearly toppled from the top of the high vehicle before righting herself, turning and charging, with an unearthly squeal of pure hatred, at the man who shot her.

The gun went off again, this time producing a heart-sinking *click* of a sound. Jermaine sighed. The girl leaped at him. And Paul stuck his hatchet in her path and felt it find brittle obstacle, then sink into her chest. The beastly cries of rage turned to a single restrained groan as the vampiress' forward momentum carried her, with the blood-smeared blade buried in her, past Paul and into Jermaine. They both fell over the side.

Paul heard another scream. Freddie. He looked up. Somehow his friend had escaped being pitched from the balcony when the flaming bus hit it. He'd curled one leg over a jagged railing and hung on for dear life. He also held onto a chainsaw with both hands. He had Paul locked in his gaze and was making tossing motions with it.

Paul held out his arms and caught the heavy tool amid fresh shivers of back pain. Freddie nudged the air with one hand, pointing out the front of the bus deck.

Duane Purcell had risen from a crouched position at the front of the flattop and was now taking cautious steps toward him.

Paul's hands felt for the pull-cord, his eyes never leaving the rebel leader.

The vampire had somehow lost his ubiquitous ball cap. Without it, his dark hair was plastered flat to his scalp except where strands clung wetly to his low forehead. His eyes were small and hard and kept shutting tight and opening again in a nervous twitch. Glints of white light twinkled in his irises as if the reflection of a hundred battlefield fires. There was not a glimmer of intelligence or leadership about him, only the unstoppable instincts of a powerful predator. He was the strongest of a clan whose brightest didn't matter.

Behind Purcell, Paul could see others climbing up to join him, using the open passenger door as a ladder.

Paul pulled the cord and the chainsaw roared to life. It shuddered in his hands so that he almost dropped it, taking off his own two feet, but he finally got it under control.

Purcell kept coming. He took slow, sure steps that ended just out of arm's reach. The vampire's nostrils twitched as nervously as his eyelids.

Paul swung the saw in a feeble batter's chop, nearly fainting from the torment it caused his back. Jolts of electric fire coursed up and down his spine and into every pain center on his body. With trembling arms, he heaved the cumbersome tool back onto his right shoulder and waited. He'd black out from one more wild swipe like the first.

Purcell took another small step, and then went rigid.

Here he comes, Paul thought, wildly wondering what he was going to do.

Wrong again. Purcell's hand went behind him and came up with a small pistol. He smiled as he lifted it chest high, Paul now thinking sulkily, as Freddie had done before, about the unfairness of vampires carrying guns. Without a moment to lose, he stepped suddenly forward and swung the roaring chainsaw with everything he had.

Purcell fired wildly. He threw a hand over his face as the saw snarled in his clothing, taking his gun arm neatly off at the elbow.

321

He howled at the spray of blood, tissue and fine bone matter.

Paul didn't wait to see or hear more. He launched himself from the back of the big deck and fell hard onto the wet ground next to Denver.

Chapter Sixty-Two

The roar of gunfire and the confused cries of men and women drew him until he was close enough to the action atop the steep rise to hear the whine of bullets breaking through the rain. He never tired and he saw well enough that his feet never tangled in the slippery brush. Small, hard raindrops continued to pelt him, singeing his raw skin, but it never mattered.

He could still taste the blood of two dead men on his gums and in the far reaches of his mouth. The stuff worked like an energy supplement. Working his tongue over his teeth, he found them all intact. He surged with rageful power and the overwhelming need to feed again. His nostrils led him unerringly the way he'd come.

Zeebe.

Todd dropped silently behind the base of another ancient elm and studied the nightscape for an explanation for the stale smoke and lung rot his nostrils had unearthed. Then he saw it, the hulking shadow just across the creek bed, crouching near where the ground rose to become the ravaged backyard of the Sundown Motel.

Todd rubbed his jaw, only partially aware that the agony of the bullet-pulped mass had dulled to the nagging ache of a bruised chin. The gut shot was like heartburn, the hole in his hand scabbing over.

The figure stirred. Jim Zeebe turned slowly as he rose from his crouched position. He stretched his legs as though conscious that he'd need them in prime working order. He shook the dirt from his jeans and chuckled softly.

"Rookie vampires, they forget they ain't the only ones got the know-how."

Todd stepped away from the tree, feeling a little foolish at expecting to take Zeebe by storm. No problem. He could do it this way, too. "You and me," he said.

Only, instead of the *mano y mano* confrontation his mind had conjured, Todd caught a flicker of movement from the other vampire's arm. The gun roared and the bullet picked Todd up and threw him to the ground.

Once more he found himself staring up at the white clouds and trying to keep the rain off his face. In the same way that sex was never so tense after the first time, the third shooting in the space of a quarter hour was almost anticlimactic.

Not that the lead burrowed into his left shoulder blade didn't hurt. He bit back a groan and tried ignoring the bone splinters churned up at the site of the neat red hole.

The splash of heavy footfalls brought his mind back to more pressing concerns. He rolled to his right as three more bullets slammed into the ground, sending up mud and rainwater geysers dangerously close to his skull.

He kept rolling until he got behind that gnarled elm again. As he did, he felt the blunt weight of the gun he'd grabbed from McConlon. Once behind the tree and on his knees, he ripped the nine out of his waistband and fired off three wild shots without looking, hopefully in the general direction of the vampire. Something to slow him down, at least. Make him think.

He heard Zeebe hit the ground with a grunt and scramble into the brush.

Wincing at the tongues of fire emanating from his ragged shoulder, Todd hugged the tree and waited for whatever came next.

Big, dumb Zeebe wasn't so patient. With a roar, he crashed out of the brush and charged straight for Todd, spraying gunfire. He ran with a sideways, lumbering gait, his thick legs seeming to pull the rest of his big body reluctantly forward.

Todd's finger froze on the trigger. He watched in helpless panic as Zeebe let loose with a barrage of five, six, seven shots from a dozen feet away and closing. One whining shot splintered the tree, shooting bark chips into Todd's left eye and the zinging missile after that kicked him high in the cheekbone.

Dammit, it hurt.

Time slowed as he felt the hard little metal crunch easily through bone as it angled toward his brain.

This is it, he thought as a pain flare went off behind his closed eyes. His fingers lost the gun, then lost all feeling as he toppled slowly, gracelessly to the ground.

Again, the wet sky and the darkness, his thoughts on how peaceful the night felt even with the steady chatter of small arms fire and the sharp crackle of gasoline bombs in the distance.

Todd blinked against the sudden glare. He shifted to see the vampire Zeebe thrashing and jerking his flaming limbs, sending tendrils of white fire into the dark heavens.

He watched with no emotions. A mental numbness seemed to separate him from what he saw. It was time to sleep.

Footsteps drew nearer. He looked up, not really caring.

"Joy?" he asked.

She knelt beside him, cradling his head, and that was the best moment of all. He tried to touch her, but his fingers wouldn't move. He watched the fiery, screaming ball that was Zeebe; watched it as it finally crumpled to the ground and brittled with ash.

Joy kissed him. His wife smelled of gasoline and flame, sweat and exertion, and never smelled better. She put another beer bottle bomb and a plastic lighter in her lap next to his head.

"This one's for us," she whispered.

"No. Fight them," he croaked before the unyielding darkness closed in.

Chapter Sixty-Three

There was a period of time that must have been no more than seconds when the battle dimmed and his body hurt no more. A beautiful, serene space of time, but it ended all too soon.

The pain brought him back, lightning bolts of it. The air reeked of acrid smoke and rain.

Paul lurched awkwardly to his feet, clamping a hand over the liquid warmth at the top of his hip. He'd wrenched his shoulder killing the girl, and now the whole area was numbing so that he couldn't make a fist of his right hand. His foot tripped over the fallen Denver Dugan, whose huge hand still gripped the section of balcony railing he'd brought down with him. Paul locked an arm around the big man's waist, and tugged. Doing so, he clenched his jaw, but a moan still escaped.

A scuffing sound distracted him, a murmur nearly lost in the cacophony of fire and death. Paul looked up as Purcell dragged himself a step closer to the top edge of the stranded blood bus. One arm stub dangled from torn tendons. He bent his knees. Sprang.

Paul's hand somehow found the sheared metal railing section in Denver's unconscious grip. He grabbed it and plunged one end into the muddy ground before rolling awkwardly and painfully aside.

Duane Purcell seemed to sense what was coming. Plummeting, he waved his arms like wings in a futile effort to stave off gravity and the awaiting metal spear. It ran through his torso with ease and reappeared the next instant on the other side, pinioning him like a tortured bug. The vampire's mouth fell open in an eruption of black blood.

And the sky went white.

It was like the landing of the mother ship in a UFO movie. The blunt, stabbing light ended all sputtering gunfire. A chainsaw slowly whined down to a conclusion and the screams of dying men and women softened as even they seemed to show an interest in upcoming events.

Purcell squirmed on the metal stake, his chainsaw-severed arm forming new tissue before Paul's eyes.

Paul stumbled away. He walked alongside the blackened, smoldering bus, now leaking radiator water and the machine's other viscous life fluids. He glanced up to assure himself he wasn't going to be leaped upon by any more night creatures, but the only perceptible movement was Jermaine Whittock disentangling his limbs from those of a twitching Patty Craven.

Like everyone else, Jermaine's attention was on the long line of headlights pulling up the long driveway and fanning out so that it was almost impossible to look anywhere without seeing the high beams of cars and trucks and SUVs and motorcycles and vans and 4x4s.

Blinded as he was, he didn't see the stretch vehicle at the fore, but heard it come to a stop some thirty feet away. Heard the *chunk* as its electric door was released. Miles Drake stepped out of the long gray Lincoln.

In a crash of red and blue lights, a cruiser intercepted the old vampire, and Bill Sandy stepped out to join him. Tabitha Drake left the Lincoln to flank her father as well.

"Purcell," the master vampire said in a low purr.

Paul turned sharply at the small sound behind him.

Duane Purcell stood on rubbery legs, blinking into the car lights. He held in two bloody arms the glistening section of metal rail that had held him moments before like a mounted butterfly. It was dizzying to imagine the inhuman strength it must have taken to unpin himself.

There was no defeating a power like that.

"Get the fucker," someone growled.

Chapter Sixty-Four

Jason Penney, horribly disfigured by flame and riddled by bullet fire, disentangled himself from the crowd to stand by the bus wreckage. His hair hung limp, gray with soot.

Miles Drake took a couple slump-shouldered steps. His cheap suit coat hung loose, ill-fitting and formless, on his bony shoulders.

"Why?" he asked in a hollow voice as Purcell met him in the circle formed by car lights and dark spectators. It looked as though the entire town had relocated to the demolished front yard of the Sundown as speechless witnesses to fire and mayhem. "Why do you treat me like this for saving your life?"

The younger vampire clutched the bloody spear of railing in one fisted hand, held it chest high like a pole vaulter contemplating his kick start. In the spotlight glare of a hundred high beams, his tattered shirt glistened with his own black gut blood, but he hardly seemed to notice. His severed arm had grown back, though it was still thin and puckered and he held it as tentatively as new growth. "You're a thing of the past," he told Drake.

Then he charged.

"Die, old man!" he screamed.

Miles Drake sidestepped the attack in a flash of footwork that should have convinced Purcell that he'd underestimated his enemy. The younger vampire skidded to a stop several feet from his intended victim and slipped to one knee on the rain-slick grass. He was up again in an instant, a snarl boiling up from his throat.

Bill Sandy drew his revolver a lot faster than Paul would have expected from the overweight, middle-aged lawman.

"No!' Drake barked in a tone that left no room for doubt.

The police chief leveled the gun at Purcell's chest, but didn't fire.

Purcell came again. This time he pulled up short, feinted a thrust and waited for Drake to stop swiveling before burying the shaft in the old vampire's shoulder.

The crowd gasped. Drake groaned. He made a grab for the weapon with his good arm, but Purcell wrenched it free.

Purcell backed up, glaring into the now silent crowd.

"Look at him," he commanded, pointing an accusatory finger. "Look at what this grandpa has become. Is this what you want to follow?" He spoke gutturally, as one uncomfortable with public speech, but Paul was sure the message got through.

Drake rubbed at a slick patch of blood on his shoulder.

"Good idea, Purcell. Look at me." He spoke softer than his adversary, but his voice was strong and commanding in its lack of volume. "Duane, even before your great-grandparents were born, I walked as I walk now."

Drake slipped gingerly out of his cheap suit coat, wincing as his bloody shoulder passed through the sleeve. He flexed his injured arm high over his head, then picked with a long finger at the frayed hole in the white fabric.

"It's scabbing over," he said cheerfully. He eyed his assailant. "I can't be defeated, Duane."

"Bullshit," the younger vampire growled.

Again he jabbed with the jagged length of broken railing, and again Drake dodged impalement. His next thrust carried him past his mark once more, and Purcell lost his footing again in the slick grass.

Miles Drake sprang too fast for any warning to have been effective. Purcell had time to screech once before the master vampire landed, burying yellow teeth into his exposed throat.

Drake huddled over his victim while Purcell's legs twitched. To Paul, it looked like a Discovery Channel documentary, lions taking down dinner. You're supposed to cheer for the predators for their sheer power and grace and beauty, but you can't erase those twitching gazelle legs from your mind.

"No," Jason Penney grunted before five quick shots from Bill Sandy's gun laid him out—at least for the moment.

The police chief strode toward the blond-haired vampire, but a woman shouted, "No. Wait." Mona Dexter stepped out of the crowd, revving up a chainsaw as she came. "The bastard's mine," she said.

Paul looked away, but still heard the blade bite through flesh and bone. When he looked again, he saw shadowy figures melt quickly and quietly from the scene.

Just like that, it was over.

Chapter Sixty-Five

Ponytail Pete was dead, God rest his soul.

Jermaine Whittock had been injured in the fall, but not seriously. Just out cold for the moment. Denver Dugan knocked all to hell, but too blasted ornery to die. Paul hadn't found Freddie yet, and was hoping for the best. His side hurt like hell and was still bleeding slightly; his back felt like that of a man of fifty-two after an intense workout.

The rain had put out most of the beer-bottle flames, but five of the town's six firefighters were working on the gas tank fire that had erupted from the misused blood donor vehicle. The flames had pretty much torched the Sundown, too. Another fireman, a guy named Dave Madgett, had taken a bunch of sick days over the last week or so and was found blocking the doorway of the lobby. Or at least what little remained of the charred corpse seemed to resemble Madgett.

D.B. was okay. A little bruised, maybe. Same with Haggerty and Mona. The downstairs room Carl had been holed up in had been sprayed with gunfire, but he'd propped up mattresses and pillows to the windows, fashioned himself a shooting nest and weathered the worse of it.

Denver wasn't in great shape, according to the woman doctor in a yellow warm-up suit.

Paul heard her telling Drake, "The forearm shot's just a flesh wound, but he fractured his leg in at least a couple places when he tumbled off the balcony. Hit his head, too. We'll have to get an MRI, but I'm guessing compound fractures. Lots of blood loss, too. Don't touch him."

Drake muttered something to her that Paul couldn't hear. Something that made the woman doctor blink.

"I won't allow that," she said. "He's my patient."

Not giving up an inch, thank God.

The rain had stopped toward dawn, the clouds having parted slightly to let in a sliver of dying moonlight. The doctor had cleared a space for Denver, still unconscious, and wrapped him in a damp blanket. Flares had been lit all around the battle site, and in their sputtering glow, Paul watched Denver's bloodless face.

The older man's lips were blue, his teeth chattered and eyelids fluttered. The doctor stood and motioned for a stretcher crew that was already occupied. She was a slight woman, fiercely determined but not as young as her figure suggested. She squatted next to the seriously injured man and Drake awkwardly crouched likewise to say something more to her in a low voice.

"What was that?" Paul asked nervously over the vampire's shoulder.

No response. Drake unbent with a crackle of gristle and bone, but continued to hover and stare grimly at Denver. Paul, not sure what else to do, laid a hand on the vampire's shoulder.

Drake shrugged it off, scowling. "This has nothing to do with you," he said.

A stretcher arrived and the doctor barked orders for the careful placement of her patient.

"Stop right there," the master vampire snapped, freezing the attendants. "We have to discuss this."

"There's nothing to discuss," the doctor replied. "He's my responsibility."

"And the town is mine."

"Load him," the doctor quietly ordered.

They studied Drake and the doctor. She stood a foot shorter than the vampire glaring down at her, but her eyes met his directly. After several seconds, one of the paramedics shrugged and bent to Denver. The other followed suit.

The recent rain had turned the fires to smudgy smoke, further blackening the predawn sky except for that sliver of moon.

Drake directed the heat of his gaze first on Paul, then the doctor. There was a fine speckle pattern of blood on his chin and along one side of his face.

"You ignored me," he said flatly to the woman.

She said, "It's my job to save lives, not take them."

Then she moved off to another fallen cluster.

When she was gone, Paul said, "You wanted to kill Denver, didn't you?"

Drake sniffed the air and his eyes fell to Paul's side, the blood seeping from a makeshift bandage. He stalked away without a reply, his face chalky white in the sporadic gasoline-fueled light.

The master vampire's world was changing, Paul thought as he followed. He was about to continue the conversation—though he had no idea where he'd take it—when D.B. shot into sight.

He said, "Paul, you gotta come quick. It's Todd. Hurry up, willya?"

The vampire had overheard. He turned as quickly as Paul and followed D.B. toward the woods at the back of the charred motel.

It was Todd Dunbar, alright, or what remained of him. He lay sprawled by the creek bed at the bottom of the ravine, a layer of sycamore bark serving as his litter. His bedraggled wife hunched next to him. They both smelled of gasoline and ash.

A covering of black blood was plastered to Dunbar's shirt, more of it smeared on his face, but Paul saw no torn flesh.

"He's healing," Mona Dexter said. She stood next to Freddie and Carl and several townspeople with flashlights or guns.

Paul forgot the others as Mona's eyes traced his own.

"You know what you have to do," she told him quietly. "For his own good."

"Everyone stay away," Joy Dunbar cried. The crowd moved back as she picked up a beer bottle that sloshed with liquid. A dirty rag poked from its neck. "I done in Zeebe with one of these and I can take out the rest of you."

She jabbed her thumb at a point behind her as she said the last part and flashlights picked out the charred organic pile twenty feet away, half in the underbrush.

Paul said, "Joy, you've got to understand—"

She cut him off by raising the bottle higher and producing a plastic cigarette lighter in her other hand.

Paul wanted D.B. to take over, but the other man stood silently. Paul shifted his weight, sycamore bark and pine needles crunching underfoot. His spine sent more electric jolts screaming through his system. He said, "It's just that, there's no changing him, Joy."

Her eyes burned. "I learned that years ago," she said, missing the point entirely.

Or maybe not. Maybe just not wanting to face facts.

Paul tried to think amid his screaming pain, the wail of sirens, the mutters of the unfathomable townspeople, the rainwater dripping from the trees and whipping at his face in little bursts of wind. Not to mention approaching daylight, its threat to some in the crowd, its promise of redemption to others. And most of all, the terrible silence of the master vampire. It all conspired to keep Paul's mind muddled. He couldn't work the problem all the way out until he remembered the slim doctor refusing to turn Denver Dugan over to the vampires, and that's what resolved his mind and loosened his tongue.

As Paul stepped away from the crowd, the vampire followed. Miles Drake still didn't look sufficiently recovered from mortal combat with Purcell. His skin was papery, his mouth thin and gray. He stood so close that Paul could smell coppery death on his warm breath.

Paul, stoked by his numb emotions, said, "If you'd killed the old guy, Denver Dugan, I'd have exposed you and the town as promised."

The vampire's chalky face with its angry purple mottling held no expression. Dawn couldn't be far away. Paul could dimly make out the milling crowds waiting, needing to be led once more to the Babylonian equivalent of a moral decision.

Drake's expression hardened. "Which is it, courage or stupidity that makes you address me in such an insolent manner?"

Paul thought about it, then answered honestly. "Neither. It's fear."

There was nothing to read in the vampire's face. Paul hoped his own was similarly blank.

From behind them, Freddie said, "You don't have to threaten us, Drake."

Both turned. The Detroit attorney's clothing was blackened with soot and splotched with blood—someone else's, Paul hoped. His face was bruised, the back of one hand slashed. He held it against his department store-new jeans to stanch the flow.

"We all know how easy—how tempting—it would be for you to kill us all," Freddie continued. "We saw how effectively you dealt with Purcell, and that's why we must remind you what you're up against if we lose contact with Darby Highsmith."

The vampire's head swiveled from one daylighter to the other, then lighted back on Freddie.

"Who the hell are you?"

"He's my attorney," said Paul.

"And as such I can't stress enough the importance of keeping us all safe. As long as that happens, we have no incentive to reveal what we know to the outside world. We want nothing but peace. And if you think Paul can't simply disappear without questions, that's doubly true of me, Mr. Drake."

The words, with their politely unspoken threat layered into the promise of cooperation and mutual benefit, reminded Paul all over again why he kept Freddie on retainer.

"I have nothing to say to lawyers," Drake muttered.

Frozen in his impotent frustration, he turned to glower at the crowd surrounding them, stopping in their tracks loyal allies and former insurgents alike. "This godforsaken town," he rumbled. "It's losing all semblance of discipline. Of respect."

Nearly all in attendance took a step back.

"I'm not sure that's so bad," Paul said. "Maybe your people are learning to think for themselves. Not always good thoughts...but their own."

In the distance and drawing closer came a familiar voice. Eventually it became Bill Sandy, directing a rescue team or a meat wagon. Both were in high demand.

Paul said, nodding toward the busy police officer, "I almost admire him. The way he can walk the thin line between sworn duty and political reality. Between *the* law and *your* law."

Something squealed underfoot and Paul feinted a kick at a rat that ambled fatly from harm.

"What I'm trying to say, Drake, is that I find Babylon not to be the horror I first thought it was. It's not my kind of place, for sure, but it has its own...decorum." He waved a hand to take in his surroundings, dawn now just around the corner. "Others apparently find it livable."

The smoke and dying flames and the steady flicker of emergency vehicle lights provided unintentional irony.

"You're a fool," the vampire growled.

Paul thought about it. "Babylon offers jobs and a strong sense of community. Of tradition. Family bonds are strong here, to say the least. It's a town with a sense of right and wrong—not everyone's sense—but at least its citizens live by a code of behavior that's consistent. That shifts less than society's." He watched the master vampire's face. "I know people who might thrive here."

The vampire turned his hot gaze on Todd Dunbar, still sprawled on the ground but starting to stir. "No," he said.

"Think about it," Paul said quickly. "I'll bring their kids back. Not your traditional family, exactly, with Mom ruling the roost during the day and Dad prowling around all night, but at least they'll be together. And he'll be alive."

More or less, Paul wanted to add, but didn't.

Drake shook his head. "No. It can't be done."

"You can teach them to be normal. Normal for Babylon. There are other mixed marriages in this town, I've got to believe that," Paul persisted.

The vampire rubbed his dry face. It *skritched* like the drag of a dead leaf across pavement.

Something caught Paul's attention and he watched Joy Dunbar help her groggy husband to his feet.

"I've got to get him inside," she said, staring up at a sky suggestive of dawn.

"Let the Dunbars decide," Paul said quietly.

"And if I don't allow it?" Drake said as he watched the woman lead her shaky husband toward the ashen motel for shade.

With the fires out, the Sundown didn't look as bad as Paul had first imagined it. He could see Mona already pushing firefighters and their high-pressure hoses out of the way of undamaged portions of her motel. If she had insurance, she could be up and running in a few months.

"Let's focus on the positive," Freddie said breezily. "If the Dunbars and any of the others who want to remain here are allowed to do so, I think I can encourage the Highsmiths to sell their home at a reasonable profit and we'll all leave very soon. I think Paul here will hire me to only occasionally check in to make sure everyone who chooses to stay remains healthy and secure. As long as that's the case, no police, no reporters."

He finished with a what-could-be-fairer shrug and a big smile.

Drake's frown had grown. He shifted position to leave Freddie out of the conversation and to address Paul directly. "How do I know I can trust you?"

"Because you can," Paul answered simply. The vampire would recognize the truth in it.

Drake scanned the sky. "We have to be leaving soon," he said. Then he added, "What if they give us up?"

By the distasteful way the word rolled off of the vampire's tongue, Paul knew that *they* referred to the Sundowners.

It was a good question, but Paul had given it some hurried thought.

"Darby and Freddie and I are stable citizens with steady job histories and respectable lifestyles." He swallowed, hoping that he'd still be seen in such a light by the time his legal problems were resolved. "We don't overdrink, do drugs or tell whoppers. That's why the police or the media will believe us if they ever come looking for confirmation of some wild tale told by Carl or D.B. or one of the others. We'd say we never laid eyes on them. Sure, the tabloids with their tales of women who dated Bigfoot might eat it up, but who'd believe what they read?"

Drake took as much time as the approaching day would give him to mull it over. "What about those who've already died?"

Paul was ready for that one, too. Ready with the sad truth. "Who cares?"

After another nervous glance at the sky, Drake said, "And the one whose wife died? How quiet will he remain?"

Now they were in a minefield. Even with Purcell and his faction destroyed, he didn't think Jermaine would ever agree to peace with the vampires.

"I don't have all the answers," he finally admitted, and watched the vampire gloat. "But I promise to work on it. Will you let me?"

It might have merely been the play of the light of an emergency vehicle over his face, but Drake's head seemed to bow almost imperceptibly.

Yessirree, Paul thought. It was indeed going to be a challenge tying up every loose end. But for the first time in months he didn't feel fifty-two. He felt his energy returning, his brain revving for a hard haul. He caught Freddie's eye and his lawyer nodded slightly, his mouth and eyes set for the work ahead.

He'd made the sale.

Paul Highsmith couldn't wait to get started.

SAMHAIN
PUBLISHING

It's all about the story...

Romance

HORROR

www.samhainpublishing.com

CPSIA information can be obtained at www.ICGtesting.com
Printed in the USA
LVOW12s2312030214

372120LV00002B/99/P